ECHO

OF THE

BOOM

ECHO OF THE BOOM

MAXWELL NEELY-COHEN

THIS IS A GENUINE BARNACLE BOOK

A Barnacle Book | Rare Bird Books
453 South Spring Street, Suite 531
Los Angeles, CA 90013
abarnaclebook.com
rarebirdbooks.com

FIRST TRADE PAPERBACK ORIGINAL EDITION

Set in Dante
Printed in Canada
Distributed in the U.S. by Publishers Group West

10 9 8 7 6 5 4 3 2 1

Publisher's Cataloging-in-Publication data

Neely-Cohen, Maxwell.
    Echo of the boom / by Maxwell Neely-Cohen.
    p. cm.
    ISBN 978-1-940207-17-9

1. End of the world—Fiction. 2. Juvenile delinquents—Fiction. 3.
High school—Fiction. 4. Teenagers—Fiction.
5. Washington (DC)—Fiction. I. Title.

PS3614 .E365 E34 2014
813.6—dc23

For J, K, L, and M

PART

1

And I saw, and behold a white horse:
And he that sat on him had a bow;
And a crown was given unto him:
And he went forth conquering,
and to conquer.
—The Book of Revelation

You got no fear of the underdog,
That's why you will not survive.
—Spoon, "The Underdog"

‡　　　‡　　　‡　　　‡

THEY WERE ALL BORN after the fall of the wall but before the fall of the towers.

Eight years before the end, ten-year-old Steven stepped off the train holding his father's hand. There was an unattended bag resting beneath a bench on the platform. Which was worse? Not spotting the bag in the first place or not telling anyone? Steven always noticed, every single time, and he never said anything. Why were people always forgetting so much luggage? Was it a game? Parks, airports, sporting events, government buildings, open plazas, unattended baggage was everywhere, waiting to be cautiously removed and destroyed. His feet made the turn and his eyes rolled over the nylon.

Steven realized that if the backpack were a bomb, it would cause citizens to run the wrong way in the event of an attack. Tourists would be involved. And bombs love tourists.

It wouldn't be an incendiary device. There was nothing flammable in the station. The ceilings were so high that a chemical attack wouldn't be possible from a bag of that size. A dirty bomb would be wasted underground. The real fun would be ruining the economy of the city above by turning commercial districts into unusable radioactive dead zones for a few decades. Even at the age of ten, Steven knew they tested nuclear weapons underground. He knew they had reasons other than circumventing test-ban treaties.

Instead, the bag would be packed with a high explosive. A timer would trigger blasting caps because cellphone reception was shoddy. The device would be surrounded by jars of screws and nails. There would be an additional bomb at the other end of the platform, or maybe on an arriving train. At rush hour, one bomb could take out dozens before the second upped the count tenfold.

Simple pipe bombs or pressure cookers would probably take a few lives, but this was the big leagues. A high explosive creates a supersonic shock wave. This wave does the real work. It knocks people around, inducing internal injuries that may not be obvious in the chaos of triage. The wave would be amplified off the walls and ceilings, people would be thrown. Outdoors: the wave would go away rapidly. Indoors: fractures, dislocations, head injuries, chest trauma—half of the body count would be immediate.

Steven knew and knows the truth:

There's the blast, and then the wave hits the body. It picks you up. It impacts your internal organs, traps gasses, and forces ruptures. It exceeds your body's tensile strength. It's the air that tears you apart. Not the fire, but the boom. Then there's the debris, the shrapnel, the fragments; they rip into you at high speed. Finally, as if you're not in enough trouble already, you have to land somewhere. In the case of this subway platform, you would either drop the five feet to the track or fly the twenty to the wall.

But most bombs don't actually go off like they're supposed to. The human brain struggles to correctly wire anything.

Reaching the escalator, Steven said goodbye to the station, just in case.

Even when he was little, Steven knew all of this. He knew because he wanted to. He paid attention to these things.

◥◤　　　◥◤　　　◥◤　　　◥◤

THE AUDITORIUM WAS ONE of two venues capable of holding a full grade for assembly at LeMay Senior High School. The figure on stage was speaking with a practiced emotional edge. There were theater lights on the ceiling, jumbled black cylinders with life-giving wires snaking into the boards above. Bodies were draped on carpeted steps in place of actual seats. This was a public school. The luxury of furniture was only provided during shows and performances, where the fags and faghags who weren't good enough to get into Duke Ellington School of the Arts put on their accented voices, where the bands played too loud and the choirs sang too soft. Since the room was not big enough to contain the whole school, this specific assembly would be repeated for each grade, the show going on and on for the poor staff and faculty who had to witness several iterations. A mother, or more correctly, a former mother, sat onstage with a doctor and the vice principal, chatting about the drunk-driving-texting-slutting-drugging untimely end of her teenage daughter.

Chloe thought someone smelled like Band-Aids. Hopefully it was not Michelle, seated directly to her left. Michelle was wearing a silver shirt that slung over one shoulder and traveled under her armpit. It had a V at her collarbone. Her chest was never fully covered.

Chloe felt a buzz, the rip of vibration through cloth, carpet, skin, and floor. On her phone's screen there was a picture, a digital imitation of a photo-booth memento. Two boys were cuddling, smiling, and then kissing. One of the faces rang true and she perked and tried to find him in the room. He was sitting with some of his teammates, sort of pudgy and fumbly, but with clear eyes and an unchanging smile. This, in the picture and on the bleachers, was Michelle's boyfriend. Chloe obscured the screen and showed it to Lauryn, on her other side.

"Who sent it?" Lauryn whispered.

Michelle's eyes were fixed in the distance, unaware of her friends' conversation.

"His sister," Chloe responded by text, the frill of her top stretched to hide the message.

Lauryn's fingers went to work on the keys concealed in her pocket.

"Why?"

"He told their mom she was hiding booze in her closet."

Chloe tried not to burst out laughing as the character on the stage was summoning tears. Chloe put her head on clueless Michelle's shoulder, obstructed from the adults by a large boy taking up the space in front of them. So tired. Her eyes closed.

Chloe could not stay awake because Chloe could not sleep.

Her head bounced upward from its droop, a falling sensation bringing instant consciousness—a reflex courtesy of an ingrained genetic memory from back when Homo-whatevers were up in the trees, because that which was on the ground wanted to kill them.

Her eyes opened. The mother said something. Chloe didn't catch it. The voice was a drone. Down the bleachers, the central face from the picture was still bright and visible. Michelle was sitting there next to her as if nothing was wrong and nothing was going to be.

In her pocket, without looking, Chloe forwarded the picture of Michelle's boyfriend kissing another boy. Lauryn alone would tell something like twenty other people. Those twenty would forward the scoop to fifty, then a hundred, then maybe a thousand. Where it came from would be impossible to determine. Chloe hit send, with Michelle still in direct physical contact, oblivious.

The theater ended, the staff rising to encourage the sporadic applause. Bodies began to shuffle. Michelle was saying something to Lauryn about next period.

"Tell her," Chloe sent to Lauryn.

Lauryn did as she was told, and showed Michelle the picture on the way down the stairs. Panic. Tears.

"Does everyone know?" Michelle sobbed.

"I think they do now," Lauryn said.

"We're here for you," Chloe said, a full thirty seconds after outing him.

Chloe pressed her skin into the delineated spots for letters on the screen. Lauryn gave an almost indiscernible nod, her jet-black hair bobbing forward and back before fanning the peer-to-peer inbox brushfire with a thumb. Chemistry was next.

⸪ ⸪ ⸪ ⸪

FIVE MILES AWAY, THE very private Woodley School had a stated enrollment of six hundred and twelve. It employed one hundred and six human beings who were considered faculty, thirty-four percent of whom had taught there for more than a decade—so the materials went. Forty-three percent of students lived in Our Nation's Capital of Washington, DC, thirty-four percent in the great State of Maryland, and twenty-three percent in the Commonwealth of Virginia. Nineteen percent of students received financial aid. None of the materials bothered actually stating the student-teacher ratio or the price of tuition.

On the third floor of the C building, a boy named Efram Daniels was sitting in an office. It was 11:10 in the morning, square in the middle of what should have been his third class of that day, April 18, second semester freshman year. The heat was still on, mitigated to a slow radiating purr, driving this eastward room slightly past a reasonable climate-controlled temperature.

Efram Daniels had not completed or handed in a single piece of schoolwork in over three weeks. No one had appeared to notice. Three heads were settled upon uneasy bodies across from him: Mr. Brady, a history teacher and ninth grade dean; Megan Myers, Head of School; and Mr. Jones, the head counselor, as this was his office.

"Hello Efram," said head of school Megan Myers. "We are just waiting for your mother." Her smile was not a million-dollar smile for its aesthetic virtue but a million-dollar smile for its ability to induce donations of a million dollars or more. The door swung and Efram's mother entered the room. He had not seen her in six days. He listened to their perfunctory exchanges without turning his head.

"And who is this, Mrs. Daniels?"

"This is Kevin Longhil. Efram desired him to be present today," Mrs. Daniels said.

"I don't understand."

"My son's lawyer," she explained.

"We can assure you, Mrs. Daniels, that won't be necessary. We are going to have a friendly conversation about how Efram is doing and if there is anything we can do for him."

"Efram wants him here," she said. She was wearing all black and sunglasses—funeral ready—a skirted royal ensemble made to exude mourning. A chair was pulled for the unexpected guest. Kevin the lawyer was slick and bespectacled, with eyes designed to deceptively exude kindness to potential enemies. He gave Efram a friendly pat on the back.

"Well, Efram, Mrs. Daniels, first of all let me personally say how deeply sorry I am for your loss and how difficult these past months must have been for both of you. We wanted to make sure to meet with you in light of recent events and have a conversation. If there is anything we can do..." Head of School Megan Myers always took the lead in any conversation with a donor.

"Did Efram do something wrong?"

"No, Mrs. Daniels. We simply want to allow any concerns to be voiced."

"Often, traumatic events at home can lead to academic or social problems," Mr. Jones said. The total lack of a response left the three waiting. Head of School Megan Myers finally put her hand on Mr. Jones's arm. "As you know, Mrs. Daniels, in the year and a half we have known Efram, he has been a great student. He's made the big adjustment from eighth to ninth grade well. I see very solid grades across the board, the low nineties more or less. His work is always in on time and of good value. However, all of his teachers' comments wish for more in-class participation. His effort grades are all threes, which are, of course, satisfactory, but usually indicative in cases of academic excellence that a student is not applying himself as fully as he could."

Efram scratched his arm, concerned for the validity of his corporeal state.

"I thought you said his grades were high?" Mrs. Daniels questioned.

"Right, perhaps I should have said that Efram is very quiet, and that it can appear that he is unengaged."

Kevin the lawyer screwed his face in a fractal contortion. Efram's mother gave no immediate answer.

"Efram do you have anything you want to say about this?"

He shrugged and looked at Kevin, who replicated his exact lackadaisical response.

"Do you have any friends here, Efram? It is important to have peers who support you," Mr. Jones turned his attention to Efram's mother. "I have had conversations with Efram's teachers and they all voiced concern that he predominately keeps to himself."

Mr. Brady, the ninth grade dean who had not uttered a single word, was dragging a pen against a yellow pad of paper. He had not looked up from it once. Despite the angle, Efram shuffled to the left, attempting to see what was being transcribed or doodled. Efram craned his neck enough so he could make out—

"HERE WE GO, HERE WE GO. ANOTHER DAY, ANOTHER CALAMITY."

So, here we go Efram, second semester of freshman year.

His mother, behind her sunglasses, was a pharmacological Everest climber supported by her team of psychiatrists.

They all would say that Efram's decline started on the day after his father, C. William Daniels—mercenary fund manager, CFO, hired gun, and rogue trader—pleaded guilty to several counts of insider trading, racketeering, and securities fraud. Hours after being taken into custody, he was announced dead by suicide. He was only facing five years in prison. The family fortune had been insulated. The funeral was rushed within twelve hours. Efram did not attend.

So on the day of that meeting, a week after the obituary for his father appeared, Efram sat in fourth period biology and did not hand in his lab report. He did not pay attention to an explanation of cell walls. He scraped his hands across the metal under his desk. He stopped when the cold smoothness was interrupted by a hole that, with some prodding, he discovered to be the home of a screw. He tried his index and middle fingers first—now on to the mechanism of osmosis—but was not able to grip the circle. He pressed his pinky as hard as he could into the chasm, ignoring the pain, and squeezed his nail into the slot, twisting and hoping that the looseness was not imagined. He repeated this rotation forty-six times. As the rest took in or pretended to take in the unique qualities of plant cells, Efram gave up. He struggled to spin the finger out of the trap without causing too much of a grimace. But then there was the slightest tickle of looseness, and he snapped his hand into the shape of a cup. The tiny screw fell to his palm. Efram elevated his right ankle across his left knee just in time to save the spinning surface from crashing to the ground.

⊗   ⊗   ⊗   ⊗

SEVEN-YEAR-OLD MOLLY CORBIN SCREAMED out into darkness she could not purge. "Mooooooooooooommmm!" she wailed, wrenching for air, trying to make a sound in dead space, unable to see light or feel fabric. "Okay, okay, okay!" she heard approaching closer and closer, and then a click. The moment pressure hit Molly's shoulders, she could see the glow.

"What did I do?" her mother grumbled to the heavens. Now able to see, Molly realized she was in her bedroom, nightlight on the whole time, previously unable to open her eyes. Frozen. Molly kept her teeth clenched, her mother's eyes wide despite exhaustion, trembling in unjustified misfortune and misery. "Such a delicate flower," her mother shook her head. Molly Corbin, barely anything, skinny and bony, shivering, squeaking, with poor circulation and clammy skin.

"Say your prayers and try again," her mother released her, then walked to the door and switched off the overhead light, leaving the one origin of salvation, the small plastic nightlight, socketed in a different corner. The resulting shadows formed angry geometries. Each outline held a different fear, each silhouette a sinister design: a dresser, a chair, a drape, each angling and creeping. Molly assumed the position and then her mother closed the door.

"Thy word is a lamp unto my feet, and a light unto my path," she said, exactly as her mother had told her to. She performed it, grasping hard and letting her mind wander upward, and then climbed back into bed. Right on cue, as her legs sunk under the covers, the nightlight burnt out. The hollow sky encroached through the windows and each shadow took a different form. The room reversed its breath, it moved with each passing set of headlights, and creaked with each shift of focus. Molly shut her eyes tight, so hard that colors began to pass, racing blue streaks, then yellow, then red, her eyelids sealed to avoid the room. She spent hours or moments whimpering, until there was nothing.

Saturday morning glory, Molly was hauled out of bed rubbing her knuckles against her face.

"WAKE UP!" her mother bellowed, pinching her on the elbow. Molly shrieked and squirmed, slithering out and then dramatically collapsed on the floor, stricken. "You are not a toddler anymore!"

Molly's eyes fully opened to a green soccer uniform shoved into her field of vision.

"God, Mom—" That whiny little girl voice broke the throat's rasp, a tone school-learned, imitated, and honed.

"SAY GOSH."

Molly tried to sleep in the car, but every time her eyes closed, she felt the glare of her mother's rage. She squeezed her legs under the seatbelt, balling up, compressing her back into the seat. She contracted in every possible direction.

"Can you sit up straight, please?" her mother pleaded, Molly, shoulder's drooped and spine curved, her slightly pigeon-toed feet squeezed in the already-tied cleats and shin guards. Her brown hair was unwashed, bunched, and frayed, sticking at angles and looping down.

Molly abandoned the curl she was tugging from her scalp and instead pulled a strand of fabric from the seat. It was loose, and she unraveled it, millimeter by millimeter, hiding it between a folded leg and her body. But she looked up to those eyes in the mirror. Caught. Her mother's voice would start calm and then escalate.

"Molly—"

There was a screech—loud—a crack, and then the glass broke, the door buckled, the front seat took flight, and all that was solid encroached on Molly, except she was sideways, now airborne, then pinned. Twisting and spinning, stopping only with silence and the dark of her eyelids. Her neck was exposed between metal and torn padding, seatbelt taut, squeezing the only part of her middle not weighted by steel. She opened her eyes. She was upright, the car sideways, but her limbs were gone just as the car was gone, unfelt, as enough space barely existed for her head against the former cushion and the newly low ceiling. No sound could be made. Her mother was nowhere, only the warped steel and shredded interior plastics. Her whole body quivered, or felt like it did. Liquid trickled, mechanical and biological. And then through a small hole in the wreck, she saw her mother's empty eyes. Molly passed out.

☒ ☒ ☒ ☒

CHLOE DID NOT HAVE a clique at LeMay Senior High School. She had a team, a consultancy, a syndicate, a Super PAC.

Lauryn, Michelle, Jess, and Chloe.

They flanked her as she walked into the school.

Lauryn was the public face, the one who the untrained eye might think was in control. Lauryn was 5'8" but told people she was 5'7". She was one of the very few who was actually as skinny as the actress who would portray her in a movie. Lauryn was pretty within the context of the social structure, letting her wardrobe—her parents' purchasing power, really—do most of the work.

Michelle had been The Great Leader in the beginning, in middle school, but now she was a chatterbox, a press secretary, a messenger, a publicist. She was a dark brunette and the shortest member, maybe on a tall day reaching three inches over five feet. Michelle's makeup could have preserved her face far out from the protection of earth's magnetic field (Jess's choice of words). Her skin was so orange from tanner, her brother would try to carve her tits on Halloween (Lauryn's choice of words). Both descriptions were elegantly posted for all to see while typing away in science class.

Jess was the alien, the Eastern European princess, the unattainable stoic. Jess was slight, even skinnier than Lauryn, and taller. Willowy. She had that odd hair color between brunette and redhead, almond bordering on auburn, and skin paler than the rest.

The bell rang.

"I hooked up with Anthony Dobbins," Lauryn said.

Starting power forward Anthony Dobbins was the only skyscraping, dunking, true athletic talent that LeMay might export. He was listed at 6'8".

Chloe considered the possibility of a backlash. LeMay was anomalous: It was a public school controlled by a city that, at one point, had been the blackest in America, yet existed in its richest and ever-trending whitest quadrant. The result was one of the few unsegregated student bodies in the United States, an actual mixture without a dominant faction, the sole exception to this rainbow nation being economic—a considerable lack of rich kids. In Our Nation's Capital, families with means, and quite a few without, automatically sent their offspring to private institutions. LeMay was a public high school not held in total disgust, but was still what it was: an enclave of an enclave.

There were, therefore, certain social structures within LeMay that were implicitly or explicitly delineated by ethnicity. There were completely independent social hierarchies for certain cliques of black or Latina or white girls, but these were mitigated both by outliers and other social markers. Team, club, interest, academic level, hotness, druggieness, parental income—these other factors held certain ethnically homogenous groups together more than actual skin color.

Chloe had a passing fear that one group of particularly nasty blue-blooded attractive black girls would attack Lauryn for falling into the clichéd LeMay pattern of a black athlete dating a half-Asian white girl. Then again, the social structure could so easily hinge on Anthony's whims. He wanted her. All else followed.

"How was it?" Chloe asked Lauryn as they went through the doors.

Lauryn shrugged.

Jess was actually the only full-blown Caucasian member of Chloe's jeesh. Lauryn had a Chinese American mother and a white father. Michelle was the child of a very light-skinned Panamanian father and a

New York half-Jewish, half-Puerto Rican mother. And Chloe, well, Chloe confused people. She had at different times been asked directly what the hell she *was*. In all, people had accused her of being part or full Italian, Afro-Caribbean, Filipina, half-black, Ethiopian, Brazilian, Sri Lankan, Romani, Indian, other Indian, Lebanese, Dominican, Turkish, Indonesian, or just "what?" Chloe usually responded with a noncommittal shrug and possibly added a flirty smile, depending on who wanted to know. Boys asked you to your face. They seemed to care. It mattered to their score cards and fantasies. When Michelle's ex cheated on her with a Catholic schoolgirl, the fact that she was an Asian Catholic schoolgirl made it far worse. The skirt and everything…

In the relative terms of LeMay, Jess was white. Despite her frenetically maintained, attempted tan, Michelle was considered a sort of white Latina, and Lauryn was usually Asian or half-Asian, the latter meant as a compliment of fetishized hotness.

Chloe was a wild card, which had certain political benefits.

Chloe collapsed to the floor of the hallway and curled up on Jess's cross-legged lap. Her body was cold.

"Seriously?" Chloe heard Michelle laugh. Lauryn shushed her.

Chloe's eyes closed, and her awareness drifted to nothing. She was still in the hallway, but it was different. There were voices and footsteps, but the space was devoid of figures. Chloe was standing, moving. Then, through all available windows and doors, there was a blinding flash. The dark hallway became whiter than daylight. She squinted at the split-second spark, and then woke up.

Jess's arm and hand were over her face, having snapped a picture.

"Shhhhhhhhhh," Lauryn said. "The queen is sleeping."

But Chloe opened her eyes. Sideways, she watched five members of the baseball team stroll past, giving their looks.

"Hey Lauryn," one called, but Chloe did not turn her head to see her friend's reaction. Michelle popped up and scurried after them.

Jess's hand offered Chloe an unwrapped granola bar.

"God, you never eat anything," Lauryn said.

Chloe closed her eyes again.

‡   ‡   ‡   ‡

STEVEN'S FATHER WAS NAMED Norman, and Norman made deals. He made deals between countries, militaries, corporations. Steven had been encouraged to say that his father was a "traveling salesman".

Eight years before the end, Norman brought Steven along to Kolkata. It was the ten-year-old's first trip to India. He drifted in and out of jetlagged sleep as they navigated through the mass of commerce. The streets were as much for people as they were for vehicles. The hired car crawled, only accelerating when they reached the river and sped over the bridge, the afternoon light beginning to fade. The city was low.

The hotel was on the perimeter of a large square. When the car door opened, Steven could hear a crowd of voices. He craned his neck. Organized chants seemed to be rising from a small street between two buildings on the far side of the expanse. A megaphone's barks were weaving in and out of the unamplified yells.

"They lost the election," Norman said while letting a man in a white khaki uniform lift the bags. "They aren't happy about it." The Union Jack flew alongside the flag of India on the hotel awning above. The lobby was covered in gilded, flowery trim.

In their room, Norman colonized the desk, clicking on a small lamp and spreading out his papers. Instead of going to the TV, Steven walked to the window. He cracked it, unmuting the sound. By sitting up against the recess at one end, Steven could see them. Even though the sky still had light, two bright streetlamps highlighted the group behind the barrier. There were a few hundred of them, all wearing red, packed onto the border of the square. Four military police stood guard on the other side of the barricade in front of a dark green jeep with sirens on top. Two of the guards faced in, two faced out. They held batons at their waists. The chanting became hypnotic. Steven's eyelids drooped, his cheek drifted toward the glass, but a sudden rush of figures on the narrowing outskirts of his peripheral vision jerked them back open.

A group of twenty red shirts trampled over the line. The four soldiers turned and raised their batons, but

realizing the number they were up against, retreated away
into the open. The swarm took the vehicle and started
breaking the windshield with the remnants of the police
fences. One man climbed on top and stomped the sirens
to sand. Norman turned out the large overhead light in
the hotel room, making their window indistinguishable
from the street.

"It happens all the time," he said to his son, and
returned to the papers on the desk.

At the other end of the square, out of sight from
the crowd of red shirts, Steven noticed another group
gathering. They were mostly wearing black, and some of
them had mismatched helmets. They all wielded sticks
of one sort or another. They poured in from the fringes,
running in lines, cutting in and out of the dissipating
traffic. They formed up in the middle of the street fifty
yards from the now-burning Jeep, and then they charged.

Steven watched a metal club collide with the first red
shirt's head, the faintly visible pink cloud of liquid misting
out on impact. The victim fell limp to the ground, only
to be trampled.

The red shirts who were still behind the barricade
split into two groups. Half, in total panic, fled while
they still could, escaping the dead end through the
only open side street. The other half took the poles
that had been holding up their signs and banners and
met the charge.

Steven saw them crumple one by one. A man in
red was pulled into a circle of the helmeted aggressors,

their raised weapons coming to the ground in a flurry of blows. When they moved on, he looked like a pile of rags ringed in a pool of liquid. His head had been deformed.

There were seven bodies on the pavement, two of them still crawling and reaching in agony. The rest of the trapped red shirts formed a physical barricade in their nook, constructing a defensive line with the wreckage. The armed men with helmets hesitated, then reformed ten yards away to wait.

Three of the red shirts who had attacked the police vehicle were now isolated on the other side of the square, running from twenty men with sticks who were giving chase. The three made it to the open stairwell of an apartment building. Steven did his best to catch glimpses of them on their way up. They reached the roof and emerged into open sight. Hearing the footsteps behind them, they started to scale the large rectangular concrete water tower, the only place left to go. One helped boost the other two then went tumbling back to the ground. The pursuers reached the roof and descended on him. He was mauled, dragged, fingernails against the paint, the first swing coming down onto his torso in between kicks. Steven saw his chest become concave.

The last two made it to the top, trapped on a small platform maybe eight feet wide. Tossing his helmet to the roof, the first black shirt began to climb. And then the second. And then the third. One of the red shirts tried to push off the first attacker when he reached the top, but the second came from a different angle. Steven saw the second's clenched fist, a hand holding something sharp, impact the protestor from both front and back at least a dozen times. The black shirts nudged his body from the water tower onto the roof where it lay still. Since his shirt was red already, Steven couldn't make out the blood.

The final red shirt hung by his knuckles off the edge of the tower, planning to drop back down to the roof and find another escape. But, by the time his hands let go, there were at least six waiting for him. Fists, clubs, boots, staves, and shivs assaulted his body, and then, whether still alive or already dead, they flung him to the street, nine stories down. Steven heard the faint cry of another obscured onlooker.

Sirens rose up, and Steven saw the troops begin to flood the square. The first pops of tear gas landed between the remaining groups on the ground.

Norman stood belatedly, shut the window in front of his son, and then went back to his desk.

⊗   ⊗   ⊗   ⊗

A COLLAPSED LUNG, PUNCTURED, internal bleeding, a ruptured spleen, clean breaks in each arm, a dislocated left shoulder, three fractured ribs, a dislocated hip, a chipped right kneecap, a broken right femur, a four inch laceration on the left thigh that missed the femoral artery by a fraction of an inch, four broken toes in the left foot, a broken left tibia, additional cuts and lacerations, and a mild concussion. Fifteen hours of surgery, sixty-seven stitches, four days without true consciousness, two weeks awake in the ICU—Molly Corbin, halfway to orphan, had been given enough drugs to please a junkie for a lifetime.

She woke up with her legs hanging from the ceiling in traction. She started at the bottom, wiggling each toe, left, one, left, two, left, three, left, four, left, five, the whole foot, then the other leg. She sucked a gulp of water from the tube, she tensed each part, each muscle, anything she thought she had, one by one and then in groups, against the pain of healing bone and the coarseness of the cast. At her hips, she had to be careful with the hamstrings and quads—what miniscule muscle mass there was of them—to flex without disturbing the hanging threads.

"My name is…" the nurse said, but Molly never remembered them, white coats and trained soothing voices. "What's yours?"

"Molly," she replied. Molly knew that her name was written down in their folders and on her wrist. They were asking just to ask.

"You're a very brave little girl," the nurse said for the hundredth time, not noticing that her patient was shifting all her weight to one side. Molly let the sting flow up her entire left half. There was a pinch in the shoulder where the nerves got confused. She trained her face to not betray the pain, opened her mouth, and took in the cereal.

Her Aunt Linda entered. She was born with lighter hair, lighter skin, and lighter weight than her sister, Molly's mother Deborah. Aunt Linda leaned over, her fragrance overtaking the antiseptic nasal static, pulling a chair.

"What are you watching?"

Molly became aware of a television, broadcasting away, animated figures saving the world in costumed bliss.

"I wasn't," Molly said.

"We try to leave it on. We ask her if there is something she'd like to watch…" the nurse said.

"What are you doing here all day then?"

In response Molly began smacking her tongue to the roof of her mouth. Over and over. Click. Click. Click. Click.

"Is there anything I can get you? Books? Something recorded?"

Molly shuttled her head back and forth.

"You used to watch cartoons before? Remember?"

A teddy bear lay on top of a dismissed rabbit and a lopsided toad, all stuffed and fuzzy, each brought by her father during his rare appearances and relegated to the dresser.

"How old are you?"

"Seven," Molly flicked each finger under the cast.

"Are you sure?"

Molly counted again. "Yea," she giggled, "I'm sure."

"Well, I could stay here and keep you company. I could tell you stories or we could just talk."

Molly gave no effort to respond, and instead tried with all her nervous system's might to flex her hamstrings.

Aunt Linda took the silence as provocation.

"I'm sorry, baby. I'm sorry for everything. You're so strong."

Molly remembered when she wasn't strong. Her mother had been very clear about that. Before this bed, Molly wasn't brave. Before she was able to move, but she couldn't actually. Molly the Clumsy.

She flexed her left shoulder, and then her sternum popped.

"Where I live in Texas—you'll come visit when you're better—there is a huge lake in the backyard, right there." Aunt Linda looked away. "You can swim, fish, whatever, it's all there. I usually—"

Molly yelled. Loud. She smacked Aunt Linda's arm as she was trying to grab her hand, forgetting each limb was a plaster bludgeon, barely discerning her aunt's gasp of pain under the volume of her own. Her hamstrings seized and shot agony through her lower body, shaking the cords and pinching her flesh. The nurse rushed back to her, her neighbor looked up, and Molly Corbin blacked out.

$$\vdots \equiv \qquad \vdots \equiv \qquad \vdots \equiv \qquad \vdots \equiv$$

EFRAM DANIELS DRIFTED THROUGH the annex on the way to Modern History. This end of the hallway was empty, save a few bags left for dead over their owner's free period. He planted himself against the wall and waited for the class that occupied the room to be released. Lockers extended on either side, each of comical thinness despite their seven-foot height. No one could be stuffed inside them, though once Efram had tried to squeeze himself into his own. The assembly must have let out because his solitude ceased and five girls apparated, camped in a perfect circle right by the door. They ignored him completely.

A blond athletic boy named Sam Page rumbled past and Efram wished Sam had turned. He wished Sam had rotated and dangled something in front of him, taunted him about his family, thrown his bag on the floor, shoved him against the lockers, yea, that would be something. Efram would love, love, sometime, just once, to be tripped or punched in the face in front of a jeering laughing crowd. It sounded fun. Meaningful. A life affirming experience. But it never came. Bullying wasn't what it used to be. People used words a lot, but they never physically attacked you. At the most, someone would call you gay again and again, or tell you that no one liked you. Unless you were actually gay. Then you were alright. Having you feel secure enough to be openly attracted to someone of your own gender was preferable to you slitting your wrists. The latter caused a far greater administrative headache. Kevin the lawyer had once told Efram a story about a kid at some school who was told by a fellow student, "Why don't you go home and throw yourself off a building." You can imagine the shock that followed when the kid made for the roof that day and did as he had been told.

Efram liked this story. The kid had found a dramatic, timely, and extremely effective way of dealing with the situation. As for the student who uttered those words, his life was over—if not externally then internally.

"Hey Terrill?" Efram interrupted the closest girl of the quintuple, Terrill Pearson. Efram Daniels reasoned he knew the first and last name of everyone in his grade.

"Yea?" She sounded nervous.

"Do you know my name?"

"Um, yea," she said. She looked like she was not sure of the right way to answer the question. "Efram Daniels. I'm sorry about your dad," she added.

"Thank you," Efram said. He had been told by Kevin to expect this and respond that way. Say thank you.

Efram Daniels' life had the volume turned down. Sometimes someone would allow an EQ band to hit the ceiling or silence one to the floor, but the overall level remained the same. +8 dB on the highs meant -8 dB on the lows.

"She knows your name Efram. The assembly was about you." The voice belonged to a boy named Raj Chaundhuri, who was propped against the wall right behind him.

"Oh," Efram said, "that makes sense."

"Not that any of them knew anything about it all, before."

Raj read newspapers. Actual newspapers. Paper newspapers. He brought them to school, spread them out over tables. One was folded in his left hand.

The door opened and middle schoolers streamed out, totally ignoring their presence. After they left, Efram followed as the cluster infiltrated the empty cell and took their seats. They were technically unassigned but stuck to a rough pattern. Some personalities jumped around the room while others remained painfully fixed. Efram could not remember if he had remained in the same seat every class or moved around.

"First, pass up your papers on the Scramble for Africa please," Mr. Brady said. Some anticipated this while others were forced into acts of drawn-out extraction. Efram turned around to see a girl named Lindsay Biltner receiving the stapled sheets. They locked eyes as she passed the growing pile. He added nothing to the stack and passed them up. A cascade of piercing alarms went off in his brain, and he turned to the left to find Raj staring at him. Efram faced forward and stopped undoing the screw in his seat with his right hand. There was nothing on his desk. No paper or screen or book or anything. He had ceased bringing a bag to school.

"Now, we already got into the causes and background of the First World War earlier this week," **causes** and **background** were textbook words, "so today we are going to talk about why this war changed our world so much..." Efram's mind shut off as the chalkboard activated.

The clock on the wall, analog, played tricks. It was far too fast and then far too slow. One minute was traded for ten. But then the warning alarms from before sounded in Efram's head, and Efram looked to his left again. Raj's nostrils were flaring, his stance was completely forward on his desk, hands pressed to support his chin, index fingers brought up around his nose in thought. Efram tried to screw his ears back to the room, to hear what was going on, to detect what could be causing such distress in his neighbor. Eventually the audible bandwidth crawled to a discernible range.

"...you have all these new technological developments. The machine gun, the airplane, the tank, poison gas, and these all led to trench warfare, which killed so many so quickly," Mr. Brady said.

Each noun was written on the board in a list. Some led to dashes and arrows. With a sharp thump Raj pounded his desk. The class jumped.

"Do you have something to contribute, Raj?"

"I don't know where to begin," Raj said, stuttering through the sentence.

Sam Page had turned around and was giving a mocking, quizzical, what-a-weirdo look. Terrill Pearson was laughing at Sam Page. Was Raj lost? The board was, after all, a mess. Since he never took notes, maybe he did these things by total mental memorization, which had finally faltered?

"Yes," Mr. Brady said, "I know it's a lot of factors to keep track of. But it's important to understand just how many advances happened at once. And how this created a culture of bad leadership. The generals didn't know what to do."

"No," Raj said, emphatically shaking his head. Sam Page was in hysterics, smelling the blood of a full-on nervous breakdown of a valedictory-seeking unsocial psycho.

"No?" Mr. Brady parroted. He was about to continue with a more helpful explanation to his suddenly faltering, previously best student, when Raj started all on his own.

"The revisionist case regarding faulty generalship is predominately targeted at General Haig, because it was under his leadership that over a million British troops were killed. The popular British and therefore inherited anglospheric image of him is that of an incompetent traditionalist, unwilling to employ the new technologies around him. This is completely incorrect. The war was a war of attrition, a complete mobilization of industrialized societies. All that mattered was a methodical grinding of the enemy's ability to fight."

Raj's arms were flailing. Sam now looked confused. Mr. Brady's solution seemed to be to keep talking. This must be a normal exchange, Efram thought. It wasn't like he had been paying attention. Perhaps this sort of thing had been happening twice a class.

"Well, right, you mean these new machines of war, they killed way more quickly than before," Mr. Brady said.

"No, that isn't what I mean."

"Well, I'm sorry Raj, I don't understand."

"That's right. You don't understand."

"Don't understand what?"

"Any of it," Raj summarized.

Sam Page changed. He was getting excited. His jaw had extended. He clearly knew something Efram did not. He mouthed a quick thing to someone behind Efram and jerked his head upward in an anticipatory signal to another.

"I don't understand the First World War?" Mr. Brady said.

"No." Raj said. "You do not."

"Raj, I am your history teacher. I understand the material."

"You may be a history teacher, but you, sir, are an idiot."

No gasps in high school, only laughs.

Oh! Efram understood. How splendid! This was an argument.

Sam Page had gone from mocking Raj to revering him. Sam was now scanning other eyes in the room, expressing a level of sublime satisfaction with how the day had developed.

"Raj," Mr. Brady calmly said, "I am going to have to ask you to leave."

Raj did not move.

"Respect for instructors is founded upon the precept that their education and knowledge of a particular subject far outstrips their pupils'. When this is not true, that respect does not exist, and those pseudo-instructors are therefore subject to intellectual sparring. Based on your previous words, you, sir, are an idiot. My assessment is not libelous and should therefore be fair game. I would do the same in calling you a liar—which would also be a disrespectful thing to call a teacher—if I believed your words were intended to deceive. But you are not remotely capable of such intricate thought, therefore, idiot will have to do."

Raj spoke at ludicrous speed. 'Ludicrous Speed' was the speed rating of the nimblest spaceship in this one game, the title of which Efram could not remember. Still, he could see the diminutive isometric pod with its third-person perspective, zooming through space, capable of insane acceleration and always wildly jiggling, and how when selected from the menu, the computer would chant "LUDICROUS SPEED". That was how Raj talked. Like that pint-sized ship. Slowing down at unpredictable times to slap the target around. The timing was odd, off, a see-saw rhythm that didn't fit the quality of his vocabulary.

"Raj," Mr. Brady said. "I do not know what is happening but you will leave this class and we will have a conversation afterward."

Raj did not move.

"Or this class can become an honest intellectual exercise, which is, one would think, what classes are for, and I can give a statement and you then can offer a rebuttal more nuanced than simply removing your opponent from the discourse," said Raj.

"That is not what we do here," Mr. Brady said.

"I'll demonstrate!" Raj exclaimed. "General Haig and the British army greatly employed and explored technological advances. Cavalry was a minuscule fraction of the force, and within the course of the war, Britain became the most mechanized military power on the planet. Their artillery force almost tripled. But the entire view of World War I as this tragedy that no one could see coming is a pathetic continuation of distilled and misguided eurocentrism. World War I was not the first war like that. By 1865, the American Civil War looked more like the trenches of 1914 than a Napoleonic adventure. The European military establishment regarded Americans as undisciplined fools, mobs of criminals pretending to fight, and thus ignored the military lessons from the conflict with great distaste. But it was not new. As historian John Terraine put it, General Haig employed the strategy that such conflicts called for. Total war requires brutal attrition, treating men as simple statistics to be thrown into a merciless meat grinder of flying metal with such abandon that your enemy cannot compete and gives up. It was not a mistake. See, I've said that, and now you respond."

"Raj," said Mr. Brady, "You are going to leave this classroom!"

Raj did not move. By this point, even the repressed laughs had stopped. Everyone else was a bystander. No one dared.

There was no mechanism at the Woodley School for the forcible removal of a student from a classroom, tall, creepy, fourteen-year-old, Anglo-Indian-American manboy genius or otherwise. To Efram's knowledge, the only security were the two traffic-directing fellows near the driveway at morning and afternoon, both of whom had no other responsibilities. Efram had never heard of a real fight occurring that would require a breakup. It was probably presumed the teachers themselves could handle it.

"Raj, this is your last warning," Mr. Brady said.

"You are free to offer your rebuttal. Have you read John Terraine?"

"You are already in deep trouble. If you do not leave this class your academic grade will suffer considerably."

And then something unexpected happened. Efram Daniels unclenched a set of muscles in his face, and felt breath fill his lungs before beginning to speak.

"But he is right," Efram said. The eyes shifted.

"Efram, I know you are going through a difficult time, but stay out of this."

"No. Raj is right. John Terraine is my great uncle. He talked about this last Christmas."

Sam now gave a whooping laugh. Raj rotated toward Efram, then relented, took to his feet, slapped his newspaper to the desk, and walked out the door without looking at Mr. Brady.

"I apologize for that class," Mr. Brady said as soon as the door clicked. "I don't know what..."

But Efram got up, and he imitated the slap despite having no paper, and stalked off the same way. And in that moment, Efram heard a new sound, laughter directed at his actions, even though he didn't see the faces creating it. Raj was leaning in the small subhallway that sectioned off the doors from the locker banks. Efram took the position opposite him. Raj's clothes were oddly formal, khakis and a button down shirt. He got away with a relative lack of ridicule only because of the stereotypes assumed to him. Efram got rid of his slouch in imitation.

"How did you know all that?" Efram asked.

"I have the prototypical Indian father, who obsessively pushed me into physics and computer science and mathematics and, yes, the spelling bee, from first grade onward. So my method of rebellion was to become obsessively fluent and prodigious in a discipline in which he had no interest."

Efram could not tell if Raj was joking.

"So you chose knowing really big-ass words?"

"History, the humanities, what-have-you."

"But that should help you spell right?" Efram asked.

"Efram," Raj said.

"Yeah?"

"John Terraine died a while ago."

"Oh," Efram said.

✉   ✉   ✉   ✉

CHLOE CLIMBED OUT OF bed at six in the evening, the sun setting. Eyelids still stuck together, she felt her way to the shower.

She forced her face into the falling water. Her muscles clenched, revolting at the temperature. She splashed a sliver of foam against her flesh, the slipping remnants sticking to her shoulder as her fingers dug into scalp.

Alexis Ellison had told Kaela Black specifically not to invite Chloe to the party tonight. Alexis must have justified such a harsh sanction with the reminder that Chloe had once shown Onika Troy a nice handheld picture of Kaela engaged in a drunken exchange with Onika's dear boyfriend Colin. Chloe thrust her head into the deluge and let the first round of chemicals hit the tile, before wrapping her fingers around the next bottle, cupping her other hand to catch the flow.

The drier nuked Chloe's hair at the push of a button, hot air beating on her skin. Hair tossed to and fro, under and in, over and out, she moved a brush through the strands. Her face tinted, particles mashed and spread, browning and bronzing. Her cheeks changed color.

Irises ghosted with suggested tinge, every speck drawn and quartered, she molded cream then powder. Clumps of matter clinging to lashes, she moved the mascara up and through, light but firm. She blinked twice and then surveyed. Her face was now prepared for another night of manifest destiny. Soap, shampoo, conditioner, towel, hairdryer, product, lotion, foundation, concealer, powder, blush, bronzer, eyeliner, eye shadow, mascara—money well spent. The clothes still remained, a whole other process. She carefully analyzed bra and panties, then dress or top, fluctuating between memorized combinations and assortments. The mirror let her survey and judge. Then she lost it. Her consciousness went, the sky outside her room glowed white, and her skin lit on fire.

Her mirror image gazed back when she dragged open her eyes.

She was ready.

In order to feel that a high school party was as good, as stylized, as brilliantly lit, as well-dressed, as well-liquored, or anywhere near as fun as the studios make it look on screen, big or small or smaller, one needed to be drunk, high or higher, and/or delusional.

Kaela Black's house was not an expansive suburban mansion flanked by a lawn filled with drinking jocks. The basement accommodated the event as the neighborhood rowhouse density encroached and overlapped, making underground the safer zone. Bodies splattered on couches and chairs stirred back and forth through the frame, passing the vaporizer to avoid embedding the stench in the furniture. Most parties, even "large" ones, found themselves severely limited in scale for the logistical reasons of space and supply.

Lauryn was sitting next to the host when Chloe walked in.

"I didn't know you were coming," Kaela said and gave her a hug.

Lauryn smiled behind her before she returned to looking disappointed. Reality was not living up to fiction. There was such a difference between the carefully manicured and manscaped himbo bodies of the actors whose pictures she worshipped, and the ruddy typical adolescent barbarians she sucked or fucked (or pretended to, and then talked about later).

Kaela went to greet the next guest.

"Why are we here?" Lauryn whined.

"Because I wasn't invited," Chloe said.

"What? Why?" Lauryn had to yell, the whisper a dead strategy. "You're being weird, were you paying attention in class today? Wanted to fuck Anthony?"

"I'm not interested in your leftovers," Chloe said.

"Where's Michelle?" Lauryn asked.

"Michelle wasn't invited," Chloe said.

"And Jess?"

"Jess is always invited to everything," Chloe said.

Kaela followed a boy Chloe thought was named Eric up the stairs out of the basement.

"She's still into Dan right?"

"Yea," Lauryn confirmed. "Hey?!"

Chloe left Lauryn and followed the new couple up the steps. Now was when Chloe should have witnessed and perhaps documented a horribly embarrassing and possibly degrading incident, and then threatened Kaela with its release and eventual spread to leverage political gain, or used its incendiary content as a trade for devotion, or let it fly for the sake of pure cruelty. Cruelty in itself always had sociopolitical value. Terror worked. At least, it worked in high school, or, it worked in TV shows about high school.

Several steps behind them, Chloe found an ottoman placed right by the opening to the logical laundry room hideaway, figuring they were inside. But when she craned her neck into the opening, she found they were not there. The little room was empty. To her horror Chloe heard the sound of their clothes against the carpet just on the other side of a table, in between her and the exit. As quietly and quickly as possible, she slid from the ottoman to the large chair behind it. She curled, rubbing her cheek against its fabric, using the back as a shield, bringing one eye to the edge so she could see the bodies.

Chloe the voyeur watched one of Eric's hands maneuver down Kaela's stomach between her unzipped legs.

Chloe reached for her phone, instinct, carefully bringing just the lens into the field of view, only to have the backlit screen die right in her hand. No more battery.

Chloe was trapped.

Kaela peeled off her shirt. Chloe retreated fully behind the chair.

The racket from underneath surged louder. Her eyes shut. The moans faded.

The light came blasting through the windows to Chloe's right side, and she buried her face, elbows rising and head diving, meeting halfway. But in blocking out the shine, her forearms began to burn. Chloe could feel the heat rising as the more combustible materials ignited around her, the frayed carpet and flowered wallpaper. She swallowed a scream.

Kaela and Eric clambered through the entranceway. Her eyes pulled open. Neither of them noticed that she was there. Clothes sweat stained, the house around Chloe was still intact, and decidedly not on fire. Her skin was still tingling.

⊗   ⊗   ⊗   ⊗

MOLLY'S FATHER, JONATHAN CORBIN, moved with his nine-year-old daughter to one hundred and one acres in the Idaho Panhandle. The property had multiple streams, a workable growing season, low population density, and easy homeschooling regulations.

The attempt at cooking dinner brought a small army of ants.

Molly's eyes frantically searched for a weapon. Lying against the wall between two boxes was a book. She wielded it as a bludgeoning mace, crushing each group of intruders with targeted blows. She was satisfied with the lack of movement, tiny black dots dead on the floor, and withdrew to her room.

A cricket lay resting next to her sleeping bag, basking in the light of an electric lantern. It evaded the first attempt, jumping to the far wall. She tossed the book again and caught it midleap. The bug entrails smudged the fresh paint. Pulling out a paper towel, she began cleaning the cloth-covered book, but then noticed a daddy long-legs and this time, flattened it with a chop. She climbed into her bag, opened the pages, and started from the beginning.

And *In the beginning God created the heaven and the earth...*

And at breakfast again, the ants returned. A single crumb brought a swarm.

"You want to handle this?" Jon quipped, but Molly took the challenge seriously. Molly retreated to procure her weapon from upstairs. She hovered over one crowded constellation of the frenzied insects, held out her holy hammer of destruction, and let go. It reached the ground with a satisfying thwap. She then put one foot on its cover and stood on the strength of its binding, twisting, making sure those trapped underneath had not withstood the impact. But despite the casualties, they came right back.

Molly pulled a chair into the middle of the kitchen. She placed a single piece of cereal on the ground several feet away. She perched, legs under her, watching the scouts snake out of the cracks. Hand on her heart, Molly counted beats while looking at a clock, trying to slow her life down as much as possible. Deceleration as the lines of ants bent from the wall. A new collection of hammering sounds emerged from another room as her father worked. Finally, head cocked to one side against her shoulder, she was satisfied that the colony had been exposed. Molly hurried into the living room and rummaged through an open toolbox, finding a large plastic tube of industrial glue. She hopped around to each wall, plugging every source hole with a healthy layer of binding goo, sometimes trapping an emerging or returning six-legged figure in a case of thickening hell. The entrances were sealed but there were still many caught on the floor. Molly dove under the sink, retrieving a bottle of dish soap, and studied the back label. There were words like sulfonate and cocamide, and the menacing coccamidopropyl. She took the one dirty glass, and filled it with water. She then poured in some sugar, making the clear liquid cloudy. She mixed in the blue sludge last. She took a spoon, and dolled it out amongst the feeding grounds, returning to her chair.

"How are you doing in here?" Jon asked.

She pointed. Death was swift and eternal.

"Where did they come from?"

Molly pointed to the three walls. "I glued their holes shut," she said.

"You didn't need to do all that. I'm going to have to tear them out anyway. There're prolly carpenter ants and termites, the wood is pretty damp. We're going to have to burn some nests out. And I want to reinforce the walls anyway."

Molly brought her chin down to rest on her arms, which were carefully crossed on her knees.

"Let me show you something," he said.

Up the stairs, her room now had a bed, a desk, and a dresser. She took off a shoe and leapt onto the mattress, landing only on that socked foot, testing its give before descending to a seat. The book, her first weapon, still sat askew in the middle of the floor. Molly retrieved it and opened to the folded page.

"No time for reading," Jon said.

"Why?"

"You can read later, come on."

"*And God said, Let the earth bring forth grass, the herb yielding seed, and the fruit tree yielding fruit after his kind, whose seed is in itself, upon the earth: and it was so,*" she said.

"Did you do your schoolwork yet?" Jon asked.

She went downstairs and sat at the dining table and filled out the three worksheets that made up her education for the day. She left the pieces of paper on the table for her father.

"Let's play patrol," the voice called from the kitchen.

Molly rolled her eyes.

"Come on," he yipped, high-pitched, as if she were a disobedient puppy.

Molly jumped into long underwear, then a pair of blue sweatpants and a maroon down vest. Wool socks went inside velcroed sandals. Jon was in speckled tan and olive camouflage. The game was simple and stupid. Jon would lead, walking somewhere on the property, usually with a .308 hunting rifle slung for no particular reason. Molly had to stay within fifteen yards of him with no verbal communication. By the time she had emerged from the house, real dusk had begun to creep. Molly stamped her feet in a slouch for the first twenty paces. She leaned against the first tree and let him get a lead into the woods. Molly waited a few extra seconds, broke out of her slouch, and left his track. She bounced across the top of the snow, letting it absorb the noise, ending up behind a trunk, peering at him from a distance.

His feet crunched into the crust and his arms scraped branches and trees, his garments producing noise despite their design. Jon clicked the roof of his mouth, a signal to do the same, but Molly did not give her response. He turned and let loose the sound again, thinking she was still behind him, and in those seconds Molly covered another fifteen strides into concealment. *Click click* and he spun again, backtracking and then drifting toward her. She looked at the shadows cast by the trunks. She casually walked in the dark wake of the largest, unseen when his eyes crossed her direction. He gave a louder version of the call. She came to a stop five feet from her father. Molly Corbin sighed loudly instead of sending a click.

TOWARD ITS SOUTHERN AND eastern ends, Rock Creek Park becomes a series of snaking tentacles, emerald tributaries reaching into the swaths of wide-avenued L'Enfant cement. Efram's house was on one of these, in Woodland-Normanstone Terrace Park, one of an oblique series of cul-de-sac houses devoid of commercial business, mashed between Cleveland Park and the Naval Observatory, and a ten-minute walk to The Woodley School's perch in Kalorama Heights.

On the nook in the kitchen where Efram typically ate was a note. *Going out of town! It read. To the beach!* And then a horrible smiley face. *Gloria* (housekeeper/ grocery buyer/etc.) *or Sergey* (driver, helper, porter, and maybe bodyguard?) *will drive you to school this week if you don't want to walk, and call Peggy if you need anything!* Exclamation points galore. High as a satellite.

The house had been plucked clean of belongings. So many of the material goods had been his father's, or, in his mother's head, associated with his father, and therefore cleansed from the premises. Boxed up and removed in successive waves by faceless helpers while he was at school. Efram had not been consulted.

He was hunched over a screen. A miniature pixelated city was being raised toward the unseeable sky: green, blue, and neon squares appeared as residential, commercial, or industrial zoned properties giving way to animated construction sites and, finally, completed buildings. Sound effects came from the speakers. It was small so far. No mayor's house yet. Leaning over with his left hand, he heard the approaching footsteps, paused time, and leapt down.

A short bespectacled woman glided into the room beaming and broadcasting infinite affection, daffodils and sunshine and anthropomorphic animals that help princesses. Peggy Kroutil was the family accountant, hired by Efram's mother independent of her husband's financial operation and predating the marriage itself. Investigators quickly established she was not worth scrutiny. Peggy was the last one of what had been an army. Behind her was the ghost of Kevin, the lawyer's head floating in the open door.

Peggy was holding several envelopes of various sizes and hues. They faced Efram in an uneven wall.

"Did I do something wrong?" Efram asked.

Simultaneously Peggy reassuringly cooed "no" while Kevin nodded wordlessly in the affirmative behind her.

"We are here to let you know the state of things," he said.

"Both your and your mother's financial futures are completely secure," Peggy said. "Your mother obviously has control over the acute family's assets at the moment, though a considerable amount has always been and will continue to be in trust for you, along with separate assets that were solely controlled by your father and his personal company, which were specifically left to you."

"We can be pretty sure that, considering the structure of the plea bargain, no assets will be seized from this point," Kevin said. "They could try something stupid, and if your mother ever lived in New York City again, there could be a purely superficial investigation, since the attorney general still believes she was complicit, but other than that, things should be alright."

"I don't want you to worry. You shouldn't feel anxious," Peggy was a mother. "Now here is a bank account in your name, a real one, a checking account, and a credit card in your name that goes straight to your mother's account. You can use either depending on what you need to do. I will be regularly monitoring the bank account and wiring funds into it as needed but you can always call me if you need more. We decided it was better this way. You might need things and direct access is preferable, considering..."

Efram took the opened envelopes with the colored plastic still adhered to the internal papers. They reflected the light.

"You have to sign the backs," Peggy reminded. She stopped talking and lurched forward one step, placing a hand on Efram's shoulder. "Really Efram," a deliberate slow down, "you are alright here on your own? If you need anything, call. You have my numbers right?"

"Yes," Efram said.

They both vanished and Efram flung his paper life onto the unmade bed. He unpaused time in the game, and raised residential taxes while cutting commercial taxes. He employed parking meters for the developing downtown and placed a police and fire station near his first school. He cranked up the speed. He wanted to add population more quickly. A bigger city faster. The real fun was in tearing it down, making a massive necropolis with the disasters that occupied their own dropdown menu. If you sent enough earthquakes, volcanoes, and alien invasions, the computer would generate four horsemen to gallop across the map, obliterating your city. He lowered property taxes and spent into debt, issuing municipal bonds to cover the expansion.

‡   ‡   ‡   ‡

SEVEN YEARS BEFORE THE end, the table was set in Hong Kong.

Alfred Noon was Norman's dinner companion, and Steven was invited to sit at the grownups' table. Alfred was an "old friend" from Norman's former days in Her Majesty's Diplomatic Service, before he had fully embraced a private sector life. The spherical Alfred kept his mouth moving with the political talking points of the day. Ignored, Steven focused on scraping the largest possible portions of pasta into his mouth. The monologue lulled and Alfred turned to him.

"What do you think of all of this, young man?"

Steven shrugged.

"You don't care who is president?" The white haired man responded as though Steven had given an actual thoughtful answer.

"Does it really matter?" Steven asked.

"My little nihilist," Norman said.

"Ah! It is an interesting point. After all who passed the voting rights and civil rights acts? Who warned about the military-industrial complex? Who gutted welfare? Who pledged to stop nation building, only to start again?"

Steven brought a napkin to his face in a show of his mouth being full.

"So what are you interested in these days Steven?" Alfred prodded.

"Steven is interested in death," Norman said. "Typical, you might say, but he isn't annoying me with prepubescent versions of existential philosophy. He studies how we physically die."

"I'm not sure I understand," Alfred said, turning to Steven once again. But Norman still answered.

"My son is fascinated by military history, disease, biology, natural disasters, things like that."

"Ah. So a future professor, perhaps?"

Norman arched his eyebrows and curled his lips.

"Hey professor!" Norman mocked. "Want to explain to Alfred what bullets do to a body?"

Steven knows that when a bullet hits a head, even if the shot isn't lethal, the pressure of the impact is so great that the skull ruptures. He knows this because Norman gave Steven his very own laptop after he got sick of sharing with his son. Steven knows that bullets are the enemy of tissue. They exist to destroy it. They shred it, tumble through it, wrecking organs and spitting bile into ducts and cavities.

"You shouldn't really be afraid of bullets," Steven said. "You're more likely these days to get bombed."

Alfred swallowed a bite.

Steven went back up to the room and let the adults have their time. He opened up his laptop.

He learned that the day prior, in Washington, DC, a police officer was shot three times during a routine traffic stop before a twelve-year-old boy jumped from his own vehicle, ran across the street, and stood between the shooter and the bleeding victim. He shielded the officer until the attacker made the decision to flee the scene. The police department said the family of the boy was insisting on keeping his identity private, and the MPD would honor both their and his wishes. "It isn't only his parents. The boy himself has no interest in doing 'hero' interviews," a source close to the commissioner's office said.

Steven clicked the box, but the grainy video from the police car camera had been edited to avoid showing the initial shots. The boy jumped into the frame and stood, staring down the gun. The officer wasn't visible, having collapsed to the ground right in front of his own headlights. But the boy was there, as small if not smaller than Steven.

The media desperately craved the identity of this child savior. They wanted to laud him and trot him out on morning shows. Steven watched witnesses give interviews, but they all said they had been ducking during the initial shooting and its aftermath, and that once the assailant drove away, they saw the boy kneeling down to the bleeding cop.

A local business owner was the first to reach the officer and apply pressure to the wounds. On his arrival, the boy sprinted back to his own car. They all gave the same vague description—short, curly haired, and relaxed.

Steven knew he would not have left his vehicle. It wasn't the rational choice.

He looked up the ingredients of napalm next.

And then pictures of what it does to skin.

PART

2

*And there went out another
horse that was red:
And power was given to him that sat
thereon to take peace from the earth,
And that they should kill one another:
And there was given unto him a great sword.*
—The Book of Revelation

*Who's in a bunker?
Who's in a bunker?
Women and children first,
And the children first,
And the children...*
—Radiohead, *"Idioteque"*

LeMay Senior High School had enough kids that the beginning of the day resembled the mass exodus of a tribe across a wasteland. Chloe, Lauryn, Michelle, and Jess were trapped in the migration. To their left was a group of short drama-and-music girls who were all varying degrees of overweight. To their right was a group of tall, nonathletic boys talking about animation, all wearing T-shirts that did not fit their awkward sizes and all hosting large headphones around their necks.

Chloe noticed people distributed themselves, tall with tall, fat with fat, one kind of stupid with the same kind of stupid, watchers with watchers and doers with doers. All of her mother's friends were short and dumpy, unable to control their burgeoning weight. They were all locked in settling marriages based on lives so pathetic that rearing children was the only logical alternative to suicide.

If only they'd all had abortions, Chloe thought.

Reaching an intersection of cement steps, Lauryn turned and headed off in a different direction with a smile and a touch of Jess's hand. Wednesday's block scheduling meant Chloe would not run into Lauryn again. Even their lunches were different. Michelle would see her several times. Jess would see her once.

"That bitch doesn't give a fuck about any of you," Michelle started once Lauryn was far enough away. "She calls you out for being a janky-ass slut every five minutes," she said to Jess, "saying shit like 'maybe one of these guys will get drunk enough and slap her around so she'll be so traumatized she becomes a dyke and then she can be our charity case.'"

Jess laughed, and Michelle was confused at that response. Michelle pulled out her phone in an attempt to call up evidence. They stopped walking, causing a jam, to read the text. "Jess BEGGED me not to tell about Alex Bledsoe. Next time she wants to suck my dick, she should get on her knees." Chloe loved when Lauryn attained that level of poetry, 113 characters.

But Jess didn't seem to care. Instead, she was holding one of her seven necklaces in her teeth, looking at the group of boys in punk bands and distressed jeans, circling around them with the flow.

"Michelle," Chloe said, "Do you really believe that Jess would ever beg anyone to do anything? Fuck, do you really believe Jess would ever have a conversation about someone? I mean, Jess," Chloe turned to her, "Do you care about Alex Bledsoe?"

Jess jostled her head, spitting the necklace out of her mouth, her chosen punk-boy grinning and walking backward so he could keep looking at her.

"Fine, but you don't care that she's using you to talk shit?" Michelle tried to get Jess's attention. But now Jess was lighting a cigarette, illegal on school property, squinting her eyes as she inhaled and waving to a security guard on the steps. "Come on!" Michelle pleaded, still showing Lauryn's messages on her phone as proof.

But Chloe grabbed Jess's arm, snaking her fingers around the inside of her bicep, and left Michelle alone in the crowd.

After school, Chloe sat on Lauryn's bed and recited the complete record of the exchange. Chloe had purposefully gone dark and not sent Lauryn seventy messages throughout the day. It would be more convincing if given as a live performance.

"Well, joke's on her—no one's talking to that bitch now," Lauryn said.

"Wow. What a loss. That's what you think revenge is?"

Lauryn shrugged.

Chloe hopped onto the bed. She lowered the screen in front of both sets of eyes. She rifled off Michelle's password.

Lauryn squealed.

Jaw clenched shut, Chloe clicked compose, and selected Mr. Takami, the volleyball coach, from the list of contacts. Fingers did their job: "Mr. Takami, I cannot play volleyball anymore. We should have killed all you japs in the first place, xoxo, Michelle."

Chloe leaned back on the bed and closed her eyes.

The light blazed. Her skin burned. Then she couldn't breathe.

$\otimes$ $\otimes$ $\otimes$ $\otimes$

"It's so great you brought your child," the man with the red beard said. He had just spent four hours demonstrating tourniquets, sterilization, and bandaging—elevating limbs and assessing damage to dummies and acting students. Eleven-year-old Molly's favorite had been bringing the CPR manikin back to life by pouring air into its lips and pounding relentlessly on its chest.

Jonathan thanked him and talked until Molly's sagging spine was about to collide with the earth. He led her back to the car. It was three and a half hours back in one of their new vehicles, TEOTWAWKI-ready, all precomputing models convincingly retained for their capability to withstand an electromagnetic pulse. It could come from the the the skies, he said. The Iranians, Chinese, or North Koreans would detonate a nuclear warhead in the atmosphere above the continental forty-eight and knock out all unprotected electronic devices. So for vehicles, it had to be back-in-the-day Isuzu Troopers or certain serial number runs of Toyota Hiluxes—anything where there was an old-school, fully mechanical fuel injection system.

"We would be back in the Steam Age," Jon had said when he explained that an EMP could do permanent damage to circuit components.

"Should we get a steam engine?" Molly responded with sincerity. Her history homeschoolbook of that moment had a nice insert photo of Hero's aeolipile from the first century, a toy. So nukes scorching the ground meant the Stone Age and nukes scorching the sky meant the Steam Age. Good to know.

Jon took advantage of civilization and pulled to a stop underneath the bright red and yellow logo of a supermarket chain. It was a biweekly practice. A way to keep their reserves intact. He filled the shopping cart with meat and dairy—they grew their own vegetables—while Molly broke off to grab cereals and packaged snacks. Jon disappeared into the housewares aisle and Molly beelined for a rack at the front, taking the opportunity to scan the magazines, studying the chiseled faces with their clothes.

"Do you want one?" he asked when he returned.

Molly shook her head. At the register she scooted around her father, making a show of digging into his pocket for the keys, and waited in the car for the lopsided squeal of the approaching cart. The groceries were loaded. And then, finally, ignition and movement.

The river to the left side of the road was dark teal, sunken into a canyon of jaded moss dotted with drab, dirt-covered shrubs below omnipresent trees. She knew their names, Subalpine Firs, Red Cedars, White Pines, Englemann Spruces, Mountain Hemlocks, and Black Cottonwoods. She ignored the buzz of the weather radio and fidgeted with the Velcro banded tourniquet which had been used as a demonstration sample, a tactical military version made of black nylon.

Molly entered a state of suspended animation. An hour from home, they peeled off the four-lane conduit to the two-lane dividerless thoroughfare. The change in traffic frequency liquefied her eyes into a state of semiconsciousness. They were last in a string of four cars, shifting in and out of a distanced line. The group entered a large curve to the right.

Half-awake, Molly fixated on a tan minivan that materialized from the approaching bend. It clipped the black SUV that was two ahead of them and went barreling full force into the side of the hill. The noise broke her trance. If you were a fly, that was how it would sound to be swatted. The car directly in front of them impacted the back of the van and spun into the other lane. In less than a second, Jon yanked the wheel to the left, climbed the opposite shoulder, and avoided both hulks despite their deceleration and his sustained momentum. Molly's eyes followed their crunched forms as they traversed the obstacle course, spinning in her seat. The black SUV that had narrowly avoided total disaster had already pulled over, and a man was exiting, phone to his ear, ignoring the scratch on the side of his face.

Jonathan Corbin accelerated.

"Stop!" she said. But no speed was sacrificed.

"The first guy is already calling. The cops and medics will handle it," he said.

She began exhaling her response, a plea, a we-could-help, a they-might-need-us, a what-did-we-just-spend-four-hours-doing, but he answered before a coherent word could be formed—

"And if we try to help any of those people, and we get something wrong, we'll get sued."

There was an urge—needles digging into her skin, forearms itching, an energy designed to make her launch out of her seat and bring her hands to his throat and face, even if only to accomplish the annihilation of their own vehicle. Her chin turned from the back window to her father after the last glimpse of the accident had disappeared with a series of turns. She went back to being stone, flexing her muscles to keep them in place.

They took another turn onto a quieter road. And then another.

Molly slammed the car door shut and left Jon to haul in the groceries by himself. The front door was locked. She bent around the corner of the porch, slid open the far window, and climbed in, crashing to the floor in the process.

"I'm going to have to lock that," she heard him yell. The outer walls had been reinforced. The doors made double and then triple. She took the stairs in threes and fours. She reached her sanctuary and fled into the bathroom. The ancient bathtub on its majestic feet had two spigots and two handles, hot and cold. She opened up the left. With that noise she came back into her room and shut the door to the hall. It was heavy. Metal inside what looked like wood. Clicking it in for the first time, Molly spun the second knob for the first lock, and then twisted the heavy lock bolted at the top. The boxed window and skylight now had blackout shades. There had been a lecture on light discipline. She pulled both ropes and brought the room into darkness and then struck a match, igniting one of the many candles scattered around the room. They were originally meant to be devotional—Catholic, Jon had told her, wreathed in glass and tall—but were by far the cheapest to buy in bulk and therefore a favorite among preppers. Molly had stacked twenty boxes of five hundred in the basement. Multiplication table practice. Molly sent her clothes flying to the floor. She took four leaping steps and jumped into the bathtub. Wreathed in the warmth, almost scalding, she brought her head under with everything else. The world went quiet. With every minute her skin became older with wrinkles.

Out of the tub and cocooned in a towel, she took note of the wax level. It was a waiting game. She had no other timekeeping device in her room. She knew from a middle school science book that if she had a scale and a clock she could figure out exactly how long each candle lasted, and determine what interval each inch of wax represented—but she had neither. Her only possible entertainment came from two plastic shelves—euthanasia by way of Brainstorms, Knowledge Clusters, Did you Knows, Discussion Questions, and Study Guides. Jon had never cohesively kept track of grade equivalents, ignoring her age completely. The material was not tackled in the order intended but subject by subject, entire grade by entire grade, and format by format. All the history worksheets from seventh to tenth grade, all the history minitests from seventh to tenth grade, etc.

As quietly as possible, Molly funneled the refuse of life in her citadel into a plastic bag. Finished and bored again, she pushed her one plain-Jane wooden chair under the exposed timber beam that presided across her room, the roof escaping upward. She tried a pull-up. Shoulders perpendicular, she gripped one side in each hand and eased her feet off the repurposed platform. She squeezed every single muscle. Her chest inched upward, body tilting but still straight, only making it halfway before she faltered and let go.

On the ground, Molly tried to guess the time. 1:30 in the morning? 2:15? She put on a pair of gray sweatpants and a turquoise turtleneck. Each stage of the lock was undone five minutes apart, so the shuffles, touches, and clicks were divorced from one another. She freed the heavy door, allowing the slightest bit of momentum to swing it, and ground her foot against the hinge to bring it to a stop before it could scrape the outer wall. She sat cross-legged a foot inside her room, and listened.

Satisfied with the quality of the void, she took to her feet, grabbed the bag of trash, and took a long step out of the doorway. She tried to pick out pieces of the floor that would not creak. A stray glance cataloged the lack of light from under Jon's door. At the stairs, she skated each sock to the edge of each step, running fingers across the bannister for balance. She took the living room and kitchen at a glide, placing the garbage under the sink. She opened the door to the basement with a slow turn and a click. The under floor had been completed and expanded. Shelf upon shelf stretched backward to a door that guarded a whole other section. Then there was a set of half-stairs, another descent. She clicked on a battery powered lantern, brought the room into being, propping open the door with a wooden wedge.

She went first to the shelves with the gear and unwrapped the plastic from a brand new, black webbed three-day backpack. She retrieved a large coyote brown duffel that she could have folded herself into and set it on the floor. Against the wall, packed and ready for flight, Jonathan's foliage green behemoth of a backpack had a machete grafted onto its back in between several auxiliary pouches for medical gear and ammunition. Looped through one cell of the webbing Molly spotted a tan watch. She pressed the button on its face and was greeted with a green background. 3:11, it told her. It wound around her wrist.

Two twelve packs of Meals Ready-To-Eat were tossed into the large duffle. Chicken noodle stew with vegetables, pasta with marinara sauce, vegetarian chili with beans, just add included water. Not wanting to survive on wet flavored dust, she dragged the duffle down an aisle, and threw a camping kitchen set and a folding burner stove into the backpack. From the pantry, Molly retrieved two bags of white rice.

Dish detergent, soap, shampoo, toilet paper, and toothpaste all found their way into the haul. She strapped it on, adding extra feet to her profile, and let the door close slowly against her before she strained up the stairs. Rising, scraping the walls and swaying with the weight, she stopped. The dark bleed from the windows revealed that Jon had not stored all of the groceries. The plastic bags were dumped on the kitchen counter. He must have given up after putting the perishables into the fridge.

Slipping the strap of her duffle across her chest, letting herself be trapped in a web of nylon to free both of her hands, Molly grasped the plastic handle loops in twos. She became a pack animal. Each step caused a new burn in her shoulders and back, knots gnawing below her blades. The sides of her thighs felt like tangled mush. The final climb was a rush, reaching her portal without glancing to see if she had made enough racket to be caught. She deposited her cargo onto the bed, her weight landing as she untangled herself. She bounded to the door, brought the slab shut, and latched each lock fully closed. Not even trusting Jon's degree of paranoia, she jabbed the wooden doorstop under the foot of the door as a final precaution. Drawbridge up. Portcullis down.

‡   ‡   ‡   ‡

Norman told Steven they were "staying with friends" in London, six years before the end. Caroline was a widow, Australian by birth but raised in South Africa. She was an assistant at an NGO. Norman said he knew her from his life before. She had one child, Sophia, a ten-year-old with a pale face. She sneered at him as they walked through the door, despite his age and height advantage.

"Presents!" She squealed, and Norman handed her two wrapped parcels.

"For you, my pretty darling," he said.

Twelve-year-old Steven extended a handshake just like he had been taught, but Sophia ignored him and tore into the wrapping paper.

"Sophia!" Caroline hissed. "Hello Steven, let me show you where you'll be sleeping." She led him by the hand down the hallway. "Take anything you want from the kitchen. Norman says you get on well on your own."

The room was not a hotel room. A single, child-sized bed had been crammed up against the window.

"I'll let you settle in."

Steven looked out of the glass. He stared at the night over the city, imagining spitfires and hurricanes rushing overhead as Nazi bombers rumbled. He pictured the glimmer of the fire casting St. Paul's Cathedral in a dark silhouette. Steven was beginning to understand that war was different than how films portrayed it. From one of the many volumes he forced Norman to buy him, there was a sentence he kept repeating in his head. "In ninety percent of planes shot down, the pilot never even saw the opponent that got them." They exploded, never knowing. Steven imagined this, from a cockpit point of view. A racket, and then plunge out of the clouds.

He looked up at the ceiling above his bed and imagined it was the second year of the second war, and that he had not made it underground when the sirens went off and the spotlights went up. He saw the iron casing break through the roof and ceiling, pulled downward, crushed by wood and fire. He imagined being asleep and not knowing it was coming. Being snuffed out or blown apart without realizing what had happened.

Steven turned from the window and opened his bag. He unearthed the remaining chocolate bar that was the last from his air travel haul, as any airport concourse always resulted in a stockpile. He threw a cube in his mouth and heard footsteps running from the doorway. Sophia had been watching him.

"MUM!!!" She levied rage. "Steven is having sweets before supper!" Her tantrum only escalated as Norman and Caroline tried to explain. If she had asked, Steven would have given her some.

Sitting at the dining table, Sophia asked calmly, "Steven, you don't talk much. Are you dumb?"

"Sophia! Do I need to send you to your room?"

"What? I wasn't trying to be mean!" Sophia pleaded, "I was asking since he doesn't go to school or anything. Why don't you go to school like normal?"

"Steven, I think it's wonderful that your father brings you with him while he works," Caroline said. "It's like you're his apprentice. Do you know what an apprentice is?"

Steven nodded.

"See," Norman said, "he doesn't need to be normal."

"I think Sophia, that you should show what a polite and wonderful host you can be, and take Steven around to your room, maybe let him have a look at your toys." Caroline took Norman's hand over the table.

Sophia hopped down, made a show of sighing, and trudged toward her room.

"Go," Norman said, Caroline rubbing her thumb along the inside of his wrist.

Steven obeyed.

Sophia's room was entirely white and pink. A horde of stuffed animals lay piled up to the windowsill. There were five separate posters of horses taking up the walls, picture books and juvenile novels occupied a large set of shelves. There was a doll with a fake tiara on the top of a dresser. She jumped on her bed and sat cross-legged.

"This is my room. These are my toys. But I'm almost too old for them. I can't wait until I get a mobile," she said. "Mummy won't let me yet, but maybe Norman will buy me one for Christmas. Did he buy you one?"

"No," Steven said, "I don't have a phone."

"Ha! And you're twelve? You don't have any friends to talk to I guess."

"He bought me a laptop," Steven said.

Her face lit up at the expense and what that could mean for her future.

"What's your room like at home? Do you have a lot of toys?" she asked.

"We never really go home. I just have my suitcase."

"Why are you so weird Steven? When my mum marries your dad, and you become my stepbrother, you're going to have to stop being a freak."

"Our parents aren't getting married," Steven said.

"You're stupid. Of course they are. My mum told me so," Sophia squealed with a bounce against her mattress.

"They can't," Steven said. "My father's already married. He and my mother are still married."

"No they AREN'T," she cried, slapping the bed.

"Yes," Steven said, calmly, "they are."

He left her room. He heard Sophia wailing outside
her mother's locked bedroom, unyielding until Caroline
emerged.

☷   ☷   ☷   ☷

EFRAM DANIELS REPEATED HIS belongingless lean against
the wall before fourth period Latin class. Across the
hallway, Raj was planted against the lockers. Raj was
holding some all-too-important text to his face, but his
eyes were not on it. Efram tracked the line. A minute and
a half before the scheduled start, a girl named Christina
Thierry appeared. No one but Efram watched Raj
watching Christina. No one caught him focusing on how
Christina's dirty-blonde hair draped over her shoulders.
Not even Sam Page, shoulders held back, hair in his face
under a withered hat whose brim pointed too far upward,
paid Raj any mind as he honed in on the same mark.
Where Raj probed with his eyes, Sam snuck up behind
her and snapped the exposed strap of her bra. An easy
target. What the hell was this? Seventh grade? Christina
shrieked while many of her friends laughed, Christina
eventually joining in, and Sam huffed and puffed. Silence
rung out from the sidelines.

Raj appeared to be back to his reading. Mrs. McGlennon
strolled up, keys in hand, and the floodgates opened.
Efram launched off the lockers and dove, juking between
three bodies so he found himself right behind Sam Page
as they started into the classroom. He kept with him until
Sam picked a desk, Efram narrowly beating Christina into

the seat directly behind him. Once settled, Efram knelt to the ground in an imitation of tying his shoe, only to find that his laces were in fact undone. One of his hands gripped the bottom of Sam's seat and frantically prodded the metal. The two support screws came out easily. Efram retreated back to his desk and let his fingers go to work on destabilizing his own chair. Sam sat down. Nothing happened. A nice series of atmospheric notes took Efram over, an ambient and cloudy series of blips.

"Efram, where is your homework?" Mrs. McGlennon interrupted the environmental symphony.

"I don't have it," Efram said.

"Don't have it? Did you do it?"

"Nope."

The class held still, amused. An admission of this sort without any attempt to explain or summon an excuse was unprecedented. But the attention waned, the rest using the time to sneak a quick message or finish an assignment or straighten a bra or daydream about a haircut or plot revenge against a social sleight.

"You just didn't do it?" Mrs. McGlennon asked, astonished at the lack of remorse in his response.

"No," Efram confirmed.

"Talk to me after class," she said.

The rest were on the verge of lapsing into total distraction. Christina was moving fingers through a carefully partitioned section of her hair. Messages were buzzing through the air.

"Here we go," a voice whispered.

Declensions populated the board. In front of Efram, Sam Page's left foot began dangerously fidgeting with one of the desk legs. Efram heard the metal moan. Fourteen minutes into the class, Raj answered a question, and answered it normally. Nine minutes later, Sam turned to sneak a peek at someone, and his right foot came into contact with the other desk leg, Efram could see the seam split an inch apart. Sam's body slouched, curving lower and lower into the seat. His hand hit his cheek, and his elbow planted square on his desk. With that, metal let loose from metal and Sam Page found himself on the ground, pinned by two tubular steel legs and a plasticized top. Laughter was undeniable. He yelped, somehow repressing the urge to curse, hands scurrying to free himself as his neighbors fought to pull each side apart. Efram rose and offered a compulsory hand. Prying himself out, Sam chortled, "Nurse..." and sprinted from the room without further explanation.

Mrs. McGlennon seemed to need none.

When Efram reconnected with his own seat, he also met the ground with a crash.

"Uh, class," Mrs. McGlennon said, not checking to see if Efram was alright. "We're going to continue this tomorrow. I'll speak to someone about this."

The shuffle began, and Efram got up, but instead of trudging up to the board where Mrs. McGlennon was erasing, he exited through the door.

He took the stairwell down to the cafeteria, lured by the scheduled aroma of pizza that emanated from the cafeteria several times a month. He was early and breezed through the empty line to grab the laid out slices. The tables were long and connected, which made hierarchal decisions more difficult, too many overlapping seats. He chose a random spot. Within three seconds, Raj was in the seat across from him. His head was cocked to the side and tilted downward, his palms placed on the table at straight right angles. He had no food in front of him.

"Did you implode those chairs, Efram?"

"Nogh," Efram said shoving the slice into his mouth

"Are you sure?"

"Mhmmph."

Efram used the liquid fruit to clear his mouth and esophagus of tomato, bread, and cheese. School pizza didn't have grease.

Groups globbed together all over the room. Creatures furiously discussing blowjobs, downloads, games, goals, Ambien, housemates, characters, vampires, ketamine, zombies, sneakers, videos, kittens, explosions, hair, teachers, colleges, siblings, comedians, breakups, ankle-breaking crossovers, and who they didn't like.

"So it'd be cool to be able to talk like you," Efram said.

"Like me?" Raj asked.

"Like how you did in history class."

"The first centralized educational system was implemented by Napoleon," Raj started, "not for economic or social development but for the expressed purpose of political and military power. The only reason to demand proficiency of an entire generation in a more or less standardized set of subjects is to allow the fielding of industrial scale armies, both in practical concerns and political. You can indoctrinate a whole generation well enough behind certain political and philosophical ideals, but you need schools to do it. An independent school like this is the next level of that, the safety valve of the Bourgeoisie to create a managing class to oversee the masses..."

But a junior girl named Penny Gilbert was striding past down the aisle, wearing a black T-shirt and black tights that looked like leather pants, and the required expressionless face that goes with being way too hot for high school while having no worthy, straight male equivalent on campus.

"My sister knows her," Raj offered.

LAURYN AND CHLOE WERE standing in front of an acne-laden creature with a borderline unibrow. His name was Anton Hotz. Chloe patted his shoulder, and Lauryn had to swallow bile.

Chloe was always nice to Anton Hotz. She smiled at him in the hallways. No one else who mattered did. He was literally and figuratively a nobody: a sophomore, short, virginal, hideously cheesy black sloganed inside joke nerddom T-shirts that were always the wrong size (but not in a good way). In any typical dated analysis of the school's sociopolitical structure, Anton was a prime candidate for relegation to bottom-feeding status. He was removed to begin with, ghettoized in the honors classes, separated into an entire magnet division, the accelerated program.

But Anton was not a valedictory address hunting, psychotic med-school wanting, future math class suicide with test-prep parents of doom. He did drugs, and not for studying. He did not have a rat tale. He did not go to school dances and wallflower—until, finally, one year, some requisite awkward-compatible mirror-image nerd girl asked him to go with her and constellations were romantically pointed out through the gym skylight. Anton was too busy for such things. He was an engineer. And Chloe liked engineers. Engineers were useful.

Anton Hotz was LeMay's premier engineer, despite his social ineptness. So Chloe listened and held his hand as he recounted the actions of his torturers.

"Don't worry about it Anton," she said. "That's really fucked up. We're gonna fix it."

Lauryn's face contorted in confusion, a chimp attempting a launch sequence, eyes exclaiming annoyance at the inclusive "we."

"Look, they're never going to talk to you again. Never touch you. Never look at you. That's what you want?"

A curt but solid nod jerked through the dismal and wretched state of the modern teenage American boy-nobody, not an uncontrollable stream of hydrated theatrical agonized crying, but a pissed-off red-face of uncontrolled emotion.

"He's such a fucking asshole," Anton said. "I fucking hate it here because of him."

"You don't think you deserved it a tiny bit?" Lauryn spoke up.

Chloe slapped the table and snapped her eyes the other direction.

"Don't listen to her," Chloe said nicely and then, still focusing on him, "can you hold on a minute?".

There was a sniffled affirmative response. Chloe twisted Lauryn's wrist and walked across the empty classroom into a closet.

Chloe fought the urge to rake her hand across Lauryn's face.

"What the fuck are you doing?"

"ME? What am I doing? Why are we here? Are we a charity thing now? Is this community service? If it is, we're picking someone different. He deserved it! He is a total creep. Shaun found him looking at a fuckload of pictures of Lindsay and did what was coming. If I were her, I'd want Shaun to do the same thing to anyone being that sketchy."

"Let me see your phone," Chloe said.

"What? No!"

"I'm not going to use it. I want to show you something."

Lauryn pulled it from her back pocket but kept her fingers on it.

"You don't have to give it to me, just pull up your message history."

"I'm not letting you see that!"

"Exactly."

Chloe unearthed her own from her slung purse, held it up to Lauryn's face, too close in anger, and pressed buttons over illuminated skin. There were thousands of them. Names and dates and times and the first few words. She scrolled fast enough that it wasn't really possible for Lauryn to get anything, but slow enough that it appeared to be an act of trust.

"That 'creep' has the ability to control all of this, this entire thing," Chloe stopped the scroll and twirled the rectangle in her hand. "If this breaks, he can fix it. He can disguise you, disappear you, block others, hide you from certain people, make fake messages, and recover deleted ones. You can tell him someone's number and he can pull everything they write from the air. You want to know what people say when they bitch about you? He can give it to you. So shut the fuck up and be nice!"

Chloe's finger was cocked in front of Lauryn's face, a warning and a weapon.

They walked back to the table.

"Sorry! Anyway, we're going to make sure they all leave you alone. Like you can disappear from it all? That's what you want right?"

"Or why don't we help you get revenge?" Lauryn tried enthusiastically. Chloe bit her lip. "We have a lot we could embarrass Shaun with. And we could get Lindsay to like hook up with you and it would get back to him or something."

"Thanks," he said with a shudder, "but I really wanna be done."

"Alright. You're done," Chloe said.

She gave him a hug and then Lauryn awkwardly copied her, Anton grimacing through the second compression.

Chloe yawned, trying to get more oxygen as they walked away.

"So what are we going to do?" Lauryn asked.

"I'll tell Shaun to stop."

"What? Why will he say yes?"

"Who do you think told Shaun about Anton being a creep in the first place?"

When Chloe went to sleep she saw the long thin exhaust line pierce the sky before her walls crumbled and she was burned alive.

Shaun Mullendore left Anton Hotz alone.

⊗   ⊗   ⊗   ⊗

SIX NIGHTS AND FIVE days into the siege, Molly Corbin lay asleep in her bed. Her desk had become a temple complex of finished papers. Her pantry was set up in the empty corner, rations kept in their original boxes and bags. Clothes hung from the single rafter, drying, washed in the bathtub. Several dining plates sat dehydrating over a towel laid on the top of her dresser, joined by the stainless steel camping cooking set that stacked into a single compact shape.

Molly's eyes opened. The roof was creaking. Moving. Someone was up there. So far, Jon's attempts at ending her self-imposed exile had consisted of muffled vocalizations through the door—mostly pleading but once angry—all of which she greeted with silence. He knew she was alive and well by the bagged trash that would occasionally find its way out of the room, tied for disposal. Molly felt the ceiling at the lowest point of the diagonal, her fingers vibrating with the rhythm of the shifting weight above. He had not tried to forcefully attack the door in any way, so why would he go to the roof? Was his goal to simply get sight of her, pass a message, or actually to try to pierce her bunker? Molly heard the noises come closer, and then the whirr of a power tool. Making a decision, she made for her door and moved the first deadbolt, knowing she could always retreat with him on the roof. The light, the electric light, the dormant one in the ceiling, ignited her room, revealing the note that had been slipped under her door sometime during the night—

Molly,
I'm having the house connected to the grid. We'll have power all the time now. I'm also putting solar cells on the roof which can be switched to stand-alone.
We also got a satellite and a television and a computer that you can use.

Please come out,
Dad

In her hand, Molly flexed that yellow paper—a white flag—preparing to crumple it, but on second thought tucked it in the middle of the mountain of homeschoolwork. She turned instead to the strained and stained wood on the beam above. Her pull-up had gotten all the way up by now, but it was still an ugly and uneven thing, only made possible by cheating and swinging her legs.

One set of fingers tapped the beam. Molly tested her thoracic mobility, keeping her legs straight while her shoulders and head craned around to hear the possible intruder. She was an owl, head over back, her eyes wide.

She pulled her body away from the floor, ignoring the invisible grasp of earth's mass, falling away from the cradle. Recalling the image from a science book, she saw herself as a insignificant thing on the surface of our floating planet, standing at the bottom of the sphere. She would just have to plummet off into space. Her fists reached her chest in satisfaction and her eyes lay level with the splintery wood. Molly Corbin completed her first legitimate pull-up. She lowered herself slowly, finishing the motion, and then swung down kicking her legs over the chair and straight to the floor. Reaching the ground, Molly hammered a book shut and threw a pencil across the room. She punched the wall, sending pain through the fist, and swept all the academic material from a shelf into the middle of the room, her father's peace offering lost in the cascade. She collapsed to the bed, and glued her eyes to the electric light.

The next morning she saw a brown spot on the sheet and immediately checked herself for injuries, punctures, flowing blood of any sort. It dawned on her eventually. She found her least favorite and most disposable pair of underwear, slipped into pants, and washed her face.

She stripped the bed, undid the locks, and took a moment to concede defeat. Dragging the bundled fabric with edges trailing along behind her, the siege ended. Down the stairs, through the hallway to the dining room, into the library.

"Jon," Molly Corbin said three days before her twelfth birthday, abandoning the old title of Dad, first-name basis now, adult to adult, handing him the sheet where the damage was done. "So that happened," she said, mindful of the sterile language of the health and biology books on the shelf above. Jon took the sheet, stripped a new trash bag from under the desk, not willing to fight wars against stains when a few dozen sets of linens lay in the stores below.

"Follow me," he said, leading back through the pantry and down the stairs to the basement. There was a door Molly had not noticed before, and she realized that the second lower room was smaller than it should have been. There was one more, another doorway opened to reveal a large generator next to boilers, water tanks, and large metal shelves, mostly populated by hard cases. A miniature warehouse of shelves and palettes, racks and stacks. In the corner of the bunker, Jonathan Corbin directed her to a large stock of pads and tampons— labeled tubs of "feminine hygiene products" of every sort and brand imaginable.

"Why are they in here?" she asked.

"Future barter value," he said. "They'll be the third most valuable thing after the end, besides gold and bullets. Take whatever you need. I can always get more. I'll go find you some new sheets."

Molly looked at the boxes and took a guess.

‡ ‡ ‡ ‡

FIVE YEARS BEFORE THE end, Norman was able to acquire a visa for his thirteen-year-old son to enter The Kingdom of Saudi Arabia. The House of Saud approved of sons learning their fathers' businesses. They practiced apprenticeships themselves.

They left the towering spike of a hotel in the diplomatic quarter. Their black SUV had bulletproof windows, and it was not the only one. They were in a convoy. Steven could see an Apache helicopter mirroring their lumbering progression from a place in the sky. Steven knew that, all too soon, the city of Riyadh would have another four million people. He wondered when it all would go up in smoke. They reached the highway and accelerated to eighty-five miles an hour their line shifting so no tail would go unnoticed. Traffic quickly thickened and slowed to an absolute trickle. And then a stop. They rolled on in spurts, foot by foot. Their minders in suits had hands on holsters.

Three lanes away, a group of five men in long white thawbs and perfectly wrapped red and white headdresses strolled out onto the highway, passing in front of a beat up taxicab. Steven saw a woman, fully veiled and wearing all black, alone in the backseat. The men began rocking the taxi, tapping on its windows, yelling at the driver and the woman through the windows. The taps became hits, and the taxi driver opened his door. They pulled him out, and one of the uniformed men released the locks for the rest. Out came the woman, gently forced down to the pavement on her knees. Steven's convoy moved another few feet.

"The mutaween," Norman offered. "Religious police."

"I know," Steven said.

The woman and the driver were pleading with the policemen. The woman struggled to stay covered as they dragged her along the asphalt, the driver, restrained, tried to explain, panicking.

"أنا عمها, أنا عمها, أنا عمها," he cried out in repetition.

"What is he saying?" Norman asked.

"'I'm her uncle,'" Steven translated.

The taxi driver attempted to escape the hold of the three men attending to him, so the first shove landed. The other police, the secular police, arrived, creeping along the shoulder until they came to a stop. They stayed in their car, observing. The woman's knees scraped across the ground as she was moved, fabric and skin tearing as they hauled her to the side of the road.

In the SUV, mundane conversation carried on around him, but Steven kept watching. One of the enforcers brought the length of his forearm down across her shoulder blades.

The traffic lurched forward.

Six miles ahead the palace loomed above the silt.

Different men wearing the same white thawbs and checkered gutras guarded the gates with AKMs in their hands, but they were there to keep the puritans away.

Once inside the walls, fresh-faced Nigerian and Chadian mercenaries strolled to each vehicle in the procession, checking lists and whispering into hidden microphones. Eventually their SUV was permitted down into an underground snake run, past large paved caverns filled to the brim with polished chrome wheels. The driver of their SUV was instructed to pull away from the convoy, coming to a stop at a dead end.

The stairs had a red carpet. A single man in a black suit was standing there.

"Ah," Norman clasped hands with the man. "Steven, this is Ahmad, head of security." Norman actually put his palm on Steven's back. He touched him.

"I am so pleased to meet your son, old friend," Ahmad took Steven's hand. His English was flawless.

"عليكم السلام," Steven said.

"سعيدة فرصة," I'm impressed, معجب أنا., please," he gestured forward.

Steven expected all the rooms to be enormous, but they were not. Instead, they were led through a series of modest parlors, each with furniture covered in white sheets. Finally, reaching a large entrance hall that glowed red and gold, they proceeded through the side and stopped in front of a closed set of massive double doors.

"Unfortunately," Ahmad said, "His Excellency prefers not to have children at dinner. Though I can assure you, he is most honored that you brought your son into his home. I will show him where to go."

Norman made a show of slapping his son on the shoulder, and they separated.

The basement room was massive—not a basement, a ballroom. White walls stretched eighteen feet into the air. The blond teenage Viking son of a Scandinavian Ambassador clumsily spun on his back atop a constructed dance floor. Scattered among the banquet tables were heavy rugs and overstuffed couches, where two constellations of Eastern European maidens lounged or danced, outliers among the vague groups of Indian or Nepali or Filipino women. Liquor was at every table, in every hand. Steven could not tell which were daughters of the diplomatic class, business guests, and which were working girls, and which were slaves. The locals held a scattered court sagging throughout the room, passing bottles of every shape and variation. The G-8 sat lined up on what had been designed as a stage, drinking and flirting only with each other, oil babies, and immunity teens, the ultimate third culture kids, this group was almost entirely male, having had to meet the clothing requirements of the trip. The G-8 were visited by the Saudi kids, male and female, let loose in western clothing who recognized each other from the boarding schools of the world—the British exported class factories that Steven had been spared.

Steven hugged the wall.

Filipino bartenders frantically hovered, taking orders and serving up mixtures of smuggled, duty-free loot and locally created moonshine. Every Italian fashion label was brazenly represented. Imitations of turntables were in his corner, opposite the door, presided over by westerners in dark indigo denim and T-shirts, fresh sneakers, headphones coiled around their necks.

A Saudi kid approached, tearing off his shirt and pumping his fist in the air. He was undoubtedly one of the Prince's sons, his babysitter trailing behind unfazed.

Steven hid behind a speaker on a stand, a strobe light blinding anyone who might try to spot him. He leaned and counted the minutes. And then the hours.

Adults started appearing, and eventually Steven spotted Norman across the room, his arm around an Eastern European brunette. He saw another man in a suit help Norman get her a drink, everybody all smiles, then pass the pill and drop it in her glass.

A group of kids raised a metal door that connected the basement to the garage, and, soon enough, a twisting car could be seen doughnutting into the frame every five seconds.

Steven wondered what happened to the woman in the taxicab.

$$\equiv \qquad \equiv \qquad \equiv \qquad \equiv$$

RIGHT AFTER THE LAST bell on May 12th, second semester freshman year, Mr. Jones's office was consumed by a hellish brightness, a terrible almost-summer humidity, a diabolical haze of moisture and light. Any quarter the air conditioner gave to the sense of touch was invalidated by the effect of its whine on the sense of hearing. Auditioning its vibration, Efram covered one ear at a time, back and forth, listening as it cavitated in stereo, one side of his brain forced to take the brunt over the other, alternating between the two. A drop of sweat sat on the bulbous Martian terrain of Mr. Jones's forehead, an ice cap melting glob of moisture in the barren wrinkled wasteland under his combover. They had noticed.

"So, Efram, how do you organize your work?" the counselor asked. "Do you have separate binders for each class, separate folders? Do you mostly rely on the online schedules and syllabi? Please, explain to me how you've decided to approach handling the load from your classes. Because you can't stop being organized! That's how we got into this trouble right?"

"I did not stop being organized," Efram said.

"Starting last Friday, you stopped handing in all homework, did not fill out any in-class work, and responded to all in-class questions with 'I don't know.'"

"I stopped doing my work over a month ago," Efram said.

In front of him on the table Mr. Jones had laid out all his typical organizational materials, advice on how to deal with the stresses of output, digital and physical, that went along with an expensive and expansive private education. Mr. Jones put all that aside.

"Efram, you know that I am not only an academic counselor?"

If you are a student at Woodley—when your dad beats the shit out of your baby sister and you're so distraught that you don't get your math homework done—Mr. Jones is one of the ones you go to blab and cry about it and get a note excusing you.

"Sure," Efram said.

"I'm here to support students, to actually help and serve them through difficult times. Me and Ms. Martin, you know?"

Because it would be legal liability to not have a female counselor in a coed high school.

"So where is this attitude coming from Efram? You had no behavior like this before, here or at your old school in New York according to the records."

His face now demanded an answer.

"The first centralized educational system was implemented by Napoleon..." Efram said but could not remember the rest.

"Is that something your father told you?"

"No. Raj..." but Efram cringed and cursed his mistake. He should not have mentioned Raj's name. He stamped the floor.

"So something must have changed recently. You can talk about it with me. What you felt about what happened to your father. Tell me what happened. Tell me in your words."

"I actually can't do that."

"I assure you that anything you say will be one hundred percent confidential."

"Don't lie," Efram said.

"Efram, if you are going to be a part of this school, you are going to have to work through these issues. You are going to have to show us you can do it. So please. How did you feel when your father got caught? How did you feel when he died?"

Efram's answer was to fiddle with his hands under the table, twirling his phone onto the surface while it was already ringing, **KEVIN** emblazoned in white pixels on the screen.

"Yes, your eminence?" answered Kevin's disembodied voice.

"You're on speaker, Kevin. I'm here with Mr. Jones, the school counselor. He wants me to talk about what happened with my father and how it made me feel—" But, before he could finish with the part about it being all supposedly confidential and shit, sunny and shiny and secrets intact, Kevin was shouting.

"DON'T TELL HIM ANYTHING. Mr. Jones! School counselors, no matter what their qualifications, enjoy no legal privilege with their students. My client will not be answering any questions about his father. If you attempt to compel my client to answer any more questions I'll end your career and skullfuck your soon-to-be-former employer's endowment, drowning them in a shithole of legal fees they can't hope to escape. Pick up the phone, kill the speaker, and leave the room right-fucking-now, Efram!"

Efram Daniels scooped it up and trailed out the door, the troll inside still sitting jilted and shocked.

"You didn't say anything did you?" Kevin squelched in his ear.

"Of course not!"

"Alright, good. What did you do to piss them off?"

"School…"

"What's wrong with it?"

"Kevin, do you remember it?"

This was the most loaded of all loaded questions. Efram knew Kevin had grown up in Lawrence, Kansas, and that being a gay teenager in the seventies couldn't have been fun anywhere, let alone there.

"Fair point. Do whatever you want."

He took off to warn Raj of his misstep, locating him on the sidelines of the large athletic field behind the buildings. Parents and fellow students, who were the only fans, stood on one side of delineated grass as the uniformed and staffed benches took up the other.

"Do you get panic attacks or something?" Raj said abruptly, responding to the look on Efram's face.

"I gotta talk to you. I was in Mr. Jones' office. I messed up."

"Hey Efram, I'm Anjali," Raj's sister broke in. She had eyes so light brown they twinkled gold, long, highlighted ochre hair, skin much darker than Raj, and a different bone structure altogether, petite.

"That's the nicest she's ever been to anyone associated with me," Raj muttered.

"You have no one associated with you," she said. "So you committed a crime?"

"Raj, I had to go to Mr. Jones for the whole, yea, not doing work in front of everyone thing and I said what you said about Napoleon and he asked me where I learned it and I said you. So if they go after you or anything—"

"Go after little Raj!" Anjali exclaimed. "Do you play lacrosse Ef— " but she cut off her question with a high-pitched "Wooooooooo!!!"

A single crimson blur dodged through green and white mesh jerseys as they hacked and slashed to no avail, a demon sprinting down their sideline. You could clearly read "Van Ness Varsity Soccer" on his shorts in contrast to the rest of his teammates. He flipped the ball behind the net to a teammate and cut across a picking midfielder to get the rock right back, turning the corner he, in one motion, caught and threw the hard rubber into the lower ninety opposite the natural resting position of the goalie's stick. Six to two. Anjali cheered wildly each time this enemy magician obliterated the Woodley defense. Raj read the question on Efram's face.

"His name is Joseph Kaplan," he said. "And yes, she knows him. He's my sister's boyfriend."

Van Ness Day School's away colors of unbroken brownish red were the perfect foil to Woodley's home white-accented emerald, but their team was not so complimentary. While Woodley ran through their offense, setting up a series of designed picks and called plays in machinelike precision, Van Ness looked fragmented and ragged— except for Joseph Kaplan. They rushed the ball up the field and tossed it straight to the star player. They didn't need a strategy. No set ups. No picks. No waiting. Give the ball to Joseph Kaplan and get the fuck out of the way. His legs had pistons. He flew past two retreating midfielders and let a defenseman twice his size bounce off his momentum, seeking out the hit, clobbering the giant to the ground. He spun, and let the three last defenders catch their bearings. Sick of being embarrassed, they all closed on him. He calmly passed the ball, a laser through the traffic to a teammate. Open shot. Goal.

The faceoff won by the losing team, Woodley once again set up their offense: precise, disciplined, running clock, and now down eight to two. Chaos versus order. Joseph Kaplan was chaos. And chaos was winning.

Even with his helmet to enhance the look, he did not fit Central Casting's requirements for a lacrosse player. He was short, with a diminutive torso, and unkempt floppy hair coming out from underneath the protective plastic. He did not implement exaggerated movements of his stick when he had the ball, no fancy cradles or face dodges. The defenders kept trying to hit the crap out of him, hard, but he was never where they thought he was going to be.

He was too...*low*...

His bottom half was stocky, thick almost, with fire hydrant-like legs and wide flippered feet sheathed in shiny low-top cleats that also belonged to soccer. Once, a Woodley midfielder managed to knock the ball out of Joseph Kaplan's stick as he was surging forward. Gasp.

Cheer. But, instead of lowering his shoulder and fighting for the scoop, Joseph Kaplan merely kicked the ball and accelerated away from the assaulting body, then smacked the orb again with the toe of his cleat, flipping it up and catching it in his stick.

Anjali yipped and clapped three more times, two more goals and an assist. Eleven to four. At halftime, the creatine infused bugs huddled around water and Gatorade while listening to their respective scowling or lauding coaches. Joseph Kaplan only needed to play for half of the third quarter, the contest long out of reach. The final buzzer sounded at twenty-one to ten, mercy employed for most of the second half. Joseph Kaplan jogged toward them, helmet off, a little boy prancing having ditched his tools. Anjali squealed in the apologetically sweaty hug. Joseph winked at Raj, so much taller than his sister and her older boyfriend. Efram was spinning though, eyes on everything else. There were people pointing, upperclassmen. They were looking at them as Anjali gave Joseph a kiss after she fake pouted.

"Great job destroying *some* of my friends," Anjali said. Joseph left to catch the bus with his team.

Anjali dropped them at Raj's house in Wellesley Heights and left immediately to meet up with Joseph. The neighborhood was six by eight blocks of light residential zoning, a postwar planned community engorged by the fruits of the global and political economy. The houses were big. Efram was trying to build a chair out of books in Raj's room while Raj stayed fixed to a laptop, reading about sixteenth-century mercantilism.

Efram heard it first. The cars were not passing like the rest but idling. He looked out the window onto the street. Teenage bodies emerged and began throwing eggs.

"Um, Raj?"

One pulled out a paintball gun and began peppering the Mediterranean style five bedroom with hideously arced inaccurate shots. Raj shoved Efram behind the wall before one of the pellets careened through the window. It didn't shatter like in the movies.

"What do we do?" Efram asked.

"We wait," Raj said.

They got closer, and the hiss of a spray can took over when the eggs and paintballs stopped. Then footsteps. Raj peeked out and Efram followed. Raj grabbed a pad of paper and started frantically writing down plate numbers.

Someone would talk.

Raj did not know enough of the upperclassmen to recognize the eight names that were offered as those who had been in the cars. None had fessed up to spray painting "PAKI SLUT" on the side wall. But Raj's parents decided to accept monetary reparation and letters of apology and forego harsher criminal action.

The next day, a recognizable rendering of Anjali opening her legs with a speech bubble extolling, "Who's got next?" filtered through the school's network. She did not show up to school the next day. Or the day after that. Raj said she might never return.

"MICHELLE HOOKED UP WITH GABRIEL," appeared in the rectangular box.

"That's weird," Chloe responded.

"Why weird?"

"Weird because she's a fucking hag that's why."

"Right. She has the grossest arms I or you or anyone has ever seen. She has flabby arms like my grandmother. WHAT THE FUCK"

Lauryn missed punctuation often.

"Bingo wings."

"What?"

"Bingo wings."

"…"

"Michelle has bingo wings," Chloe repeated through her device.

"What does that mean?"

"Like when an old woman is playing bingo and she wins and raises and shakes her arms and yells and all the flab is moving around. Bingo wings."

"[insert abbreviation regarding the digital transmission of laughter here] The new title!"

Across the room, Jess looked up from her notebook, lifting it in the air to show Chloe that she had written "WIZARD SLEEVES" in large letters on the page.

"Or wizard sleeves," Chloe typed to Lauryn.

"WE SHOULD EAT SOME BUFFALO WINGS," Lauryn said.

"*BINGO WINGS,"

"ASKASDLKFJASLKGH,"

"…"

In the mob of shoulders and heads and the occasional tall torso, the morning rush, Lauryn rotated her head over her shoulder and yelped, "BINGO WINGS!" as Michelle walked past.

"Ugh, Lauryn, that's not the way to do it," Chloe said.

Chloe had changed the name on Michelle's profile page. Bingo Wings has accepted your friend request. Bingo Wings likes this. Bingo Wings commented on your photo.

Lauryn had been pressing touchscreen letter keys all day to make sure that it was everywhere. Memetic infection. STD viral.

"I don't care," Lauryn said, peeling into her classroom.

Ahead, two adults were standing in the middle of the hallway.

"Chloe," assistant principal Timothy Winters greeted her by name.

"Yes, Mr. Winters?"

"I'm going to need you to come to my office."

"Sure," she said, "Do you mind if I use the bathroom first? And could I put a couple things in my locker?"

"I'm sorry but you have to come right now," he said.

"Alright," Chloe relented.

She used her body to shield her hand between her bag and her back, thumb on the screen. Keypad memorized, Chloe sent one last message to Lauryn and Jess.

"MAKE UP WITH MICHELLE RIGHT NOW," it said.

Then Chloe flipped Anton's digital switch. The phone changed, the messages given a different history. They reached the office. She took a seat.

"Chloe, we have been told that you are responsible for some very nasty harassment."

"I am not," Chloe said.

"No?"

No resistance was the doctrine. Before he could lay out his allegations, Chloe simply slid her phone across the table, rifled through her bag for a pen, tore a sheet of paper, and scribbled several passwords and account names on it. She folded it, popped out of her seat, gave him a smile, and placed it in front of him.

"Check for yourself," she said.

"Just like that?" he asked.

"Yes."

"I'll have it back to you at the end of the day," he said, now smiling. "You may leave."

The hallway bare, five minutes into the period, Chloe went the opposite direction of her classroom. On the way to the gym, she opened a door to a small closet, with a carpeted floor, filled with chairs used for PTA meetings and conference days. Behind two chairs, she curled up on the padded surface.

Her eyes closed like the doors to a vault.

There was darkness. Then blindness. Every single atom was bleached beyond white, frozen through any tolerance of reflection, the source bathing all existence in pure glare. This was fleeting. There was orange, red, and black, and a noise so deep it felt like matter itself was rumbling, grating through her skin. The light gave way and the air accelerated, nitrogen and oxygen and that remnant bit of argon were propelled, like a wave of thunder thumping against and through, the big bad thermonuclear wolf finally blowing down everything but reinforced concrete. She only caught half of the gust, wind knocked out, not enough to stop seeing. Heat, then steam, sweat, and fire itself. Flash, flash, two more, bang, bang, triple the effects, and the air itself began to scorch, burning crimson and tangerine and alighting all that still deserved any energy. It all melted, but she was stuck there, eyes open, trying to breathe. The world got punched and it ended.

She awoke in darkness.

By the end of business that day, Michelle was welcomed back into the fold. Mr. Winters returned Chloe's phone and cleared her of all wrongdoing. The school year refused to accelerate. Chloe flipped Anton's switch back again.

⊗   ⊗   ⊗   ⊗

THREE-QUARTERS OF A MILE up the grade there was a slight clearing that dead-ended into the side of a burgeoning hill. Cans were set up on tree trunks. A couple empty file cabinets tossed on both sides, riddled with holes. The treeless floor was muddy where he made her stand.

"I really don't need to learn this," Molly said, but Jon was setting out the triangular zipped black bags on the makeshift table, alongside the colored boxes of bullets. Metal met skin. Her father's instructions were dampened, the isolation booth headphones placed over her ears. It had already been hours of lectures around the kitchen table. He had made her draw sight pictures. Recite stances. He brought the guns down to the table the second day and started her with cleaning. Learning how to clean a gun implicitly meant learning how to load, unload, clear, assemble, disassemble, reassemble. Never point a gun at something you aren't prepared to destroy, he told her repeatedly.

He offered her the .22 rifle, which Molly yanked from him, peppering cans before he could give instructions. It may as well have been a BB gun. Knocking them down and finishing and certifying it was empty, she set it on the flat duffle bag, casting it aside. He said something about how she was not practicing any sort of memorized form. Molly put her hand on her hip.

"I'm going to go back," she said. "You have fun."

Before she could turn he unzipped one of the other triangle-shaped pouches and held it in front of her.

"This is yours actually. P229. This one is a .22, for now. It's on the slimmer side, good for small hands. Double-action. The trigger is ten pounds."

Automatically, like cleaning at the dining table, she checked the chamber. It had a pulse. Her hand fit the gun, not the other way around. Jon shifted behind her while saying something about moving her right foot behind her left and straightening her right arm. He was about to place his hands on her shoulders to forcibly turn her when she extended her arms out, bringing her weak-side foot slightly forward, letting her knees be a mobile platform, while keeping her hips totally square to the target. Her father told her that was a more difficult stance, but she did not listen or retort, sensing it was right and knowing for sure from her father's lack of criticism. He stood behind her, ready and waiting, half expecting the kick to send her backward despite the petty caliber. Within her trance, Molly heard her father giving the go-ahead.

Her breathing slowed and she let her eyes focus straight down the sights. Jon was educating on the difference between pulling and squeezing. Molly pretended the trigger was a straight line, a straight piece that she would split in two under pressure. She wanted to control it as it went backward, exactly in line with the barrel, which was in line with her eye, which was in line with the target.

"Okay," Jonathan Corbin's lips said, "Fire."

Molly lowered her arms forty-five degrees, relaxing for a moment, then raised them as quickly as possible to the same position as before, exhaling and squeezing as if her index finger were still extended, its nail a laser. It hit too far from the millimeter dot she had picked. With the next round chambered, trigger under control, and a straight back, her eyes followed the front sight and the picture of the target. Molly fired again. She blinked her lashes at the Glock 9mm in the holster on Jon's hip, and the .357 on the table.

‡   ‡   ‡   ‡

FIVE YEARS BEFORE THE end, Steven and Norman were trapped in Heathrow. A three-day fog had lifted, the string of cancellations wreaking havoc on the remaining schedules. Their flight to Johannesburg was delayed six hours. They had already missed their connection from Johannesburg to Windhoek.

Norman put down his phone.

"The company can get me out on a charter," he said.

"The mining company?" Steven asked.

"Yes."

"But not me," Steven said.

"No, only me. One seat. You good taking the normal flight on your own? I will make sure someone is there to collect you when you arrive."

"Sure," Steven said.

Norman looked into Steven's eyes for five seconds, got up, and slung his briefcase over his shoulder.

"And don't forget my luggage," Norman put his phone back to his ear, and walked down the concourse.

Once his father was out of sight, Steven opened his laptop. With Norman's lifted credit card number copied and pasted, thirteen-year-old Steven fingered the keyboard and bought a ticket to Baltimore-Washington International Airport. He had a frequent flyer number tied to his father's. Free upgrade.

Holding both tickets, the obsolete destination and the new, no checked baggage, already through security, the airport in chaos, no one did the math. Steven at thirteen easily appeared eighteen. His face was made of stone, his shoulders too broad, his hair buzzed to a militaristic crop. Airlines were only required to supervise unaccompanied minors traveling internationally through age eleven.

There was no announcement in-flight; no air marshal or crewmember grabbed him, and no agents at the arrival gate prowled for the runaway child. Norman would be in the air for another twelve hours.

Even though he liked his UK passport best, Steven slotted his blue American variation into each set of hands. He pushed the dramatic windowless doors past customs, cutting into the throng of huddled drivers and family members, and walked to the cab line.

Norman had purchased the Maryland house seven years prior, and Steven's mother Marie had fled there immediately, ditching the continent for good. It looked bulky and foreboding in the dark, angular, set on an inlet outside of Annapolis on the mainland side of the bridge. Dropped off, billed, Steven rang the bell. He banged. Nothing.

He circled the porch to the other side, trying each window. The fourth one slid upward in a hurry. He summoned lights every twenty feet, making it to the stairs. At the end of the hallway a faint television glow slipped from under the only closed door. He gave it a knock, but like the front door, there was no reply. Steven opened the door. Collections of water glasses lay on the side table, interrupted by pill and vitamin bottles. The only visible part of Marie was her head, barely emerged from the duvet, from under a towel turned into a hood.

"You can't do that. Can't run off from your father," she said. "Why did you?"

Steven gave no answer.

"Well you know where everything is," she said and rolled back over.

"Everything?" His room held no possessions. The hours spent selecting furniture and paint color and curtain fabric, room by room, they meant nothing in the dark. "Why are you in bed?" Steven asked, "It's like seven o'clock."

"You're exactly like your father," she said, veins spidering out from her pale shoulders, eyes reflecting back the television screen. "Just like him."

Steven retreated.

Norman met him at BWI two days later.

"Why are you angry with me?" Norman asked.

I know what you did, Steven wanted to say.

"I know your mom and I have a complicated relationship," Norman said.

For the first time in his teenage life, Steven rolled his eyes.

"Do you want to stay here with her or do you want to fly?" Norman asked.

Steven got up.

"Let's fly then," Norman said, slipping into a fake American accent.

THE WINDSWEPT FRONT LAWN of The Woodley School had been usurped by a white tent, an ugly chimera. Every year Woodley threw a perfunctory open-to-the-neighborhood festival on the preexam Saturday in May, when the school engaged its community. The parents of each grade were assigned to run a station: grills, cakewalks, carnival games, raffles, and other over-designed distractions.

An amplified voice erupted from underneath the canopy, explaining that Head of School Megan Myers would be making an announcement. There was a large screen with the school's original coat of arms projected, a dim illumination crushed into faintness by the invading sunshine. Refreshments were passed around, decadent enough to be a full-catered society party, at least in Our Nation's Capital. Efram unexpectadly spotted his mother, wine glass in hand, taking pleasantries from a cadre of parents who seemed to be intent on engaging her. Head of School Megan Myers walked over to the wooden lectern where attached microphones resembled the spindly black legs of an enlarged bug.

"Parents, students, neighbors, friends! Thank you all for coming. I hope you are enjoying this beautiful day. We usually do get lucky with the weather for these events, so I'm glad that despite the wind, the streak has continued. Once again, we are about to conclude another wonderful year of learning, playing, performing, creating, and growing here at Woodley, and I for one want to personally thank you all for being a part of that.

We have a surprise for you today! After a great deal of planning and intense discussions, I am pleased to offer you the first look at this school's next step. As you all know, last year's complete redesign of the C building was a resounding success, and our students made excellent use of the beautiful new facilities. Today, I'm thrilled to announce Phase II, a complete renovation of our Upper School facilities, a comprehensive reimagining of our campus that will include new science and computer labs and wonderful new spaces for the arts." The projector image changed and the screen was filled with an artist's rendering of the new façade, bigger and whiter, and now in proportion with its grander counterpart.

"The B building will be expanded and extended all the way to the Lower School building, allowing our youngest students easier access to certain amenities outside of their classrooms. Pickup and drop-off will be streamlined by—"

The speakers began emitting a horrible hiss, a rising whine that rose beyond feedback, cutting in and out of her words. A flunky rushed to the podium and handed her a different microphone, but this one cut in and out as well. A garbled "sorry" emitted, pieces of the words from an apology for technical difficulties barely escaping the distortion festival. Ears covered en masse, someone mercifully pulled the plug on the speakers outright. Head of School Megan Myers did not panic. The slides morphed to show alternate angles of the theoretical building, a new atrium covered in glass, the backfield raised to a turf terrace.

"I am so sorry everyone, but I think my voice is loud enough. Despite the inconvenience of construction to the neighborhood, I can assure you that Phase II will greatly improve traffic flow in the future, making the morning and afternoon rush more efficient and cutting down on the number of cars on the surrounding streets. The new theater and band room—"

But now the projected image had melted into a sketchy, low-quality, pixelated mess on the big screen, not helped by the constant glare. One of the fast moving clouds came into position overhead, and the shroud killed the contrast, making the image more visible, but Head of School Megan Myers was already pressing the button for the next.

"—I am so sorry everyone. Clearly we're having some technical difficulties."

The next slide was the same thing, only now with the shadow it was clearer. It was a cameraphone picture of a blurred body hurling something on a dark street, the outcroppings of a Mediterranean style house on the fringes of the image. Efram swiveled his heard around and found Raj toward the back, Raj's height allowed him to locate Efram just the same. The next slide showed a higher quality image of an egg stain on stucco. Then the graffiti exclaiming "PAKI SLUT." Then the drawing of Anjali with her legs open. The projector was snapped off.

"Well anyway folks, I'm so sorry for our problems but am still so happy to share with you this announcement and those first looks at the next big step for Woodley! Enjoy today!"

Head of School Megan Myers retreated fast, moving toward her administrative entourage and temporarily postponing the many conversations with prominent parents she was about to have. The audience murmured to each other while the kids filed out first, eager to escape, and Efram and Raj locked in on a beeline. They met on the edge of the tent, right by one of its supporting poles, and before Efram could ask, Raj's arm shot forward almost smacking him.

"Look!" he exclaimed, but by the time Efram turned Raj was only pointing at a short hooded figure sprinting into the B building.

"What?" Efram asked.

"That's Joseph Kaplan," Raj said.

"Uh, what is he doing here?"

"Efram..."

"Oh. Right. But how would he do all that?"

"He's sort of an anarchist," Raj said.

"An anarchist lacrosse star?"

"Yes."

"Is doing your sister?"

"Yes—"

Raj was interrupted by a piercing whine from the B building followed by a constant ringing. Fire alarms are a normal feature of scholastic life, unheeded by all the surrounding students and even their parents. But this was different. The LED's on the red alarms did not blink. A security system had been violated. Joseph Kaplan was assaulting The Woodley School.

"We have to stop him," Efram found himself saying.

"What? Why?" Raj said.

"He could get in real trouble for this. He isn't a student here. He could go to jail. Jail sucks, Raj. Go find him! Get him out of here."

"What are you going to do?" Raj asked.

"Doesn't matter. Now go and get him out of here. And if they catch you, deny everything, both of you."

Raj sprinted in the direction of the alarms, and Efram turned and maneuvered around the perimeter of the tent. The gusts accelerated through the trees, moving the branches. The rest of the activities had been instructed to resume. The engineering team gave rides up the driveway on their crank driven hovercraft. The softball team had a dunk tank. Cotton candy was swirled together and handed to siblings.

There was a cauldron of staff around Head of School Megan Myers. Efram pierced the line and leaned against a tree.

"I'm sure it was someone retaliating. I'll call and there'll be a witch-hunt. Someone will know, it'll be online somewhere. The fire alarm will give it away, too. There's dye right?"

"If someone pulled it. It could be an accident. They are welding something in the cafeteria today. Smoke could've set it off."

"Two kids are running between B and C. We could close the gates now and if we don't catch them, try to account for everyone. But they're headed now to cut them off. The police are already en route. It isn't the fire alarm. Someone somehow turned on the motion detector and then it went off."

Efram pulled his shoulder blades together against the tree. A green uniformed member of the maintenance staff received muffled updates from the chase on his walkie talkie. Efram was five feet away from the group of adults, standing still, ignored.

"I want to know who is responsible!" Head of School Megan Myers said, losing her cool.

"I am," Efram said. Alarm bells still going in the background, radios hissing. Mr. Jones started first.

"You set off the alarm, Efram?"

"No," Efram told the truth before lying, "But I put the pictures on the screen."

"Really Efram?" Head of School Megan Myers asked. "Why?"

"You were friends with Anjali?" Mr. Jones asked.

"She was nice to me," Efram said.

The air rushed past harder now, a cloud encroached, not threatening downpour but bringing an angry wind that whipped across the lawn. Children marveled in delight, but the cries turned fearful as the tent began to sway, the few still under it escaping, fearing the worst. One half of it deflated, a pole nonviolently drooping downward to the ground.

"So you ruined the speakers and collapsed the tent! Destruction of property."

"No!" Efram told the truth and then lied again, "Just the pictures."

"Sit down," Mr. Jones said pointing to the curb where the grass ended. Efram obeyed. The circle of parents around them had dissipated with the wind, finding children or getting a better view of the chaos, rubbernecking at the crunch. Gasps wrung out from every angle as the tent continued its semi-implosion, the resumption of festivities ceased. Water had begun to trickle from B building's lower entrance door, a new development in failure of the days activities for the crowds.

"There's a flood. Definitely not from sprinklers. A pipe burst on the bottom floor," the green suited man reported.

Raj and Joseph erupted from the other side of the administration building and sprinted across the driveway onto the lawn, a green shirted maintenance man in pursuit. Suddenly Raj tackled Joseph into a kiddie pool that had been used for hunting rubber duckies. The maintenance man reached them and hauled them out of the pool but after only a few moments of mouths moving walked away. The walkie talkie squacked again.

"The running kids were playing tag," someone told Head of School Megan Myers. "Unrelated."

Two police officers trudged up the hill to where they were gathered, Efram still sitting on the curb. Right on cue, Efram's mother arrived, wine glass still in hand. Efram watched Head of School Megan Myers shriek at the officers, and his mother cock her head in an attempt to grasp the situation, bringing her checkbook out of her bag. An audience had begun to gather, not of parents but of kids, kids with faces he knew, high schoolers, all years. Lindsay Biltner and Sam Page excitedly pointed and jumped up and down in hysterics. Terrill Pearson buried her face in her hands. Mr. Jones' arm reached down and pulled Efram up. They had formed a half-circle: Head of School Megan Myers, Mr. Jones, the green-suited head of maintenance, Efram's mother, and two police officers.

"He did all of this," Head of School Megan Myers was saying.

"He confessed?" one of the officers asked.

"Yes," she said.

"Only to the pictures," Efram said.

"The rest of this just happened? No. You sabotaged the speakers. Hacked the computer and somehow changed the pictures. Set off the alarm. Broke a pipe and started a flood. And collapsed the tent."

"He couldn't have caused the flood," the maintenance man said. "The pipe was three feet above his head, he would be soaking wet."

Raj had tackled Joseph into the pool...Efram craned his neck and saw their two silhouettes standing by the main gate, watching right back, ready to bolt.

"I'm sure he could have found a way if he found out how to do all this other stuff."

"Hold on a minute, ma'am," one of the cops said. He looked at Efram. "What exactly did you do?"

"Right before the presentation, I switched the plug from the computer to a hacked drive, which had photos on it from the night a crime was committed and then covered up by this school," Efram lied. "I didn't hack into anything. I didn't mess with the tent. I didn't set off the alarm."

"No! He must have armed it first!" said Head of School Megan Myers.

"How would he know the alarm code? And, ma'am, I'm sorry, but the wind knocked over the tent." The swirling had not stopped. The crowd swelled.

"I want to press charges!" she was getting really mad now, her famous composure waning.

"What charges? It sounds like he pulled a prank that had no physical effects. You want me to arrest him for showing some pictures by switching a plug?"

"Look around at everything else! This wasn't all coincidence. He caused major damage to the school! Ask people if they saw him sabotage the tent or go into the school! Dust for prints!"

"What's your name?" one of the cops asked Efram.

"Efram Daniels."

They looked at each other, and one whispered something, then looked at his mother's face. Efram pulled out his student ID and handed it to them.

Head of School Megan Myers' fear continued unabated, "What are you going to do? I want him out of this school right now! You're expelled! Off this property."

The cops moved, turning, and put themselves between Efram and the others.

"I'm sure we can work something out," Efram's mother said. "It was only a prank and as you know,

Efram has had a very rough time." She was wielding her checkbook again.

"We are way past that. Will you two start investigating! Interview all these witnesses to his crimes!"

"Ma'am, we aren't going to do that. There isn't any reason for it. The wind has been downing trees all day. Your man over here says he thinks the flood is an accident. Unless you've been giving your kids your security codes, the alarm has to be a glitch. My partner is going to escort him out of here."

The cop did not take his arm forcefully, but placed a hand lightly on his spine and steered him away. The sounds of Head of School Megan Myers' demanding badge numbers and superiors faded into the howl of the wind. Another cloud passed over, another fast, temporary shadow. Efram's mother stayed behind to plead her case.

"They're gonna kick you out." The cop said. The hiss of the crowd was barely audible. Twenty feet from the gate Efram turned. Raj and Joseph had thankfully retreated to a car down the street, but they were watching. "Are those all your friends up there?" He stopped and turned, motioning his chin at the assortment of underclassmen gawking and ranting and texting and capturing it all.

"Well, take a bow," the cop said.

Looking back up, he extended both arms outward, in a long-range visible shrug, bowed, and then turned. He caught a few of the waves and could hear the slightest static noise as the wind began to die. The word spread to

every nook of Woodley and beyond—the myth born—
that in anger, Efram Daniels had destroyed a speaker
system, hacked into a presentation, set off an alarm, and
caused a major flood, and then, somehow, gotten the
cops to protect him from the angry administrators and
let him go free. Efram Daniels started there.

"You were telling the truth right?" the officer asked.

"I didn't do any of it," Efram said. "None of it."

The officer gave him a card.

Efram took a left and vanished from the fence line.
Raj and Joseph launched at him from behind the car,
shocked, wondering how on earth Efram had escaped
unscathed. Joseph Kaplan soaking wet and Raj, now
trapped in that state with him, caught up. One week
and an insurance claim later, the fundraising drive for
Phase II officially began, the ever-expanding campus on
the prowl.

Efram Daniels was officially notified of his expulsion
the following Monday.

PART

3

And I beheld, and lo a black horse;
And he that sat on him had a pair of
balances in his hand.
                    —The Book of Revelation

This is our house.
This is our rules.
And we can't stop.
        —Miley Cyrus, "We Can't Stop"

⊗　　　　⊗　　　　⊗　　　　⊗

J ON LEFT FOURTEEN-YEAR-OLD MOLLY at the metal detectors with an awkward hug. There was no babysitting airline official waiting on the other side, but she did have a very specific set of typed instructions. The crowds flowed around her, those close to her age embroiled in their devices, ears covered and eyes on screens. Her father believed that all of these people were going to die, save a few getting by on pure wit and whim.

Molly stopped in a newsstand and looked down the shelves, her fingers walking across the colorful pages, picking a fashion magazine emblazoned with tips and tricks and a gun magazine with bright fonts obsessing over tangential tactical accessories.

Her head was trapped in know-what-to-do mode—assessing where to run if the airport collapsed in a heap of explosive art, how to burn her clothes in case of radiation.

Molly eyed the zombies during boarding, the man in the dull blue collared shirt squawking into a microphone, the red eyes and the comfortable shoes. Down the jetway, she touched the skin of the plane as she stepped across the threshold, palm pressing against steel and rivets. The printed stub placed her in an empty row, window seat. Jonathan Corbin probably scheduled the least busy flight on purpose, minimizing the likelihood of an adjacent conversation widening Little Miss Corbin's world. She glued herself to the window and focused on the painted lines, the signs, the runway and taxiway designations, trying to guess with each turn whether the engines would rev and the saunter would explode into altitude. Finally, it happened, the noise escalated into a shriek. Molly turned from the window and pushed her back into the seat, trying to feel the moment her feet lost contact with earth.

A few seconds later, the climb became steep, forces pressed her downward, a thermal hit, and bumps started. They rolled, still pitched upward, now askew on every geometric plane. There was the beep, and then a brief announcement.

"Ladies and gentlemen we seem to be hitting some choppy air here. Please keep your seatbelt fastened and we'll try to get above it shortly…"

It got worse. The plunges became deeper and the g-forces multiplied. The air caught and then released the steel. Her waist pressed into the seatbelt. There were muted exclamations from neighbors, whimpers of fear or expletives of shock. She could see to the right a fellow traveler's eyes closed, hands gripping the armrests in a concentrated attempt at prayer or meditation.

But Molly Corbin loved it. She had never been on a roller coaster. This was better.

She turned around in her chair to peek at the anguished faces seated behind her before closing her eyes.

Safe on the ground, Dallas/Fort Worth dwarfed the chaos of her origin, hordes of tin moving on designated taxiways. The multitude of soldiers in the terminal

brought the familiar camouflage patterns from her
father's wardrobe: MOLLE, ALICE, ACUPAT, MARPAT,
MultiCam.

Fourteen year old Molly was taller than her Aunt
Linda. Their car zipped through concentric circles of
contracting sprawl.

"How many kids do you have?" Molly asked.

"Your cousins you mean? Two," Aunt Linda said,
"Eliza and Simon, six and nine."

"And your husband?"

"We're divorced," she said. "Martin, he was in your
hospital room a few times, you wouldn't remember, you
weren't really awake and then he had to come back. He
teaches high school chemistry."

The two lane highway reached a town that
manifested itself out of nothing. At the center was a large
courthouse, flanked by an empty commercial center and
surrounded by houses, some dilapidated but most clearly
inhabited.

"Is this still a town?" Molly asked.

"Yup. It's alive. You should see West Texas," Aunt Linda
said, "West Texas makes East Texas look like Rome."

⊠   ⊠   ⊠   ⊠

CHLOE WAS THREE STEPS into science class when it
happened again. "Report to the office of Assistant
Principal Winters," they said.

Some kids became as close to the teachers and
administrators as possible, as a means of insulating

themselves from the consequences of their chosen social style.

Chloe thought this strategy not worth the risk. Fellow students tended to grow very angry when they saw an authority figure mistake a sinner for a saint. They would do everything they could to unmask your dirty wretched soul and rat you out to that teacher who stupidly thought you were above it all.

Part of the secret to Chloe's success was that she got decent grades. Educational institutions associate bad social behavior with bad academic behavior. Chloe knew this was comically naïve. Did they actually believe all the people who got straight A's were more moral than those who disrupted class and ignored homework? She wondered how many teenage rapists got away with it by being National Merit Scholars.

Chloe herself had a carefully developed and honed strategy. She made sure to churn out B's like it was her job, but she also made sure to never demonstrate greater aptitude than that, not wanting to risk being labeled "a hidden genius who could do better if she only applied herself." She made sure to struggle for a while at the beginning of the year, so each surge toward the norm looked like an improvement.

That way, the faculty and administration left her alone, and she left them alone.

Chloe did not know anything personal about Mr. Winters, and she liked it this way. Whenever she was in earshot of bitching and gossip regarding their teachers and administration, she drifted off, choosing not to hear.

Denial to a stranger was easy.

Assistant Principal Winters greeted her at the door. She forced him to spend a few moments in a dead vacuum while she manipulated her hand in her bag, pretending to silence her phone while really she was letting Lauryn know where she was. Lauryn would warn the rest. They would be ready.

"Chloe."

"Mr. Winters."

He led her into the office, but they were not alone. Mrs. Washington, acting principal or interim principal or maybe straight-up principal—Chloe could not remember—was sitting at the conference table.

"Chloe," she said, monotone, in lieu of hello. Mr. Winters moved back and took a seat. Chloe took the hint and sunk into the chair provided. The possible charges against her scrolled in her head. She strained to discern what particular sin might have been discovered, or even manufactured. Was it internal or external? Had Lauryn decided to usurp the throne singlehandedly? But Lauryn was nowhere near bright enough to assemble a sufficiently thorough scope of information. Had Michelle stopped being a sheep and decided to take revenge? Was Jess going psycho warrior assassin on all of them?

"Mr. Winters wanted to go out a limb," Mrs. Washington said to Chloe, sneering and sarcastic toward him, not her. "So you, apparently, are here to help us."

"You were very candid with me in our last meeting Chloe. You didn't mess me around, so I wanted to ask you about something," Mr. Winters spoke very differently than last time, with a tone that slowly gathered momentum, straining his eyes with each utterance as though every syllable required deep thought. "We have a student who has been receiving threatening messages, anonymously."

"Call her 'Student A,'" Mrs. Washington interrupted. "So we won't get confused."

"Earlier, Student A was involved in a situation where another student, Student B, sent messages suggesting her boyfriend would physically attack Student A." The gendered pronouns gave clues, but Chloe could not think of who they could be. "Both were ordered to keep their distance and refrain from threatening each other. But after a week, Student A began receiving intimidating messages again, this time from anonymous sources."

"I'm certainly not sending them," Chloe said.

Mrs. Washington laughed, and once again looked down at her underling.

"We aren't accusing you," Mr. Winters said. "We need to figure out who the threats are coming from, if it is still Student B, Student B's boyfriend, or someone else entirely, and then assess their legitimacy."

"Threats?" Chloe asked.

"Yes."

"What does that mean?" She knew they wouldn't actually tell her.

"The kind of things we actually have to investigate."

So that meant physical destruction, injury or death, saying someone's gonna get fucked up. Public schools tend to be pretty sensitive to such things. The white ones are afraid of active shooters taking out a dozen or so and the black ones are terrified of a gang war erupting. LeMay was both, former murder capital represent. Two-Oh-Two.

"I don't understand," Chloe said.

"Yes, you do."

"This isn't working, Mr. Winters," Mrs. Washington said, though Chloe could tell Mrs. Washington had almost slipped and said his first name. Chloe tried to sneak a peek at the small backlit screen within her bag as the two adults shared a moment.

"I thought you might be able to help us," Mr. Winters said.

"Why would I be able to do that?" Chloe asked.

Mr. Winters laughed very hard, and Mrs. Washington did not like it.

"Chloe," he said, "don't play dumb. Do you know how many dumb kids I have to deal with every day?"

"No, I'm pretty dumb."

"Chloe."

"I don't get how I would help you. It's not like I'm going to snitch around until I find out, I don't know how I'd do that anyway. If it was one of my friends, I'd know about it, but it's a big school so how could I know?"

"You misunderstand. We want your opinion. Think of it as a scenario, a level in a game, it doesn't matter who they are, tell us what you think is happening." Mr. Winters said.

"What?" Chloe's hand moved under the desk, slinging her bag down from the perch into concealment between her legs. She had to update everyone that they were in the clear, and not about to be gestapoed and hauled in one by one with parents and consequences and all.

"How likely is it that the threats are from the same girl who did it the first time, Student B? And even if it was her, how would we know? Would someone attempt a second infraction anonymously, knowing they couldn't be caught? Wouldn't they know there were ways to track these things?"

"This is a waste of time," Mrs. Washington stood and faced him. "Kids attempt things all the time despite warnings to the contrary. They don't care about consequences. Consequences don't enter into their calculations. SHE," and Mrs. Washington pointed emphatically at Chloe as if she was some lower form of being, an object, "she certainly wouldn't entertain anything complex, or be capable of educating education professionals about it."

And inside Chloe, her own switch flipped, and she let slip her reserve.

"Educating education professionals?" Chloe mocked.

Mrs. Washington stopped, but before she could chastise, Chloe started again.

"What do you mean by messages? In terms of the anonymous ones? Texts, posts, groups, notes, what?"

"We can't tell you that," Mrs. Washington said.

"The students in question," Mr. Winters resumed, "could very much calculate based on consequences." He faced Chloe and ignored that his boss was still standing.

"It's possible that the girl who started whatever the first time is doing so now, but it is just as possible that she isn't involved at all. In fact, it's more likely the victim herself, Student A or whatever, is sending anonymous texts or emails or whatever the hell they are to herself as a way to get her enemy in further trouble. Neither could be involved, someone totally different could be trying to damage either or both of them in the same way, just by knowing what happened, and since you all got involved, I'm sure there was enough noise made for that to be possible."

Mrs. Washington regained her seat.

Chloe kept going: "But during the first thing, are you sure Student B actually posted the first threatening message?"

"What do you mean?"

"Did she, herself, Student B, personally confess to threatening Student A that her, Student B's boyfriend, would like kick her so hard she'd get pregnant or whatever?"

The two adults looked at each other.

"No, the two of them had had problems in the past, so in the meeting we simply discussed the threat and informed them that they must calm down and keep their distance."

Chloe brought her palms together.

"You have to be careful. Friends know their friend's passwords. Many others figure it out. Phones can be stolen, borrowed, whatever. Even if it was unanonymous, that doesn't mean it was necessarily the person who owns the account. So she may not have done it in the first place. It could have been her boyfriend pretending to be her and threatening that he would beat the girl up."

"Would someone, knowingly under the threat of expulsion, send anonymous messages after having gotten caught so recently? Would you?"

"Sure, but, I would never have to. Why risk it when I could get a friend to do it. The message would still happen and in a way I 'sent' it, but why would I risk involving myself when it's just as easy for someone else to do it for me."

A sense of deep and petrifying panic solidified her limbs, eyes spiraling around the office, brain craving a way out of the revelation game.

"But you should be talking to some super-nerd kid, not me. Someone who knows how to... what are they called, the computer address thingys?" Chloe was back in ditz mode.

"Gut feeling?" Mr. Winters asked as Chloe got up without permission. "In what we laid out, who is sending the threats?"

"The victim," Chloe said. "The victim is trying to get revenge by using you to attack her enemy."

With that, Chloe bolted.

On the way back, she looked out the windows, hallucinating contrails between the clouds, a rainbow of death taking up the atmosphere above the city.

☷   ☷   ☷   ☷

THE VERY FIRST DAY Raj came over to Efram Daniels's house that summer, Joseph Kaplan appeared at the gate. Like magic. Summoned. He was sitting on the hood of a matte black sedan. Efram had not told him where he lived.

But Efram Daniels had secured acceptance to Van Ness Day School, where he was slated to join Joseph Kaplan, who was entering his final year. Raj was to remain at Woodley, unaffected and unimplicated.

So Efram had done his homework: He found out that everyone who actually knew Joseph Kaplan seemed to refer to him by the name "Asshole Joe," distinguishing him from "Jewish Joe," another rising senior at Van Ness Day School. Jewish Joe was known as such not because he was Jewish, a beyond-unremarkable distinction in the private educational institutions of Our Nation's Capital, but as a simple way to separate him from the constant chatter regarding the behavior of Asshole Joe.

Asshole Joe was less an asshole than he was a provocateur, just as he was less an anarchist (as Raj had described him) than he was a hacker, though it is possible both were appropriate since he clearly had no respect for any organized governmental system. Efram and Raj walked out to open the gate.

"Bzzzzzzzzzzzzzzzzz2ZZZZZZZZZZ," Joe said.

They got in the car.

Efram and Raj learned that first day that Asshole Joe behind the wheel was an exercise in uncertainty. Filled with sugar and synthesized energy drink caffeine, he hunched forward and jerked the wheel back and forth, kicking the accelerator and slipping behind the next car or truck. They learned that if he spotted an abandoned storefront at three in the morning, he would hit the brakes and sprint out of the car, leaving it running, door ajar, in the middle of the lane and, using that prodigious athletic talent of his, he would, in a series of leaps, launch over the sidewalk and scale the wall, yanking himself up an awning onto a second floor balcony and, revealing a spray can from a nowhere pocket, throw "AJOE" in spraypaint on the biggest, most visible, flat surface available. They learned that if he spotted a group of college girls, he would roll down the window and slow to a crawl, loudly calling out some mastery of crudeness—"I want to finger your asshole," or, "Do you like being choked?"—said matter-of-factly and without laughter, deadpan, horrifying his passengers even more than his targets. They learned that if Joe needed to relieve himself while driving, he might pull over on the side of Massachusetts Avenue and quickly make use of the bushes of an embassy. In those sorts of moments, Efram and Raj were certain that, at worst, they would all be killed in a hail of diplomatic-immunity-legalized automatic gunfire or, at best, end up in prison. But Asshole Joe, as always, got away with it.

Despite all of this they learned that Joe, as previously observed, had an immense and unexpected talent for attracting and dating very upstanding pretty girls. Raj's sister was a temporary example, followed by a cascade all summer from Holton, Sidwell, St. Agnes, and Madeira. Efram and Raj were not clear as to how exactly this functioned, or to what extent his assholeness, intelligence, or disinterested athleticism was the integral feature in his success.

So Efram filed away the information:

Joseph Kaplan, aka Asshole Joe: athlete/libertine/hacker/malevolent force.

Asshole Joe promised to teach Efram how to solder and circuit bend, how to lock pick and infiltrate a network, how to find the G-spot and build botnets, even though Efram had not asked to be taught any of these things.

Three days before the start of the school year, Asshole Joe hung on a bannister at Efram's house with an opened laptop teetering on his legs. He found a picture of a random teenage-looking-but-probably-overage girl flashing in her bedroom and posted it on /b/ and reminisced that "when you find a wife, she will have done the same thing as this whore" and then refreshed to see new threads, finding an underwear self-portrait of a relative fatty asking, "Am I pretty?" and, after one response of, "MAN THE HARPOONS" and another of, "I would rape you," Joe inserted the tried and tested image of the North Tower smoking from its cavernous, jet fuel, burning hole, with the bold accompanying text, "9/11 JOKES AINT FUNNY SIX MUSLIMS DIED HERE."

Two days later, Raj and Efram watched Asshole Joe help an old lady cross a street.

On their last night, they spread out in the middle of Efram's lawn at four in the morning, and Raj spoke first, a rarity when unrelated to some subject of literary, political, or humanistic merit—

"Couldn't we invite over some other people?" Raj asked, dead philosopher's tone.

"I don't know any," Efram said. "You can if you want."

"I mean, I can, but none of them are interesting." Raj said.

"All the kids are fucking boringgggggg," Joe bellowed from the tree that he had climbed. "Where are all the cool motherfuckers? Hiding or they don't exist! You guys will learn: You aren't going to meet anyone fucking interesting. Maybe one or two if you're lucky, but the kids here, they fucking suck."

Joe had a habit of getting drunk with the twenty-somethings at Columbia Heights house parties. Joe also had a habit of climbing bridges or construction site scaffolds and painting AJOE upside down with his off hand, and then trying to steal credit cards from Estonia, sometimes successfully. So his definition of "interesting" notwithstanding, Joe said this, and unlike other things, Efram kept running it through his head.

"Where are they?"

The next day, underclassmen at Van Ness Day School had a morning of orientation before the real fun. Asshole Joe was nice enough to give Efram a ride.

"It's exactly like Woodley," Joe said. "You can't ever hit anyone."

So here we go, Efram! A new school, first semester sophomore year...

‡   ‡   ‡   ‡

FOUR YEARS BEFORE THE end, fourteen-year-old Steven was over Baghdad. Steven was ready. He guessed that they were at about nineteen thousand feet, except they weren't twenty miles out like normal. They were right over the airport. Out the window, the Tigris split the beige and scrub green into unending rectangles.

The cockpit made the announcement.

"Please fasten your seatbelts and brace yourselves for a combat landing."

Steven started laughing, half hidden under a mandated hood.

"What?" Norman asked.

Norman was reading a magazine. The pseudo-flight attendants had already taken great care to collect all the beverages and rubbish. Steven wondered if Norman had heard the announcement.

The hydraulics made their noises in the wings. Steven pressed his hand against the bulkhead as it tilted. It was slight, but then the speed picked up. They banked to infinity, spiraling to the bottom. Steven knows it's the easy way to avoid a missile. Start at an altitude out of surface-to-air range and then coil down as tightly as possible, straightening out at a random low point to deploy your gear and grab the tarmac. Norman labored to keep the lines of his face from betraying distress. Steven was on the low side, pressed to the window, seeing the city spin from every angle, a full panorama. Bridges stretched the river and apartment buildings scaled into the air, but, like London, no towering landmarks. You could tell Baghdad was Baghdad by the shape of the river, a straightened snake.

Steven knows that Norman stopped working full-time for Her Majesty's Government twelve years before the end. Certain contracts and consults were at the ultimate bequest of his former employer, but he was a free agent. In those first few years, Norman split time as an independent consultant between Lawton Global Analysis and Trusk, Inc., which catered to both public and private sector clients. He retained his seat on a USAID advisory board concerning Economic Development In Sub-Saharan Africa, though the meetings were sporadic. Eight years before the end, Norman became a partner in Merrimack Group, a global marketing and economic forecasting firm that split off one department to service government and defense clients and their private sector brethren. He did forecasting and risk-assessment. Copying all the others, he joined a motley crew of State Department dropouts, ex-academics, military men, Silicon Valley transients, wayward futurists, and financial industry refugees. Merrimack had been consulted to determine which security firms would be contracted to protect foreign diplomats in Baghdad after the withdrawal. And it was time.

The Emerald Club was a small group of the elite, a collection of non-Iraqi [typically G-20] minors who had seen the Green Zone or renamed International Zone with their own eyes. Steven was a member, and the group in formal terms only existed in Steven's head. Most thought the risks of ambush, killing, kidnapping, car bombing, mortaring—and maybe even the spin of those combat landings into the former Saddam Hussein International Airport—were reasons enough to leave the kids at home. But Steven knew that he was not alone. He had met the European diplomat who snuck his daughter in as one of his aides, a father acquiescing to teenage political dreams. Norman had told him the story of the CEO of the private military contractor bringing his two sons to see what their Dad really did for a living. Most of all, Steven knew there were stories he did not know. Wars were littered with unlikely travelers. Young men from Kansas ended up in Wehrmacht ranks, American college kids fought with Libyan rebels over spring break, and teeny boppers took plunges in the pool at one of Saddam's former palaces.

Steven knows that back in The Good Old Days, Norman was briefly tapped to sell Iraqi banknotes. The Coalition Provisional Authority milked him for what he was worth, asking him to use his position to pimp Iraqi Dinars to foreign investors—a good deal when the 'inevitable juggernaut' of the Iraqi economy got moving again.

"This is a country with so many resources! Not that long ago, it was the largest tank army in the world,"

Norman would pitch. Steven knows that pitch paid for the house in Annapolis.

It took hours to get their bags out of the luggage netherworld, the moving piles of gear going every direction. Steven waited on a bench overlooking the air traffic. Blackhawk, Apache, C-17, lover, giver, killing machine. Steven wrapped a black shemagh around his neck and the lower half of his chin, overtaking the collar on his shirt. He salvaged the tan cap from his backpack, a requirement, and put on a pair of sunglasses. Norman was being collected.

"I'm Skip," the contractor said, a vest over a black T-shirt and a leg holster over a pair of washed out jeans, tattered gym-ready sneakers and a floppy black baseball cap, a clear plastic wire coming from his left ear. "And you're the aide?" he looked Steven up and down. "A simple back and forth correct? Nowhere outside the wire?"

"Exactly," Norman said.

"Alright, let's go," Skip said.

They put a vest on Steven in the SUV, a vain precaution for the eight-mile drive through unsecured urban sprawl.

"It used to be a lot worse. But they stuck two-five Cavalry on it and that shit ended," Skip said. "And now Airport Road is one giant fucking traffic jam."

Steven's vision was obscured by lines of skyscraping trucks on both sides, rows of cement walls when they finally stopped, the city invisible. The checkpoints were all paperwork. No questions.

Approaching the Republican Palace felt more like pulling up to a train station or resort than a hub of geopolitical intrigue. Steven left the vest on the seat. He ignored the suit waiting for Norman. Steven was an aide not worth an introduction. The main rotunda looked like the fake reproduction of a magnificent palace, the quick work of someone trying too hard. The room clogged with bodies. Steven followed until Norman turned to stop him.

"You can wait by the pool," Norman said.

"I've already heard all about the pool," Steven said, "seen pictures of the pool, read about the pool."

"You can't wander around here." Norman brought his face close.

Steven wondered if getting caught wandering meant being thrown into a CIA private jet and cast into a Syrian prison. He opted not to vocalize this question. The suit sensed the problem.

"Your assistant can wait up those stairs," he pointed. "There is a new office lounge set up, your first right."

Norman glared with a *stay the fuck there* insistence as Steven took the first step. There were four gray tables pressed against the wall opposite a bank of windows, that yes, overlooked the pool, which yes, had bodies lying around it or frolicking within, yes, not Florida or California but yes, Iraq. In the corner, two men and a woman were speaking Polish. The only other person in the room was an Air Force Staff Sergeant huddled over a flowering galaxy of paperwork. LIVINGSTONE her nametape read. Steven sat in the corner. He took off his sunglasses, his hat, the wrapped piece of cloth around his neck. He breathed. Steven broke for what looked to be newspapers on a counter. Blank pads of paper greeted him. He returned to his chosen seat. LIVINGSTONE was watching him. She stood, and was at his table. Steven pretended to search through his bag for something. She sat down.

"How old are you?"

"Guess," Steven said.

"What are you doing here?"

"Waiting for my boss to finish a meeting downstairs," Steven said.

"Are you part of some special program or something?"

"Don't they have teenagers in the Air Force?" Steven said. "There must be some seventeen-year-olds around here."

"Are you seventeen?"

"No," Steven said.

There was terror on her face, pale and ghostlike. The room darkened as clouds rolled. The recycled air flowed over and around and down. The eyes in her skull worked overtime, a ferocious digestion going through the possibilities. LIVINGSTONE was still standing right in front of him, so Steven walked to the window and pointed up to a nonexistent point in the sky.

"What are you looking at?" LIVINGSTONE asked.

Steven waited, a gray speck, from that altitude, the needle, this one unarmed, a Predator drone, MQ-1, a lazy track across the angle. Steven did not tell her he had seen it. He put on the sunglasses. Aviators.

"I'm almost fourteen," Steven said.

"How tall are you?" she asked.

"I dunno, five-foot-eleven," Steven guessed.

There was no imagining this time. Steven watched the one thing he could not have seen during a flag-waving football pregame. Not a fighter flight or strategic bomber or airlift wing—those you could see out on parade. Steven witnessed the total silence of a Predator drone circling overhead. Steven felt one step of the dance of the automated army, life and death in the age of intelligent machines. After the fall of the towers but before the fall of the sky...

$$\underset{\cdots}{=} \qquad \underset{\cdots}{=} \qquad \underset{\cdots}{=} \qquad \underset{\cdots}{=}$$

VAN NESS DAY SCHOOL's campus was a single white brick building that spiraled into four arms, like the wings of an insect sunken into a flat piece of ground, fenced in and green. First semester sophomore year, Efram had Algebra II with Trigonometry every single day at 8:30 a.m., his first unmovable engagement. It was followed on Mondays, Tuesdays, and Fridays by fifty-five minutes of Music History. The other two days Efram had Digital Storytelling, which was a lame educational attempt to act as if the school was adequately preparing students for the twenty-first century. English occurred next, four days a week, excepting a free period on Friday. The latter half of his afternoon was dominated by the daily presence of a history class that mixed civics with a borderline pre-law style of curricula. His last class was Art, passing over the specific offerings for the basic fare, four days a week with free periods alternating. It was, as Joe had said, just like Woodley.

But on the Thursday night of his second week, Efram found himself facing the stage in the auditorium waiting for the fall talent show to begin.

The phone in his pocket chirped.

"Where is Mommy Daniels now?" Asshole Joe asked. "St. Barts still? Aspen already?" The pantry was still stocked. The house was still cleaned. The bills were still paid. The credit line was open.

Efram had selected his seat randomly, arriving too early. He was alone. Sitting with the center aisle on his right a cavalcade of seniors rushed into his row, followed by the general deluge.

"I can move?" he offered to the girl who had taken the spot next to him, arranging their numbers from her point.

"Are you fucking kidding Efram Daniels I'm totally sitting with you, it's ridiculous, you are a guerrilla terrorist and way cooler than all these losers," she pointed emphatically to all of her friends. "So Efram, what's the deal, why aren't you hooking up with your entire class? Or are you, and everyone's keeping their mouths shut because you invalidate reality?"

"I probably invalidate reality?" Efram guessed.

"I mean, I get it, you are like, originally from New York, right, where there are actually, like, lots of hot girls, and your prospects here aren't exactly rich kid music video harem material."

"You'd recommend a harem?" Efram asked.

"It's such a bummer, kid, that I don't fuck people I go to school with—don't shit where I eat, you know—because rolling around, conquesting with you would be the most hilarious shit ever. You don't even know."

"I don't even know," Efram agreed. "Where do you shit, I mean, where do you eat?"

"Fuck boys. I'm over them. Fucking idiots. Don't turn out like them. You're rich, so be more creative than stupid LA TV heir mopetards. Or Israeli soldiers. Except the girl ones are incredibly hot I guess. Better than this place. Remember how hot all those girls seemed in middle school? What happened? And god, it will only get crappier. It's good you aren't up there though. Everyone up there is trying to get laid." Her finger extended toward the stage.

"That's why people do it?" He asked. "Does it work?"

She was fumbling with her phone now instead of answering, so Efram did the same, punching in, "There's a crazy senior girl next to me wearing leopard print tights and a feather in her hair. She is talking to me."

"Zoe. Weiss. Man." Joe replied.

"Zoe the Wise Man?" Efram asked.

But the curtain went up and a teacher took the mic. Efram's pocket vibrated. "The talent show doesn't have any," Asshole Joe sent back and it gleamed in the lower light. Zoe spied on the exchange, and, as if this were normal behavior, she snatched the phone and started pressing buttons. "Joe you are such an asshole go get herpes from a shitwell bitch and then cut your hair. Please. Xo. Love ya. Z." She then frantically added her number in Efram's phone as "Zoe the Wise Man, your new best friend."

A junior girl was first onstage, and tortured them through a Broadway tune. A gruff freshman boy strummed and sang a bland original, then there were piano concertos, a senior jazz trio, and a weirdly dressed senior named Eugene Sculetto who dressed in pants and shirts that did not fit and talked about being the only Republican in the school as an intro to his standup comedy set. Four dance routines paraded in a row. All of this was greeted with kind applause and whoops from the specific friends of each act. But Efram watched their eyes and their phones say different. She's so fake. He's an alcoholic. You can't trust her. He's using everyone. Fake ass wigga. Politically correct nazi. Feminazi. Lesbian. Drama queen. Efram became aware of the constant noise and the constant signals. The messages bouncing back and forth and to destinations not in attendance.

Benny Eaves sloshed his right foot to the beat as he pounded out a dreamy guitar solo dangling his blond hair and slaved-over body. Zoe whispered something about the experience being profoundly overrated.

Four stringy figures ambled on stage and screeches erupted from the youngest among them. More dancers, Zoe said, baby dancers, freshman dancers. The four strained in their ready position, chins down and arms pinned to their sides. But unlike normal, apart from the barbies, a fifth figure walked into the corner of the stage, barely visible, smaller than all the others, trailed by a cable. She was holding a rectangular box that had buttons. She sat in a plastic schoolchair and plugged in the gadget on her lap. Efram could barely discern the reflection of shifting red lights off of her glasses, and the lack of makeup on her face. The whoops of the fellow freshman girls were drowned out, almost purposefully, by a hissing morphing monster of an oscillating siren, an alarm that sped and slowed as this miniature being twisted a dial.

The wail gave way to a bubbly noise of wet splotches in the same key that then pitched up or down at a finger—

"I'M SO INTO THIS FREAK," Zoe whispered, pointing at the messy, bespectacled, petite, nymph birthing the noise from the chair.

One of the still figures turned their head and barked an order and the movement started as the distorted synthesis gave way to a stripped down beat. Utter glee passed over Zoe the Wise Man's face when that first set of bass hits fled from the speakers. After an awkward pause in the routine, out of that beautiful distorted chaotic shoegazing refrain came the rising beat of a club-ready poppy disaster of a teenage girl anthem. Then the routine really started, a carbon copy of the others, and the same disappointment becae visible on Zoe, Efram, and even the girl with the box on stage, contrasted with the forced smiles of the moving bodies. "Bring that back," Zoe kept whispering. "Please bring that back! Ugh please please please please miniature weird freak girl bring that first part back!" The pre-Millenial *Tiger Beat*-ish girl power cut ended abbreviated, only like forty-five seconds because, unlike the pros, they could only dance about that long. And the freshman glitterati started applauding again but Zoe turned her hand over his ear.

"Let's go bring that back," she said. "The real part." She got up and he followed her, rushing up the aisle as the claps subsided. Efram copied her hoist onto the platform. The four pint-sized dancers were walking into the wings. Zoe pointed Efram to stage left so he took that direction while she made for the bald science teacher host. He could hear the whispered lull from the crowd. Backstage, the four baby dancers huddled in happiness, jumping up and down, but their shorter counterpart was on her own, packing up.

"No, don't do that," Efram interrupted her. "Set it back up. We would like you to play more of that first part."

Now the four dancers stopped their mutual masturbation and assessed the intruder, but neither Efram nor the miniature one on the floor was willing to give them the gift of eye contact.

"Ummm. Excuse me but someone is going on after us. There's a program and there was an application process…" one of them had protested until the other three must have stopped her. Efram Daniels was no longer a bottom feeder. Seniority ruled. Unclear whether in a state of terror or bliss, the tiny one removed the red tinted rectangle with its drumpad buttons from her bag along with a smaller box. Behind her glasses, her right eye was a gray blue while her left eye was an almost orange brown. She was maybe a shade over five feet, but Efram got the sense that asking her for the actual number would be discourteous. Her hair, a confusing auburn, was drawn behind her head, and her slightly freckled face rendered itself far too childlike for high school. She looked like a twelve-year-old girl mad scientist behind her thick, square-framed lenses.

"Ummmm she can't go on again without us," the dance ringleader said. "You can't do that, Jennifer."

But little Jennifer stood up and grabbed the power and audio cables she had discarded. Zoe the Wise Man had finished her negotiation with the teacher. The crowd only knew the disorganization of adolescent performances. Efram Daniels dragged the chair from where she had sat the first time, against the wall, into the center of the stage. She sat down again and Zoe grabbed his arm and led him to the edge, where they sat with their legs dangling.

"Um. We have a late addition. Ms. Jennifer Savage."

Zoe mouthed the last name in amazement with an inserted middle name and an exclamation of the inclement sex-laden nature of such a given title—but there was new applause of that old perfunctory style, without exclamations or enthusiasms of recognition, except Zoe started throwing her hands upward in invitation for more noise, and it came, first from the people, and then—

The little Savage's fingers went to work. She made it louder from the jump. First a dead, atonal almost-note, a sound not of music but of sound itself. For maybe ten seconds it wavered alone, until a phasing distortion brought in the marauding familiar of that first siren from before, starting slower but now looping and let loose in a building whirlwind, begging for the beat that would come. But a voice joined the fray, a ranting, dancehall, hyping, Jamaican accent uttering words indecipherable in the vibrating wind. A line of dry and torn, low-end rips came next and Zoe bounced her legs in a thundering four note progression that cut into the siren like a razor. Jennifer took that repeating refrain and twisted two knobs at once, diminishing the low and raising the high, imprinting a whine on that melody, a ghost of what was left of it at the highest end. And out of that came the drums from before, the happy and excited torn down and built up bass and clap and hi-hat accompanied by a ghostly marauding tune and Zoe was off the stage, dancing down the aisle with her arms raised.

Sixteen bars of that and Zoe was joined by her upperclassmen row romping as the melody stripped away and the drums beat through a dubbed haze before the disembodied voice came back. Jennifer sensed she did not have forever, and let this second derivation spool over the next eight bars, bringing back that initial siren belting alongside the distorted voice, swinging both clearer and louder into the middle. And all of this rolled, the slow, replicated, not-quite-discernible spoken chatter doubled with the crescendo, becoming a machine gun of the first syllable that sounded like "bam, bam, bam, bam, bam." Then it all ended, except for a wraith, a quiet, resonant reverberation of the Caribbean ditty behind it all, something that might have been there the whole time but was now vanishing into silence.

The crowd responded the way they did for all the rest, except for Zoe's excited troupe enacting a psychotic episode of exultation in the middle. From his perch on the stage, where he had spent most of the performance crooking his neck back and forth, Efram could see the rest looking at her and hers, disparaging such jubilation in thought and message just as Zoe had judged the emphatic cheering of the previous act. Jennifer Savage vanished into the wing and Efram appeared back in his real seat. There were two performances remaining.

"Everyone is acting like nothing happened," Zoe said. "This is retarded. No one even wins this show. It isn't a competition. A competition would be too competitive. She would win. And fuck her friends, who were probably like 'we're going to do this dance and you should bring your electroboard thingy and be on stage with us like our bitch-dog,' typical fucking freshman girl crap."

Efram had trouble focusing on the stage. The remaining ten minutes were withdrawal. They didn't hear the violin or the last attempt at a rock band. Zoe and her posse shuffled out behind Efram with the flow. They finally reached the door, when Efram noticed groups of freshman girls flying through the hallway, carrying shopping bags full of wrapping paper, scissors, and tape. They were running to certain lockers and encasing the doors in multicolored decorations, finally writing, "GO (*insert name and number here*)!" in sharpie.

"It's pathetic. The team is terrible. And yet every fucking day before a game, no matter how many games we lose, a bunch of freshman bitches gotta pretend we live in Texas and rove around decorating lockers of the froshes who made varsity. There isn't even a junior varsity!"

"Mmmmmmmmm," Efram said.

"Who are you taking to homecoming?" Zoe asked. "Or you're too cool to go to a dance right? Yea you're too cool, that's the right decision."

"When is it? What is it?"

"It's a really shitty big school dance in the upper atrium that's all decked out in bad lighting. It's the only big dance on campus. Prom is always outsourced. It's at a fucking eighties-themed club this year. How stupid is that?"

"Very stupid," Efram was afraid to disagree.

"And it ends super early at like midnight."

"Is a student DJing?" Efram asked.

"No. Kentaro Ikegami did it two years ago and now the school won't allow it. But you can't ever have a real DJ at a school dance. It defeats the purpose," Zoe said. "But we're throwing an afterparty this year," Zoe the Wise Man said.

Here we go Efram, first semester sophomore year.

THE RANCH IN TEXAS wasn't a real ranch, but a large, sprawling, single-floor house on a considerable acreage, the land passed down for four generations. Molly Corbin lay in the grass. She picked the ground with a pocket knife lifted from a kitchen drawer.

"Molly you out here?" Aunt Linda called.

Molly cringed. She wasn't low enough to go totally unnoticed. She should have found a burrow or climbed a tree.

"Yup," she sat up on her knees, letting her dress encapsulate them in a cone.

"There is a PTA meeting tonight. Can you help look after the kids? Our neighbor Luke is going to come over to babysit them. You don't have to do anything. We'll be back by dinner."

"Sure," Molly said.

Molly ended up in a tree, a few hundred yards out, scoping the house from an angle. The closest bank of the large lake was on her left. The supporting bark was perfect, rough enough to grip her clothing, but smooth enough that it did not uncomfortably impale her skin. The perch gave the best long range view, the gravel of the driveway and the peak of the curved access road. Her cousins were playing on the paved square next to the garage. Her ears caught the vibrating refrain of an approaching vehicle, but then it vanished on the wind.

A figure without propulsion came into view from the southeast. Walking along the fence, under a hood, the silhouette turned the corner to the access road. She tracked this new outline instead of the children. By the time the visitor had almost reached the house, Eliza was compacted in a wicker porch chair and Simon was pushing a toy truck along the grass. Molly leapt from the tree.

He made the last turn. Simon leapt for him and tackled him with a hug, the hood flying backward. The neighbor looked like a puppy dog, shaggy straight sun-streaked hair and a body too big for his nervous system. He was tall, large despite being angular and rangy and he wore a zipped sweatshirt and boardshorts. Here was a teenage, Texan surfer, or something like it. Simon was delivering kicks to his tan leg as if they were pillows, his short body flailing with fists deployed in front of his face, balance not always steady. She abandoned her sneaking approach, ambling toward them in a straight line. This new boy was barking words of encouragement to the whelp. Molly extended her spine, trying to stand up straight.

"You're Molly," Luke waved, and Simon stopped and jumped.

"I am Molly," she said.

"Do you want to introduce me to your cousin?" he asked Simon.

"This is Luke," Simon said and began pummeling his leg again.

"Don't snap your foot," he said in his particular twang, a collision of a West Coast beach bum stoner and laidback Central Texas linebacker.

She took a few steps forward and Simon ceased punching and kicking again.

"What? Are you scared of her?" He asked with a rehearsed, instructing tone. Simon struck again, hesitant, obliging, but still with an eye tuned to Molly's presence.

"I'm not scared!" Simon howled.

"Then don't stop. And kick harder."

"Does Eliza also beat the crap out of you?" Molly asked, pointing to the girl watching from her porch chair.

"Wanna attack me E-Liza?" he asked.

"No, thank you," she said politely. Her brother suddenly bolted away from the two tall bodies and collapsed on the seat with his sister. She laughed and then burrowed her face in her hands. She heard footsteps and a slam, and the kids vanished. Luke began walking up to see where they were, but Molly took the initiative. She took four long strides across the lawn, met the porch and boosted herself onto it, eyes darting into the window of the living room, where she saw the screen was on, colorful, animated, anthropomorphic figures dominating the flat screen. Luke had stopped on the stairs.

"They are watching TV," Molly said, hopping back down onto the grass.

"Alright, alright, alright..." he said slowly in a higher voice, imitating, accent accented to a much sharper form.

"So you're training Linda's children to be killing machines?" she asked.

"Yup," he said with a smile. "Wrestling, grappling, boxing..."

"All of them?" Molly made a face.

"Yes ma'am," he said. His disheveled mop seemed incomplete without sunglasses. "You want to learn?"

"No thanks, I'm good."

"You don't need to know how to defend yourself?"

"I already know how," she said.

"So if someone came running at you?"

"I'd shoot them."

"Shoot them?"

"Two in the chest and one in the head," she said

"What if you don't have a gun?"

Molly drew and flicked out the pocket knife as fast as she could. His version of laughing was smiling brightly and swaying his head, the slightest break in his throat.

"So that's why the kids run away from you," Luke said.

Molly folded the blade and rolled her eyes, walking over in front of him, lifting her arms in her best imitation of a boxer. He turned, feet now slightly greater than shoulder width apart, arms upward in front of his face, with his hands curled into half fists—suggesting that hands were not important in that moment—hips unlocked and chest balanced, elbows cocked and loose. She mirrored him, recognizing the position from firing a handgun: aggressive, arms and legs ready to react with mobility.

"Okay," he said as she adjusted and avoided his eyes, "Okay, that's alright."

He took her left hand in his. Molly fought a reaction to pull back. He formed her first four fingers into a fist, and Molly instinctively pushed her thumb under them. Luke shook his head nicely, soft upward smile again, wordlessly pulling her hand apart and holding the thumb separate, curling her fingers in and then moving her thumb to rest against the second segment of her middle finger. He now held her smaller fist in his hand and gave it a resisted tug.

"Relax" he said. "When you punch you want the point of impact to go directly onto these two knuckles," he placed the heart of his open palm against the flat edge of the fist created by her index and middle fingers. "You almost have to flex downward to do it right," he shifted over so now it was his chest the fist was pressing into, that flat part pressing into the cloth of his sweatshirt. "What you don't wanna do is hit with the point," he rolled her wrist back so it was striking at the knuckle joint, and she gave a nod of understanding. "In real fighting, not boxing or MMA stuff, in real fighting, it is all about what works. In many cases that is running away, or talking your way out of it, or avoiding a dustup in the first place, because anytime anyone comes to this shit, there's risk. You and I could fight right now and I could lose." He put his hands on her shoulders and relaxed her into a normal position standing across from him, his eyes an inch above hers. "Eyes," he mimed a gouge in front of her face. "Throat," he slowly faked a snap at her neck. "And groin," he slowly motioned his palm like a tennis racquet downward. "There're other weak points, 'course—joints, ears, nerve endings—but as far as what you do striking with your hands, that's the rub, those are the targets. You can strike with a fist," his fist flew toward her throat only to stop, "an elbow," again, "a flick," he gave a snap at her eyes, this one slower, "a palm," miming again, "or, as you've already shown," a pen flew out of his pocket held in his hand toward her face. "It doesn't have to only be punches, I guess is the point." Now he stood straight. On the last one she had flinched. "So go slowly, and don't make full contact, but I want you to step with your right foot, pivoting on your left, and throw two strikes at eyes or throat, any combination, mix it up, then end with an elbow to my neck." He simulated the motion of a proper elbow.

She went eye poke, throat punch, and then the elbow, letting her feet turn her body for her.

"The feet were really good," he said. "On the elbow don't arch or turn," he held her arm again, his palms not rough like they should have been, placing her back straight and turning her torso, not her arm, to show the proper way.

"Again," he said.

And again.

And again.

And again.

And a few more times after that.

ASSHOLE JOE WAS WAITING in his car, idling, having finished tearing turf with his cleats at Friday soccer practice. Raj was riding shotgun, a collection of ever-harsh, obscure metal blasting through the speakers. Opening the door to the back, Raj tossed two stapled papers into Efram's lap.

"They are for Monday," Raj said.

"Have fun, sweetie?" Joe asked.

"Joe, somewhere there is a directory of lockers right?"

"I don't know. Do people even use lockers anymore? Do they use books?" he asked facetiously, accelerating forward. Efram oriented the papers so he could begin reading, but the music and conversation caused too much distraction.

"I need a directory of all the lockers."

"Why?"

"Have you ever heard of Jennifer Savage?" Efram directed the answer at Joe.

"No," Joe said. "Who is she?"

"A musicological demon."

"A what?"

"A freshman."

"Decided to go finger a frosh?"

Efram had been assigned two essays, one where he had to make a constitutional argument, and another where he had to contrast the Old and New Testament versions of the character of God. They were in his lap. Both were due Monday. Efram now had two days to read them and cover his ass if asked about their contents.

Raj had unleashed a linguistic fury on both, ignoring any attempt to compensate his language to Efram's in-class presentation. He did accommodate for personality, or at least stereotype of personality. Raj extolled that federal income taxes were in violation of the First, Fifth, Thirteenth, and Fifteenth Amendments, (somehow working in a tidbit about a case in Texas where a strip club tax violated First Amendment rights for not letting chicks go topless), and then ferociously reminded the reader that the English Bible translation assigned to them (the King James version) was an abomination for not extolling the eventual heretic William Tyndale, whose translation of the Bible was absolutely pillaged by the editors of the King James Version, Raj addressed the actual topic by discussing possible reasons why Tyndale's original words had been plagiarized to the tune of eighty-three percent of the New Testament and seventy-six percent of the Old Testament in the King James Version. That was the fucking difference in the characters, Raj argued, and then wrote that he considered the question both meaningless and also a perfect allegory to the psychological experience of the Protestant Reformation—substituting the language and behavior of one God for a completely incommensurable new version.

Shuffling into the basement, Efram tossed Raj his next week's math homework. The past Monday, a student named Isaac Ming had been suspended for "serious acts of plagiarism," which resulted in an additional assembly on the topic. They were told that they could only cite online sources when explicitly permitted, and that plagiarism was a serious crime. Efram told Raj and he fumed.

"These incompetent fucking losers. The nature of information is different now."

"Wait till we all get the chip," Joe said bringing his finger to his temple. "Would you take the chip?" he asked.

"The chip means the end of humanity. Robot takeover," Raj said.

Joe took in a breath to start his fight, but the unexpected Efram answered.

"The world is not going to end," Efram said.

Joe and Raj shared a stare.

Efram played with a doorknob mounted on a loose two-by-four, picking the lock on a table, unlocking it again and again without the aid of a key. Joe posted a picture of various furry children's television show mascots and puppets engaged in a variety of sexual acts, with the superimposed caption stating "US CONGRESS," while watching a blonde beauty hack to death a masked army with a samurai sword.

Asshole Joe had given Efram one of the secrets to his (partial) success. Not only did they easily secure the teacher's editions to their math textbooks, but two years prior, Joe had worked on a large, open-source community project for a computational search engine. His particular contribution and focus was in creating a program where, when you inputted a math problem, it would not only give you the answer, but show you the human steps to arrive at that answer. Coincidentally, it was Asshole Joe, during his sophomore year, who convinced the head of the math department to permit gifted students to submit problem sets electronically, so long as they showed their work. The disparity between homework and test results could be explained away as nerves, learning disabilities, extra medication, divorcing parents, deadbeat siblings, bad breakups, and away losses.

"Joe," Efram said, "find me the locker directory."

"No."

"What can I get you in exchange?"

"Zoe Weiss," Raj cooed.

"Fuck off Raja Bell."

"Stop being an emotional midget, get him the unfathomably insignificant locker number whatever it is, and then he will help romantically merge you with this Zoe girl. Though from the sound of it, maybe you just want to gaze longingly at the stars with her. Or you already have and you are grappling with a need for catharsis?" Raj said.

"Like the catharsis from when I fucked your sister in the ass?"

"Yes," Raj said. "Exactly like that."

Asshole Joe lifted himself off of the beanbag and collapsed into a desk chair and rolled it halfway across the room. He started punching deck with fury, clicking keys, and bouncing around sections of the Van Ness Day School website.

"Like at the beginning of the year there had to be some sort of transmission of a locker directory to at least some of the teachers, right? It isn't sitting on paper locked in someone's desk?"

Joe answered by cracking the login to the faculty webserver and haphazardly browsing through the contents, scooping everything there. He got sidetracked upon discovering the Faculty Handbook, scrolling straight to the section regarding sexual harassment and reading intently.

"Joe, Joe, Joe, Joe, Joe, Joe," Efram said and Joe relented. He pulled up a new terminal window and scrolled through a massive directory Efram didn't understand, finally landing on a list of copied gibberish dotted with various forms.

"Was that whole thing a keylog?" Efram asked. Joe didn't respond.

Raj was looking over their shoulders. "Who is mfreegan?" He asked.

"One of the deans, I think?" Efram said.

Asshole Joe studied the page of repeated insanity, shortcuts, correspondence, and everything else, merged into one giant text file exactly how it was typed. The guy obviously had his passwords saved most of the time because there was nothing there. On the fifth page Joe spotted it. There "cassi124" sat, in between a failed misspelled derivation and the accompanied uses of the enter key. Joe switched windows to a faculty mail login, entered the username and password, and scrolled through the mail.

"Why aren't you just searching for it?" Raj asked.

"Search terms are for pussies."

He clicked through the archived files until he settled on a batch in late August and began, one by one, looking at correspondence concerning scheduling blocks and calendars. Joe focused on the messages with attachments and found it on the fifth try, addressed to the freshman advisers and bundled with schedules for athletic tryouts. The list was only half the battle.

The locker numbers were all three-digit values that started mysteriously at 128 and skipped portions of the sequence matching the end of each hall. The highest hallway had lockers from 832 to 886, a number that had no basis in reality as there were nowhere near that many students.

"Where is 342?"

"You'll have to wander around and figure it out."

"Now I need you to drive me to get wrapping paper and tape and markers."

Efram expected difficulty but received none, and the three filed into the Joemobile, skidding around corners to the nearest drugstore. It required an actual shopping cart. Efram loaded thirty-eight rolls of wrapping paper and piled a few dozen magazines into the cart. He moved down the aisle creating an amalgam of tape and glue brands, several pairs of scissors, and an assortment of stuffed toys from the bedraggled kids aisle. They joined cans of sugar and energy, soon merged with several bags of chips and candy.

Efram paid.

He arrived at Van Ness an hour before his first class. A test run: a dozen magazines in a backpack instead of wrapping paper. The Savage's locker was found on the fourth floor of one spiral, and he covered the ground in candy bears. He built a monument of magazine images: pimped out cars, muscled lads, bikinied babes, previewed digital worlds, thrashing guitarists, and advice on how to organize your closet. Efram tore out a piece of paper, wrote on it, and jammed it into the locker through the angled slit—

> DEAR J. SAVAGE,
> WANT TO DJ A PARTY?
> E. DANIELS

‡   ‡   ‡   ‡

GENEVA. SWITZERLAND. COCKTAIL PARTY swank, chandeliers and caterers, all dust vaporized from the residence; Steven stood tall and broad and flexed the brawn he had done nothing to attain. Three years before the end, Steven looked like Death: black suit, white shirt, no tie. Norman had taken him to the haberdasher, but Steven rejected the more playful English colorways and tailoring, opting for simplicity. A pianist stroked keys in the corner, real ivory, old world. Norman beelined for the loud laughing circle of men, legitimate businessmen, moguls, and job creators. All had their trophies on their arms.

A waiter halted to the right and offered Steven pâté. He refused. He watched Norman talk to a drug kingpin who was also a telecommunications giant, a Balkan football owner who took rips off of kidnapping and enslaving crews. Drug money was building schools. Sex traffickers were investing in small business. Steven knew a programmer working in Eastern Europe earned better money and benefits queuing up keyloggers and botnets than he ever would banging away in Silicon Valley. Steven was a wallflower. Norman was escorted for the night by an East Asian who introduced herself as "Jean." She had been selected because this was new Norman: post-mid-life-cool Norman, Norman who stayed in boutique hotels and actually went shopping for clothes. She claimed she was a "photographer."

Steven found himself trapped by a Cambridge undergraduate. She was fresh out of her semester's festival of postcolonialism and global intertextualities, traveling with daddy for the summer, and chatty. She asked him what countries he had traveled to in Africa and he rifled them off, one by one, as best he could.

"Oh wow," she said, "that's a lot. So what do you think we should do about it?"

"Do about what?" he asked, though he knew exactly what she meant. People who treated Africa like it was one singular place deserved a special kind of intellectual derision.

In response to her question, fifteen-year-old Steven suggested that Africa was in dire need of an indigenous empire to unite a fractured corner, preferably in Central or Southern Africa. "Someone needs to find the time to go Genghis Khan," Steven said. "Build some tanks and then pave some highways."

She then began lecturing Steven on the extreme importance of a "more compassionate" brand of Western aid. But Steven knew that to Norman, and, more importantly, to Norman's employers, "aid" meant economic development. And economic development meant emerging markets. Always plan to get a cut.

He said nothing, and, when she was distracted by a selection of drinks on a proffered tray, he escaped to the other side of the party.

Stuck behind a white haired man, a late arrival tried to get through the door. The new girl was dressed in a leather jacket, weathered and clearly from another time. She took it off in an attempt to blend in, revealing a black tank top that passed within the tolerances of the more casual dressers present. She turned, and on the edge of her back, right under her right shoulder, a tattoo interrupted the plane of her tan skin—

"Free France," Steven said. She turned with a raised eyebrow, rotating fully on the spot.

"Most people get it wrong," she said, "and think it is because of Joan of Arc."

She told Steven her name was Raphaelle Guerin.

Raphaelle lifted her shoulder under her chin to bring her fingers to the inked skin—a pose that caused those in the room who were not looking at her before to certainly look now—her caramel eyes smouldering as they struggled to peer at the mark over the delicate structure of her collarbone.

Unlike Norman, Steven was not looking at her that way. He was not breathing heavily at the light reflecting off her tan, or the perfect flatness of her stomach; the angle of her hips, the sleek form of her legs, or her large, oval eyes. Nor was he focusing on the strong jaw and immovable hairline of her boyfriend, who was embroiled in his own conversation several feet away—a blue-eyed Spaniard of Steven's height.

"My grandfathers fought for the resistance," Raphaelle said, her French accent thick and her English unpracticed, but her attempt without fear or failure. She took a quick survey of the room, a movement suggesting that the rest of the Frenchmen present were not of such noble roots and ancestry.

"You know what it is called?" She asked pointing to the tattoo.

"The Cross of Lorraine," Steven said.

"What did your grandparents do in the war?" She asked.

"Le père de ma mère était dans la marine, sur un cuirassé dans l'Océan Pacifique. Il est mort avant ma naissance."

"And the other?"

"Trop jeune," Steven said.

"You trying to practice your French with me? Trying to be impressive? Hear my accent and decide to have a go?"

"J'ai besoin de pratiquer?" Steven asked, sheepish, eyes down.

"I was teasing," she said.

She looked him up and down. The age question was coming next.

"My father," Steven pointed him out, "he signed up to fight in a war, but was too late and missed it."

"Which?"

"The Cold one," Steven said.

Norman was looking at them still. At her. Smiling. Pleased that his son was talking to a girl.

$$\vdots \qquad \vdots \qquad \vdots \qquad \vdots$$

THE GUEST LIST WAS controlled by Zoe the Wise Man, Raj, Joe, The Savage, and Efram.

Ninety-three lucky souls from Van Ness Day School had their lockers decorated over a sporadic two-week period. They found invitations inside official school business envelopes, typed on acquired official school stationary. Eleven students at Woodley, predominately sophomores, received the same treatment. Direct links to the semiprivate event page were sent to eight students at GDS, seven at Sidwell Friends, twelve at Field (someone had to bring the ill hydro), two at Maret, one at St. Albans, four at NCS, three at Holton Arms, four at St. Stevens-St. Agnes, none at Potomac, none at Mclean, one at Georgetown Prep, none at Landon. Joe invited ten from

Woodrow Wilson Senior High School. One was tapped from LeMay. Public school would be let in the house.

The digital messages came from an official Van Ness Day School email address.

The heading remained the same regardless of the form—

YOU (might be) [i.e.{in essence}] are invited to THE OFFICIAL Van Ness Day School Homecoming Formal AFTERPARTY!

The chosen were given a phone number to text. Directions would be sent the night-of to all who responded.

In addition, various physical flyers were discarded on hallway floors, school desks, and taped to walls. But these did not include the location or the host identity. They did not all have the same text, instead encouraging or advertising "getting wasted" or "tons of drugs" or "free pony rides" or "petting zoo on location" or "moon bounce" or "male strippers" or "onsite pharmacy."

Searching for "the OFFICIAL Van Ness Day School Homecoming Afterparty" brought up a long domain with that exact name, which, when clicked, revealed a page with a blank black background, interrupted only by a gigantic white hollow diamond. A move of the pointer within its borders revealed a star vaguely in its northwest quadrant, which corresponded to a certain house, in a certain park, in a certain diamond shaped city, which had

had one fourth of its diamondness sawed off, though on the page the shape was still complete.

If they could figure out where it was, they would be admitted.

Fuck wildfire—word spread like a Biopreparat genetically modified biological superweapon. But no one knew if it was real.

First semester sophomore year, Efram Daniels skipped the actual Homecoming Dance.

⊗   ⊗   ⊗   ⊗

MOLLY HAD TO WAIT until Friday afternoon. Luke showed up after school, and they went off about a half mile from the house, right next to her tree, almost to the lake. It started with the same repetition.

"Now," he did that same thing: pressed his hands to her shoulders and got her out of his stance. "After your first two and then your elbow, I want you to eye-gouge, and then grab like this," the elbow strike became a hold of the shoulder where the elbow pressed against the neck, "from there we will go…" Molly started the motions and he was a willing dummy, but on the second rep he started distracting in progress, either a test or habit.

"So Idaho?"

"Yes."

"Homeschooled?"

"Yes."

"How is that?"

Molly flexed against his throat slightly harder. His right arm shot a poke into her side, her jump was half repressed.

"Did Linda tell you to be nice to me?" she asked.

"Yeeeeeaa," he said.

Molly's tongue held as she finished another hold. Luke was apparently the least nervous person on the planet. His body held no tension as he moved.

"Now at the end of that," he flew through the strikes and grabbed hold of her shoulder, arm in contact with esophagus, "bring me down." He let her feel how his feet shuffled under her, around her exposed calf, skin on skin, and he gently threw her to the ground, leading her body downward in the only trajectory it could go and catching her right before she hit the grass. "When you do it to me, you can go as hard as you want with the throw part," he said. "Weight is working against you."

The first time she flubbed it, tangling her right heel behind his, as opposed to engaging the calf, but she reset and tried again, launching him to the ground as hard as she could, a release from the slow motions of fake fists and elbows. The takedown had no effect on her target. Luke was still relaxed, now on the grass, having landed and quickly positioned one hand behind his head in a proto-pose.

"Show me what it really feels like?" Molly said

He held out his hand and Molly looked down at him, cocking her head again, dirty strands of hair covering his eyes. She took it and gave a slight pull. He gave his head a hair-settling shake. Molly imagined him with four legs, a tail, and his tongue hanging out of his mouth. He dispensed with the first few strikes, went straight to the elbow across her neck, and then paused.

"How fast should I go?"

She rolled her eyes.

She didn't feel his foot move this time, only the rush of air as she was catapulted to the ground. Of course, with feet already planted, she was able to instinctively drop her left arm to take the brunt of the momentum when it hit the ground.

"What the hell are you doing?" A voice seared from around the corner of the house, charging with a familiar gait. Molly rolled and stood with a hand from Luke, facing the other way.

"Hi, Dad," Molly gave that much to Jonathan Corbin, and then quietly cursed that her senses had not noticed the grinding sound of rubber against gravel when the car approached. "What are you doing here?"

"I drove down who is that?" He merged two sentences into one.

"This is Luke, Jon," ten feet away now, "he is a neighbor and he babysits the kids." She pointed at the window. They were watching. "He brings them home from school when Linda can't. He is a... What are you exactly? He knows how to fight. He was teaching Simon and then he was teaching me."

Jonathan Corbin's legs still steamed ahead, so Molly started that way too, right as Luke mistakenly extended his hand to the oncoming parent. Luke was taller, bigger, and she repressed a laugh.

"Who is Simon?" Jon yelled again.

"Simon is Aunt Linda's son, your nephew, you know, family, blood, sister-in-law's son, all of that stuff." She reached her father, who was still fixated on Luke, and placed her hands on Jon's shoulders just as Luke had done to her.

"Ummm, see you later," she called over her shoulder, forcing Jon to turn around, pressing her hands into his back and pushing him.

Eight hours later, in the darkness, Molly Corbin left the fold-out bed in the sitting room. Her feet adjusted to the tiled floor, each rounded square of clay with a sloped apex, her socked feet sticking to a pattern memorized to avoid fabric catching on the mortar around each smooth brick. She peeked around the corner to check that the lights were extinguished, skin prickling from the clay as her hand traced the wall. She wore safari shorts, long and baggy, contrasted with a soft and thin undershirt, her current sleeping and sneaking clothes of choice.

There were voices in the kitchen. She shuffled closer to the wall.

"Please keep your voice down," Jon was pleading.

Molly poked an eye around the corner, seeing her father's back across from her arms-crossed aunt, a praying mantis poised against the counter.

"That's the point. I know to keep my voice down with sleeping kids in the house. I raise children. I'm a mother. I'm a real parent. They go to school. They have friends. They have hobbies. They aren't being raised to believe the whole world will go to hell at any moment," Aunt Linda's voice broke.

Molly edged closer.

"I refuse to lie to my child," Jon said. "And who are you? Parent of the year? She said you were letting your son fight with that teenager, not to mention leaving my daughter alone with him! Where did you get the right to do that?"

"She doesn't have any friends, Jon! And while that might be standard procedure for you, it isn't the way to raise a child. It's not what Deb would have wanted for her daughter."

"What is it you want?" Jon escalated.

Aunt Linda took a breath, gears winding up.

"I think you know that I have options—legal ones— and that I could make this messy for you. The way you live puts you in an awkward position…"

"You already threatened me to get her down here. Have you even asked Molly if she wants to live here?"

"No, I haven't—"

"Haven't or wouldn't?"

"Jon."

Molly attempted to find a closer, still-concealed viewing angle.

"What I really want is for her to want to come live here, and you to let her. To want that for her. But I know I'm not getting that."

"I'm not a control freak. She has more real freedom than any fourteen-year-old girl on the planet."

"And you do nothing, make no effort at all, to make her happy or fulfilled."

"I can't regurgitate illusions that I don't believe. I can't live in a fantasy land of endless good times and stability, and a life supported and taken care of. I've taken responsibility for my own existence, which includes her."

"Have you ever asked her what she wants?"

"She is a fourteen-year-old girl! She doesn't actually want anything."

"So you haven't ever asked her, 'Molly, what do you want?'"

Molly stepped out of the darkness, strolling into the kitchen. Aunt Linda's expression collapsed into shock. Jon's jaw flared.

"What the hell are you doing?" he asked.

Molly gave her most annoying smile. She brought her arms out to her sides all the way, stretching her neck and showing her wingspan. Holding her back straight she stood on her tip-toes and began to pitch forward, a rigid plank tipping over. There was a woosh as Linda let out a gasp and Jon leaned off the counter, but Molly had caught herself in a push-up, fully horizontal and absorbing gravity's blow. After one to the ground and back, she shifted off her hands and feet and curled on the kitchen floor, her head resting in her hand.

"Dad, why are you here?"

He didn't answer.

"If you leave right now and let me fly back when I'm supposed to, I promise I will actually do it and be there."

Aunt Linda began to open her mouth.

"I don't need to be rescued," Molly said to her. "Alright? Great! I'm going to bed."

She rose and navigated around the counter, muffled whispers renewing when she reached the hallway.

Molly stayed in her room the next morning until she heard the truck pull away.

CHLOE STOOD IN THE circle. There was roughly a quarter of her grade standing on the gym floor. No Lauryn. No Michelle. Jess, separated from her, was stuck on the far side.

"Now we are going to start our exercise," the woman said. "If you were born in Washington, please step forward." Chloe stayed rooted. More than half collapsed inward.

"No one from DC ever calls it Washington," Chloe typed in her back pocket.

"Now step into the circle if you were born outside of the United States." Some went. Some did not. Some lied. "Now the point of this is to understand and respect each other as individuals, to understand how different identities are a part of all of us. This is a safe space. We all agreed earlier that everything that happens in this room, that is said and that is seen, will stay in this room. Step into the circle if you are an only child."

Roughly one third relented, Chloe making her first movement. She touched Jess's hand in the center. The woman was orbiting along the outer ring. They all stepped back.

"Step into the circle if you are a girl," Chloe had barely made it back to her place, and reversed direction. Jess stayed on the outside. Hand on hip. Exhausted. The woman did not punish her, and instead made the boys step in too, even though the separation had already been made.

"Now please enter the circle if you have a gay or lesbian family member."

Chloe wondered about the ethics of outing a parent or sibling. Several kids stepped in as a joke. She heard them mutter about their dad or their brother being fags.

"If you are Jewish, take a step forward." Then, "If you are Christian, please take a step forward." Then, "If you are Muslim, take a step forward."

Chloe was actually straining, really trying to pay attention and listen to her peers as they shared their insights, thinking she could reach some brilliant political epiphany about the modern scholastic social structure. Instead, Chloe's eyes could see the woman's moving mouth, but no sound came out. Her stomach ached. Something gnawed and clawed against her insides. Though she was still standing in the gym, stationary, fine, breathing, her entire nervous system went through the visceral feelings of vomiting, but violent and full of blood, uncontrollable. A phantom caretaker's hands stroked her hair like she was a drunk girl poised above a toilet, but her hair went with them, ripped out like it was nothing. The smell, rancid and burnt, was clearly from her—not solely from her now naked scalp, but from all of her skin. It wasn't falling off, but peeling away in strips, shimmering from heat worse than the burn from the sun.

"If your parents are divorced..." But what if your parents were divorced and then got back together? What if they were separated? More than two thirds of the class stepped into the circle. The adults must not have done the math, had not considered that this particular sample contained a large statistical aberration. After the flock retreated, it appeared like they knew what was coming next.

Still standing, consciousness left her again and the exercise faded away entirely.

There was no prologue or preamble, no need for an introduction. A missile, a light, a smash, a teetering on the knees, a loss of balance, and a crush of her ribcage. Whether by wind or the collapse of buildings already shattered, she was knocked down. She was on what had been a street, she thought, but no longer. She lay pinned on the ground under rock and metal, unable to move except to feel her skin burn hotter and hotter, and worse, unable to scream, unable to block out skin searing and clouds blooming, unable to retreat into darkness or soft bedroom light. A mushroom cloud hovered.

"If you were adopted," the woman said, "please step into the circle."

Chloe balked.

‡   ‡   ‡   ‡

Six weeks after they met, Steven met with Raphaelle in Rome. Norman paid for his flight and put him up. She was spending her nineteenth year filling her Trastevere apartment with sketches and volunteering for a small NGO that provided assistance and shelter to prostitutes and victims of sex trafficking. Her parents were not aware of the second part. Her new boyfriend was Italian, named Jacopo but euphemistically called an Americanized "Jim" by his friends and family. Jim followed her around like a drunk puppy. Jim and Steven took leaning seats on a railing next to one of the public Roman drinking fountains, while Raphaelle and two colleagues, a married couple, slowly rolled down the avenue in a retired ambulance, stopping every now and then to hand out free contraceptives, testing kits, and medical care. The girls did not all come at once, but approached in small groups, coats over shiny or dark dresses. The occasional man whose job it was to watch did not interfere. Once every few minutes, a car crawled near and then pulled to a stop, a lean in the window and an opening of a door. Raphaelle worked hard and fast, and looking decidedly alien in her army green jacket and jeans relative to those she was serving. Jim did not say much, no faith in his own English, and assuming on principle Steven could not speak any Italian. Steven could not in fact speak Italian. He'd never had the need. On its loop, the van came close to the boys' central position. After the constellation of patrons dissipated, Raphaelle walked over. With her in front of him, Jim tried his English in deference to their guest for bonus points.

"Where are they from?" he asked her.

Instead of answering, Raphaelle shifted her eyes from him to Steven, inclining her head.

"Moldova, Poland, Romania, Slovokia, Albania, Lithuania, Ukraine, Russia maybe…" Steven said.

"The whites cost more?" Jim asked.

Raphaelle looked disgusted—more at how Jim had asked the question than the question itself—his assumption coming from a less than academic place.

"Nigeria," Steven continued. "Ghana maybe. Colombia sometimes. Argentina."

Seven years before the end, Norman and Steven had zoomed past Falkland Road in the human swell of Mumbai. There, the young girls were stolen from Nepal, or Bangladesh, or any of the outer regions in the country. Five years before the end, Steven had seen a bus in Istanbul full of Eastern European women being shuttled into an alley, past a briefly opened metal gate.

Now, the two others working in the van had disappeared. Jim got up and put his hand on Raphaelle's back. He received no touch in return. Behind them Steven saw the husband emerge and enter a slow jog toward them.

"Raphe," the husband said reaching them, "Sbrigati." She turned and followed, and they went back twice as fast, mouths moving. They vanished into the parked vehicle, and Jim rocked on the balls of his feet like he wanted to follow but relented to the gravity of Steven's seat, remaining still. Gotta babysit the wayward, fifteen-year-old American kid.

The moment dragged. Strained. Refused to die.

Raphaelle finally poked her head out the back and waved them forward. Jim wanted to sprint but Steven settled into long-striding walk. The husband came out with her.

"Parli rumena?" He asked Jim.

"No. Perché vorrei? Ma non è proprio come italiano?" The husband exhaled and turned back, but Raphaelle paused him with a hand.

"Steven," she said. "Can you speak any Romanian?"

"A little," Steven said. "But I thought they were close and my Italian is nonexistent, it's some Latin mixed with French and Spanish, which means your actual Italian probably makes your—"

"How the hell do you know 'a little' Romanian?" Raphaelle did not hide her skepticism.

"My dad made this rule when I was eleven or twelve that if I wanted to go out and see things without him when we we were traveling, I had to speak the language. We were there for like a month when they were joining the EU."

Silence, and then Raphaelle nodded to the husband and nudged him forward.

"Alessandro," he introduced himself, "Driver." He was proud of his English title. Raphaelle split off and corralled Jim who was asking her incessant questions in Italian. Alessandro knocked on the back of the van. The wife opened it, and stared at him.

"Raphe!" She yelled.

Over his shoulder, Steven saw Raphaelle holding both of her hands up for Jim to stay put.

"Steven, this is Lia," Raphaelle said introducing the wife. The two women hoisted Steven into the van. Boxes lined both sides on metal shelves. It took him a moment. He did not notice it at first, but beyond the first set of shelves a pair of legs stuck out. A box of bandages had been knocked to the floor. There was a ragged girl, ripped on the lip with circles under her eyes and a horrible bruise visible below her left knee, maybe indicative of damage to the bone. Raphaelle's voice got very quiet.

"She saw the van and ran to us. Probably escaped. Not from the street. Won't speak. Doesn't respond to anything we say. We can't get her name or anything."

"Why can't you take her to the shelter?"

But then Steven saw it. In her right hand were several bundled syringes, gripped tight and ready to be wielded.

"Lia tried some Romanian but that's a guess," Raphaelle said. He took a slow step forward.

"She won't let us look at the injuries. We have to..." and now Raphaelle struggled to find the English words... "calm her."

Steven got to the end of the shelf on his side, taking care not to let his legs come close to hers, and slid his back down so he was crouched diagonally from her. The girl's hair was faint, not blonde but a neutral brown, skin pale and veins visible. She did not look at him as he sunk to the position on the floor. Lia came to Steven's shoulder, ready with a slung medical bag. Raphaelle watched by the door.

Steven rubbed the tips of his fingers against the bristled hair above his ear. "Hi," he said, an instinct, and then a vain wave, but there was nothing, no acknowledgement of his voice. He looked back at Raphaelle, who nodded at him to actually try.

"Care este numele tau?" Steven asked. "Pot să-mi spui unde ai apărut?"

Her eyes and neck twitched. She was definitely conscious despite her slack.

"Permiteți-ne ajuta."

Nothing. Time to cycle. Start with the harder ones.

"Dobry wieczór. co masz na imię?"

She used her left hand to scratch her neck then returned to nothing.

"Polski?" Steven checked one last time and then moved on.

"Mi a neved?"

"Ako sa voláte?"

"ПРИВЕТ. КАК ВАС ЗОВУТ?"

Her eyes were at least looking at him now. Dead moments waiting for each reaction.

"ПОЖАЛУЙСТА, ДАЙТЕ НАМ ПОМОЧЬ ВАМ."

"Olá. Vamos ajudá-lo? I have no idea if that was right."

"Ки. КАКО СЕ ЗОВЕШ?"

"What was that?" Raphaelle asked.

"Serbian, I think. Don't worry. It's the only thing I know in it. Did you guys try straight Italian?"

"Per favore, mettili giù e farci aiutare," Lia said edging closer breaking the girl's unarticulated threshold.

The girl raised the hand with the syringes to her neck, and Lia leaned backward.

"¿Necesita ayuda?"

"Lia already tried that," Raphaelle said.

"Fuck," Steven let himself say softly.

"مساعدتك لها السماح."

He could see the needles skimming the pores on her neck. "你叫什么名字?"

But she did not like that. There was a whimper and she was trembling by the time he completed the phrase. Her eyes strained and her legs began to move under her.

"I'm sorry," Steven said. "I'm sorry, I'm sorry. No more, I promise."

She stopped, but now at least her eyes were focused straight on him. The bottom of Steven's palm was scraping against his forehead in frustration. Crouching on the balls of his feet, his hand settled above his orbital bone and his thumb streamed through his brow. She held his eyes.

Something changed in that moment of study. She let go of the syringes, placing them carefully on top of a box, and climbed out ninety degrees toward Lia.

Steven tiptoed around the bodies to exit the van. Jim was sitting bored on the curb. Alessandro slapped Steven on the back and got in his driver's seat. It was apparent Raphaelle's work was done for the night. Lia and Alessandro left for the shelter without them. The three caught the last tram across the river.

They edged west from the stop on the end of Viale di Trastevere, knifing through a set of half-alleyway streets, bending left as they met wider thoroughfares. Jim now ranted descriptively at Raphaelle in rapid Italian, stories and exploits, but she kept silent, failing to acknowledge him, focused on leading them back. They reached the square: the nice, almost-rectangle that preceded one of the more ancient churches on the planet. The minor basilica Santa Maria in Trastevere was tall and squared off, a larger residence-style building on the right and the double tiered church on the left, the two split down the middle by a campanile tower. Angling through the piazza, it was only one and a half streets over, west then north, where Raphaelle keyed the metal security door before the real door on a street level flat. She tossed her bag and her coat onto a chair. Jim was still chattering away, this and that and a mess that Steven could not decode, names of friends or mutual whatevers thrown in and out like nothings. With his flight instinct running high—fueled by an unsettling notion that time was up—Steven turned to say whatever awkward goodbye he could muster before scrounging up a cab back to the marbled center and his hotel. But reading his mind from across the room, Raphaelle held up her perfect palm and pointed to the sofa. Steven sat. She took the prattling Jim by the arm and led him back the other direction, ushering him through the front door and closing it behind her, leaving Steven alone. He only could make out the muffled syllables. She returned through the door alone.

"I hope you didn't have to listen to that," she wiped her feet in a compulsive series of movements.

"I couldn't have understood it if I had," Steven said. "I still can't speak any Italian."

"No, just everything else," she said.

Raphaelle walked to the corner of the studio, where open accordion doors flanked a pseudo-closet. Without any warning or hesitation she stripped off her sweater and the top under it, again revealing the black Cross of Lorraine, the tattooed cross an island runway in the sea of her bare back. She tangled a black baggy T-shirt spotted with flecks of paint over her head. Steven looked at the blank wall as she kicked off her shoes and peeled off her pants. She walked back, bare legs, panties, and drooping eyes, collapsing on the couch with one foot under her and one dangling over the edge. She moved her hair around, cajoling the strands the wrong way across her part.

"How did you do that before?" she asked.

"I didn't do anything. I didn't get her to say anything. Didn't find out where she was from."

"No. Part of you is bullshit," she said. It was a statement, not a question, a declaration of founded fact, observed and recorded and empirically proven. Steven did not know what it meant. He shrugged, sinking lower into the furniture. She looked at him harder.

Raphaelle brought her hands to the fabric on her sides and began to shift her body, a freeing of her leg and a shuffle, and then a lean toward Steven's torso. An all-out retreat ignited in his every nerve and limb. Steven flinched as she approached, a subconscious retraction, a crawling of his skin.

"Hey," she said, "it's okay. It's okay. I'm not going do anything." She let her shoulder collapse onto his chest, pushing him back into the cushions, bringing her hand to his side. Raphaelle, with her eyes closed, took her free hand and grabbed Steven's wrist, hooking one of his arms around her torso. It lay there slack, a horseshoe caught on a hook.

After a few minutes, she bit the cap off of a pen, and brought the sharp point to the soft skin of his captured forearm. She scratched the ink into thick lines, one bar crossed twice with stripes of equal length, the other Cross of Lorraine. Branded, Steven knew Raphaelle was not the type to wait for someone else to make the first move. She was unafraid.

Maybe Raphaelle did not try to kiss Steven because she could sense what she was dealing with. Maybe she could perceive the dissonant uncanny radiating from his skin. Maybe she could feel the way the universe warped around him, the dark pull on mass and energy, the frigidness of the surrounding sphere, the hell of the world converging and bending toward him. Maybe it scared her as much as it terrified him. An embrace felt like a daring act—a challenge against instinct. Each would have to weather the horror that all-too-human gesture might unleash. Maybe in that touch, in that nuzzle, in her natural squirms and adjustments seeking comfort, she knew she had brushed up against a bottomless pit of cold and decay, the antithesis of energy, destructive antimatter. Maybe she found answers in that. Answers and restraint, insulation against the collapsing field.

⁝⁝ ⁝⁝ ⁝⁝ ⁝⁝

THE LOWER BASEMENT WAS not for the faint of heart.

Transformed into a pit of desperation, your ears would have heard a beeping, synthesized, three note refrain, had you been there at midnight on November 13, first semester sophomore year, showering snares rattling back and forth in your head as if you were caught in a sealed metal cube. "THE SOUND YOU HEAR IS THE SOUND OF AN IMMINENT NUCLEAR ATTACK," and rough clamor drove out from five angles. Bodies packed the room wall to wall, a thin layer of dust and mud covering the cement floor from the pounding footwear. Zoe the Wise Man jerked her collarbone to the sky as a rush of what might have been originally guitar noise exited through the middle. A new set of thumps dove through the shifting legs, dodging in and out gliding inches above the ground. It was this almost-but-not-quite breakbeat riff blinking across the software effects processors and drum machines that were hard wired into a second mixer. On the other side of the stage, two Technics 1210 MK2 turntables and a Rane TTM 57 mixer made up a nice trio of all matte black gear, complemented by several laptops that formed a cloud of cables, snaking back and forth across the folding table. The four speakers

and two subwoofers could shake anything shakable, and
there was a mini-earthquake caused by every bass drum
count of one or three, or an all-out apocalyptic tremor
when it hit four to the floor. Raj had wanted to set up a
seismograph. Six-foot-two Malik Rahman backed away,
changing the guard, handing off to that tiny thing waiting
next to him. The headphones remained plugged in.
Switching them was pointless, the sweat already shared.
He was leaving her uptempo. The Savage had her hair
slick, darkest crimson in the light, shimmering, braided
from her temple down the shape of her head, past her
ear, glitter strewn over her face and skin. She wore a
paint-flecked, original old school Air Jordan T-shirt that
had belonged to someone much larger, as on her it was a
dress. She went straight wax on the next one, the needle
hitting actual real analog sound when cued in her left ear,
having to turn the gains down, no digital manipulation.
At the modified pitched up count of 132 beats per minute,
she cut the low-end of what had been playing and started
sliding her right hand in a blur, vinyl across the cloth of
the slipmat. Thunk, thunk, thunkity, thunk, thunk, the
water droplet sound created by The Savage slithering the
record back and forth in quarter and then eighth notes,
with one set of fingers and cutting the fader in and out
in the other. And then her hand released the spin. It was
relatively quiet at first, gained down and EQed out, a
slow upslope revealing a cha-cha beat: a boom-boom—
boomboomboom-boom-boom—boomboomboom,
hand claps joined it after two bars, the previous song

and sound now euthanized, vanishing range by range into nothingness. "Hit that ass from the back, girl how ya make yo pussy jump like that?" appeared for two bars, chanted, no melody, Baltimore club, the Mid-Atlantic Brotherhood made the forty-five minute drive, a DJ Technics, DJ Johnny Blaze, and Blaqqstar tribute came with that and the next three records, the same cha-cha beat rained down with kid cartoon themes and doo-wop barber shop refrains, substituted for the repeated come on. She switched again to the unruly chant of "WHERE U FROM?" with the repeated alternating answers, "NORTHSIDE, SOUTHSIDE, WESTSIDE, EASTSIDE," but The Savage wasn't normal, and did this thing she did a lot where she took the stripped down sound of Bmore Club, Miami Bass, or Chicago Ghettotech and threw in massively distorted Detroit or German techno tracks on the other side, dirty electrified vibrato synths merging with the nasty lyrics and teutonic dubplates: hedonism meet hedonism. But The Savage wanted to go slower, so she let one of the techno tracks ride out, then turned on a reverb effect, and flipped the "ON/OFF" knob on the turntable which cut the motor out and allowed the spinning platter to grind to a halt over about seven seconds. It's momentum drained, the sound slowing and pitching down into oblivion. She prolonged this process by ringing her finger around with the label, making the deceleration take even longer—a grinding disintegration of what had been. Zoe the Wise Man clattered to the floor in fake collapsed death, hanging off of Asshole Joe in elegant ragdoll style. And right when it was about to totally cease, right before the empty buzz of unoccupied speakers would be revealed, up came "slow motion for me, slow motion for me, move it slow motion for me," pitched down past its original eighty-seven beats per minute, tired and drawling, chopped and screwed—the first step on the race back uptempo. In the upper basement behind the closed door, the former office kitchen was now a bar, except for the freezer stuffed with frozen pizza products. The frankenstein system was countermanding the extra noise from below by blaring tone-deaf dubbed-out stoner fare of ambient doom, a piece of music software hacked by Efram and Joe, into a robot selector, to find ways to categorize spacey and chill music from the rest through signal analysis. Efram Daniels held court sitting atop a desk while a thin, taller-than-him senior Woodley girl named Serena Hendrix draped her arm around his neck, and her Jamaican-consulate-daughter-Washington-International-School-friend Victoria rested her head in Serena's lap, wearing a gas mask around her neck, an accessory stolen from the top of an improvised lamp. Christmas lights were everywhere, complimented by coils of uninstalled track lighting pillaged from hardware stores, to be hot-wired and plugged-in, housed in disused file cabinets and buckets, or bolted or taped directly onto walls. In the lower basement, a fake chandelier had been created by mounting floor lamps to the ceiling. All the screens and monitors upstairs were glowing with different muted videos and films on loop: instructional primers, historical dramas, science fiction landscapes, childhood commercials—save for one, where Efram devoted his attention. It was divided into four quadrants, each providing a different angle of the street and driveway. The stairs further upward were barricaded. The rest of the house did not exist. The Savage stormed into the upper basement, slamming the door and spinning to avoid a stumbling cluster of male behemoths, banging her hand against a pillar. This meant that JP Urquiza, an El Salvadorian, was up there now with Malik, two local legend late-twenties DJs that Asshole Joe brought in. The Savage looked fake next to the two them. There had been loose twenty-to-forty-five minute sets in casual fashion, house party style, no set-times or rubric. She escaped to this other room, and Efram could hear a faint cavalcade of vintage hip-hop, sensing the rhythmic structure through the wall and floor. The Savage fled past them, toward the back nook that held Efram's bed.

"Some stupid drunk girls kept going up and requesting things and giving her shit," Raj said. Occupational hazard. Raj went after her.

A pair of headlights began crawling down Efram's surveillance footage view of the street. There had been the occasional car, but this was moving too slowly. It was creeping. Efram slithered forward and keyed that view to fill the screen. His eyes saw the outline of the faint lights on the roof. MPD typically left their lights on, after a far-gone police chief visited Israel and decided it was a good tactic to steal. Efram bounded to the floor, his companions almost collapsing with the shift. Dodging through bodies, he reached his bed where Raj had buckled and The Savage was pacing back and forth.

"I hate that. They all have their zillion songs, they all know what they want to hear next. Why am I up there? They wait around for their repetitive trash to come on so they can cheer and get off on their own obsessions..." The Savage was fuming, but Efram had to stop her, interrupting by jumping up and down waving frantically.

"Fire drill," Efram said.

They moved through the room and to the stairs, down another level, ears adjusting to the other fray. The Savage dodged to the platform to relieve PJ and Maliq. They would hurry upstairs, bypassing the controls, and hide there, exiting to the side path if the worst were to occur. Their car was parked blocks away. Raj retreated back up, ready to hide the contraband, whispering in Joe's ear on the way. Efram entered the cold air and looped around the house. The headlights had not yet hit the fence. Two came through the portal behind him into the relative silence.

"They coming for us?" Joe asked. "You keep being so fucking paranoid dude. It's a closed gate in a totally fenced-in house the size of an aircraft carrier with a party in a bunker sunk into the ground. We can't even hear it here."

It was an absent buzz, faint echoes with certain highs and lows, or maybe that was the remnants ringing in their ears. Two specks of flashlights appeared probing the hedge the few hundred feet up the driveway.

"I can handle it," Zoe the Wise Man said. "I'm super good at talking to cops."

"No," Efram said.

"Why do guys always do that? Why do you think you're better at getting out of shit than girls are?"

"It's not cause you're a girl," Joe clarified. "He'd say the same to me. Watch. Efram, I can handle it."

Trudging up the driveway Efram waved his left hand in a plea for the two of them to hang back and hopefully remain quiet. The lights lingered for a few moments every ten feet or so before moving on, searching for a path or a door. The swinging electronic keypad controlled driveway entrance opened with the push of a button in Efram's hand. A streetlight streamed a dark shadow in the new canyon, and Efram hit the sidewalk. The moving metal brought the two bodies to him. In his head he theorized how the conversation would go, the, "Is there a problem, officers?" followed by the bartering and obfuscating, and Joe and Zoe possibly saying something dumb. So Efram preempted it. They asked if he lived there and he handed them an ID and a thicker plastic card.

The first gave no recognition. But he handed the pieces to his partner who looked down, and laughed loudly, signaling his partner back to the car.

"All grown up, huh?" he said, surveying Efram.

"Getting there."

"The neighbors are catching on. We've been circling out here the last two hours. This time they really must've paid attention. If only I'd known it was you. You're pretty quiet."

"I try," Efram said.

This one, slightly wrinkled in the light, gave Efram a card with a number and told him to call if there was any trouble, if anyone got out of control or unmentioned shit went down. The engine fired up and the silent blinking lights streaked away. Efram closed the gate and pulled out his phone, hailing Raj and The Savage to retrieve the overage talent.

"HOW?" Zoe asked.

Joe took her hand.

Efram tried to avoid being close to Joe and Zoe walking back. He skirted flowerbeds and walked on the stone limit of the driveway, dodging bushes in negative light.

CHLOE'S BED WAS A command center. The screens streamed and scrolled the messages.

"Can't handle having a refrigerator, too many options," said Natalie. "Going home," said Ruby. "Ladies: Belts can only do so much to combat hipster tummy (tm). What happened to corsets?" said Emerson. "fbgm GCK," said Ian. "How do you know MA?" said Murphy, initials, not state abbreviations. "Fuck bio," said Amy. "TR IS GOD," wrote Ani. "What teenage girl doesn't want to be fucked like an animal?" commented Carlos. Ani liked Carlos and Carlos's comment. Ani's forty-five-year-old half-brother also liked Carlos's comment, since he was actually old enough to remember the recording in its natural era, made when he was a teenager. Ani and Carlos didn't realize they were being nostalgic. Chloe scrolled on. "Arab spring break?" asked Graham with photo attached. "This seems cruel...but the enjoyment level is so high," said Shannon with video attached. "Doesn't he own a shirt?" Beth wrote. "Swag to the maximum," James said. Courtney aka / getfasterpeoplegetfaster added a topless female form to her daily digestible photographic redirected appropriations, lifted from a European fashion mag editorial someone had ripped and scanned. In a world in which they were all transmitting nude pictures, the models had to compete.

In the next venue, Anonymous asked Lauryn how it felt to be an ugly bitch, and Lauryn guessed who it was in response, but who it was asked again, saying it was not who it was, and so Lauryn became anonymous, and asked who it was (who had been denying that she was who it was) how it felt to get really drunk at a party, start blowing Trevor Stout, and have him borderline lose consciousness and start pissing—and then that account went dead. Point to Lauryn, and someone else, a New Anonymous, asked Lauryn for advice for her first time. Lauryn urged the New Anonymous to message her directly.

Chloe watched Aaron Martin and his boys cover OFWGKTA, though she was not supposed to know what or who that was.

Twenty-seven new pictures of Jess were posted in a cluster, already tagged, all from a party. A real party.

A party that actually looked like the movies. A party in a mansion. Jess danced. Jess chilled. Jess played dress up, ironically adopting a pair of dual lettered logoed sweatpants as if she was going to visit a mall two decades before, and hoisting a letterman jacket onto her shoulders over nothing but a nude lace bra. Jess lay on the ground while three artists covered her bare skin in pastel paint pens, dazzling lines and bubble letter messages, tag after tag, temporary tattoos. Jess posed for the camera. Jess posed for her own camera. Jess kissed a stuffed animal. Jess held a disco ball above her head like she was holding up the whole world. Jess bit her lip while closing her eyes. She splayed on a couch in the middle of a mosh pit, red cups and bodies with their heads cut off, flanked by a white boy wearing a white masquerade mask, and a pink T-shirt with a picture of a naked leggy thing armed to the teeth, flipping off the lens.

Lauryn now unanonymously told Marisa (pronounced MarEEsa), not Marissa E. or Marissa F., that the acne around her lips looked like herpes. Matt Peres said "Fuck school," and wasn't the only one. Chloe stopped forwarding and closed it all and shrunk into her bed. The sound and imagery and text stopped. Replaced.

This time it was planes, airliners, and they floated the way they do when you watch them landing, moving slower than you would think they should. When directed down, they did not only erupt in their own fire and wreckage. They had the glare, the atomic sunrises, the blinding, binding force that rendered her sightless

before she felt the wind knock her off her feet. Her body tumbled and smashed against a corner at whatever speed, whatever pressure would cause her ninety-seven pound frame to eject at such velocity. Her back crunched and there was a blackout, but she was inside it, and so she watched the black screen as an intermission before the curtain went up or the lights went on, and she crawled out of the wreckage of a mangled steel frame, coughing and looking at her mangled legs. Vomit hit the dusted pavement and she rolled. Another plane dived, much closer, and she watched the airline logos descend and heard the city inhale and braced herself for the burn. The mushroom clouds watched over, the true gods of that world.

Then she woke up, and opened it all up again. No one said, "Don't trust anyone over thirty," but several of her followers or friends or wayward tumbling portals said "Don't trust anyone." The screen in her lap heated her thighs through their fleece sheaths.

She put it away, and reached again for the covers.

⁝⁝   ⁝⁝   ⁝⁝   ⁝⁝

MR. FREEGAN OCCUPIED THE middle of a large conference table, meant more for business meetings than scholastic affairs, flanked by Mrs. Harkness and Mr. Adams. They were just names. Suffix, surname. Again and again. Revolving door. Efram sat on the other side.

"Your mother should be here shortly," Mr. Freegan said.

Kevin walked through the door instead, and took the seat next to Efram without looking at him.

"Where is Mrs. Daniels?"

"She is out of town."

"This is very serious. We need Efram's parents to be here."

"Parent," Kevin corrected. He opened a briefcase, a serene sound of clicks, ancient, and pushed a piece of paper across the desk.

"Power of attorney. Kevin Longhil."

The adults all made their glances.

"Efram, you understand why you are here."

"No," he said.

"You hosted a party that advertised binge drinking and drug use. You used the school's name without permission."

"You are trying to police an event that did not occur on school property?" Kevin asked.

"He tarnished the name of the school. Pictures are all over the Internet. We will be taking down the pages. This will not be tolerated."

Efram covered his mouth, laughter suppressed.

"I don't understand," Kevin said, "what proof do you have that Efram advertised anything."

"I'm not telling him that," Mr. Freegan said.

Kevin let himself laugh.

"It really isn't a laughing matter," one of the others said.

"We will determine the extent of Efram's punishment once we complete our investigation. Before we talk about

that with Efram, he needs to go down to the nurse's office, right away, and take a drug test."

"No," Kevin said.

"Sure," Efram said.

"Sit down. My client will not consent to a drug test."

"It's fine," Efram said.

"Mr.... Longhil? This is a private institution. We are free to drug test our students as we please."

"Sure you are. But this is preposterous. There is no evidence Efram violated any school rules. You cannot punish him for a private event off of school property."

"Efram will have to take the test to continue to be a student here."

Efram got up.

Kevin followed.

⊗   ⊗   ⊗   ⊗

MOLLY CORBIN LOST HER virginity sixty-six days after her fourteenth birthday. Luke had chosen the spot without that direct intent in mind, a tree dotted landing on his side of the lake. They swam clothed first, Molly not owning a real swimsuit, wading out in a baggy borrowed T-shirt and a long pair of red mesh shorts, her favorite, the fabric adding a pulse to each submerged kick. There was a patch of soft grass thirty feet from the water, a landing shielded by slope and flora where they had laid out two towels and Molly had left her backpack. He teased her habit of constantly carrying it, swiping a toe at her heavy-grade boots, not realizing the fortunate reality:

that an enclosed red nylon medpack included condoms in addition to antibiotic ointment, Band-Aids, and eye-flush. Jonathan Corbin's preparedness to the rescue.

There was no slaved-over lead-up lust, no sweat-stained dreams, or aspirational internal ultimatums to show hidden affection. Four days of learning how to kick, block, choke, float, and how to move with purpose; this process had made his touch so routine that a graze of skin to skin warmth gave her no unnerve. He first gave her a real hug after accidentally catching her with an elbow, a knock to the forehead that caused Molly to fumble back. She had the urge to shove him away and hurl a foot into his chest, but his shaggy twang gave voice to apologies and his fingers traced the target area, ensuring no damage was done. Later that day Molly didn't respond when he draped an arm on her shoulders, but she also didn't flinch or resist, and maybe leaned the slightest bit toward him. Luke was lax in his pursuit, whether consumed by fear or out of genuine confidence, no clumsy, frenzied moves of rushing teenage boy hormones, only light fleeting embraces and scratches, none of which compared to the contact from when they drubbed each other.

Four days later Luke taught her how to get out of being pinned by an opponent. It didn't require brilliant leaps of logical analysis to understand that the situation would only occur in the case of attempted rape. With this he was different, cautious, teaching by having her demonstrate on him, sitting on his stomach, feet under hips and knees angling to the side. She pressed her hands down on his wrists, and he showed that even with a strength advantage he was not able to gain freedom by straining his arms upward. Instead he traced his hands along the ground, skidding back and forth, making her balance difficult and forcing her arms to cross, eventually skewing her enough to release with a twist and a tackle. When it was her turn to try, for the first and only time, Luke really held back. His strength was muted as he pressed her wrists into the grass, and he looked away, taking weight off of her torso and hips. There was tenderness in it, his face pale, a pall in his eyes that wished Molly would never be in a situation where she had to use these tactics.

His sass and swagger had been replaced with arched eyebrows and a softer handling, but not out of fear. Molly saw his concern was not concern. It was not Linda thinking helpless or Jon thinking doomed. It was somewhere between care and worry. So when that lesson was over and the day was up, when they walked the mile from his lawn to hers, when, a hundred yards from Aunt Linda's house he slung an arm around her shoulders and whispered a joke, she brought her left hand up and lightly scratched his neck. A motion sensor triggered a light and he released his arm. But Molly kept her hand on his neck, stepping on a toe. Ten yards from the door, she stopped him by putting her palms on his shoulders in a pointed imitation of the way he would reset, and without warning brought both her hands under his cheeks and unleashed her best attempt at a kiss, pulling away mere milliseconds after her lips had touched his, swiping at his hip with a kick as she turned away.

Two days later, after swims, ambles, and conversational self-descriptive exposition, Molly leaned into him, pressing her head down into his shoulder. Her fingers traced the inside of his forearm, tissue moisture interrupted by thin strands of sun-lightened hair. After years of tinkering, focusing, learning the function and structure of her own body, Molly focused on someone else's, outlining the curve of his hand and the dents in his back. Molly whispered her intention, stating her inexperience with a a nip on the neck. And he asked her if she was sure.

Molly didn't lose it after five drinks with a contentious, dramatic boyfriend or a party hookup, no one gossiped and no one fretted, and no one was nervous about what friends were doing or saying they had done. There was no soundtrack, no growl of an air conditioner or whine of an idling engine. There was no occasion and no dread, no advice experts and no panicking parents, no talking heads bickering over values.

She learned about him.

He had started wrestling at age five, happy parents driving him to successive classes and disciplines, thrilled to have a son with talent. He told her stories of teachers and lessons, of teenage friends, of high school, where he became a laid-back sentinel, easy-on-the-eyes and easygoing. The day before they had sex, Molly had asked him mid-make out about the girls he had dated or been with, and he talked about his history: when he was young and small and crushed hard to no avail, when he entangled the competitive, Taekwando hippie, and was hunted by the cheerleading stoner. Molly tried to take no offense when he did not return the question, smart enough to know the answer, respect for the cloistered.

Molly Corbin steeled herself when he started, acting and doing what felt right. After they finished and went once more into the lake, a cool plunge, Molly buried into his side, light dying under Texas sun, her hand gripped on hip flexor and bone, wrapped in his unbuttoned flannel now permanently thieved. Despite the sting, she only regretted not having done it in her own bed—if only she could have given her father another set of bloody sheets, sending him careening over the edge. Molly Corbin was vindictive, at the very least in theory and dream.

The next day, she flew home.

PART

4

And I looked, and behold a pale horse:
And his name that sat on him was Death,
And Hell followed with him.
　　　　　　—The Book of Revelation

If I die before I wake,
Please rejoice this song I sing,
As I lay me down to sleep,
Pray the lord I rest in peace.
　　　　　—A$AP Rocky, "New York
　　　　　　　Bittersweet Symphony"

(As sung to the tune of The Verve's "Bitter Sweet Symphony", which samples
Andrew Loog Oldham's "The Last Time", originally by The Rolling Stones.)

☰   ☰   ☰   ☰

FRAM DANIELS WORE AN "Evergreen Academy
Football" letterman jacket to his new new school,
even though they did not have a football team.
They barely had a basketball team. But they rooted hard
for the tall hippies and rebel jocks who could not dunk,
who wore Chucks and Vans instead of Jordans and Air
Force Ones. Evergreen Academy was different, they told
him. It would be better for him there, they said.

Efram Daniels and a girl named Ami Virilio pulled
around a path to the auditorium and took their seats.
Having friends in the cast, they had been cleared to watch
the dress rehearsal (which doubled as a performance for
the many students who couldn't make the real thing with
seats at a parental premium). So it was really the first
performance. The lights came down, and then up.

It was the 1930s, all over again, and a sixteen-year-old
with rich parents was playing an eleven-year-old orphan.
She woke from a bad dream on a metal bedframe, stage
lighting giving birth to a whole sleeping dormitory. These
other teenage girls playing little girls pretended to sleep
until they tossed off their sheets and began to read notes
from dead or fake parents. And then, most unfortunately
for Efram and Ami, they all started singing. Little orphan
Annie hatched a plan to escape in song, and therefore
so did Ami and Efram, except Ami was specifically
interested in the sexual dynamics of this particular
performance, so they stayed. Offstage, the actor playing
Daddy Warbucks was doing the actress who, onstage,

was playing his future adopted daughter. This merited Ami's attention. She planned on writing some extensive literature on the subject for immediate posting on one of her semianonymous, world-famous, miniature media empires: not the one where she curated a selection of photography—a mixture of erotica, fashion editorials, amateur pornography, and sexual ephemera—but the one where she prodigiously answered solicited advice from the pubescent masses, and theorized extensively on the aesthetic and practical matters of modern sexuality. She got more hits per day than her school's website. Ami Virilio was the greatest fifteen-year-old sex therapist on the planet.

Onstage, orphan Annie got caught leaving. The evil old bitch (played not by an evil young bitch, but by the sweetest socially awkward theater disaster victim in the school) scolded all the teens playing children and said they had to clean the whole orphanage, which in this case was still a stage. They took mops and rags and buckets, all dry.

The piano was about to start playing again. But, instead of the lonely unamplified tones of black and white keys struck by the hands of a performing arts teaching professional, amplified sampled drums erupted with a different piano—a ghost piano, the same tune that should have been there, *A Hard Knock Life*, but pitched and sped up, ringing out of the speakers on the ceiling. "Take the bassline out, uh-huh," the not-yet rapping voice of The Almighty Jigga blasted through the room, and the actresses on stage gave panicked looks to one another, and the real piano joined in, trying to keep up. "Let it bump though," and the ghosts began to sing, not the real teen girls playing little girls, but old women who once played the same little girls, stolen from a record and sped up and looped, but it was only the instrumental, so the holy J Hova didn't come back after they finished chanting that it was, indeed, a hard knock life. Chaos still raged on stage and off, the mad dash to figure out the source of the invading recording and end it. The show must go on, they always say. Ghetto anthem of five-figure tuition.

"I hate theater kids," Ami whispered, thrilled beyond belief, her arm now hooked at the elbow around Efram's neck in appreciation. She had once authored a treatise regarding the drama kids' incestuous sphere: how half tended to fuck each other profusely, regardless of attractiveness or social status, while the other half drowned in the quicksand of their ever-expanding, manufactured personal dramas without ever getting any. Trained and told to "emote," and starving for the spotlight, those teenage beings treated their friendships like overproduced life or death spectacles. They watched award shows liked they mattered. They were not, therefore, in Ami's opinion, deserving human beings. So some had sex. The rest sang and complained.

With the illegal, unintended beat now polluting the auditorium, it fell on the character of Mr. Bundles, who was, in this case, a five-foot-nothing freshman, first name Sadeq, last name recently changed to Maple. Sadeq's almost elderly Iranian father, in one fell swoop, had cashed out, left the country, divorced, and married this American heiress who was considerably nicer than daddy was, so Sadeq changed his name to hers, court and everything. Ami had once told Efram that Sadeq had learned English solely through popular culture, culling his middle school adopted tongue almost exclusively from various music video sources. She also had made out with Sadeq's new stepbrother, though, she confessed, she actually wanted his new stepsister—her real target had escaped that night too soon. Sadeq heard the music and figured it was his cue to save the show. So he started rapping, from memory, the actual original Jay-Z lyrics, not missing a word.

Here we go Efram! Second semester sophomore year...

Ami put her hands in the shape of a triangle in the air. Posters, stencils, and stickers sprinkled the hallways and alleyways, inside lockers and on the backs of signs, propaganda style, a war manufactured. They all, despite differences in medium, included a cartoon image of Efram's face with evil red eyes, which were made giant and creepy for the noncolor stencils, culled from a photograph with an overzealous flash.

"EFRAM DANIELS IS THE ANTICHRIST," the posters and stencils said.

The rest of the show passed without incident.

⊠   ⊠   ⊠   ⊠

ASLEEP, CHLOE SAT IN the middle of Dupont Circle, waiting for her shadow to be burnt into the side of the fountain right when the cascading water vaporized into a screen of steam. Instead a white van slow-motion exploded, throwing shrapnel and dust toward her in a cloud, breaking every window within half a mile. Four fires started in four directions, a slight breeze carrying the caesium, cobalt, and plutonium southwest. The exposure was enough that, within minutes, Chloe's stomach was exploding onto the pavement, her internal organs melting and head pounding from a molten fever. The field went black before the firefighters ever got there. They would've gotten it the worst.

Sitting on her bed, convinced she was awake, Chloe looked out the window of her room, and watched six ballistic missile exhaust lines impact the city in succession, each blinking the hemisphere into artificial daylight, and she was crawling on the ground, no room, no house anymore. Her elbows felt dirt and pavement and gathered splinters and glass. She writhed on her stomach, struggling, chest heaving.

She reached out, feeling something, and hoisted herself up.

Chloe sat in the computer lab.

Jess and Michelle were on the other side of the desk.

"Nuclear nightmares," Chloe typed.

Articles came back titled exactly that, the "Nuclear Nightmares" of environmental groups and political campaigns, activists and pundits, most of them concerned with nuclear power plants melting down.

"Nuclear explosions dreams," Chloe tried again. First, there were a couple of open posts by random users in general discussion locales, badly worded stories ending with question marks.

The next combinations brought Chloe to several dream dictionaries, and she continued even though each address yielded annoying pop-up windows that she dismissed with the trigger of an enabled finger. She tabbed up the appropriate categories, which seemed to vary from site to site. There was only ever one term for the countless variations of the thought—"nuclear explosions," or "nuclear bombs," or "nuclear war." But the interpretations and definitions were even worse. "If you are dreaming of a nuclear bomb, this implies you are suffering from extreme helplessness. You feel like there is no way out of the finality represented by the bomb." "To dream of a nuclear explosion suggests you are frequently in a state of anger and self-destruction, and wish to annihilate parts of yourself." "Nuclear war dreams can allow the unconscious to view and warn of big changes in your life."

Nowhere was the literal fear of the bomb itself.

"Every night I dream about the end of the world," Chloe typed.

In a video, a man said that the only people who could accurately dream about truly horrible things (fields of dead bodies, mass rapes, firebombings) were those who either were victims—and therefore survivors—or perpetrators. You had to have seen it in order to dream it. Normal people, people who had not lived through war or plague, were not very good at having nightmares about mass death. They might dream of the end of the world, or might themselves be the victim of a mechanized genocide or another 'cide of some sort, but it was always scaled down to a few individuals, usually family or friends. He said that none of us had horrific dreams of a proper scale. We didn't see killing fields. We didn't see hundreds of motionless bodies we didn't know, or thousands of starving, walking-wounded carcasses with pulses trying to escape—unless we had seen that same fodder on TV. We didn't see anything except the color-corrected dazzle and the CGIed mushroom clouds. We didn't feel the fire. We didn't smell the skin as it peeled off our bodies.

Jess's eyes dug into her, and Chloe cleared the history.

‡   ‡   ‡   ‡

TWO YEARS BEFORE THE end and it was time for another DSEi in London, the largest arms convention in the world. Norman did not dare pretend sixteen-year-old Steven was his young-ish aide, the event strictly eighteen-plus and checking IDs. There were no protesters that year, the non-powers-that-be focusing their energies elsewhere.

Norman had two briefcases, one a traditional leather, fancy-handled rectangle, which he kept, and one more modern, messenger-style sling, which he gave to Steven to hold until he needed it.

Steven stood outside the convention center and watched his father melt into the crowd of suits and uniforms. Steven could have snapped a picture in the general direction of the entrance and caught officers in the full military dress uniforms of China, Kenya, Ukraine, South Korea, and France all in the same frame.

So Norman went inside to help buy or sell some guns. And Steven cut away. He hugged the river, deciding to forgo the Overground and walk to the Jubilee Line station at Canary Wharf, which he knew was theoretical ground zero for a future resumption of hostilities with the IRA, not to mention a nice ripe target for an intrepid jihadi. Under the shadow of the low-yield, thin fuselage traffic into London City Airport, Steven crossed Royal Victoria Dock to hit the northern riverbank, coming into sight of the alien Thames Barrier. Steven began the bend on the side westward, reaching the park anchored along the water.

And then Steven saw her and ducked. She was walking with her friends along the railing. Sophia, the girl who thought she would become his stepsister, who Norman had given gifts and vacations before running away. She was beautiful now, beaming, holding hands with a boy and laughing at jokes.

Steven hung back as they passed and averting his eyes as they faded down the bank of the river. Steven had a phone now, and on it his father summoned him back.

Norman was sitting with four men in a courtyard between the two exhibition halls. Three of them were in Eritrean Army uniforms, the fourth wearing a beige Italian suit. His badge was actually readable, exclaiming the fact that he was The Minister of Defense to the world.

"...would Parliament have to approve the sale?" The Minister was asking Norman as Steven came into earshot.

"In some cases they would," Norman answered, "but in this case, the Prime Minister and Foreign Office can give approval without the need for a vote. And of course, I would be more than willing to facilitate that without an additional fee. No EU embargoes or international laws are a factor here, so you wouldn't need to worry about that, either."

"And what would be the timeline?"

"Depending on the size of your order, one-to-two years," Norman calculated. "You also must consider the logistical realities of operating and maintaining modern armor. You will have to think about fuel, replacement parts, mechanics, training, all of which I can assist you with."

"For a price," The Minister smiled.

"Yes, for a price," Norman smiled back. He beckoned to Steven for the second briefcase. "You can take these with you. They wouldn't give you these in there at the booth. This is an actual organizational breakdown of how it would look from your end, how you would set up and train the forces predelivery."

But The Minister and his generals were beginning to notice they were not alone. Four new suits were closing around them. No uniforms. British suits. Cheap British suits. They strolled toward them from three angles.

Panicked, the Eritrean Minister took to his feet, as did his generals, and so Norman popped up.

"I'd be happy to come to your country to discuss it further," Norman pretended all was well.

Three of the cheap British suits now surrounded the group, and one hung back, tossing an apple up and down. Norman quickly handed The Minister the sheets of paper and forced him into a handshake.

"Don't worry about them," Norman reassured. "I look forward to doing business together."

But the man with the apple let loose a loud laugh that became a cough. And the delegation shuffled off, looking at Norman with distress and skepticism. One of the generals tried to maneuver his shoulder into one of the cheap British suits, only to be evaded at the last second.

"We have a right to do business here without intimidation," the general said, and the suit with the apple laughed again. He tossed the fruit into the air.

"Aye Norman," he said in a deep Scottish brogue.

"I can get you in deep fucking trouble for this," Norman said. "One fucking phone call."

"Did I cost ye some money there?" The Scotsman said. "Well, here listen, ye tell me how much I costed ye and I'll have someone deliver a cheque."

"The terms of the deal were, and ARE, still up in the air," Norman said.

"I don't know, I think I costed ye some money. Let's see, four million quid a tank, say a couple a companies of fourteen tanks each. That's a hundred and twelve millions pounds. Who knows what yer cut would have been from those lunatics."

"Actually," Steven joined in, "He was going to give them a discount and give them the tanks for three million eight hundred thousand."

"Aye? Norman, yer goin soft in yer old age," the Scotsman said.

"Stop," Norman said. "You can't prevent me from going down there and finishing the job. They're tanks, not chemical weapons."

"I don't think Her Majesty's Government likes the idea of arming Eritrea at the expense of Ethiopia," the Scotsman said, tossing the apple again.

"Since when has Her Majesty's Government ever cared about the welfare of Ethiopia?" Norman asked sarcastically.

"Aye, there was once a time when randomly selling an African country a battalion of tanks wouldn't push the needle, but sadly Norman, those days are behind ye."

Steven let slip his reserve.

"They're tanks," Steven said, "Tanks are overrated pieces of garbage. They're not very good at killing people. Sure, at the beginning they freak people out, but once you get used to them, you wait for them to pass and then throw a grenade down the hatch. If Eritrea wanted a lot of trucks—trucks and men—then it would be trouble. But tanks? You might as well be selling them satellites without the rockets to launch them. Take the money. Take the jobs."

"If I'm honest," the Scotsman replied, "our concern isn't the tanks, it's where they got the money to buy the tanks."

"I don't know anything about that," Norman said. "That's your job."

"Aye. Ye know what else is my job, Norman?" the Scotsman asked, playing catch with the apple again.

"What?" Norman asked. "Are you going to gun me down here, in the middle of London?"

"They have subtler ways," Steven muttered, just loud enough.

The Scotsman finally approached closer, cocking his head and raising an eyebrow.

"Who's yer young friend here Norman. It's not like ye to have new friends. Not in yer nature, if ye know what I mean?"

Norman pulled Steven by the arm and began his skulk back to the entrance. The Scotsman winked and threw Steven the apple.

⊗   ⊗   ⊗   ⊗

BACK HOME IN IDAHO, piles of her clothes were strewn all over her room. The sky emitted gray, a silent din, dark through the window, curtain pulled. Molly lay in bed, well past noon, scratching her arm. There was a knock on the door and Jon turned the handle himself, but she did not stir.

"Do you want me to make you something to eat?"
Jon attempted.

Molly rocked to her feet, rolling the connective
tissue against the wood floor as she spread her toes. She
tilted her head with her hands and cracked her neck in
both directions.

"I'll do it myself," she said, walking past him before
he had a chance to respond or offer.

The egg hit the oiled pan and singed within seconds.
Jon followed her and stood in the kitchen. The egg was
one of a potential thousand, Jon having converted a
section of one of the sheds to be a possible coup, but
the animals were not yet acquired. He was more a
hoarder than a farmer or forager, intent on enduring
instead of building.

"Want to go shoot?" he tried.

Molly shook her head. She flipped the egg and let the
other side fry, wordlessly counting the seconds.

Salt and pepper were added, the fried egg was
plopped onto a plate and consumed with a single fork,
a mechanical meal. When the fork met the plate in
completion Jon opened his mouth again.

"I gotta show you one thing," he said.

He walked to the sliding door and stepped through
it, waiting on the other side. Molly followed, bare feet
transferring to the porch and then the ground. He
led her around the house and then to the makeshift
storage garage, off to the side forty feet from where
the other trucks and cars were parked. It was only a

roof with no walls, camouflage net on one side faking a surface. He pulled a green tarp off of one of the parked creatures, revealing a white car, an extended trunk and a clean interior.

"When you get your license, this one will be yours," he said. "If you want to practice in the driveway let me know."

Molly dragged her toe in a lazy circle.

"I'll race you back to the kitchen," Jon tried.

Molly rolled her eyes.

"Come on. I always see you running, show me what you got!" Jon contorted into a ready stance.

He was going to attempt to lure her either way.

"One...Two...Three... Go!" He took off. For that split second, Molly watched him, wishing herself to stay still and then stroll back into her dark fort. Her body, after a full two seconds, had other ideas. Five strides ahead, before he could have the time to look back and know she wasn't moving, Molly was on the tips of her bare feet, lurching legs pounding into the grass. She was level with him in four strides, passing him with another six, having to leap to avoid the gravel on her skin. Well in front of him, she heard his breathing grow shallow and faint in the distance, kick after kick providing separation. Around the corner to the back sliding door, she heard coughing and turned around to see him stop twenty feet behind her. He hunched over, hacking away, raising a hand to show that he was not dying. He picked himself up and made his way back, passing her up the stairs to the porch.

"You would've won if you'd kept going," Jon said, passing through the door and thus technically winning the race. Molly walked straight through the kitchen and back to her room.

⚏   ⚏   ⚏   ⚏

"SOMETIMES I'M LISTENING SO hard," The Savage said, "And I can't decide, is anyone else hearing what I am? And I think about every time at a party, how people fight over what to play, plugging in so they can put on their version of what would be good. 'Put on some good music to dance to,' they say. And I don't get it. There's no such thing as good music to dance to and bad music to dance to. It's like they're scared to decide for themselves. The worst part is the songs that can make people look good when they dance, really good, those aren't those songs that make the woo-girls and the fist-pumpers go. Everyone thinks they know."

The Savage gave life to the droning rise and fall of a wrecking-ball, downtempo intro, then the opening drums of a thug life instrumental, and into the drawling guitar of a live cover that fit underneath in an echo effect. But the whole time, there was some difference in the way she moved, a break in what she should be. She arced her hand through her hair and held her head in a way that was adult, fierce, and intimidating—a knowledge of a body that should not be had. And she, the smallest and youngest looking, was suddenly the oldest and most mature, sultry, and sexy and all those words meaningless to them. Adolescent sex is really just mutual masturbation plus penetration. No one really knows what the hell they're doing, even the ones who know what the hell they're doing. The Savage wasn't consciously biting her lip or rubbing her cheek against the inside of her bicep or swinging her hips to throttle Raj and Efram with the sight, not that they knew what they were looking at anyway. She was the only one correctly interpreting the power of amplified sound. She shifted with the fader again, and now it was somehow the creepy violin of an Avant Garde post-ambient Scandinavian classical composer, but she was still moving, and it was more religious and more sexual than all the porn or worship they could have ever possibly witnessed up to that point. Her eyes closed and her head tilted back and her body rocked with an occasional spin and she sank to the ground. Real agony. The boys knew they were young because they did not know how to touch a being like that. They searched for anything—scratching a head or pressing against the back of a neck or caressing a cheek or really, actually, embracing a living breathing human being with sufficient feeling—that might be remotely meaningful to such a creature. Efram and Raj took a peek at each other and took seats on either side of her against the wall. She drooped her head onto Raj's shoulder, nuzzling with gravity right on the incline of a bass driven crescendo. It was much louder over there. She took Efram's hand. Lightly. A friendly gesture. No, more, a sisterly gesture. A yes, I care about you too, don't worry, but she leaned into Raj with a different weight. After a moment of tilting to her much taller companion she rotated her head and opened her eyes toward Efram. And she did know that, at least to some extent, Efram could hear the same thing she did, but that it could not matter less. Not only ecstasy and despair, but noise, true noise.

"Thanks for building all this," she said to Efram, and let go of him.

Her fingernails were moving up and down Raj's arm. And just as neither boy could fathom where she had come from, she looked at Efram, and could not fathom how to get him to the place where she was with Raj. She knew it impossible, that Efram's loneliness was a death sentence, complete, because no one would be able to compete with all of this. And she knew Efram knew it in that moment, too. And Efram got up to let them be.

In the other room, Efram asked Joe where he was hiding. In response Joe linked a picture of the Emperor Hirohito visiting Gerald Ford with the superimposed caption, "AWKWARD. WE DID NUKE YOU."

Ami was sitting in a beanbag in the bathroom scrolling through images, deciding what constituted the very epitome of hot for that specific day for her 40,000 followers. She settled on an appropriated ad originating from a surf apparel company in New Zealand, where a brunette with ski poles for arms wore a kaleidoscopic dress and shot water into her mouth from a neon gun, standing next to a naked Maori warrior holding an assault rifle.

Another girl, Anna Lee, was reclining in the bathtub wearing a purple, one-piece swimsuit and matching goggles.

"I need to be rebranded," Efram said.

The beat collided off the tiles, ricocheting under his words.

"Come wash my hair Efram," Anna Lee said.

In one world, Anna Lee or others talking about Anna Lee had to explain that her name was simply "Anna Lee" as in Lee, Anna, and that there was no additional last name needed. In her other world this was unnecessary. In the first world, her normal high school life, being 5'11" at seventeen made her a freak. In the other world, her modeling career, this was normal. She was fluent and familiar with additional parallel universes, but in those, naming conventions and height were not as important. Torn out of Pleasant Grove, Utah by a budding scout at age fourteen, her everyday values had degraded past the point of convenience for her Mormon parents, so, still supportive, they sent her off to the nonbeliever cousins in Northern Virginia, where she could train to book jobs in New York on evenings and weekends.

Efram moved his fingers through soaked golden hair per Evergreen senior Anna Lee's instructions. He squeezed moisture to the floor, unconcerned with flooding the whole room.

"I don't know who I was in my last life, but I think I was a humpback whale," Anna said.

Shampoo was not supposed to smell like it did in Anna Lee's hair. Scent was not supposed to be capable of overwhelming a nervous system to that degree. She sunk her narrow face under the water, shutting her eyes. Right above the cut of her bathing suit, there was a stretch of skin that shined more than the rest.

"And I don't ever want to shoot anyone because I have a machine complex," Anna Lee said emerging, rising out of the tub. Ami wrapped a towel around her.

"So you would use a knife?"

"Exactly," she said.

She walked back into the basement void, picking out a Himylayan plateau of cushions to perch herself upon, using the towel as a robe and replacing her goggles with bulbous sunflower sunglasses. Ami climbed to the top and sat behind her, wrapped around, nuzzling into the towel.

"You need to start doing things Efram," Anna said.

Somewhere in the corner, The Savage put on a distant wind, religious chant, ambient trip-hop record, spinning knobs upward and quaking the walls.

"Do what sorts of things?" Efram asked.

"Girls like guys who do things," Anna educated. "Except when they like girls."

"She's right," Ami said hidden behind her, returning Anna's kiss. "Studies also show that most straight women are attracted to men who do not smile at them, but who brood and look serious and tortured. So stop looking so nice. And you need to start doing something. Actions."

"Perpetrate some actions," Anna agreed. "Do some things."

Ami had recently finished researching, compiling, and publishing a database of suspected authentic female pornstar orgasms, complete with her analysis, much to the general acclaim of the assorted underground erotica newmediasphere and a famous New York sex-positive feminist writer who proclaimed Ami to be "the chosen one." Raj had finally accomplished his goal of reducing every single Woodley School history teacher to tears. The Savage had started playing out in the greater world, opening for the big boys in bars and clubs, ready to dash to the back room if the cops showed up, underage talent. They all were doing things. Efram Daniels, on the other hand, only reacted.

The Savage turned a guitar wall of suicide and husky death out from the speakers.

"Do what you do best," Anna suggested.

"Do what you do," Ami said.

"What's that?" Efram asked.

Asshole Joe's name appeared in his pocket bearing a picture message showing a naked girl covered in paint pen graffiti. Her inner thigh told Efram to "cause chaos."

"Thou shalt set the children free," Anna Lee prophesized behind the bug eyed glasses and the purple towel. "You will give them miracles. You will show them what's wrong with the world."

Efram triggered a whirlwind dash, a thump into a rolling office chair propelled across to a desk.

"And there he goes," Anna Lee hollered after him.

He drummed fingertips to keyboard keys. The Savage let a song play for more than a few dozen seconds as she set herself next to the display, cocking her head, questioning the sudden action, and staring until he elucidated.

"What are you doing?" she asked with a poke.

"Any market needs three parts," Efram said, "buyers, sellers, and a clearing house. The clearinghouse matches the buyer to the seller and authenticates the purchase and any capital holding requirements to back the content of the security."

Raj took the other seat and joined the audience.

"You're buying stock?"

"No," The Savage said, "he's making a stock market."

"Sort of," Efram said.

The Efram Daniels Expulsion Index (EDEI) was a hybrid futures and prediction market. It was a game. The commodity was Efram Daniels being in school. Originally he defined the positive value as "staying in school" and the negative value as "being expelled, and therefore not in school," but he flipped it. So you could buy or sell a future considering whether or not Efram Daniels would be in school on a specific date. Suspensions counted as not being in school. The value of the security would therefore directly correlate with the expected duration of Efram Daniels remaining a student of a certain institution. The EDEI allowed participants to add additional students for trading, those with an expectation of dismissal very low to have low valued stocks and those who had a more immediate threat to their enrollment were given an ascending value.

The message to Asshole Joe returned an image of a bear flying off of a trampoline. The site took form within four hours. Miami Vice colors were ringed by twinkling GIFs, all of it topped by an animated psychedelic ticker crawling across the bottom of the window. Participants were each given five million fake dollars. Raj, The Savage, Ami, and Asshole Joe all allowed themselves to become traded commodities, and all except Joe bottomed out with the initial trades from price fixing robot sellers. The true genius was that no one needed to *actually* get expelled: Trades and short sells were made on fluctuations in opinion. The high performing traders got a standings list, a top ten, a competitive invented game incentive. And announced from the beginning: "Not only will the top performer receive a prize each semester, but a correct prediction of the date of Efram Daniel's expulsion from a given institution will result in an additional five-hundred-dollar bonus prize."

"This is a thoroughly unregulated market," Raj said. "What's to stop someone from allowing themselves to be traded, buying a huge whatever-you-call-it on a specific date, and getting expelled on purpose?"

"Nothing," Efram said, "But you would only get fake money. Then again if anyone actually does that, they deserve their place in the standings."

"It won't matter," Ami said. "People will only trade other people."

Raj wasn't so sure.

Anna Lee was still in her bathing suit.

The EDEI went live, second semester sophomore year.

⊗ ⊗ ⊗ ⊗

FIFTEEN-YEAR-OLD MOLLY OPENED THE car door. She did not know where she was going. She wondered briefly about where her father would escape to between now and when he picked her up. Had he considered a plan if the dollar ceased to exist at that particular moment? His truck faded into the pines.

The Willow Creek Church Community Center was a crooked attempt at a rectangle, faux timber leading to a sloped green metal roof, an annex to a larger building topped by a spire in faux deco granite, parking spaces on all sides as if it were a strip mall. She scratched her nose and opened the door. Benches were trimmed by the walls, red upholstered cushions, all surrounded by clashing wood paneling with a walnut finish. Textbooks had taught Molly that churches, even with their adjacent community centers, should be old, as old as possible. In order to become old, something had to have been new at some point, but this one did not deserve to survive and become a historic landmark. God should have wiped it off the face of the planet out of sheer aesthetic sensibility.

There were three women on the bench closest to the window, with their purses and nametags. Two blondes (one real), one brunette, two grossly overweight, and one only pudgy.

"Oh look at you! You must be Molly!" The fake blonde (the least obese) got up and clasped her hands together. "Look how tall you are! Your father wasn't kidding!" Molly held out her hand but was given a hug, the woman's forehead ending near Molly's chin. She gave a pat, crying uncle.

"We're so happy to have you join the Backridge Homeschooling Community!" The woman took Molly's arm and started walking, dimples excavating her cheeks. Molly expected to go through the hugging ritual twice more, but the other two women remained seated, whispering as she was led away to a set of stairs.

"So today is sort of a hangout day, something to get you kids talking actually face to face, it's hard these days with technology and everything!" the woman's head bobbed about six inches when she spoke while moving. "But a pretty girl like you won't have any trouble, I'm sure!" she went on, finally liberating Molly's arm. "You know, most people feel bad for the plain ones, but I feel more sorry for ones like you! So much more temptation at such a young age! Not that I mean for you dear! Here we are!"

They reached the top and it was one large room, benches on the sides and windows opaque. There was a fold-out table with food ignored by the scattered groups, most appearing to be aged somewhere between eight and twelve.

"Well, here you go! Have fun!" the woman said, and trotted down the stairs at high velocity. The older teens were crowded into the northeast corner, a couch jammed up against the non-bench wall. They draped themselves all over, five boys and three girls, four with black logoed T-shirts. Below them on the floor sat three girls, these one's Molly's age, but smaller and younger looking, playing cards intently.

Molly shuffled forward, and then backed toward the stairwell until she hit the corner and flattened against the wall to her right. She leaned. And took a breath. They weren't staring.

Every once in a while someone in the room would look up at Molly for a few seconds and then return to whatever they were doing.

Molly's attention shot to the right, then to the west, the compass in her head still working. She began to isolate their conversations.

"That episode sucked... he thinks he fucking knows everything... I hate it... it better come out soon..."

There was a spot on a bench, not all the way in the corner but far enough, separate from the distinct masses, a forward operating base. There was a lone girl reading on the stretch of wood, disregarding the room. Molly went for it.

"Do you mind if I sit here?" she asked.

"Nope," the girl answered without taking her eyes off of the pages.

The stairs creaked, Molly hearing before the others and automatically turning to check it out, ingrained.

Someone taller than her entered. He had a cheek-stretching smile, with cropped dark brown hair over a rectangular head attached to the most massive frame Molly had ever seen. He was a tower, with way too much additional meat and muscle for a high schooler, or homeschooled high-schooler, or whatever he was. The younger kids flocked to him. They recited his name as a hymn. "Tommy! Tommy!" The boys jumped and worshipped at a new altar. The whole room reacted, except her neighbor on the bench, whose head remained in her book. Molly broke attention from the celebrated hulk to see if she could discern the title that was capable of retaining such attention. But suddenly, the girl next to her spoke.

"You're going to ask me who he is, so his name is Tommy Tewell, and he's *the* quarterback, plays at Northern but is homeschooled, serious missionary parents, all that, will go to University of blah-blah-blah and have a wonderful life on cable or never be heard from again…hopefully."

"I actually wasn't going to ask," Molly said to the reading girl.

"All the girls do."

Before Molly could refute the generalization, she became peripherally aware of Mr. All-American, who was walking toward them. Molly made sure to not look, to lean back, trying to calculate what response would not satisfy the expectation the reading girl had in her head. But when he stopped in front of her, he turned away from Molly.

"Hey Lane," he crooned and sat next to the reading girl.

"HI!" Lane oozed with faux enthusiasm. Tom beamed and gave her a fake punch on the elbow.

"Lane, you don't want to socialize instead of hiding in your book?"

"You wouldn't understand."

"Here, I'll show you," he demonstrated turning to Molly and holding out his hand. "I'm Tommy," he held that same smile, now already annoying, one hundred percent sincere, "and this is my cousin, Lane."

"This is Molly," Lane hummed.

"Umm... How did you know that?"

"Does this look like Rocky Mountain High?" Lane asked, finally closing her book. "The parents told us you were coming and to be nice and welcoming."

"Then why aren't all of you being nice and welcoming?" Molly asked.

"Well, I am," Tommy declared, beaming once again, but Lane shushed him.

"I'm sure even you can tell you're not exactly entering the, like, most socially intelligent flock. And they're all scared of you," Lane yawned.

"They are?" Tommy asked, looking around frowning at everyone. "Really? Are they scared? Are you?" He started to yell to the room but Lane shushed him again. "They are all very nice, I promise," he said.

"They don't know how to deal," Lane whispered as Tommy turned into the room, six and a half feet tall and two hundred and twenty pounds, lumbering, "and apparently neither does he." Lane was too late in grabbing him—

"HEY EVERYONE, THIS IS MOLLY!" Tommy outstretched his palm to Molly. She didn't take his hand for the second time. "BE SURE TO WELCOME HER WARMLY!"

He came back vibrating with extremely-pleased-with-himself glee.

"Well Molly, I'm glad to meet you," and his face lit up even more. "Hey! My family and a couple of friends are going to this food bank tomorrow to help them pack and organize things, if you want to come." Molly looked at Lane, but she was studying Molly, waiting to see how she would respond.

"Oh, Lane isn't coming, but it's fine," he gave a reassuring pat. "My Father's sister lost her faith, but she'll come back."

"Oh please, she was over your crazy dad."

"But yea, we take all the donations they get and pack and form them into crates so they can be shipped out. Feels great to help others." The last line was made for his future interviews, the throwaway human-interest question after the interrogation as to why he checked down on third and five in the fourth quarter, when the D showed blitz.

"*Although they cannot repay you, you will be repaid at the resurrection of the righteous...*'" Molly said.

Tommy the quarterback was shocked, like a twelve-year-old boy discovering masturbation, but before he could exclaim in victory, Molly spoke again, "but alas I will be busy tomorrow doing my best to 'honor thy father,' and therefore cannot attend the cleansing festivities."

"That means no, Tommy," Lane exhaled.

"It means she can't, Lane!"

Four of the smaller boys walked up and grabbed Tommy and he let the cadre lead him off as their prize.

"Sorry. He didn't realize you were making fun of him. You're good practice for college, but I'm sure you loved it," Lane said.

"I didn't actually."

"No?"

"Quarterback, so dreamy?" Molly tried sarcasm.

"I mean it's true if you took him into the bathroom right now and tried to give him a handjob he would be terrified and run away," Lane said. "Not that I'd blame you when the only other options are Andrew and Joe." She gestured to two curly haired brothers who were loudly imitating pro-wrestlers in an enclave of furniture. That's pretty much it," Lane tilted her head back into the book.

"And that's why you spend your time reading about..." Molly did not know the right words to describe the angled faced pouty boy on the cover of the book.

"Not everyone looks like you," Lane said.

She appeared to start to read again, but was only holding the book in front of her face.

Lane was peering up every few seconds from the pages, darting glances across the room. Tommy the quarterback had hit the ground under a pile of boys' tackles. Behind the ruckus, there was a new boy, or at least she hadn't seen him before, leaning against the wall by the staircase. He was still, like a corpse. Lane looked again. He was only an inch or two shorter than Tommy, but of a different species. He was stretched, skinny, wingspan greater than height. Black pocketed tactical pants, a tan T-shirt, and sunglasses hiding eyes.

"What about him?"

"God, am I that fucking obvious?" Lane closed the book in self-disgust.

"Well…"

"Well what?!" Lane snapped the book down on the bench.

"Do you know him? Does he like you? Et cetera, et cetera?" Molly looked again. That's what she was supposed to ask right?

He had not moved.

"Yes I know him. This place is small, don't you get that? But he hasn't 'shown any interest' or whatever. I don't know." Lane opened the book again.

"What's his name?" Molly asked.

"David."

Molly's legs extended to the ground.

"Where are you going?" Lane asked.

"To talk to him for you. I might as well use my newness for something." Molly cracked her knuckles and started across the room before Lane's breath could form a protest.

Molly made sure not to look at David as she traversed the fifteen paces. She focused on the stained wooden ceiling and the angled windows. She turned to lean against the wall right next to him, spinning ninety degrees to her left and settling. He was taller up close, unseemly, elevated, rail-thin, ellipses of raw but small muscle on each arm, and indented cheeks on his face, hair buzzed down so it was stippling on his skin.

Molly got impatient after a few moments of waiting for him to move. She reached into her pocket and realized she had nothing to fiddle with.

"Hello," she said.

"…" he still hadn't moved.

"I'm Molly. David right?"

Nothing.

"Where's Goliath?"

It was like she had woken him up.

"Nice, yea, that's really what we need, what this room needs." He took off his sunglasses and with a stretch, looked at her. "Another dose of salvation humor from a teenage Bible thumper."

"What? I was kidding," Molly said, "No pity?"

He yawned, and gripped his fingers around air and tensed them.

"Saved or doomed?" he said.

"What?"

"Are you saved or doomed?" He seemed totally unsure of how to pause between words.

"I don't really understand the question," she said.

"There are only two kinds here. The lefties who believe in freedom for their children or whatever, they don't count, they wouldn't send their kids here. That leaves the parents who took their kids out of school because going seven hours without prayer is totally unacceptable, and parents who think the world is going to end and live in the middle of nowhere. So, saved or doomed?"

"*And the kings of the earth, and the great men, and the rich men, and the chief captains, and the mighty men, and every bondman, and every free man, hid themselves in the dens and in the rocks of the mountains,*" Molly quoted.

"Fucking great," he sneered. She had actually gotten him to unfreeze from the wall.

"No. I'm the second kind. I promise. I'm the kind that isn't interested in dying. I'm doomed."

"To be fair," he cleaned his sunglasses with the bottom of his shirt, "almost all the survivalists say they're men of faith or whatever."

"Not mine, I don't think," Molly said.

"Good for him," David said. "That's consistent." He finally looked her in the eyes. His were green.

"Which are you?" Molly asked.

"An atheist."

"Then why are you hanging out in this building?"

"It's mine. It's my dad's church," he looked away.

"So you just lean against the wall the whole time and what… stare at girls?"

"What girls exactly?" he gestured out to the room.

"What about Lane?" Molly looked over but she had reburied her nose in the book, too nervous to keep looking.

"She believes in God," David said.

"Man shall not live by bread alone, but by every word that proceedeth out of the mouth of God," Molly poked.

"Yea, we're done," and he went down the stairs.

◹   ◹   ◹   ◹

THE ASSEMBLY SPEAKER TOLD Chloe to be nice to her peers. Treat each other with respect, they said. Obey the golden rule. A group of entrepreneurs realized it might be profitable to bring social justice not only to the starving children half a world away, but to the rich, poor, fat, and skinny, in their own minivans. Chloe knew parents loved buying anything that made them feel better about themselves.

But there was also the panic. Moral panic. The unbroken cycle of OH FUCK IT'S ALL GOING TO HELL WILL SOMEONE THINK OF THE CHILDREN! When in reality, all was well, we'd had a pretty good century, they'll have a better one, and whatever you were worried about won't kill them any more than the old ways would have. So they got on TV and walked into those lecture halls and said, "Oh! Children are so cruel to each other now, so harsh. Especially the girls." Counselors, teachers, and educators dedicated to the empowerment of young women, unwittingly or wittingly (who knows which is worse), created a pervasive logic for acceptable sexism. Girls were worse, Chloe had been told, over and over. The boys at least said shit directly to faces, got in fights. That was bullshit. No one said anything to anyone's face anymore. Who needed vocal chords? Who needed a physical presence?

If Chloe, Lauryn, Michelle, and Jess were a clique, they were a clique at the end of cliques. They were a noble family with their country manor on the eve of World War I, the canals before the railroad, the monarchs eyeing the Medici bankers, Hollywood ogling Silicon Valley.

They sat outside the west steps and the crowd parted, and Chloe watched this boy—man?— emerge, and all of their conversation stopped. His hair was buzzed short and his eyes were dead gray lights so gorgeous it hurt, his lips cold but perfectly formed, and his jawline a scourge of angles. His torso was a perfect V, jutting up, but not overly worked, no veins popping or bulging neck, and his shoulders sat back, two perfect ovals. His walk, at its natural relaxed pace, was faster and more upright than all those moving in the opposite direction. He wore a long navy coat, a modern reimagining of a Commodore made mean, and a black hoodie's hood poked out, unused, around his neck. His legs were covered in black denim of a far-too-high quality for high school, his whole outfit without a label or a logo. He looked at no one. The collar around his throat, under the first two layers, shimmered with a just-pressed formal white, made more stark by a death-black tie. Chloe expected weapons to fly out from his hands or explosions to follow behind him. In her head flashed an image of this boy, or man, all too beautiful, reclining on a European deck, cigarette smoke encircling his perfect features as he advertised the clothes on the page. But then, he vanished, and it was like no one else had seen him. Michelle was singlehandedly chattering away while Jess was propped against her back looking the other direction. Lauryn and Anthony had started fucking again.

And Chloe watched Lauryn say goodbye to all 6'8" of Anthony for the day.

Every movie and television show Lauryn watched could turn the dumbest fuck-around sexual teenage relationship into high romantic opera—but this didn't have the right soundtrack for that. Airy, ambient post-indie-rock didn't mumble from the screen as Anthony walked away. No witty text messages came in as Lauryn rode the bus home alone, gazing thoughtfully into the camera as trees passed, rain only coming in for scenic effect when someone was about to make out or the world was turning grim. Life without a cinematographer, editor, and musical accompaniment left a dissonance, the sort of chasm that then motivated Lauryn to bat her eyes at poor teensy freshman girls, flirting and complimenting to make them squirm, then strategically ignoring them in public social situations.

Asleep that night, Chloe was subjected again. Our Nation's Capital was wrecked completely, with her inside its limits, multiple independent reentry vehicles stuck on repeat in multiple independent dreams, incinerated, starved, crushed, bled-out, and throwing up guts from the radiation. Again and again. Infinite. Sitting at school, lying in bed, or walking along—and then the spark and the blast. Literal hell on earth. This earth, once upon a thermonuclear war. Chloe died over and over as the city around her was destroyed.

Awake and on a break from attempting sleep, Chloe got a message from Lauryn. "Yo you have been gone way too fucking long from my life. Bleh. Expect mad rape in art tomorrow, if I decide to go."

The next day, a junior named Beau Jones spent a skipped third period hidden in the band room writing and recording a song titled "Reynold Gay" about Reynold Meachem, not the most liked human being in the place, a grade-A douchebag who had run out of hail-ass girls to pretend he had fucked. Beau grabbed Lauryn and Jess to be the background dancers for the music video version, body shots only, dancing in bathing suits with the frame ending at their necks. Plausible deniability.

Chloe received constant updates from the cafeteria where a whole table had engaged in a game of not passing the water to Brandon, the typical fat kid, passing it around to each other back and forth.—"(insert name here), would YOU like the water?"—and never letting him have it.

The "Reynold Gay" music video had 188 views by fifth period. Catchy shit.

Chloe fell asleep.

This time the hallways of the school did not collapse after an airburst. She walked into her math classroom, third floor, west side, and heard the first shots from her desk, waiting for the teacher who would not come. Active shooter, the PA blared. "Reynold Gay" played over the loudspeakers, a soundtrack for the gunshots. No missiles needed.

Reynold Gay,
Reynold Gay,
Lies about janky asses every day,
Have bullet holes?
Stripes in your leg?
Be sure to hit up Reynold Gay…

The scene changed and Chloe crouched around
a corner, blood streaming down the floor, men with
no faces and women with no limbs, and she saw him,
moving. He was tall and lanky and dressed in all black,
not the mystery boy from before, not with a trench
coat or a nerdy T-shirt, but menacing cargo pants and
an armored torso. He was not holding his assault rifle
like in a videogame, jerking back and forth, but smoothly
fixing it here and there like it was a biological limb. Chloe
collapsed down further to crawl away, across the liquefied
floor, dodging the bodies, but enjoyed a split screen and
could appreciate that he wasn't alone. Chloe saw her,
an amazon, and she was even more terrifying. She was
the one killing, shooting, snapping. Tall, towering with
no effort, her skin a fabric of cream, hair of every color
coming perfectly down onto her shoulders. Michelle got
a bullet right between the eyes. Lauryn had her head
cleaned right off by a large curved knife. A grenade
landed in Jess's lap. No SWAT team yet. No opposition.
But they were not massacring. They were fighting. They
had objectives. They moved, detached and together, and
then they multiplied. Eventually the war started, and the
missiles came. Like always.

Chloe woke up.

And Chloe fell asleep.

⁚⁚ ⁚⁚ ⁚⁚. ⁚⁚

MONDAY, THE FOURTEENTH OF March, second semester sophomore year—

KILL ALL

CHILDREN

—the T-shirt said, a rip-off of the Tom Sachs KILL ALL ARTISTS, exactly like the original with a giant handgun after the KILL ALL and before the CHILDREN.

Either the original or Efram's version would work great on Fridays at MoMA, or your not-so-average liberal arts college. But walking through Evergreen's half-arcade hallway from lunch, Mrs. Freemont stopped him and told him he was not "allowed to wear anything with a weapon on it."

Efram prepared to apologize and say it was a mistake and offer to turn it inside out since he had no other options, but then he remembered the new initiative. He was supposed to do things. Say things. Be someone.

"What? Why?" he said. "We don't have a dress code?"

Six freshmen stopped their journey to watch.

"Inappropriate imagery is prohibited. Drugs, alcohol, weapons..."

Efram tilted his head to one side. Ami came skipping up, phone in hand, and said that Mrs.

Freemont was wrong, that in fact only "racially and sexually offensive clothes" were unacceptable. But then, Mrs. Freemont pointed out the part before that where it said that students had to "dress appropriately" and that the definition of appropriate was up to each division head. She sent Ami off and dragged Efram into the faculty lounge, a dingy hell of an imitation office conjuring memories of large corporate cubicle floors. The brownies left on a plate next to the water cooler probably had pot in them. She searched like a rodent for Mr. Westwick, technically in charge of the glorious tenth grade, rifling through the miniature fake walls and miniature plastic desks. Nothing.

"Turn it inside out!" She said. "I will inform Mr. Westwick."

Efram complied, and it was better that way, the smiling faint outline of the menacing handgun barely visible if you looked hard enough.

Tuesday, the fifteenth of March, second semester sophomore year, Efram Daniels repped a purple picture T-shirt, with an orange Diana Rigg in an early sixties jumpsuit holding her Baretta 950 jetfire. Dear Mrs. Peel was pointing the gun right at you, right at Mrs. Freemont and Mr. Westwick and Ami and blunted seniors with minor STDs. No one objected. During fifth period Ami asked for it, so Efram took it off mid class and spent the rest of his day shirtless under a sweatshirt.

Wednesday, the sixteenth of March, second semester sophomore year, it was long-sleeved and

V-neck but had a nice AK-47 and two grenades on the back, assembled like they were the crest of a science fictional military order. The science teacher, Mr. Murilo sent him to Mr. Westwick.

Efram texted Raj on the way. Raj had his back. The wonderkid manchild demagogue contrarian reached his long digital rhetorical fingers from his AP History classroom at Woodley (where he was the only sophomore in the room), now a star student again, his blips of antiauthoritarianism blamed on an unwise friendship with long-gone Efram Daniels.

Raj told Efram to say it was political: "Say that you were making a statement about how we ignore conflict diamonds. Make it about the symbol." Raj reminded Efram that the flag of Mozambique has an AK-47 on it.

"So if I were from Mozambique, and I wore my country's flag, I would be in trouble?"

"No, Efram, well, yes Efram."

"So if I show up tomorrow with a Mozambique flag in any form I will be in trouble? Because I'm pretty sure the *Post* and the embassy would LOVE to hear about that."

"No. Flags are appropriate."

Efram read another missive from Raj under the table.

"What about Hezbollah?"

"What?"

"Their flag has an AK-47 on it."

"They are a terrorist organization."

"But I could wear an Israeli flag?"

"Yes."

Efram made a show of pulling out his phone and mashing letters in the open.

"Efram this is not the time for that..."

"Oh. I'm sorry. I just think Noor should hear about this."

"The senior class president?"

"Yes."

"Why?"

"She's Palestinian."

"Efram you cannot wear violent and sexual images on campus."

"So I cannot make political statements on campus?"

"Not when they involve violence, sex, or race."

"Jennifer Lauryntia has a 'Make Love, Not War' patch on her backpack."

"That is different."

Efram took off his shirt.

"Thank you Efram. Do you have something else to wear?"

"Sure!" he said, but went out shirtless.

Sadeq ran into him and asked what the fuck, and Efram stretched out the offending T-shirt and Sadeq gleefully retained it. Thug life. Guns, bitches, and bling. The true nature of the world. He squeezed into an emerald halter-top lent by this junior, Liza Kelly, and let Anna Lee and Ami wreath him in eye shadow. No one jeered at him. They cheered and laughed. No one called him a fag. It didn't work that way with Efram Daniels.

Thursday, here we go, Mr. Westwick checked his voicemail to find a message from the Embassy of

Mozambique returning his call in regards to a geography class taking a field trip to visit, kindly agreeing and urging him to call back. Efram wore a black zippered hoodie. On the back was a straight black and white photo of a fully topless female body: Brazilian, Rio in the late seventies, with what Ami described as, "the greatest tits and nipples I have ever seen ever." The memo had been sent around. Ms. Merrimack in first period noticed and made him put it in his bag, and said he would have to go to Mr. Westwick straight after class. He looked to his left and handed it to Ami, who stuffed it in her duffel. His shirt was also black, and Ms. Merrimack didn't notice but it too had a stylized photograph of a woman on it, this one only wearing a T-shirt, using one hand to stretch it down over her bare legs while holding a microphone in the other, except the head of the microphone was squarely, or circularly one should say, in her lips.

Shirt confiscated and a two-day suspension.

Friday, with Efram at home, Ami wore the 'greatest tits she'd ever seen' sweatshirt. Summoned into the office, her phone broadcasted the whole thing to Efram and Raj, the video image showing darkness but giving sound. Mr. Westwick reared again.

"Did Efram give you that sweatshirt?"

"No, I don't share clothes with boys."

"Ami, both the handbook you receive at the beginning of the year and the code on our website clearly state that offensive imagery on clothing is inappropriate."

"So me liking naked women is offensive?"

"Yes."

You didn't need to see Ami's raised eyebrow and crossed arms. He backtracked.

"I mean. The naked part is offensive."

They could hear the shuffle. Ami got up.

"Your parents can come retrieve the confiscated item."

"Keep it so you have something to jack off to, you bigoted fuck," she said.

Efram fell off the couch in the midst of axing a dragon to death. Raj's hidden earbud in the back row of the room coughed. The file was saved. Conversation recorded. Legend born. Ami never had that sick feeling in her stomach when she flaunted authority, no creeping childhood neediness to prevent real action and cause massive apology. She never had that because she had never needed it. The rules had always worked for her. So tear that apart, and it's like a Band-Aid, straight off. Mr. Westwick smartly let the curse and insult go.

Monday, fresh from the suspension, Mr. Westwick was waiting for Efram at the front to ensure compliance. Students milled around, moths to the light, not wanting to go inside, an audience. Efram leapt from the car in a white on black graphic masterpiece of two bleached-blonde girls reaching for a kiss, barely touching lips, both topless but pressing their breasts together to avoid showing nipple, black underwear wreathing round asses, absurd, plastic. He took enough of a moment for the audience to see, to acknowledge, enough of a beat for Mr. Westwick to lurch forward and maybe open his mouth, but before sound, Efram took off the shirt and threw it in the backseat, door still open. This revealed a bleached, staticky-soft, well-worn, pink T-shirt underneath. It took a moment, then gasps and howls. The new image was of two shirtless, ripped, perfect-bicep, Adonis men kissing. The kiss was a chaste one, no extreme additional body contact, romantic. Westwick said no, and did not let Efram come in.

Bedlam.

The GSA staged a walkout by second period. They invaded the president's office by lunch. The City Paper called by 1:00 that afternoon. The *Post* by 2:30. Emergency assembly. In the large theater the student body was assured by the president and the counselor that the problem was with nudity and not sexual orientation. Please you are encouraged to wear rainbows and display pride and not get us all fired. Also, if you could please not all kill yourselves that would be great. If you want to commit suicide please graduate first, attend some prestigious institution that we can brag we got you into, and then commit suicide so it is that other institution's problem. Yes, you can wear rainbows here. But the school has to have some acceptable standards to function. So no naked people please. During the time for "dialogue," Evergreen's only Young Republican, Alec Yergin, raised his hand. Alec got by because of a mean streak, angry libertarian, legalize drugs position, and kindly inquired as to how straight people were supposed to show pride for their orientation, and then quickly pivoted to ask what the appropriate way of expressing political advocacy for the legalization of marijuana would be, since drug imagery was also expressly inappropriate.

Phones out, The Efram Daniels Expulsion Index spiked. There'd soon be an app for that.

The school failed in their attempts to contact Efram's mother.

The following Tuesday, Efram wore an Armani suit. EFRAM DANIELS IS THE ANTICHRIST, the multiplying stickers warned. Ami's older brother was studying printmaking at MICA and banged out a shirt for lil sis. Simple text. Helvetica. Clean lines. Black on white.

MR. WESTWICK IS A BIGOT

Nothing they could do about that. She wore it unhindered.

On Wednesday, Efram wore a teal sweatsuit, horrible, baggy, mom sweatpants, and a matching hoodie. A walking oceanic puffball. The BIGOT shirts cloned themselves. The printshop did work. Ami went with something new—

I LIKE KISSING GIRLS

But on Thursday, David Yergin showed up with a white T-shirt he had hastily inscribed with a Sharpie—

I LIKE SMOKING WEED

David was made to take it off. Three silkscreening machines manifested themselves in Efram's basement. Straight cash, homie. Boxes from streetwear companies, boutique brands, and colorway obsessed hypebeast initiatives around the world piled up. At lunchtime David received the replacement—

MARIJUANA SHOULD BE LEGAL

Not sharpied. Printed on the press during a lucky upperclassman's free period. White tee, black text. It was permitted unhindered as an appropriate political statement. The MR. WESTWICK IS A BIGOT shirts were fruitful and multiplied. Panic mode. Board meetings. Evergreen was not the sort of place that could consider a dress code. In two years, during a slated staff reorganization, they were going to encourage the faculty to begin using first names. This genius artist couple, Amy Lin and Iman Redmond, tall white girl/short black guy, attached a file to Efram unprompted. On Friday, he rocked it. It was a woman against a mugshot lineup, except in a model pose, hands behind head. Her body was covered in black censoring rectangles that each said GUILT, obstructing any guesses as to the presence of a wardrobe. One last rectangle went along her eyes.

On Monday, Efram's kind Chemistry teacher Ms. Wilson grabbed him after class and in a whisper pleaded with him to remove his shirt showing Bluto taking a swig of Jack in his COLLEGE T-shirt.

"I won't tell them," she said, "I don't want to get in trouble."

Efram obliged. She was nice. Out of the room he replaced it with a graphical set of framed vignettes showing an attractive nose smelling, holding, and smoking a rolled joint. He was thrown out of fourth period, but spared the office.

Next was a black T-shirt with Tyrone Biggums counting rocks in a baggie of powder. That was it. Ballgame. Over the line.

"Last warning," Mr. Westwick said

Tuesday morning. Another regular Tuesday. A black shirt with Jules Winfield holding his 9mm Star Model B. Back to guns. He was led to a different office.

"We cannot reach your mother, but Efram, you have been expelled."

Bilal Khan, junior, Van Ness Day School, took the index and won the 500 dollar grand prize. The posters self-replicated.

Asshole Joe graduated.

And then vanished.

⊗   ⊗   ⊗   ⊗

MOLLY SPOTTED DAVID LOADING the car. Lane joined in, faces pressing against the church glass. They were sitting on the long cushions on the wings, in between the gamers and the gossipers, second floor in the strip mall house of God.

"I'm going out with his friend Keith now," Lane said from under her book.

"David has friends?"

"They all go to real school. They were neighbors growing up. There are all these cute pictures of them together as kids."

"I thought you liked David?"

"I thought I did too. But Keith is more my type. He's like, a real guy."

Molly could tell by the way Lane put away her book that she was about to elucidate a moment-by-moment recounting of her relationship with Keith. The way he looked at her on a fast food run, the minutiae of wording of the first text messages. It could go for hours. Molly excused herself saying she thought she might have left her bag in the lobby. She sprinted down the stairs of the community center. The three women were guarding the entrance hall so Molly went the other direction, backward, landing in a small kitchen next to an office with a fortunate side door. She took the ring around the lot at a gallop.

"Wait!" she shouted, throwing both her hands up before he could pull away.

David rolled down the window.

"It's hell in there," she said. "Are you like going to get food or something?"

"No," he said. "I'm just driving around."

"Well can I come? I have to be back by four."

"I'm not actually just driving around."

"Whatever. Please?"

He opened the door, tossing into the back a black
sling bag emblazoned with an ACU-Dark Velcro patch
on its hilt reading—

INFIDEL

—above a second emblem, an X within a clover.

"You're an infidel?" She asked.

"From both my parents and durka durka's point of view."

Molly reached back and ripped the patches from
their places, proudly sticking them to her sweater below
her collarbone.

David made a face and turned his eyes back to the road.

"Sure, help yourself," he mumbled.

He took two rights around the house that was next
to the church and then down a path of gravel. After three
miles, they turned into a clearing next to a hill. Tires on
grass, he stopped the car where the field ended against a
tall rising slope. He reached into the back seat and fumbled
on the ground, retrieving an empty plastic bottle and a
black velvet ringbox. He opened the door and put them
on the ground without leaving his seat. They reversed for
hundreds of yards, and then he stopped again, this time
for good, and suspended the bag over his shoulder. Two
long, hardened cases came out of the trunk. He rolled a
towel out on the ground. A box of cartridges was tossed
to the side. The first box opened. He handed her a set of
orange earplugs.

David balanced the scoped rifle with his hands, elbows
temporarily making a four poster with the attached bipod,

settling, chest to the ground, legs twisted in a rehearsed pose. The miniature mountain was the backstop. She could only barely see the bottle target. He let his eye through the scope three hundred yards downrange. The sound shook Molly so hard she blinked uncontrollably. As best she could tell, the bullet passed straight through the bottle. He handed her a set of binoculars. The next one tore through the ringbox, shooting up a tuft of dirt behind it.

"Most of the time, if the targets jump, you missed them," he said. "The force of the bullet hitting the ground kicks them up. When you hit it directly, the bullet cuts right through."

"I thought you didn't think the world was going to end?"

He pulled the trigger again.

Crack.

"I don't. It isn't going to. I'm joining the marines at seventeen," he said.

Crack.

"You can do that?"

Crack.

"My parents will have to give consent, but they'll have no choice. They'll look stupid if they don't. I already have my GED."

"Do you ever miss?" she asked. He was in a different class from her father.

He put the first rifle aside and opened the second hardcase, a parent cradling children when replacing and extricating them from their cribs. Next was a carbine. After reentombing the first, he now was on one knee, shoulders straight, and pressed the new metal to his shoulder. He painted ten rounds in a figure eight around the targets, a semiautomatic spread, laying down a cover hail, catching each at least once in the vicinity. He put it down, clipped and safetied.

"Your turn," he said. "You know how to handle this?"

She nodded.

"Let me try the rifle first," she said, and he set the carbine aside, unloading it completely. He sat the sniper rifle in front of her and came to his feet.

She did what was comfortable, slithering down to the ground and gripping the wood. The way the scope was mounted, she made sure to move her head back so it didn't hit her in the eye.

He was kneeling next to her. She expected a hand lightly on the middle of her back, but it did not come. She controlled her breathing. The barrel was really a barrel, a long extending line from her eye. Molly did not know how much to relax and let the gun sit there and how much to grip and suppress the coming kick. A juggling act without knowledge of the variables involved. The finger depressed into the trigger, and through her plugs the shock made her eyes blink again. It was like before, a whole other process. She was positive David's lids never twitched. The scope hit her orbital bone—not back far enough—but she repressed the burn and ignored it. The whole rifle had somehow yanked to the right, a hand guiding it out. She pulled the bolt.

"How long until you turn seventeen?" she asked.

"Nine months," he said, "and fifteen days. They have a special program for homeschoolers."

"How about for atheists?"

"They can bury you in Arlington with a different symbol, an atom encircling an A."

He showed her a picture on his phone.

"So in death you get to be an atomic anarchist?"

It was a trial at first to get David to laugh, that low heart rate an obstacle to forcing any reaction. He kept quiet as though any banter might give his position away. He waited patiently, looking for the shot to come. She let it loose. This one got the bottle, or so Molly hoped and assumed, since it was hard to tell as the scope disappeared with the kick and the sound blinked her eye.

"Four inches down and right," he said.

She pulled back the bolt. David adjusted the scope. She trained the crosshairs on the ring box. She snuck a peak at David, shifting the few degrees to the new target. Remember that bullets arc, that bullets drop. A breath of wind hit her left ear, so she guessed a few inches to the left. That time, only her closed eye spasmed from the thunder.

HEAT BLASTING AS THEY emerged, the flight attendants gave emphatic goodbyes to the tiniest business class passenger. Seventeen-year-old Steven did a three-sixty, blurring the fringe vegetation and low architecture, one year before the end.

The hotel was only three floors but had miles of carpeted hallways, an octagonal series of buildings encircling a manicured attempt at a Floridian lagoon. His room had been covered in plants, as if water was not a scarcity. The only order of business was to turn on the television. Steven flipped channel by channel, ruggers and soaps, grazing the heaps of remnant airport acquired snacks. There was a knock. Steven relented and opened the door. Norman stormed inside. Some of the plants looked like they had died in those few hours.

"Dinnertime," Norman said.

"I'm not hungry," Steven said, surrounded by duty free chocolate wrappers. A documentary on an oil platform was the current selection lighting the room, blackout curtains were drawn. Norman opened them, and the desert glare broke in.

"Come try at least." The picture ceased.

A new woman was in the restaurant with them. Norman was eager. He was showing off. The woman was American, New York bred and born, weaned from law school into the globe trotting arts, IR, however it is it always starts—liberal guilt, Peace Corps in Kenya, grandiloquent prognostications on development policy. Modernization Theory. She was in her early forties, though you would never know it—pretty, dark brown hair, and thin wrists. She was, to the best of Steven's knowledge, not being compensated to be there.

"Oh hello precious, I'm Kate," she said. "So you're Norman's tiny terror."

Steven sat at the table, with a disconnected, unentertained smirk.

"Terrorist more like it. Beautiful. Tall. A killer," She said. "Look at those eyes."

"He's tired," Norman said.

"Or not hungry," Steven replied.

"Well, don't let us spoil your fun," Kate said. "Go and wander. Find some trouble. Let us be boring adults."

They ate at the table while Steven plopped himself in the fake grassy knoll outside the glass, staring into the untouched pool. To the left was a tall boundary fence that obscured the setting sun. Steven switched his angle so he could see through its one gated opening. It was parallel to a highway, which, despite its automobile traffic, was dominated by pedestrians hiking up and down the shoulders, weighed down by belongings, economic refugees struggling with all that they had to move despite the heat. He moved forward to the crack in the wall, and wedged his body through it.

He crossed the sand-blown asphalt in step with the emaciated travelers. Across the road was a police station, and then a ten-foot high wall. He walked its perimeter until he found a break. Behind it, shanties extended in every direction until they met the horizon or another wall. Steven entered the alley, stepping over the green sludge of human waste that flowed out toward the thoroughfare.

The houses were made out of every imaginable material. Aluminum was grafted onto wood then balanced on hastily baked clay. Sparks flew as toothless children worked a spinning metal wheel, forging and pounding scrap into something usable. The few elderly sat rotting in front of their structures, wrapped in layers despite the heat, stuck watching in gutters. Flies swarming infants' faces, children weeping and coughing, wounds festering from infection, rodents picking from the living and spreading the dead.

Steven watched a woman with a child on her back fill a jug from the hideous toxic mess of the river. He did not glance away when he passed the child with a sore so bad the bone was visible. He smelled the dead, the dying, the decaying, heard the woman yell for her lifeless child, and felt the trash ignite in flames. He looped back around.

Steven squeezed back through the hotel wall into the courtyard with the pool. He sat on the flat part of the reclining chair leaning on his hands and looking at the clean water.

Kate emerged from the building holding a wine glass without Norman.

"Oh! There you are!" she exclaimed, toasting to him. "Your father had to make some calls. It's been over an hour." She sat down with her hip against his. "How is it that someone who looks like him fathered someone who looks like you?" she murmured, stroking the line above his ear. "It's astonishing. I'm astonished." Steven could see Norman prowling behind the doors, still talking on the phone, but watching them.

"Are you bored? Do you want to go back to your room?" She brought her lips to his ear. "Do you want me to come with you?" She giggled and put her hand on his knee. "Have you been with an older woman before? You must have. You look so much older than you are."

Norman finished his call and stalked through the doors toward them. Kate set her glass on the tiled floor and rose to her heels, running her arm along Steven's back as she stood.

"Come on," Norman growled. Kate took his hand, but looked back at Steven and rolled her eyes as Norman led her away.

Steven retreated through the lobby and up. He closed the shades again and gave the screen life once more. At four in the morning he silenced the set.

⋮   ⋮   ⋮   ⋮

FIRST SEMESTER, JUNIOR YEAR lasted approximately seventeen hours. Lansdowne was a school with Mission and Values and Philosophy and Civility and Conduct and Moral Character. The social development of young men, boys, specifically. Hemmed pants. Jackets and ties. Loafers. Thirty-five percent were boarders.

A few years ago, Zoe the Wise Man started hooking up with this boy, her cousin's friend, whose brother had ended up at Lansdowne after his family moved to NoVa from Atlanta. The brother hit the big time when he and eight of his friends got absolutely hammered on a Saturday night and were aimlessly driving around in a van videotaping their escapades. Utterly gutted as to the complete lack of girls to abuse, they therefore decided, in their infinite, wisdom to fuck (read: rape) one of their quiet male friends. Shit got posted before the injunction brought it down. Ami alone forwarded the story to like a hundred and fifty people.

All boys will wear a fully tied necktie. The tie must be pulled up. Honesty. Respect. Ethics classes.

The papers didn't get a sniff of the drunk-boredom-van-rapes, but Lansdowne did receive local news attention for creating a region-wide fantasy sports-style league for prospective female hookups. Within an hour and a half, Efram created a stock market to the same effect. Except his new fellow classmates didn't understand that it actually included both genders, and these dudes were about to get short sold to all fucking hell once it got going.

A more disciplined environment would do him some good, they said.

Despite the rigorous demands of orderly and respectful conduct while on campus, the first week of junior year, as a celebration of the impending doom of irreversible grades that truly mattered for one's college future, the tradition of Assassins was permitted with a blind eye. Every member of the junior class was a participant, whether you wanted to be or not, with around six-to-ten declining to participate every year and quickly getting slaughtered, and another six-to-ten having better things to do and submitting themselves for execution to a treasured friend. The senior prefects served as referees, exempt, and an honor system was used. A "kill" constituted the purposeful bombardment, application, or striking of a target with a liquid, almost always water. Once every few years someone would coat a doorknob in Vaseline as a "poisonous" kill, but this was rare. Nerf guns were allowed, but they required several objective witnesses for a clean kill and had limited, unreplenishable ammunition, and therefore had all but been phased out. The majority of the combat was accomplished with small water pistols, concealable in a pocket, pulled out at close charging range like late nineteenth- and early twentieth-century political assassins. The competition typically took all week to sort through the eighty or so students, as the survivors became paranoid, sprinting between classes and disappearing from all social situations, planning their next assaults over class schedules and campus migration patterns. There were no rules that dictated the boundaries of the game. Theoretically, one could ambush a target within a class, but disciplinary rules still applied, so no one risked such punishment. Once you were dead, it was your responsibility to inform a prefect as to the fact and nature of your demise, and who dispatched you. The list would be updated. Cheating meant social suicide. If you got hit, you told.

Antonio E. Battle, a senior prefect assigned to show Efram around that first day, informed him of these rules in the afternoon. He handed him a clear neon plastic water pistol.

Morning number two Efram was carrying a nondescript brown duffel bag. 8:05 that morning marked the beginning; a homeroom-like period dubbed "Community Period" that shapeshifted its purpose throughout the week to accommodate advisory meetings and special character classes. The fire alarm went off at 8:07 a.m. Don Monticiewitz, an English teacher and associate dean, was told within 30 seconds that the alarm was triggered by the automatic system. Nothing was pulled. As the crowd filed out, ears covered, the faculty dispensed to deal with an apparent electronic error, no structured supervision needed for the upper schoolers in the courtyard. Pistols came out as soon as the teachers left. With the high-pitched soundtrack, the freshmen and sophomores and seniors all became cover, obstacles. People were running in circles, one climbed a tree. But then the mayhem ceased with a splat on the grass. People turned. Where was it coming from? Water balloons were flying over the buildings into the courtyard, not off of the roof, somewhere else, no line of sight, artillery death. They started to arrive in clusters, striking more than one at once. On the far side of the colonial buildings, at the base of a steep hill, Efram Daniels was yanking backward as freshman Ronny Jefferies and sophomore Terrance Seguin were holding the giant slingshot into place. Next to him were another three, making up another battery. They accomplished a round every six or seven seconds. The second launcher, manned by the large but sweet offensive lineman, Daniel Gwo, wearing his letterman jacket in September heat and squalor, had figured out how to launch two-to-three balloons at once. They ceased with a battle cry, "Huzzah!," and sprinted off. Twenty-six of the eighty-two juniors were assassinated in the initial close-quarters pistol combat. Someone would kill and then be killed, instantly. A furball. Another twelve had surrendered to friends as soon as they hit the courtyard, and were kindly squirted on the arm or shot point blank in the head. The water balloons took out an astonishing twenty-four students. Then again, when you consider even the slightest trace of liquid counts as a kill this was better than might have be expected. The collateral damage was, of course, considerable. Seniors vowed revenge upon whoever had been responsible. Except the ones who recognized true genius. The prefects loved it. They trolled the courtyard pointing out splotches and exclaiming, "Death!" and "War!" and "Chaos!" and "Vengeance!" They soaked themselves in berserker rituals. Duty. Honor. When the water balloons stopped, the survivors made for corners and human shields, until the teachers showed up.

The battle ceased, but the faculty relented for a slight moment, standing among them, unsaid peacekeepers, extra time given for the heat to dry them off. Between 8:07 and

8:13 a.m., Efram Daniels had engineered the demise of sixty-two students. Twenty remained. The prefects updated the list, putting a "?" next to the water balloon fatalities. Some faculty expressed concern, but then realized the scale of the initial onslaught meant the rest of the week would be quieter.

With a new fury of unexpected aggression, the game changed, and the remaining chose hunting over surviving. Two were tagged with point blank water gun shots in the hallways between first and second periods, friends asking friends about friends' schedules. During midmorning break, Carlos Aguilar had a mug of water poured on him from behind by Drew Kolodny. A clever kill. Drew knew he would have to clean it up to avoid discipline, and the cafeteria staff handed him towels, only to have starting whiteboy small forward Jeffrey Lane double wield his pistols from around the corner and nail him in the head while shouting, "Don't let your dick fall off." Drew finished mopping, a dead man. Efram left his classes at a gallop. He hid in closets. He stayed in empty rooms. He climbed through windows.

Sixteen students remained.

Cross-referencing the list of the survivors, Efram acquired (read: Asshole Joed) the class schedules of the remaining fifteen. Five of them would be sharing both fourth and fifth periods. A second bloodbath. Efram came under fire after third period on the way to lunch, knifing behind a locker and a sophomore, pirouetting and connecting with two shots, killing Theo Wilson. His face an unknown one, the new kid, he walked straight up to Paul Madison in the cafeteria and shot him from the hip, and told him his name. Two more fell elsewhere.

The rumor spread, twelve students remaining. The prefects replaced the "?" on the water balloon casualties to "E. Daniels." They also put an asterisk next to the courtyard kills, acknowledging that if the alarm was set off on purpose, some of the credit belonged to the instigator. The five contenders sharing fourth period together all showed up late in successive waves. As the class ended, they eyed each other in the rhythm. One smartly was first out of the room, making for the door when teacher uttered the first syllable of completion. That was genius. The rest played a waiting game of trying to find cover in their dead classmates. Waiting too long in the room meant being trapped, or worse, being unprotected by the human shield of a teacher. It was a convoy war between their next class. A stray shot almost hit a very displeased Mr. Matheson in the hallway. Next to him, Mrs. Brown thought it was pretty funny. The game would be banned next year regardless of her opinion. One went down en route. The four contenders arrived at their fifth period classroom for Spanish, relieved that the teacher was waiting. Blissful, they took their seats, only to find the asses of their pants completely soaked through.

Efram paid a freshman fifty bucks to skip his class before to set it up, and plead first week ignorance.

Seven students remained.

Geoffrey Eastburn got Tim Craighead in the locker room before football practice. Isaac Houghton bravely squirted a water bottle at Geoffrey Eastburn between hitting drills. It was legal.

Four students remained.

The student directory, the public one, not the one he ~~hacked~~obtained creatively, said that John Kester lived at 2113 Washington Ct. Great Falls, VA. The package on his doorstep exploded when he opened it, a projectile trickle, fortunately not having a mom who would have opened it herself.

Three students remained.

The two besides Efram were dorm kids.

The plastic oval keychain had a button and a small switch, the toggling of either emitting a shriek made to debilitate rapists and assaulters. Efram pulled the pin and tossed the plastic into the opened diagonal of Jesse Shore's first floor dorm room window. He waited by the door, and shot him (and his already dead roommate) in the face at 6:37 that evening. Off campus students had to be out by seven.

Sam Foreman, FBGM, an A&F sociopath—the kind of guy who would be hooking up with a girl who said she would only give him head if he told her when he was about to finish so he couldn't cum in her mouth, who instead would hold her head so she couldn't move and cause her to throw up, and would himself not only be feeling A-OKAY about it but think it was funny, yea, that kind of guy—was cowering in his second floor dorm room, locked, seeing the last update as Jesse texted a prefect and the text changed.

Two students remaining, Sam locked the window shut, despite the heat, and barricaded the door, despite his roommate's absence. If he won, it would mean so much. He would be top fucking dog. But then, this Efram dude was serious. Maybe he should surrender. But then he'd be a little bitch, and everyone would make sure they knew he was a little bitch. The Neanderthal brain turned through its options.

The opaque glass in his window fractured into a thousand pieces. Sam let down his shielding elbows to see a ski mask climbing through the new portal in all black, with tough gloves and tactical boots. Sam reached for his gun, but Efram Daniels shot him with the puny neon water pistol. It was unclear if the urine wrecking Sam's gym shorts would have counted as a kill.

Efram showed up to the administrative offices with a blank check in hand for the window.

Kesting, Assistant Head, VP, Director of Discipline, the harrowing man with no face, no introduction or prefix needed, always warned about, tore into Efram for fifteen minutes. He waived the right to an honor code hearing of his peers. Kesting rebounded in his dead brain, community service, expulsion, criminal action, and eventually vacated the room. A secretary led him into another. Old and leather, white in all pigmentation, Dr. Kimball, Headmaster, was a genuine English Schoolmaster. Rugby School alum, he eyed over glasses, patches on elbows.

"I don't think this is going to work out, Mr. Daniels," he said, kind smile enforcing spare wrinkles, a lifetime of relative stoicism giving flatter skin.

"I suppose not, sir."

"It's a shame you don't have an athletic talent in which you could channel such aggressive skill."

He held up a printed out page of the prefects' tally.

"Quite a shame, sir."

"And a shame your academic record is so spotty that attending a British boarding school, where your sort of talents would be appreciated whilst being simultaenously ground out, is impossible."

"If only," Efram said in a fake English accent. He handed the check over the desk. His signature had two stripes and three dots floating above the space between his two names like a crown. Memo: Broken window.

"Ah, yes, that will do it."

Daniel Gwo won the five hundred dollars on the EDEI despite the fact that Efram had not been technically expelled. In an unprecedented move of kindness Dr. Kimball refunded Mrs. Daniels the tuition money not that she noticed between the Xanax and the Paxil and the wine, overlooking the water. Between his four institutions, New York early childhood, local celebrity, hedonistic parties, and networked presence, Efram Daniels had three thousand, two hundred and forty six friends. He never turned down a request. They asked in droves. Where are you going Efram? Where the f are you? Come to ____! The collective student bodies of Sidwell

Friends, Maret, St. Albans, GDS, Landon, Georgetown Prep, McLean, Potomac, Gonzaga, DeMatha, Burke, WIS, Field – they all cowered in fear or wonder or wish.

Now kicked out of Woodley, Van Ness, Evergreen, and Lansdowne...

Where the fuck was Efram Daniels?

Where had he gone?

Where would he go?

PART

5

And they cried with a loud voice, saying,
How long, O Lord, holy and true,
Dost thou not judge and avenge our
blood on them that dwell on the earth?
                    —The Book of Revelation

Paranoia, paranoia,
Everybody's comin' to get me,
Just say you never met me,
I'm runnin' underground with the moles,
Diggin' holes.
                    —Harvey Danger, "Flagpole Sitta"

MOLLY WAS RIDING SHOTGUN as they left the church. David drove slowly. Lane and Keith had invited them over.

"So what's he like?" Molly asked.

"Who?"

"Keith? Lane said he's like your best friend."

"Not best," David said. "Oldest. He lived next door when we were kids."

"So, what's he like?"

David braked, and looped into a driveway.

"He's alright I guess," David said.

But there was a wail and then a sputtering series of thumps under the hood. The wheels jolted. David turned the keys to silence.

"You go knock," he said. "I'm going to look."

"Do you know anything about cars?" Molly asked.

"No. I'm just going to make sure nothing is on fire."

The door to Lane's house was ajar. It was one floor, split roof, small, a failed child's tricycle rusted into the gravel that split the pines.

Molly made it a game. She slipped into the house without disturbing the door, making herself thin. She took each step with less and less gravity. Her boots did their best to not squeak on the kitchen tile. Music was playing, or maybe it was a television, ambient fuzz. A half-wall divided the kitchen and a small room with a dining table. She threaded through the furniture toward the visible portal. Shoulders skimming along the hall, she could sense she was getting closer. Prey was around the corner. She would jump out to screams and laughter.

A crack and she spun, and David was through the door behind her at a stroll. She did not need to keep her rotation long for him to bumble forward and see her finger brought to her lips. He received the message and shrunk into a sneak, following seven or eight feet behind. She homed in on the source of the noise, reaching the edge of a large break in the wall that was broader than a normal doorway. And instead of lunging for it then or peeking around the corner, she took quiet steps inward, creeping in like a passing shadow. Lane and Keith were at the opposite end of the living room, standing in front of a couch pushed against the wall. Keith was holding one of her wrists in his hand. They had not sensed the intruders, consumed with each other, actors on a stage ignoring the audience. David made his way around the turn at the exact moment Keith's clumped hand descended onto Lane's face. Her yelp overwhelmed the digital noise. It was not a slap. It was a blow, a pound, a real connection. But with the follow-through, Keith saw them, and with the force from the impact, Lane saw them, blood starting to escape. And then it took over. The beast awoke. For three of them, there was a moment of looking at each other wondering what was going to happen next. That was illusion. The fourth was exempt from that pause. Not a decision.

Molly had already been moving. The seal opened. An electrical storm entered the nervous system. Two strides of her body completely weightless, slack muscles released to the ultimate capacity of human tissue, the pure, relaxed sinew of a hundred massages, an athletic dream. The room was crossed in those two steps, so quick that it occurred within the computational lag time in the others' brains. Face-to-face with Keith, 6'2", 210 lbs. vs. 5'11, 130 lbs. (*Ding!*) Arms not in some exaggerated combative stance but slack at her sides, Molly started by planting her left foot to his side, as if she were moving to save Lane, and then swinging out her right arm in a sweeping arc, a tennis forehand without the racquet, the hardest part of her palm meeting the soft skin right above his crotch but under his stomach, the Hammer of God into his pelvic bone. He immediately, uncontrollably hunched forward, partially due to the defensive assumption that she was gunning for his balls, his too-late, too-slow hands protecting the wrong target. In that bent-over microsecond, Molly reset. That was the prologue. The trailer. The buffer.

She extended her left arm straight to his now-vulnerable face, flicking out her fingers at his eyes with a snap. With her right hand, she punched Keith in the throat. The knuckles of her index and middle fingers impaled his Adam's apple with a forced three-quarter extension, a hydraulic shot of her bicep and forearm, bludgeoning and then folding back. Post-punch, her right arm formed into a sharp elbow, which she aimed straight into his throat again, a double hit. She flexed, her weight transferred, and blunt weapon of bone connected with laryngeal tissue. Her right hand caught onto his shoulder, the elbow flat against his esophagus, his arms now starting to react in an attempt at defense. She slapped his right arm away with her left and briefly let go of his shoulder to quickly claw her fingers across his face. His nerves could not keep up; they did not know that her left foot had rammed into his right knee. Leg behind leg, Molly wrecked him to the ground, dropping him with a crash. Then there was no sound. His open mouth made nothing. She discerned, in the wake of her significant acceleration, a slight writhe of anger. Molly stamped her right foot onto his chest, a diagonal crush across his sternum. She did not hold him down after the implosion, but stood, as if he was a beam, and swung her left foot in a wide kick across his cheek.

It had taken two seconds to cross the room.

And five seconds to conclude the confrontation.

Seven seconds.

Lane had not moved in those seven seconds. By second three, David was taking his first step forward, and he only reached the other side by second eight.

Lane's eyes were wide. Keith was done, a trapped soul lashed down to the floor in pain, blank expression, brain searching for ways to interpret the signals his broken body was giving him. David skipped Molly completely and brought an arm around Lane, pulling her into a seat on the couch. He then returned to the floor to survey the damage. Staring down at his friend, he could not find a starting point. Molly turned and fixed on Lane's face, unmoving, until Lane turned away. Molly made for the exit. She did not want to see David's face when he looked back up. She sprinted from the house.

It was a mile run to a gas station. It took her four minutes and forty-eight seconds. The clerk let her use the phone. She called the number no one called, and after a thirty-five minute wait on the curb, Jonathan Corbin picked her up. She told him that the car had broken down and the other parents had gotten there quicker, that she could have gotten a ride from one of them, but he had already left.

She stole the landline and called Lane six times that night. The rings all ended prematurely, the abbreviated symphony of an ignore button. The next three days were the same.

Her room became a prison again. Molly blocked out the skylight and the window, duct taping sheets from the walls and ceilings, accepting the shroud of the covers.

Molly heard the growl of Jon driving off in the morning. Three hours later, the knock was light on her door. It came again. And then again. She must have been unconscious and not heard his return.

"Go away," Molly said. She could only hear the muffled voice through the reinforced metal.

She opened the door after the fifth overture.

"It's Thursday," he said.

Molly rolled her eyes.

"I'm not going."

"Fine. But if you don't go you're helping me go through all the seed stock. The replacements came."

David was sitting on the hood of his car in the parking lot when Jon dropped her off. She faked the steps up toward the door as her father drove away, and rounded about, stopping in the blank asphalt in front of him. Distance kept, she studied the paved landscape. She gave in to the standoff.

"Is Lane alright?"

"Yea," he said.

"Is she here?"

"No."

Molly crouched onto her feet, a ball with two bird legs in the parking lot. David had chosen the side without the windows looking out. Smart.

"She's pretty freaked out."

"Yea. So I what, give her time?"

"I guess. Yea. She's in shock. To be honest she's more freaked out by you right now than by Keith. But she'll come around."

"Great."

"And, in case you want to know, Keith is, well, he's alive and all that."

"Well… the cops didn't come…"

"I'm sorry, Molly."

"You don't have to. It can be easy. You don't want to see me ever again.."

"Why would I be the one who doesn't want to see you ever again?"

"Because I'm the girl who beat up your best friend, and freaked you out, too, maybe."

"I thought you wouldn't want to see me ever again."

"Why?"

"Because I'm the asshole who saw his friend hit a girl and didn't react. While you did what you're supposed to do instantly."

"You would have. You were behind me."

"Not the way you did," he said.

Molly stood up and dragged a rubber sole against the ground. He rolled off the car, stood tall, and wrapped Molly in the trap made by his long arms, even though she kept hers at her sides.

"Come on," he said.

They checked in with the women at the front desk. Faked the move up the stairs, snuck out the back, got in his car, and drove to the shooting hill. David brought cans for targets.

‡　　　‡　　　‡　　　‡

THREE MONTHS BEFORE THE end, the island was one of those few locales that seemed to contain every type of climate in one compact space. Desert flowed into forest, and beaches into taiga. Rock outcroppings worthy of a resort town were covered by immense frost. There were desolate cliffs and strange meadows.

There were no roads on the island, only sparse paths marked by wooden planks, laid down forty years prior so cars could traverse the sand and dirt. Their guide and translator had been introducing Norman, wrapped in a scarf, to one of the few locals who existed there. It was unclear how the ninety-year-old Russian woman could get food and survive in this place. Her shack was ancient, brown wood puzzled together across the frame, weathered by decades of every possible form of storm. The few other houses on the island stood in groups, or at least in sight of each other. This one was all alone.

Steven wandered away into the adjacent glade, short grass for half a mile that mutated into a patch of desert that crashed into rolling hills. Steven saw the posts first, a few sparse pieces of thick wood still standing tall. Where the dirt gave way to weeds, there were piles of blackened timber on the ground. A few more steps and curved planks covered the grass on one side, a relative highway on this island, worn with use. Then came the smell, still lingering, even though the fire had been extinguished decades before. He hit the first slab of shitty cement, seeing there were several more foundation blocks among the burnt wood, the wreckage. Some walls, obviously scorched and then demolished, lay in concentric rectangles.

"What was it?" Norman asked.

"You don't know?"

"No, Steven. I don't know what this rubbish in this wasteland is. Don't be an insufferable know-it-all."

Steven ignored him, and bent to feel the ground, to sift through a mound of ash. He picked up a fragment, a bronze button, holding it high in the sunlight, letting it glint.

"What the hell is this?" Norman pleaded with the broken ground.

"лагер," Steven said and then rose and extended both arms and spun in a circle gesturing to the whole land around them- "in a зона."

"No," Norman panicked.

"Да… ГУЛАГ," Steven said, "gulag."

"How do you know?"

Steven did not answer.

"So this is why you fought?" Steven asked instead as he threw the button and stood up.

Norman did not answer.

Their minders, their watches, told the translator to tell their guests that it was time to go. The men held outstretched hands in the direction of the formerly military helicopter, its off-white paint having overtaken camouflage years before. They said nothing about the site they were hurrying away from, no acknowledgement as the liftoff gave a clearer look at the foundation's outlines.

They flew. They flew to Irkutsk, and then boarded a commercial flight from Irkutsk to Moscow, then Moscow to Dubai, then Dubai to Nairobi, then Nairobi to Juba. Steven saw airport concourses and hotels that did not require going through immigration. He looked down from window seats onto farms and dunes and shipping lanes.

Fresh off the final leg, straight from the airport into the provided and escorted car, Norman and Steven opened the doors and walked to the point where the road stopped in South Sudan. The pounded not-quite-pavement stretched forward, but a flowing spiral of barbed wire blocked the way. Red signs with skulls warned of mines. In the distance on the right, the White Nile bent away. There were birds everywhere. Steven knows minefields have a tendency to produce unrivaled nature preserves.

The city wasn't visible, but there were still several dotted lines of winged metal cylinders in the sky, each waiting for its turn to land and unload the burden of aid. Juba had become one of the busiest airports in the world in a manner of months. In fact, if you compared incoming air traffic to poverty level, Steven was sure this was the highest contrast in human history. Norman was there with two men surveying the prospect for capitalizing on the world's newest country, and using it to create a transportation hub that could cause development to sneak northward—a pipe dream. Soldiers flanked them on the side, wearing boring green fatigues with no clever disruptive pattern. They were holding Type 56s pointed at the ground with no bayonets fixed.

"You see, it's going to take years and years. They might get a rail connection to Uganda and Kenya, but don't hold your breath," one of the men said.

"Not if the Chinese have anything to do with it," Norman offered.

The city was flooded by Beijing's agents of state capitalism. Half the continent had been covertly inundated. At least the areas that had oil or coltan or anything minable. Steven knew not to be fooled. China could give a fuck about India and Pakistan. They were too busy exploiting Africa for its resources.

The three men kept their huddle. Steven gazed through the fence on the other side of the car, grazing his fingers against the metal in between the barbs.

"And do we really think they'll be able to hold it together?" one asked.

"Like it's together now…"

"What do you mean?"

"Won't Sudan come after it as soon as anyone turns their head? Won't Sudan flaunt the UN and start shit again?"

"Steven," Norman called him back to the group, "could the North invade?"

"Is it take-your-son-to-work day?" Steven asked. The two men laughed. They were not dressed for this outward jaunt beyond the city lines. Dust infected their pleated trousers. "They could invade, but that's not what you're asking. I don't think they would get anywhere. And if they did, that would be really stupid on they're part. Not that we should ever assume rational actors."

"Right," Norman started, "but—"

"What you're asking, what they are asking," Steven pointed to the two men, "what you are all wondering, is if one day Islamic militias and suicide bombers will be lighting up Cape Town, and the answer is no."

"Why won't they get anywhere if they invade here?" One of the men asked. Steven squatted.

"Have any of you ever built a road?" Steven asked.

Norman's colleagues said they had not in fact built a road.

"If you ever ask someone who builds roads 'How do you decide where the road goes?' they'll tell you: 'What do you mean? It just sort of goes where it has to. The land makes the decisions for you.'"

Steven could not tell if Norman knew where he was going or not.

"People like Norman don't like to hear this," Steven continued, calling his father by his first name, "but wars are overdetermined events. Armies can only go certain places because roads can only go certain places. And soldiers need food. Trucks need gas. Guns need bullets."

He started drawing the new border between Sudan and South Sudan in the sand. He put checked dot marks around Abyei on both sides, to show it was disputed, and then snaked down the only four roads between them, only three that really connected between Juba and Khartoum. He kept going at that scale, shifting on his feet, filling in the entire lower half of the continent.

"So what do you think we should do?" The men were talking directly to Steven now. Norman crossed his arms.

"Well, what is your goal?" Steven said.

The men looked at each other.

"I mean there's nothing left here, they already got the oil, so what? What is it you want?"

"To stop the spread of Islamist militarism in Africa, possibly utilizing this fine country as a means to that end," Norman droned like the answer was obvious.

"But what's the real goal of that? You either kill them all or you don't. Unless you're willing to nuke Mecca and Jerusalem, what's the point? It's better to let them try, let them extend, let them overreach, let them burn themselves out or go too far and unleash a sleeping giant."

"So you're saying we do nothing?"

"Wars are overdetermined," Steven said, "Save your money."

Norman scowled.

Steven drew arrows from the south attacking north. He rubbed out borders. An empire spread.

"But doing that means standing by and not worrying about people dying," one of the men said.

Steven finished his map.

"Yes." Steven said, looking at each one in turn. "You're all going to die."

⊠   ⊠   ⊠   ⊠

A HAPHAZARD SYSTEM OF mounted televisions had been installed around LeMay Senior High School, sporadically placed above entrances and in public spaces. The screens streamed static lists of scheduling reminders and event calendars. This week is a "B" week. Today is Monday! Practices are on Blue schedule.

At first, Chloe thought she was discovering new televisions that she simply had not noticed before, but then it became clear they were actually multiplying, that without warning or explanation the screens were breeding and affixing themselves onto new walls and ceilings.

"Where are they getting the money for it?" Chloe asked.

Jess shrugged.

Michelle showed horror on her face as if by asking a serious question, Chloe had confessed to murder. But then Lauryn said that she had heard a girl in her math class ask the teacher about it, and the teacher was as confused and didn't know what was going on either.

Chloe passed Mr. Winters in the hallway and took the shot.

"What new televisions?" he said.

She pointed at the one in sight, one that had not been there before, gleaming with the same message as the rest.

He tilted his head to one side, and then walked in the other direction.

By lunchtime, Michelle and Lauryn had decided they weren't talking. Mutual this time. Chloe didn't care why.

So Michelle sat with Chloe and Jess while Lauryn took up a few tables away, rubbing her hand up and down Byron Singleton's thigh. Lauryn was confident— she knew that, at a moment's inspiration, she could flip it and force Michelle to be the odd one out, the alone one, so it was almost better this way because Michelle sat in anxiety, waiting for it.

Chloe instead focused her attention on watching fellow juniors Becca Checkoway and P. dub. Ballard execute their distract-bombard-cover-advance plan of throwing food at the anorexic girls in the cafeteria. When Becca caught her eye, Chloe pointed at the veiny form of Roberta Costa six tables over. The camera came out. She could humiliate the humiliated by spreading it around, or go after Becca with evidence of her wrongdoing. Control. The video uploaded though capacity was low.

She scrolled through images to delete. An unfortunate amount of space on her phone was taken up by the nude images of others, both sent and forwarded. In three days, there was supposed to be a big, open-forum town hall to "engage the students in dialogue" on the topic of sexting, but someone had hacked into about a dozen teacher and administrator cellphones and excerpted raunchy texts, messages, emails, pictures, and voicemails. The school was having trouble putting out the fires.

The lights surged off, the new televisions going dim. Power outage. The rest were cheering, hoping the catastrophic maintenance malfunction meant their early release into the waning moments of mild winter, but Chloe glanced around for evidence of a school shooter, a bombing, a nuclear detonation, a terrorist, or an invasion. Of course the attack could have been hundreds of miles removed—a jumbo jet flown into a power plant, a ravaging virus taking down the grid, a strategic strike leveling adjacent cities, an earthquake in the wilderness—all these things could have destabilized the system far away. Then she thought about a storm drowning them all. She saw the seas rise.

Mercifully, the lights came back on.

"What the fuck is going on today?" Michelle said.

"I don't know. But it's all been weird. Maria Price-Marcos came in like a Maserati."

"Wait. What?" Chloe said.

"She smells like she's being smuggled," Michelle said. "Maybe her parents won the lottery."

"She did not get dropped off in a Maserati," Chloe said. But Jess was expressing confirmation.

The phone image was held for Chloe to see, and sure enough Maria was emerging from a car with doors that did not open the normal way.

Nothing else happened that afternoon. No other power outages. No other strange public upendings of the social-romantic order. But the school had changed. Something was wrong. The televisions said that softball would begin indoor tryouts on Thursday.

LeMay Senior High School was founded only seven years before the end in response to the changing demographics of NW Washington, DC, another brick in the mass reorganizations of the endless mess that was the DC public school system. It was not really founded, but refounded, recycled. The building had been a shuttered shell for six decades. There were no pictures on the walls of class after class, no cases holding skyscraping cities of trophies. Chloe was only its second or third regent, or, depending on how you appraise her total domination and ability, its first true empress.

But now it had ghosts. It had entropy. The electric surge had made the walls crawl. Chloe was sure the building was going to collapse at any moment. Over and over again she felt the floor vibrate, the P-wave suggesting an earthquake without the punch line. The sky looked like it was on sped up film, color-corrected, a CGI orange tint on everyone's skin. Not even Jess brought comfort. All the other faces seemed to be looking at them, looking at Chloe, like they knew. They stared like they had figured it out.

On the screen under her desk, Michelle claimed that Lauryn had gotten herpes from making out in the bathroom of a Mexican restaurant with a drunk University of Maryland student.

Chloe unplugged the battery from her phone, and kept her head on a swivel, expecting a detonation. LeMay had become cursed ground. She remembered watching a group of actors playing soldiers use a laser guidance system to paint a target (of alien invading bugs), guiding in missiles launched from far above. And Chloe knew LeMay was being painted. Marked for death. Or something like it. The gravity was coming from the inside. Not a controlled implosion. Something else. Chloe heard the static from the PA system. It took every part of her, every disciplined neuron, to not scream, to not plead for it to be turned down during English class.

Whatever was happening to LeMay, it was happening at the smallest possible level. Molecules were getting knocked off their orbits. There were four kids in math class Chloe could swear she had never laid eyes on. But she knew everyone. That was her job. After the last bell, Chloe watched three people try the wrong lockers. The draft was flowing the opposite direction than she remembered. The proles, the sloths, the fat, the socially awkward, and pussing oiled skin masses—on the walk out, they were all standing tall.

Chloe tried on purpose not to sleep. With her phone off, the inboxes full, ALL CAPS odes inquired of her and fake worried, needy of guidance or gossip or action. She would make up a story of technical malfunction. With that as good a last thought as any, she let loose control and slipped into what should be nothing.

The mushroom clouds hovered that night. No big explosions. No burns. The clouds hung in the distance, watchful sentinels, dust kicked into the air, a brave new world. She sat at a café in the shrouded suburb, ordered coffee, and kept still as the small child in line pulled off a jacket to reveal a suicide vest, the glass cans of nails, the blocks of plastic. She smiled at Chloe and pressed the button.

⊗　　　⊗　　　⊗　　　⊗

TWO WEEKS BEFORE MOLLY got her driver's license, David agreed to give her a ride to the community center. Jon said it was okay. She would be driving her own car soon either way. Jonathan Corbin did not get to stand face to face and discover he was a foot shorter than his daughter's new friend. It was pouring. Jon gave a wave from the porch and ran back into the house. Molly took the five wet steps and pried the car door open. It smelled like teenage boy. Traces of deodorant and processed food and mass-inhabitation. Trash filled the bottom of the back.

"So that's him," David said as soon as she shut the door.

"Yup."

"I thought he was going to interrogate me about being a good driver. Or what my interest in his daughter was."

"I don't think he knows to do that," Molly said.

David began the three point turn. His sedan treated the dirt and gravel like ice as it lurched back and forth.

"So what is he going to do when you leave?"

"Like right now? I don't know."

"No I mean when you leave for good."

"What?"

"Like what are you going to do after?" David asked.

"After what?"

"I don't know. Your homeschooled equivalent of graduation."

"I'm already finished," Molly said.

"So what are you doing with your life then?"

Fear seared. What did that mean?

"I'm 16?"

"Yea but. What do you want to do? Are you going to be sent off to college by your dad who thinks the world is about to end?"

"We've never talked about it," Molly said.

"Well what do you want to do?"

"I don't know," she said. "I don't know how any of it is supposed to work. I have my aunt. I always thought I would talk to her about it."

"But you don't have a plan to move to New York and start a band or something? Join the Marines?"

Molly raised her shoulders away from him. Eye contact ceased being a factor. She shrunk into the seat, curling arms around knees under the seatbelt. A disease infected her nerves. A takeover of embarrassment, a need to explode with tears, a lump in the throat. Nails dug into her own arms. And now that she had betrayed emotion, a new terror descended that now he would try to comfort her with the faux therapy of debunking her living situation. But he went somewhere else.

"I have this cousin who grew up in Indiana." He said.

"Is she fucked up like me too?"

David pulled into a patch on the shoulder between two trees. The key turned. He, with his seat back all the way already to accommodate his height, did his best imitation of her curl, of the regressive self-cornering shrink. He leaned his head on the window as if it were a pillow.

"This one uncle and aunt. I never met them before they died. They were black sheep, but they had Kelley, my cousin. She's seven years older. She ended up going to Purdue. She got in with these people, basically like... Okay, there were a bunch of rich kids, and they were friends with a few agricultural majors, like my cousin, and one of them inherited this massive plot of land in the middle of nowhere. So they started going there over the summer and breaks to hang out and scheme about growing there after they graduated. And it started like that. Organic farming. Selling at the farmer's markets within driving distance. And they also had all these friends at University of Indiana, Chicago, Notre Dame, and a few from other places, too. So then they started bringing people as friends, to hang out and work, and a bunch were engineering and tech people. And they started messing around building windmills and solar panels and that led to all this do-it-yourself stuff, robots and a hardware hacking lab. They started tutoring some of the local kids when they were around. And then the next year a bunch of artists started coming too, putting up sculptures, making a studio space. One guy founded a software company there one summer, like, he and two friends coded the whole time on all these projects. The rich kids incorporated the place. Gave it a budget. Made it a real thing. And it snowballed. Now most of them have graduated, and while some moved away or went to grad school or got jobs, a bunch stayed and kept building it. And younger students trickled out. And it grew. And now it is totally self-sufficient. The agri kids grow all this food. Culinary kids cook. Econ kids run the budget. A bunch of kids are EMTs. There's a nursing school grad who couldn't find a job, lots who couldn't find jobs. One of their friends who is a member or whatever is almost out of med school. And though some of them aren't living there the whole time, they have this place, this totally sufficient and resilient community. My cousin and two of her rich friends were on a road trip and stopped to visit my family last year. And they invited me."

"So you're going to go live in a hippie commune after the Marines?"

"It's not like that. It really isn't. But I mean, it will be an actual place. It's the only place I'm spending time when I'm on leave. I'm sure as hell not coming back here."

He looked at her the moment that last part had come out of his mouth like it had been wrong.

"Why would not coming back here be bad? Of course you won't."

"I know. Right. Good," he said.

Molly faintly brought her lips to her own knee, a jerk reaction.

"I actually told her about you the other day," David said.

"Who?"

"My cousin Kelley."

"Why tell her about me?"

"She said she wanted to meet you. And that you could come, too."

"Like come check it out?"

"Yea. And be there if you wanted to. Be a part of it. She said me vouching for someone was unprecedented."

"Why me?"

"Well you are a real-deal survivalist, in your blood, so there's that. But they'd want you for the same reason they'd want me. Every village needs warriors."

"But why me?"

Now she actually looked at him.

☒   ☒   ☒   ☰

THE EYE IN THE storm arrived. The school exuded a better aura, less doom and gloom, calm, normalcy.

Chloe couldn't decide whether to let herself be fooled by it or not. Tuesdays were one of those lucky scheduling masterpieces where Chloe and Jess shared every single class. Thursdays were the same. Blessings. Jess was wearing black boots that each had three buckles on the sides, sheer black tights with menacing, geometric doodled designs reaching up her legs—evil flowers and climbing vegetation. Her skirt was actually a dress which was actually a shirt: an off-white with repeated clockwork eyelash graphics across the chest, the top half obscured by the black high-necked lace top pulled over it and covered by the dozen necklaces ornately dangling down her front. Her hair was up, never straightened, wild, dark and wavy, red burnt-almond strands launching from the knot held in their sporadic trajectories. No makeup except thick eyeliner. Dangling from her bag was a red and black plaid button-down, stolen from a boy—or that was the suggestion—an added layer ready when warmth was needed. There were four bracelets covering almost half of her right forearm: one of wooden beads, one of faux bones, one leather band, and one metal chain. Jess's nails were painted almost-black, shadow with hints of obsidian.

The true secret to Chloe's (and by extension Lauryn's) success had been the early high school adoption of direct confrontation as a strategy. Chloe had the epiphany in the ninth grade, back when Michelle was still warm from the embers of true power, straight out of middle school, when Michelle told Starsha Greer that she wasn't pretty enough to hook up with Harrison Drummond, a prowling, targeting senior. Michelle then of course followed up with the ubiquitous "just kidding" followed by the reactive statement that Starsha needed to be able to take a joke. Michelle was afraid even then to go all out. So Chloe started being honest. It was that simple. If a girl was stupid enough to ask, "Do I look fat?" Chloe told the straight up truth. Lauryn caught on within two months. She was always the best mimic. Chloe practiced honesty before she practiced deception.

Walking down the hall with Jess, Michelle dogging them from behind, Kendall Beal shot a nice message asking Chloe if it would be okay if she hooked up with Anthony—if Lauryn would be mad—and then apparated on the lockers to ask Chloe in person.

"I don't want to start shit," Kendall pleaded.

"Why are you asking me?" Chloe said.

"Because you're friends with her and…"

"If you want to fuck him fuck him. It has nothing to do with me. Don't bring me into it. Don't ask for my permission."

"But do you think she'd be mad?"

"Would you be mad?"

"Yes."

"Well then the question you have to ask yourself is, 'Is Lauryn as weak and pussy as I am?' Like, would she get pissed and turn all her friends against me and make it so bad that I kill myself and then my parents drag her into court and that gets so bad that she kills herself?"

"I wouldn't do that. That's not me."

"I know," Chloe said, "I was just kidding. Can't you take a joke?"

"Oh...Okay..."

"Go ask Michelle. She'll know better."

Of course Michelle would tell her to do it because Michelle was still mad at Lauryn for reasons that Chloe was still not paying attention to, because they were surely boring beyond belief. Chloe texted Lauryn the news of Kendall's interest in her on-again, off-again fuck buddy.

The passing students did not have faces. They were demons, drones, and cloned machines. Chloe and Jess accelerated ahead of the waylaid Michelle. Lauryn texted back: "OF COURSE I'm okay with it what do I care" which meant she wasn't okay with it, and then said, "but she hsud have asked me" which meant she wouldn't have been okay with that either—spelling aside.

The hallway became clogged with a frenzied rush. Between steps she heard boys inarticulating something about someone who had left a massive cube of new sneakers on the football field, like ten feet tall, free, for anyone to take who got their first. Jess was tempted. She slowed. She walked to a window that only partially showed the field. Chloe grabbed her and led her away.

"It's some stupid marketing trick or a team prank," Chloe told her.

Jess rocked her head like a zombie. The believers made for the prize. Maybe someone was filming a commercial. But she would have heard about that.

They were late to math class by three minutes. The teacher didn't acknowledge it. The rest were seated. There was an eerie line of big boys, some athletes, some slobs, all tall, who were blocking off a corner of the room from her sight. The entire back half of the room had smiles. What the fuck was that? They took the two programmed empty seats.

Chloe forgot that Angela Griner and Brittney Pope were in the class. Angela was alright, but Brittney had a tired and unrelenting little-miss-perfect act: How are you?! Oh my god!! How was that test?! Did you hear about...?? She always sat next to and talked to Jess whenever they were there. Jess didn't respond of course, vow intact, but smiled and played along with a sincerity that only encouraged discomfort.

Jess was everyone's favorite white girl. That was her job at LeMay.

Brittney whispered something to Jess while the teacher was turned. Hidden in her pocket, Chloe started venting to both Lauryn and Michelle— someone needs to take Brittney down a notch. There was an annoying buzz in the room. Not a fictional or metaphorical buzz, an actual buzz, a real sound. Chloe did not risk bringing it to the teacher's attention, general policy, but it was there. She glanced backward but could only see the few rows of normal doodlers and attention-payers.

"I like BRI" Michelle said under Chloe's desk. Ugh. BRI. Even worse.

Lauryn was better, "Yeah she sucks but who cares."

On her own, Chloe started typing again, inviting Angela to come with her to the weekend's pleasantries but saying there was only one extra seat in the car so only she could come. Steal the friends, divide and conquer. After she finished, she would ask about what the hell was happening on the lawn. Her thumbs flew over the invisible non-keys, but then Chloe was descending. The metal under her buckled. The world was rushing downward. Chloe found herself on the floor entangled in the remains. Her desk had collapsed.

(Here we go Efram, second semester junior year.)

═   ═   ◱   ◱

EFRAM DANIELS HAD HIS driver's license second semester junior year. This meant that he pillaged the thirty or so automobiles that had been kept in storage, selecting the dozen he wanted— rich kid dead father Christmas—and so he pulled up to LeMay Senior High School for his public school debut in a set of wheels with a sticker price-worthy of a large house. Well, worthy of a large house post-crash, or a large house thirty years ago, but still…

"Be careful," they told him, Raj and Ami and The Savage. Raj wanted him to calm it all the fuck down, to try to blend in, but Ami told him that honesty was important. "Don't act like you aren't rich, that's worse." Ami had to convince Raj that Efram was not going to get shot. The Savage didn't really care, but was there the whole time anyway, composing a minimoog ambient drone sad symphony as if the bleeps and bloops accurately reflected her opinions.

You can be a rich kid, but you can't be an asshole about it. That's all. That's the strategy. But Efram did know how to make entrances, sunglasses and woofers ringing and, at first, plain white T-shirts, tweed trousers, and pointy wingtipped shoes.

Chloe could not understand how this boy, this skinny scrawny boy, this rich, white, privileged, asymmetrical, curly-haired wonk was not despised on sight. The opposite happened. Within three days, Efram Daniels was best friends with the male elite, cross-race and cross-class. The worst part was that it seemed natural. Like he hadn't tried to do it.

Marcus Worthy, aka Senior God—a perfect teeth pretty boy of charm, headed to Howard or Georgetown or Harvard, a black male Casanova, linebacker / scholar— decided that Efram was going to be his sidekick for the first few days. He showed him around.

"My super-duper magic wigga, my super-duper magic cracker, my super-duper magic honky," Marcus joked. The manufacture of MAGIC WHITEBOY SIDEKICK T-shirts was discussed.

But Efram Daniels did not fold into a particular group. He sat at lunch with a group of seven freshman Latina girls. Every single fucking day, Chloe had to watch it, and all they did was laugh and joke and what the fuck.

"There's whole sites about him," Michelle said. "Do you know—"

"Yes," Chloe said. Everybody knew. Everybody knew that Efram Daniels was super rich and his dad got caught doing sketchy financial shit and committed suicide and Efram went crazy and got kicked out of every single private school in the known universe. Everybody knew the aggregated stories and the hypertexted histories, the mountains of video from parties so retarded they belonged to the wildest imaginations of horny film producers, who wished they could go back in time and legally fuck teenagers.

"The stories are exaggerated," Chloe said.

"What do you mean?"

"He did not rappel from the roof of his last school and crash through a dorm window with a water gun."

"I'm pretty sure he did. Why else would he be *here?*"

The EDEI reached extreme volatility, the market unsure how to adjust to a public school. Conventional wisdom was that he might not be capable of getting kicked out, as his antics never seemed to involve violence, drugs, et al, and would be obscured in a student body ten times the previous size. Efram Daniels would not be a name to those overseeing him. To his teachers, he would be a number on a list. A few took the other tack figuring Efram would account for this, or suddenly start playing politics, or get into it with the wrong sort of students and have to remove himself to prevent physical harm.

Michelle walked up to Efram and Marcus and a whole nonstandard crew in the courtyard like a miniature rat

dog, shivering with excitement. Lauryn, Jess, and Chloe
followed.

Chloe hung back to the greatest possible degree.

Marcus and Efram sat on the cement step, leaning
back, flanked on each end by a buzzing group of disciples.
There was another new television in the corner under
the roof of the passageway.

"Hey," Michelle said, and Chloe already wanted to
vomit. Lauryn moved up to Michelle's side.

Marcus and Efram yanked their heads from the
nugget of deep conversation, the whole group taking in
Michelle's pose.

"Ummmmm, hey," Marcus said but Efram stood up
and extended his hand like he was a fucking lawyer.

"Hello," he said. Michelle had no established response
to this, she barely took his fingers.

"Hey." Again.

"So, what is your name?"

"Michelle," she said.

"How do you spell that?" Efram asked.

"Um, M-i-c-h-e-l-l-e."

"What is your full name?"

"Michelle Allyssa Castens, my family calls me Ally."

"A-l-l-i-e, A-l-l-y, or A-l-i?" Efram started to ask, "Or
maybe it is O-l-l-i-e."

"Sheeeeeeit," The Great Toscano said lying down
on the cement. "I wish it was Ollie. Butter. Ollie Butter.
New name for future pornstar wife. Ollie Butter. Buttery
ass Ollie Butter."

The Great Toscano was black, but Italian. He had been born in Italy to Ghanaian parents who had made it across the Med, who were the slightest percent, the lucky, the exception, who then managed to grab a successful asylum application when he was only two or three. LeMay almost exclusively called Mario "The Great Toscano" or "TGT."

The Great Toscano was fully assimilated, and no one knew the wiser until he gave his real name, which he never gave. The Great Toscano wore tight black jeans with a fake squirrel tail peeking out his back pocket, fresh turquoise dunks and thick black glasses that had completely translucent frames, a lime green plaid top over a "chicks and kicks" fonted masterpiece and a Nats snapback. He played soccer, but not on the team. In the street.

"Ally with a 'y'," Michelle said.

"Whyyyyyyyyyyyyyy," the chorus behind sang, eventually in harmony.

"Interesting, Michelle," Efram said, the pinnacle of polite. "And what is it that you do?"

"Uh, what?"

"What is it that you do? What do you do with yourself? How do you spend your time, Michelle? Why are you worth anything on this planet?"

"Ummm. I don't know," was all Michelle could come up with.

"Like TGT over here. What do you do TGT?" Efram asked him.

"I make beats son."

"TGT makes beats. That's what he does."

"Why always me?" TGT said.

"WHY ALWAYS YOU MARIO?" The chorus hit him back.

"Man, always me."

"And Maria over here," Efram gestured to the corner to the ultimate offender, the scab, Maria Price-Marcos, Stinky Maria, "the trailer," they called her for years, unloaded on since the sixth grade for being too poor to afford deodorant or laundry detergent. "Maria makes art."

"The best art," TGT said.

In fact Maria Price-Marcos made strange visual representations of digital motion, disjointed frames of broken screens, symphonies of noise and caution—paintings and drawings that were the concept art for a God planning technofacistic human decay—a really pretty descent into a new underworld. It had been hard for Efram to get her into sunlight. Get her to hang out with other people. She refused the social sphere, instead sending her friends recordings and videos of her noise-music alter egos, a new one every week. So you'd ask her "What's up?" or "How are you?" and in response you'd get a recording of frothing static, clamoring uncontrollably under a trill acapella.

"If we're honest," Maria said suddenly, "the new TGT mixtape sucks. But if you play it four times simultaneously with the slightest of delays, it's epic."

"Why always me?" TGT said as Maria started grabbing their cellphones and arranging simultaneous delayed recordings in a discordant symphony—

all with Michelle still fucking standing there.
"And Marcus. Marcus hangs out and looks really good-
looking. That's what he does."

"Hey!"

"Yea, he gets good grades and shit. But Michelle,
in my personal opinion, I don't think grades are any
indicator of intelligence. Do you?" Efram asked.

And the spotlight went back to Michelle.

"I don't know," she answered.

"So Michelle, back to the question at hand. What do
you do?"

"I go to school. Hang out with friends."

Lauryn winked at Chloe, and then advanced forward.

"Hi, Efram. I'm Lauryn."

Here we go.

"L-a-u-r-e-n or L-a-u-r-y-n?" She broke him off with a
confident nod. "Interesting Lauryn with a 'Y'. And what is
it that you do? Why are you worth anything on this planet?"

The courtyard was almost an amphitheater. He was
on a stage.

"I kind of see myself as a style impresario," Lauryn
said. Chloe chortled. Where had she stolen that word? "I
really want to have a reality fashion brand for myself, star
in something, maybe move into music eventually."

"Ooooh, Ooooh, Oooh!" TGT was raising his hand
frantically like a kindergartner.

"Yes, The Great King Toscano," Marcus called on him.

"I know the answer teacher. I know what she does.
Or she did. Or she do. Woooooooo!"

"I was thirteen," Marcus said in explanation.

Before Lauryn could attempt to continue her crafted, acted answer, two whirring machines, four rotors suspended in a diamond structure, descended and curled and hovered around Efram's shoulders. They made threatening movements toward both Marcus and TGT, the former unflinching in his photoshoot ready pose and the latter swatting and rolling away.

Michelle and Lauryn took steps backward.

"What, like, are those?"

"They are his quadcopters," Maria said, still constructing her lo-fi symphony in a psychological corner. "Flying robots. The cops are starting to get them. They'll be watching us all soon. They're already all over the border. Best to build your own now while they're still legal."

"My apologies," Efram said, "but it's time to go. Nice meeting you." .

And he began to tilt off the map. The clock said they still had ten minutes. Efram reentered the cafeteria, eight informational schedule-updating TVs now sixteen informational schedule-updating TVs, darting through with his two flying friends. It looked like they were chasing him. He barely avoided crashing them into loaded trays of refuse. Howls. Not wanting to look like a douchebag in the more compact hallways, at a touchscreen command and they followed him more indirectly, distanced, buzzing slowly on a skim of the ceiling, almost unnoticed to the traffic below except when someone looked up and giggled. He took his seat, and they orbited over him, angels.

The English teacher glanced down at her list—

"Efram those are not appropriate for school. Please put them away."

"They aren't mine," Efram said, "but they keep following me around."

She walked down the aisle from the desk, and reached out, only to have the two quadcopters sense the threat and climb quickly. The class started to fill. Another audience.

Efram walked over to the window, slid it open, and set them free. They took turns going through it, an arranged exit, an algorithm trained for portal navigation.

‡   ‡   ‡   ‡

THE HOTEL LOBBY WAS decked out in wrought iron framing that had glass bubbles trapped inside the beams. These two-inch dots extended wall to floor, radiating dull copper light. The ceiling was burnt to the darkest, red-finished walnut. Steven bypassed the large arched green leather thrones and headed straight for the elevator, which was done up in a sequential progression of grayscale stripes. His coat was like a commodore's, leather buttons on two sides, royal navy of gloom, covering a black thermal-lined sweatshirt and a shadowy woolen button-down shirt, heavy for wear and tear or climate resistance. His hair had been sculpted down to a faint hologram, his face shaved clean. On the fifth floor, the carpet switched to burgundy.

One month before the end, Steven knocked on the door. Norman opened it wearing sad slacks and a white shirt, the top of his head only reaching Steven's shoulders. He led him in, the first room of the suite adorned by two long couches. A series of beeps and vibrations emerged from the desk in the corner—a polished piece of mellowed cherry broken up by bright white drawers, a silver vase of roses clashed with Norman's effects. Norman walked over to glance at his phone.

A woman emerged from the bedroom door, putting in an earring while passing through the portal, dropping the second in shock—

"Who are you?" she yelled. Steven turned his head toward Norman, and inclined in that direction.

"Cynthia, this is my son," Norman said coming back into her view.

"I thought you said he was a teenager," she said, relinquishing the tone of dread and the confusion in her eyes, finding the earring and then the couch.

"I am," Steven said.

"You must make a lot of girls cry," she said.

"It's not genetic," Steven responded.

"You found us alright?" Norman asked.

"Yes, murlyborne mallerybone merelyberne…" Steven went through the various possible mispronunciations—"Whirlybird!" he exclaimed as an ending.

"Mar-ly-bone," The woman offered the correct form.

"He knows," Norman said.

"Oh! Taking the piss were you?" She laughed. "So do you have a girlfriend?"

"No," Norman answered for him.

"Oh, why not?" she asked.

"Yes Steven, why not?" Norman echoed.

"I'm terrified of accidentally getting with a half-sibling," Steven said.

She didn't get it.

"I was summoned?" Steven stretched his arms outward.

Cynthia looked at both of them from a kept seat.

"I need you to go back," Norman said.

"Back where?"

"I need you to go deal with your mother," Norman said.

"My mother, your wife," Steven raised a fake glass.

"It's serious this time," Norman said.

"Serious for her, or serious for you?"

Norman's cheeks had hollowed out. His hair had frayed as it faded. His torso had gone soft.

"Alright," Steven said. "Define 'deal with her?'"

"See her. See how she is. Check out what it's like and let me know."

"Alright."

"When can you leave?" Norman asked

Steven answered by giving a fake salute.

"I'll send you the confirmation number," Norman said.

Steven knew the way to the airport.

THERE WERE MISMATCHED COUCHES, loveseats, and chairs—Archie Bunker thrones and plaid cushioned chesterfields.

The basement floor was cement, the giant studio door raised up revealing the driveway. Kids were skating both inside and outside, a wooden box against one wall presented as a ledge. Fifties and sixties rock was playing, sparking odd reactions like, "That shit is tight yo," when *Hanky Panky* by Tommy James and the Shondells repeated over the standard D, A, E riff. Each time, they said they were gonna skate to one song and one song only.

The loungers sat unbothered by the loud snaps and thunderous lands of the skaters when they collided with metal and cement. Housewives were projected onto the walls. Closed captioning. Jimi Hendrix came on, *Are You Experienced?*, the speakers inquired, and time reversed with the beat, and the skaters asked one another "the Pharcyde sampled this shit right?"

They reached the stairs and the giant God of shuffle presented them with a low down Houston chopped and screwed drawl, a pitched down acapella yawning over a decelerated blues guitar loop that had a bit-crush and roll effect applied.

The Savage had once told Efram that all music was based on mixing. Even without recording, alone, at its most basic level, a voice or instrument mixing with the air, entering into competition with the ambient noise, the sound of your own body living. Voices mixing and instruments blending, evolutionary step by evolutionary step.

The stairs had a turn in them, a corner, and they stretched horizontally over the scene to the second floor, still subterranean. Lauryn was instantly visible standing on Lil' Jack's skateboard, his hands resting on her hips and her arms on his shoulders. Chloe knew Meredith Pulaski would be fucking pissed. Meredith was Lil' Jacks's main on-again off-again jump-off. Lauryn almost fell, caught while unleashing a half-sober laugh, suspended from his arms as his foot caught the escaping wood and wheels. Lauryn had changed. Black leggings under this gold skirt that was only a strip since her shirt was so long, a white frilly thing squeezed by a leather belt at her stomach. Less makeup, pink blocky sunglasses with neonish holographic lenses, worn indoors. A ring with antlers on her left hand and an ironic cross hanging from her neck.

Lauryn brushed Jess on the cheek European style and gave Chloe a hug, light, grazing her lips against Chloe's neck while she filed past with her new friend Lil' Jack, back downstairs. Moving the opposite direction, Chloe and Jess came across an alcove in front of two desks, where two kids in headsets were bopping with their first-person guns, flying around frantically unloading clip after unrealistic clip into enemies that took more damage than an elephant could before they finally fell. Chloe noticed the gravity physics were off, that the arena, which seemed to consist of two large pillars, allowed the players to shoot upward if they jumped. It only became clear when one reached the top that the map was of the World Trade Center, lost architecture given new life. A sprite resembling an old lady in a frock connected with the player on the left, freezing her menacing, rocket-launcher-toting frame on screen as he died, and had to wait out the countdown clock to respawn.

Efram Daniels walked over wearing large, oval, bedazzled women's sunglasses, a neon pink and turquoise floral print button-down shirt, gray sweatpants, and a pair of AstroTurf flip-flops.

"I'll give you twenty dollars if you can get everyone to peacefully gather in the center of the map without saying anything to any of the other players," he said to the first-person shooters.

Respawned, player one walked to the center of the map, stopped, and turned around until he was killed. He tried again. Maybe they'd catch on eventually. He had been in the lead. It did not look like an error. Everything was on purpose.

The insults and curses could be heard bleeding from his headphones. The taunts and laughs. But the player kept his mouth shut.

"Greetings," Efram said.

"Hi," Chloe said. Was he going to ask what they were doing here? Did she need to add the 'Lauryn invited us' to not get thrown out by some butler? But Jess knew him. They shared a hug, a real one, and Efram grabbed Jess by the hand and led her forward into the more psychedelic reaches, where the real gathering was.

Marcus was sitting with his legs hanging off of a metal filing cabinet. The Savage, Maria, TGT, and two others were in the far corner, playing with paper and machines. Anton Hotz had a real chair. Ami was on top of a bookshelf, her small frame in a perfect L on its thin width, back against the wall holding the corner, perched high above the rest. Raj had stretched out over a series of pillows. Three girls and two boys had made a Martian landscape out of sheets and bedding, and that quadrant looked like a camping trip. Chloe stayed back standing, unready to commit. Efram balanced his arm around Jess's shoulder, and she did the same, chums.

"So you know Chloe?" Anton asked Efram.

"He hasn't asked me how it's spelled yet," Chloe said.

They laughed but Efram absorbed it. Totally unaffected. Idiot savant. What could you possibly say to this one to break him down?

"So Jess," he said, "I want you to meet Raj, because we've told him about you, and we can't decide if he will find your vow of silence to be the sexiest, most genius thing ever, or he will hate you. And since he's sort of the arbiter of all judgment in the universe, it's important."

Chloe snatched Jess's hand to move it off of Efram's shoulder. They were headed toward a row of discarded cushions against a wall, so Chloe made a move to position herself in the middle when they sat down. Efram extended his hand, vertical, fingers curled, thumb up, wanting to have a thumb war.

Seriously? After the Chloe death stare, Jess reached over Chloe's lap and took the battle, winning in quick succession.

"See," Efram said in impressed defeat as they started again.

"You know she isn't always silent. She talks," Chloe said.

Raised eyebrows. Jess shot Chloe a disagreeing look. Yes I am! I haven't spoken in years. Don't lie, Chloe.

Raj rolled over to watch the conclusion of the match and presented himself with a wave.

Jess took Raj's fingers as if he were a maiden, and lightly kissed his hand.

"See, the question comes to this." Ami said from above. "Do you have a reason for your vow of silence or not? Is it even a vow? What is behind it?"

Marcus's pure white teeth illuminated the room, helping the candles, dimmed bulbs, and discarded track lighting coils.

Jess gave this wonderful shrug where she turned her chin toward her shoulder as if she were naked and trying not to show anything.

"It's a mystery at LeMay," Marcus said.

"Will you type things?" Raj began.

Jess shook her head.

The Savage walked over and sat cross-legged on Raj's back like he was a piece of furniture, the size difference allowing such a position. She leaned down and entered into an entwined position in his arms, just as focused and fascinated on the subject at hand.

"So perhaps it is a regressive antitechnological statement?" Raj said. "Though being a luddite is so last century. So maybe it is not really antitechnological or antisocial but more nuanced? Maybe you have given up speech as a counterweight to the inane and endless communication of your peers? The last bastion of genuine humanity might be in closing the mouth and quieting the soul to be with people without the blabbing twittering cacophony. Maybe you are consumed by something else? Purely focused on the development of an art or craft? Moral philosophy? Geopolitics? Computational Neurobiology? Sculpture? Maybe you are a voyeur. You want to watch? Maybe you are really an angel of death, a vixen trained her whole life in combat, death, and destruction waiting to be pushed over the edge and kill us all. Maybe you are the smartest one here, the smartest one at the school, and what is the point of engaging with the intellectual insects you are forced to socialize with? And what is the point of dealing with all the school crap, because if you are that smart, then you are smart enough to know it is all crap, so you coast along with the minimum possible energy and effort until you escape. Or maybe you are a scientist? You are observing us diligently in the service of a grand social theory, and attempting to limit your effect on the outcome of the experiment and fieldwork by keeping silent? We are all your ethnographic subjects? Maybe you do talk, Jess, and we don't notice? We created a mythology of you not talking because it was a better story. Or maybe you had been talking, but then you realized no one was listening, so you stopped to see if anything would ever change. Or maybe your voice is so powerful and destructive and seductive that you learned you have to be careful with it? Already you have broken too many hearts and shattered too many souls, and have grown sick of your power and wish not to inflict it. Maybe you are undercover? Maybe you are a spy?" ("Narc!" TGT gawked from the periphery while Raj kept going. "Shit. Girl could be five-oh.") "You are deep cover, a sleeper—but no, then you'd try to blend in, so you wouldn't shut up. Maybe even better, you are an alien? A Von-Neumann probe. Or maybe you don't have a reason. Maybe there really isn't a specific inspiration. Maybe you go home every night and inhale every literary work in the canon. Or maybe it's the opposite. You haven't read Nietzsche or Marcus Aurelius, you didn't hang out with monks or yogis, maybe you started one day. Or maybe slowly, over a few years, you started saying less and less. One less word a day, until, nothing…"

"Maybe," Jess said.

"I could see there being something numinous and transcendent—" Raj started saying to The Savage in his arms before Marcus finished his sentence—"in saying fuck it, and not responding to anyone and letting them figure it out."

"That's a possible plan, Efram," Ami said.

"Plan?"

"Are you going to start a cult where everyone suddenly stops talking all at once. No one answers questions in class. No one says anything to one another. Is that how you are going to destroy LeMay?"

"Why would I destroy LeMay?"

"It's what you do Efram. You go to a school and find a way to destroy it."

"He doesn't just do that," The Savage said in the midst of a post-speech Raj kiss.

"You go to a school and you identify the most hypocritical thing about it, the evil or absurd part of it, and you totally fuck with it."

"Make a mockery," Raj said.

"I don't want to make a mockery of the teachers," Efram said.

"You seriously think they're doing a good job?" Marcus asked.

"Not really, but they aren't the deal, they aren't in control."

"True," Marcus and Raj said.

"So what is the evil in LeMay?"

"The social order," Marcus said.

"Who could Efram hook up with to totally shock everyone and upset the social order?"

"No one. No one would really be surprised at anything."

"Well then who would be the funniest?"

"Chloe," Marcus, TGT, Maria, and even Anton said all at once. Jess nodded.

"I want a prince not a jester," Chloe said, and oooooooh, there they went. Fast shoot-down lyrical response. Raj gave a golf clap. An actual victory of the night in the fast language of the room.

"Well is LeMay like that hierarchical?" Ami asked Marcus.

"No it isn't like that," Chloe took over. "Everyone is mean to everyone. Being popular, pretty, good at sports, whatever, like it doesn't matter anymore. People will still fuck with you if they're jealous or don't like you or just feel like it. It's not controlled or built."

"Says the fucking queen of the school," Marcus said. But he said it nicely at least. Like it could have been a good thing.

"Not the queen. She's the CIA. The NSA. The Federalis, uhhhhhh, what's that FBI fucker's name?" TGT stumbled.

"J. Edgar Hoover?" Raj tried.

"Yea, but he was a queen. She's like that uh, like…"

"Rasputin? Machiavelli? Kissinger?"

"Yeaaaaaaaaaaaaaaaaaaaaa," TGT jumped up and down.

"I'm none of those, and I'm not the queen either," Chloe said.

But Marcus and Anton and Maria laughed. The nation-state may have already declined. Hollowed out. But the people still looked at their leaders as if they were in control. Save us! They cried. Fix it! They bargained and elected, still thinking it mattered. Because the alternative, being stuck on your own, being undefended by the mythical power of protection, that was unfathomable.

"The greatest trick the devil ever played…" Raj said.

Chloe was technically staying at Jess's that night, and Jess decided to stay at Efram's with the rest in the fake camp they made, snacks in the center, pillows and bedding covering the floor. The ones that had to left, curfews and clearances and lying skills depending.

Couples absconded to other reaches of the house for a period but then returned, wanting to be a part of it, aware that the rest of their lives would not be so full of such nights.

A hardcore ten had the freedom or the lies to remain for the entire night.

Chloe slept on an air mattress with Jess next to her, pushed right up to a set of stolen cushions on which Efram's sleeping bag unfurled in a mummy shaped blob, unzipped due to the heat. The music never stopped, it became quieter and more ambient, deconstructed, atonal. The Savage left on a looping series of lullaby beeps before she wreathed herself in a corner of Raj's torso and entered her stiff-as-dead sleep. Though down the room in the alcove the gamers were still going, the bodies next to Chloe all fell into patterned droops. Efram had rolled, and was splayed on the uneven edge of his not-bed with his arms crossed over his head in a knot. He twitched over and the palm of one of his hands landed on Jess's shoulder, totally unflexed. It sat there, three square inches of body contact. It was not as if Efram tried some insane snuggling trick out of the blue, he did not slowly escalate flirty contact or wrap an arm around her waist. In his sleep it landed there. And Jess grabbed it and wrapped it around her and Chloe, a seatbelt, but Chloe separated, lightly, understanding the movement was not under his control, leaving the hem of her shirt sitting at the verge of Efram's fingers while she scrunched herself back in closer to Jess.

In the middle of Austin J. Tobin Plaza, in between the two towers, right in front of the sphere—different without a virtual Manhattan surrounding it—sixteen deathmatchers stood motionless in the center of the map. Sprites of soldiers and leather clad objectified sirens and aliens gathered, despite the guns they could not holster, and let the server go fragless. Peace, for a brief moment. Efram would give the twenty buck reward in the morning. But once you accomplish it, what's the point? You're just a bunch of fuckers built to kill, standing there. Balance would be restored. Someone would leave and a hopped up twelve year old would join the game, throw some grenades, spray some bullets, curse, laugh, taunt, and then quit for another option.

Chloe tossed and turned, or dreamt that she tossed and turned, either way afraid, clutching to Jess. The background soundtrack of digital killing seeped through her exposed ear canal. Sleep paralysis. Not enough nerve control to throw the pillow over her head and block it all completely. The sea levels rose. The tide rolled.

⊗   ⊗   ⊗   ⊗

Sixteen-year-old Molly woke up with her face cornered in aqua green nylon. The crunch in her eyes pulled them back closed. She rotated away from the wall of the tent and slipped one arm around David's hunched torso, becoming the big spoon despite the fact that she was smaller. This was an accomplishment. A bottle rolled around at their feet, now inert, having been filled with boiling water as an added heat source. His skin was paler than hers, reflective, bright, and she tucked her off arm against his back while her free hand traced up and down his stretched biceps. His arms were these strange, flat, ninety-degree pistons, riddled with strength, but not defined in the typical way. There was nothing spherical or bulging about them; it was a hydraulic system. Molly lifted her head, unintentionally brushing her nose against the slope of his back, and lightly brought her teeth onto his shoulder. She tapped them in rhythm against it and then, bored, closed them more readily and pulled on the skin. There was no chance of discerning the difference between David awake and David asleep. He would talk in his sleep. He would slumber with his eyes open. You really couldn't tell.

Her teeth still at work tapping his shoulder, without a stir or budge or breath or roll, the sound came out of his mouth.

"Do you have to go now to sneak back in?"

"Not yet," she said. The watch read 4:14 a.m.

The night before, Jon had stayed up later than she had expected, pacing in his office. She used an alternate strategy. She had made no big scene out of going to bed, announcements and obvious door closes and lights turned off. Only when he finally retired did she make the room dark, give the big door its fortress powers, maneuver out onto the roof, leaving the window open enough so that she could squeeze her arm inside and turn the crank, and then scale her way down. She had stashed her car half a mile from the house. She was two hours late. The fire David made had become a low demonic landscape of frightful embers, cities of burnt paper and remnant carbon. He was crouched over it, a sentinel, prodding the volcanic landscape with a stick. The tent had been set up. "Sorry!" she said annoyed and jumping from the car. And then they didn't talk.

Now four hours later, back in the tent, Molly stopped biting his shoulder and pressed her face into his upper back. She realized that her hair might be bothersome in that position, but did not relent or reposition. She burrowed and slithered her arm under his body, now wrapping him up completely, and squeezed. Her arms were then matched during a long inhalation. The intake took time and muscular effort, the sound a failing engine.

Three weeks until he joined the Marines, and never came back.

"We don't have to talk about it," he said.

"It's okay."

Molly released her grip and he spun onto his stomach, and she collapsed back onto her shoulder blades, a quarter roll, heads turned to meet in the middle.

"Yesterday, my dad asked me what verse I would like to be read at my funeral," David said.

"Ha. He's that pessimistic?"

"I'm sure he meant it more generally."

"And I'm sure you started a horrible theological argument that would bore me to death."

"I was probably about to, but then I told him to read the part of Revelations with the horsemen. He said that verses at a funeral was supposed to provide comfort through faith, 'a reaffirmation of God's power in the face of tragedy' or whatever—Him," David's sarcasm coming into effect at the capitalized pronoun, "reaching down to hearten his crying worshippers. 'I don't think those verses would inspire that sort of comfort,' he told me. Then I told him it was the only part that ever comforted me."

. Molly could imagine elementary school David sitting there in Sunday school Bible study, flipping through and thinking—boring boring boring, Matthew Mark Luke boring boring boring Romans blah blah blah John boring boring—Oh! Wait! What's this with all these angels and seals and lambs and stuff? End of the world? Oooh, I like the end of the world. This is totally kick ass...

"I told my dad it was the only part that I believed in," he said.

"The revelation and the apocalypse?"

"No, just the horsemen. I believe in the horsemen. They are probably real."

"How does that work? See, I could believe in Cain. That would make sense. He's out there somewhere. Still wandering. Banished," Molly shifted into a ghost-story voice and waved out of the tent. He laughed. But she asked the question again. "How do you just believe in the horsemen, Mr. Atheist?"

"Like, it's a good story. I'd like that part to be true. That's what that means. I'd like it to be true."

"Well how could it be true?"

"Every generation there'd be four people," David said, "waiting for the end of days. Over thousands of

ECHO

OF

THE

BOOM

years they'd be born and die having never gotten their chance. But they'd keep popping up, designed for that purpose, and eventually, one set of four would get their chance."

"You really could write your own religion," she said.

"A great way to make money."

"You think you're a horseman?" Molly rubbed her nose along the side of his torso.

David opened his eyes, picked up a pebble that had accidentally invaded the tent, and tossed it over his shoulder, hitting the red backpack, the only clear target, dead center, the exact middle point.

"No, I'm not."

"But you are Robin Hood," she said.

"Or Lee Harvey Oswald..."

"Who's that?"

David did not take the bait.

Two hours later her car crawled to the inlet off one of the driveway tributaries, a hunched parking space ringed by trees. Backpack on and sleeping bag in hand, she started her hike. The house appeared dead, empty shadows, nothing from the chimney, no slivers of early morning electric light. The fields were fallow, the vegetable patch dormant. He was slacking. She took the stairs to the porch, planning to drop her things there, assault the roof from the back, and then open the front door to nonchalantly retrieve her pack and sleeping bag. But she reached the top step, and Jonathan Corbin swung open the door.

He had atrophied. His torso was soft. His hair was turning a gray that was almost green, patchy, and his eyes and hands were no longer steady. Pupils were sad. Molly considered sprinting for the climb and resurrecting siege mode. But he spoke softly with a hand raised to the sleeping bag—

"You don't have to sneak out to go to a slumber party," he said. "I'm not that horrible."

"A slumber party. Yea, with Lane from the church. I thought you would…"

"It's fine," he said. "You were close. You could get back if anything happened."

Molly left her things there and turned to walk around the house.

"Where are you going?" he asked.

She had to climb back up the roof and through the window so she could unlock her bedroom door from the inside.

Jon watched his daughter easily yank her way up the overhang the way he might watch an orangutan scale a towering tree—an impossible species difference—an ant looking at an eagle, a turtle trying to race an antelope.

⋮⋮   ◹   ⋮⋮   ◹

PRESIDENT'S DAY, SECOND SEMESTER, junior year, there were only nine adults, all maintenance staffers, present at LeMay Senior High School. The dividing line was a crack in the pavement, an odd fluke of construction that bisected the central courtyard, and then was extrapolated on the other sides of the surrounding megabuilding by the large, honeycomb, middle stairwell windows on the wings. On the flanks, there was an effective neutral zone, but the sheer size of the map made this acceptable. One hundred and forty-two players showed up. The team defending from the center to the back fence wore orange. The team defending from the center to the sidewalk wore purple. Pennies had been raided from the storage area under the gym bleachers for those who did not come with prepared dress options.

Maria Price-Marcos was the referee. The Zebra. She made sure each flag position was legal. Legal meant an actual game of *capture* the flag, as opposed to a game of 'let's see who can place the flag in the hardest-to-get-to place and run around pointlessly for three hours.'

Time ticking down toward the start, numbers so large, Marcus brought together the purple huddle with his bellowing voice. He and Anthony took up, as the athletic senior class elite, as the de facto leadership. And the yawning division into offense and defense occurred, the tainted psychological reality being that most everyone wanted to play offense, especially the gifted. You could see the mixture of relief mixed with disappointment on the faces of those who would be defending. Seventy-one was a large team. The wise queen stepped forward. Constitutional monarchy.

"Flip it," Chloe said, but no one heard her. So she moved into the center and screamed it.

"What?"

"Have everyone you've picked for offense play defense. They're sending their best people on offense. In our territory we have the advantage, so focus on that, let them come."

They started to argue among themselves, but Chloe crossed her arms, and there was silence.

"Huddle up!" she yelled in her higher voice, the dictum of the sovereign.

She divided the seventy-one into seven squads of ten, distributing athletic talent evenly.

"We aren't going to attack at the beginning." she commanded. "We are going to catch them, one by one, and then swarm the fuck outta them once they have almost no one left."

She paused. Marcus smiled.

"We are going to starve them to death," Chloe said.

Three squads took the line. One for each of the grass flanks and one for the courtyard. One squad guarded the flag and one squad guarded the jail. She then allotted Marcus and Anthony each a squad, and told them to wander around terrorizing anyone who might step over onto their side. The other squads were to hold to their assignments and let the rovers take out any who evaded easy capture, and then take up nonstrategic positions in hostile territory. The squads on the line were instructed to have three of their fastest runners each make scouting charges across the divide, gain information, and yank backward, so it at least looked like they were trying to attack.

Marcus unzipped his purple track jacket. He had a T-shirt that said TEAM CHLOE over a rectangle with a lightning bolt through it.

"What, what is that?" Chloe asked.

"Efram thought you might need to be rebranded," Marcus smirked.

Maria let the megaphone siren blaze, loud in the courtyard and faint on the wings, and leaned against a pillar for an eye-roll and a snack.

‡   ‡   ‡   ‡

SIX MONTHS BEFORE THE end, Steven entered the airport lounge. Burgundy granite walls were inlayed with track-lit shelves of magazines. Sets of square leather chairs, alternating black and white, arranged facing each other, blocks in a grid, each rectangle playing host to a businessman or frequent traveler. The news, crawling on television screens, repeated over the expansive landscape of wheeled carry-ons and waiting bodies. The window to the left showcased takeoffs and landings. Snacks were laid out on an island.

Steven made for the emptiest cell, only to find a boy in one of the chairs, obscured by the height of the furniture. The child traveler was maybe ten, his family was one booth over, several siblings with thumbs to their screens. But the boy was sitting over a travel chess set, spinning the board after each of his moves, playing both sides himself. Steven took the cushion diagonal from him, keeping the greatest possible distance.

"Will you play with me?" the boy asked. Steven inclined his head, his muscles moving independently from his brain, and shifted across from him.

"Do you know the rules?" the boy asked him, rearranging his pieces back to their starting positions.

"I think so," Steven said.

The boy removed the two kings from the now-ready battlefield. He put them behind his back, shifted them an unknown number of times between his hands, and then extended his closed fists so Steven could choose.

Steven pointed to the left hand, and the palm revealed he was black. Steven smiled.

The boy moved his pawn, and Steven mirrored him, so the boy moved the one right next to it, letting Steven take it, trading material for position. The diagonal now open, Steven let his queen fly, forcing the boy to move his king the one space over, giving up the ability to castle. But the boy's pawns and knights went chasing after her. And so she moved, Steven's bishop covering her retreat, until she had to move again.

⊗   ⊗   ⊗   ⊗

AND MOLLY CORBIN LAY prone, masked in the full woodland camo appropriated from the basement stores. She had the reject gun. David had offered her his—a nice, semi-auto, high-powered, well-oiled, paintball-slinging masterpiece—but she refused. David was dressed in all drab, a soil-caked mask, somewhere out there prowling. Molly's team was dead. Tagged. Lit the fuck up. She was all that was left. Her gun was ancient, its hopper lopsided and its air tank a corroded and abused aluminum. The gun had to be pumped after each shot to load another round, gravity fed. Molly sunk into a muddy rut next to a tree. She squeezed herself between rock and trunk, an impossible hole, and emerged on the other side of the brush. The taste of dirt mixing with sweat in her mouth, she let the vegetation scratch against her skin, ignoring the welt on her arm from when she had tested the gun by shooting herself.

A carbon fiber, camo-styled helmet was forty feet away, across a creek, looming outside of a fake wooden bunker. She knew she had to arc it. Three quick pumps, three quick shots, the second making a perfect rainbow in the sunlight over the water, descending and colliding with the side of a head with a thud. A buzzsaw of a circle and she killed two more, these from behind, blurring past a series of watching casualties from her own team. Next was a firefight, but Molly got one on the hand, narrowly avoiding a shot that whizzed past her left leg.

Now David was the only other one still in the game. He was out there, slanting toward her flag or on patrol defending his. Or, he might be doing what he did best, unpaintball like, a sniper in a tree, lying in wait—screw the flag. Somewhere, a shadow or rock or branch or leaf was really David's smile. She zagged. The trees, tall and noble pines, became a cascading tunnel for her to run through. And with acceleration, she let her own exhilaration creep onto her face. A collection of rusted, ancient trucks served as the enemy base. The bandana flag drooped from a stick. The shots rang out.

Molly used the tree house platform, jumped onto the roof of a truck skeleton, and took a running leap toward the pole. David's volleys splashed around her. She left the ground in a spin. Molly Corbin hung in the air, the perfect soldier, the accrued dirt drifting upward in slow motion as her body rolled with a scissor kick, her right arm blindly twisting around her body and lunging for the fabric.

⊠　　⚏　　⊠　　⚏

TGT HAD TIED AN orange bandana around his face, and was shirtless despite the two-layer weather. He wore a penny that had been stenciled in spray paint with "TEAM EFRAM" and the DC flag, a mesh cuirass over his skin. He led the orange deep-strike force, thirty strong. Half committed to back and forth probing actions on the wing, while his half snuck through a driveway path behind a line of bushes, which was technically inbounds, and hid behind the field maintenance shed by the baseball diamond, down a slope and through a faculty lot from the main field. They had expected to wage a speed war from the back, curling sprints up the hill and across the field, attempts to draw and wedge between the formations.

With thirty solid defenders staying behind, Orange had ten people as independent roamers, namely Efram Daniels. He wore obnoxious orange camouflage, a beret topping it off.

Efram Daniels tried the side door to the gym, and met with strange success.

The purple flag was on top of a hill next to the football field, fifteen yards from a curving fence and ten yards below a cement block that jutted out of the landscape. Cones were set in a five-yard circle, delineating a no guarding perimeter. Chloe stood on a wall, and spied over to the jail. She saw the right flank chasing the attempted flank invasion, the orange athletes on offense outstripping the initial patrols. They curved around the side of the building to meet with Marcus's roving band, and catch five, and the rest split between dodging trees on a route back to safe territory, pushing deeper, dragging them down through endurance, and finding hiding places to conduct guerrilla operations.

Three peeled off, and three-letter-sporter Abby Sexton came bearing down at a vicious angle toward discovery of the flag, sagging away from pursuers. She hadn't seen the high traveler. Chloe leapt from the block and pounded her feet, and this was exhilaration. Awake, Chloe's feet struck the ground so hard she made the grass feel pain, depriving the blades of oxygen. *Get her before she realizes where it is,* a heavy mantra chanted with each stride, *get her, get her, get her, get her, drive her into the fucking sea.*

Within ten minutes, Chloe's team had captured almost all of TGT's guerilla force, as well as large numbers attacking off the line. All alone, TGT retreated and then snuck up in the football field's irrigation ditch, surveying the prison adjacent to the entrance to the east wing. It was hopeless. More than half the team was in jail. The thirty-six students lay in a line, constantly touching, holding hands, extending outward toward their territory, in plea for a savior. A dying, bored, gossiping snake, being suffocated by time. Chloe stood halfway between the flag and the jail, overseeing the kingdom. Anthony and Marcus looked up at Pharaoh.

"Go," she said. And they took to their groups. They were now allowed to go on the offensive. The pincer movement would commence. The attackers disappeared over the hill. The panic could be heard as the main line broke. Countdown.

There was a clank and a murmur. Chloe jogged toward the origin.

The backdoor to the school had opened, and nine maintenance workers in their characteristic blue jumpsuits were on the path in a clump. Were they about to get busted before she won? But she had already won. The game was about control. She was in control. They had followed her. That was the victory. Rest assured, someone would lie and tell them that this was an official activity, or Efram had some other plan ensuring they'd be covered. That was his job. That was his game. The group of adults ignored the roaming purple clad teenagers completely, as if they didn't exist, a knife through butter. They took the path away from the flag, curving around the jail, to the parking lot. Alright. Just for a second. But a figure burst from inside the group of adults. The imprisoned serpent curved toward it. Efram Daniels' hand hit Erica Rios's left arm, connected to Jess's hand, and the break was on. The voices pitched high with hysteria. Fury from the defenders, now disorganized and rushing back to toe the line against their freed adversaries.

Claims that it was cheating went unanswered. There had been no rules against entering the school. Efram had used the escaping human wave as a screen and was doing his sad imitation of a suicidal run toward the flag, but TGT and a couple others were near there too, somewhere, ready to move. How many decoys… Chloe knew Anthony and Marcus would still succeed in their drive for Efram's flag, despite the prison break. The race was on. Chloe applied her trajectory and signaled out orders.

"MOVE," Chloe commanded.

‡   ‡   ‡   ‡

STEVEN TOOK THE BOY's rook with a bishop, except the boy did not return the favor. Instead, he advanced a knight to threaten Steven's line of remaining pawns, so Steven took the other rook, but the boy then slung his queen across more than half the board, forking Steven's bishops and checking the throne.

"Flight 2171 is now boarding…"

Steven looked at the board. It was over. Done. Defeated. But Steven did not despair. He focused on playing it out, on picking which pieces would live and which would die. The boy cleaved through the narrowing set of moves, letting

Steven exchange knight for a knight, bishop for a bishop, pawn for a breath, a chance to consolidate.

Steven counted a bishop, a queen, and a knight defending his surrounded and embattled regent. The scattered pawns caught in the fray.

"This is your final boarding call…"

Steven tipped over his king, and reached for the boy's hand.

⬒   ⚌   ⚌   ⬒

FOR FIVE STRAIGHT DAYS, Chloe slept without the dreams.

In the morning bug-sized quadcopters patrolled LeMay's hallways, programmed to hover silently right over teacher, administrator, and security guard heads. Laughter followed. Students waved at their new minders.

PLEASE DO NOT BRING YOUR DRONES TO SCHOOL, Chloe read the notice hastily printed and taped on each door. They weren't sure if it was against the rules or not. Or the notice itself was fake. Part of the joke.

The televisions bred like jackrabbits. Procreating. Installed during all hours students were not present.

This is an 'A' Week! Softball Game is Rescheduled For Saturday. HAVE A NICE DAY.

Outside her science classroom Chloe noticed a wet paint sign, right over a bright red rectangle that had been attached under a fire extinguisher. A box had been bolted to the wall and painted red. Chloe checked. It was dry.

She could find no obvious open or closing point, no clear reason or purpose for its presence. She placed her palm flat against its surface, and waited. It was vibrating. She brought her ear to it, and it was playing music at a whisper.

"Why are you listening to the wall?" Lauryn asked.

Chloe shushed her. A hall monitor was about to force them inside. Chloe walked to the opposite wall of lockers, imitating a spin, the adult not knowing any better, he walked right past. She felt along the top until her fingers caught a wire. And followed it to a break in the aluminum. There was a hole, and Chloe felt curved glass. Lauryn dragged Chloe into the classroom and they sat in a line with Michelle. A brand new projector hovered above them, despite the budget cuts.

"Do you have it yet?" Lauryn asked.

"What?" Chloe said.

Lauryn and Michelle held out their phones under their desks. They both had matching icons on their home screens, a rounded square around two bolts and three stars over the letters "EFRAPP."

"What does it do?" Chloe asked.

"We don't know yet," Michelle said.

"It says 'coming soon'," Lauryn said, showing her the stylized text announcement, which was paired with a rotating array of animated stills. "It's gotta be the parties. Word is he's going to start renting whole venues."

"Who has it?" Chloe asked.

"Everybody," Lauryn and Michelle said in unison.

"What do you mean everybody? Who? Who got invited? Like specifically?"

"No," Lauryn said. "Everybody has it. She gestured to the masses around them. The plebes. "Everybody."

The second the bell rang, Chloe bolted for lunch, Lauryn and Michelle chasing her.

She sat down at Anton Hotz's table, and took one look at his companions, which was enough for them to scram. Only then did Lauryn take a seat next to her.

"Oh, hey Chloe," Anton said, barely giving a look to Lauryn.

"Hey, I—I mean we just wanted to check that things were still better. No one is annoying you?"

"Oh yea, much better."

"Anton, how did the teacher's phones get hacked?" Chloe asked.

"They didn't really. Like, that isn't really hacking. When someone's pictures get stolen like that it means like, someone stole them. You can't remotely get into someone's phone to get them. Or, you can in certain situations when its tied into an email address and you guess the password, but that's probably not what happened. Like, the school obviously knew they were real cause of how they responded, but they held back. They weren't pictures that would have caused the cops to really get involved. It almost seemed like it wasn't a kid. Like a few teachers' pissed off wives and husbands stole their phones and posted it all so it looked like it was a kid."

"So you don't know who did it?"

Anton shrugged.

"But you can steal a text message out of the air, right?"

Anton had folded his arms and was rubbing them nervously.

"No."

"You can't?" She turned to Lauryn, but Lauryn was absentmindedly surfing on her phone.

"Well you can. I've read about it. But it's really hard. Really limited. And it'd be easier to get it right from their phone somehow."

"How?"

"If you can get permission to be on their phone somehow. Get them to want to use something that gives you their data…"

But Anton trailed off, the muscles of his face screwing tight, his eyes losing focus.

"Look at me Anton. I'm not other people," Chloe said.

His eyes came up. He breathed deep.

"I helped you," She patted his hand.

Anton told her everything.

The next day, Saturday afternoon, second semester junior year, Chloe told Efram to meet her at Ft. Reno.

Our Nation's Capital is a jigsaw puzzle. Forget the SW condos, the endlessly gentrifying development zones, how fucking crazy The U was back in the day, the Capitol Hill and Eastern Market dividing line transformation into Southeast, Anacostia reigning. Nothing is really there except schools on the interior and radio towers on the exterior. Pollen and bugs. Federal and tangible. "Smile, you're on camera!" the cement walls of the parking lots told them, knowing the loitering teenagers were coming. Plague of the locusts.

This particular radio tower was anchored at one of the highest geographic points—the largest, the tallest, emanating radiation for half a mile. Woodrow Wilson Senior High School loomed over the minuscule stage in the adjacent park where she sat, weathered wood containing the infinite dust of decades of summers where the others came to free weekend shows, and learned about guitars and alienation. Another school, one that was not their own, loomed a few hundred meters away, the host from which they were cloned.

"I can't believe I was summoned!" Efram said with pride.

"Are you gonna go here next?" She pointed to Wilson.

"I mean, sooner or later I'm going to have to not get kicked out of a place just to shock everyone," Efram said.

"Right. That's your whole deal. Got to keep them guessing."

"But. No. Not there next. I don't think they'd let me."

"Can't buy your way in?"

"Nope."

So that's how he did it. He never lied or fought or showed annoyance or shame at his wealth or how he acted. He laughed along at himself.

"I know what you're planning to do, Efram," Chloe said.

"I didn't know I had plans?"

"Well I figured it out."

Efram sat down where the access stairs hit the platform, gazing at the old brick turret in the background that looked like it was missing windmill blades.

"What?"

"You've been putting up all the new TVs."

"Sure."

"And you posted the thing about all the teachers sexting right before you came."

"I actually was already sort of there, but maybe."

"I read an article…"

"You read an article? Don't let anyone know that!"

"…you have no idea what I read."

"If only they knew!"

Impasse.

"I read an article about this conference, in Vegas, where this hacker guy demonstrated how he could pull text messages from an area and broadcast them in real time."

"Sounds interesting," Efram said. "But I don't think that's very practical."

"No it isn't," she said. "But you could do what the big companies do, and get everyone to willingly give you all their information."

"You could…"

"Is this what you do over breaks?"

"Breaks?"

"When you're not in school?"

"It's not only the text messages. There are cameras. Microphones. And then there are logs of every form of social network. And not just in real time. Almost everything from the past six months, sometimes even a year," Efram told her.

Chloe rubbed her arms.

Efram planned to show everyone everything. Welcome to the century. Fuck privacy. It should not exist. If you want to do something, then be willing to do it or say it publicly. That's it. It was not only going to be the televisions. It was going to be on untraceable servers in non-extradition countries, messages of every format delivered to every student on every platform. No one was safe. Efram was planning on compiling the sum total of teenage cruelty in a single school, and tearing the face off of it. This is who we are and you are. Bystanders would be documented along with perpetrators. Unlimited funds. Even at that minute, Chloe's classmates checked their phones to see if EFRAPP had gone live. Chloe reasoned there could be hidden cameras everywhere, every nook, every cranny. Hell they could've been there for over a year depending on how long he looked ahead. He, and more importantly his endless gang, could have been lounging about in voice mailboxes and hard drives for as long as they wanted. The basement had servers, she remembered, let alone the cloud. She swallowed her rage at the personal invasion of privacy. That argument would not work. He would cry hypocrisy in an instant and be right.

The weekend rush drivers formed their line, never exceeding thirty miles an hour. It was agonizing to plod through. That's what happens when you're penned in by two slave states. Chloe switched her strategy. Emotional connection. Make it like you're breaking the ice and showing truth. She touched his arm, a rub on the hoodie, and a real look in the eye.

"You can't do it Efram."

But he was mad. Or annoyed. Or some emotion that was not supposed to exist in him, let alone roar from his face and body language.

"Why not do it?" he said. "Because it will mess up your whole world by showing everyone what's really going on? What everyone really thinks and says? No more everyone talking behind everyone else's back. Come on. It will be great."

"No Efram. It won't be great." She threw a long caring sigh in there for effect. "You know how many fights there will be? Real fights, not fake fun fights. Blood. Parents will sue. People will hurt themselves."

"No they won't. No one ever gets in real fights anymore. What I'd give to once, just once, to actually have someone punch me."

"Efram, you don't understand," Chloe said. "This isn't some prissy private school. Kids walk around and say shit, racist shit, rape shit, it's bad."

"It won't be any worse than it is now. It's still happening either way. And people know it is! I'm only showing scale. That's it. I'm zooming out and showing the true size."

Chloe switched again.

"If you do it, I'll destroy you. They'll hate you either way, but I'll make sure they really know it was you."

"I don't care if people like me."

Chloe was ready to go right back at him, but then considered that that part was probably true.

"Really?" She checked again.

"Yes. And you're only afraid because everyone will be so pissed at all your crap. You're no worse than everyone else. It will be equal. Everyone will be equal. Don't be scared of that."

"Stop acting like you know me. You don't know me. I'm not scared of that."

"Well then." A wave. "Hello Chloe. Who are you? What do you do? Why are you worth anything on this planet? What's so interesting about you?"

"Hi, I'm Chloe! Every night I dream about the end of the world," Chloe said in a mock tone.

"I know that," Efram said.

"No, you don't."

"You should start playing games," he said.

"I don't play games!"

"Not those kinds of games. Start playing Tetris. Tetris is the best, they use it in sleep studies because like eight in ten people will dream Tetris if they play it before they go to sleep. But it pretty much works with anything. You play a game for a long enough time, that's all you dream, the game. Nothing else. You'll see what you want to see. You'll find peace. You'll see God, or gods, or whatever."

Chloe did not need God or gods. She believed in the bomb. She trusted in the atom. The physicists, the engineers, they had seen that religion had lost its explosive power. Fear of a vengeful heavens no longer held sway now that there were explanations for the misfortunes that rained down. Sanitary conditions caused that illness. Tectonic plates caused that earthquake. For centuries it seemed like the gods were taking revenge on you for previous action. Every shipwreck, every outbreak, every fire—this was the will and the whim of the titans. But that went away, and it went away right as we were getting really fucking good at killing each other.

So we created an actual God worthy of dread, a tangible one, one that would force us to confront species-level mortality, despite all our grand advancements of science, medicine, and art. Chloe knew this was what nuclear weapons really were: divine, uncontrollable intervention. Something powerful enough to end everything in an instant. God's will. Noah and Gilgamesh's flood, except real and subject to the whimsical political, economic, and moral behavior of millions of humans, not the whims of geological or meteorological phenomena.

No longer could you justify a too-horrible action by claiming you were creating a better world for your children. The consequence was too great. Your children might not have a world to call home.

Mutually assured destruction was not doctrine. It was scripture.

"You're going to destroy me and I'm going to destroy you," Chloe said.

We built the bomb, and then to defeat the bomb, we built the network.

Efram gave his patented shrug.

‡   ‡   ‡   ‡

THE SLEEPWALKING UNIFORM AT passport control took his time. He flipped through the pages and actually looked at the stamps, impressed, checking the dates, going back and forth to the computer screen.

He tilted his head to one side and, with a slack jaw and wired eyes, let an unsteady voice speak over the slapping crunch of the stamp.

"Welcome back."

Back in the homeland, the real one, Steven blurred through BWI, no checked baggage. Past Servena Park on the sleight peninsula north of Annapolis, he was at the house by dusk, time difference, crawling up the gravel. The door would not open. Keyless, Steven began trying windows. Mother Marie emerged in a robe, opening the front door while Steven was scaling, leaving it open and retreating back inside. No hello. She was older, wrinkles taking root on her cheeks and hair frayed and gray. Her eyes were marbles in a sunken landscape.

"I've been doing electroshock therapy at Johns Hopkins," she said, fingers along the bannister.

"I'm sorry? Or is that good?"

"Also I have heart disease I'm pretty sure I discovered today."

"..."

"And I think I have a tumor in my lower back."

The house was destroyed clean, floors rubbed with so many chemicals they had no remaining sheen. Bland furniture that belonged in drab business chain hotels in exurb districts had overtaken each room. She waddled into the kitchen flipping on and off lights. She poured a large glass of water.

"Are you doing well in school?"

Steven weighed the cost-benefit analysis of lying, and settled on saying nothing. She knew he did not go to school. Or she must have known. Up the carpeted stairs she went, carrying her goblet. The master bedroom had been stripped of everything except a bed and a television. She sunk deeper under the covers.

"Is it over?" she asked Steven.

"Is what over?"

"Are you here to take me?"

"Not yet," Steven said.

"But it's going to happen soon. I know it is."

"How?"

She pointed at the television.

"Please," she said, "don't kill me, Steven. Don't kill us all."

"I thought you said you were dying all on your own."

"Well I only discovered the heart thing in the shower an hour ago. It isn't beating in rhythm! I'll have to go tomorrow."

"You can go yourself?"

"Don't be like your father. He tried to get me committed. But despite my struggles and my health, they wouldn't keep me for more than a few days. I'm not a danger to myself. I can drive. I can live alone."

She flicked on the television, newscast on mute. Three seconds of tanks on parade, stock footage of a mountain man in rags on a ridge firing an RPG, cut back to the desk. "Parents Complain of Racist Game in Textbook" scrolled into the corner chased by a graphic of a ruler and a book. Marie mumbled something about poor people begging for handouts.

"Don't worry, you won't have to deal with your horrible mother much longer. And NOT because I'm a danger to myself. It's all going to be over soon," she said, pointing again at the TV. "But you know that. You were always good at seeing what was about to happen."

With great exertion, she fished the remote from the waves of comforter and changed the channel, the new colors rebounding off the beige walls.

"Are you staying here?"

"No," Steven said. "But I'm going to take a couple things with me."

"Of course," she said, "Just don't take me."

Out in the hallway, Steven's phone display became the only light source.

"So?" Norman's words had appeared.

"You deal with it," Steven hammered in, saw it delivered, and then pried out the SIM card and pressed it into a recess of his wallet.

Over the past two years, someone had stocked Steven's "room" with clothes that were sure to fit him. He appropriated a matte black garment bag from a hallway closet. Two black T-shirts, two gray T-shirts, one black button-down shirt, a tan duty shirt, a drab green duty shirt, a white dress shirt, dark gray denim jeans, dark gray trousers, a black suit—the wardrobe went on. He laid out the gains on the forever-made bed, and stuffed his selections into the bag. He opened the widest kitchen drawer, which held his mother's wallet, random receipts and papers, and the chaos of modern life. There were three paper envelopes of cash ready to pay the housecleaners. Steven took one of them, almost reaching for the second before jerking with inspiration, wheeling around, and nudging the drawer closed.

Marie's car was in the driveway, but there was a garage—the last vestige of Norman's relation to the house, his office having been cleared and boxed long ago. The two additional cars were all that were left, except for a file cabinet under a tarp and a blanket, but Steven knew it was there. The top drawer was nothing, but the bottom was locked. Dust taking to the air, Steven removed the upper file housing completely and flicked open the lock with a finger. Sure enough, because Norman liked to look the part, inside the lower drawer was a briefcase, also protected by a combination of spinning numbers. Steven entered his birthday. An extra diplomatic passport from back in the day, now surely expired. A Glock 17—what a poser—but then $10,000 and £10,000 and €10,000...of course...banded together like Norman actually might still need it.

Steven removed the money and stuffed it in his jacket pockets. Leaving the gun, he closed the briefcase, and left it beneath the unpacked clothes in a large plastic tub under his bed. Slinging the bag with his backpack, he chose the sedan over the SUV, opened the garage door, and peeled out, so his mother in bed could hear the departure. Three miles away, he used his Norman-enabled credit card to fill the gas tank—a bread crumb, a middle finger, a HELLO!

Four weeks before the end, Steven gunned the engine.

⊗   ⊗   ⊗   ⊗

MOLLY SAID GOODBYE TO David in secret. He would take the bus to Boise, then a flight to Georgia, and go to boot camp the next morning. She offered to drive him, even all the way, but he said no. It was better this way. The sky was orange, a forest fire in British Columbia kicking up ash and coloring the atmosphere.

Molly gave him a spent casing from their first time shooting, weathered by the fiddling touch of skin, the bronze losing its sheen. He enveloped her neck in a khaki shemagh with black stitching, British surplus, the cloth now a blanket talisman. She buried her nose in it, wrap, protector, tablecloth, desk, hood, and veil. She traced fingertips along the underside of his forearms, and he submerged his head into her shoulder. And then they broke apart and Molly drove home.

She climbed up onto her rafter, and lay across its length, arm dangling off the side.

The knock came hours later.

"Come into town with me," Jon said.

Molly did not budge.

"I gotta pick up the mail," he said. "And there's a bunch of boxes."

Molly had never been brought along when he got the mail. She dropped down to the floor.

So Jonathan Corbin sped into relative civilization to the post office. He told her there would be six boxes, three of nimH batteries and three the parts for a new water filtration system.

The post office was in a half strip mall, between two unused storefronts, lines of gold PO boxes in a grid on the wall. The man at the counter lined up the boxes for them to load, three trips better than six, he handed Molly one. Under her chin the address label read –

DEBORAH CORBIN

She walked to the car carrying the weight, slowing down her breathing, calming, waiting, underreacting. The next trip inside she grabbed the pile of mail he had removed from their locked cube, timing it so he would not see her flip through on the way out –

DEBORAH CORBIN, DEBORAH CORBIN, DEBORAH CORBIN…

Bill after bill, notice after notice …

How had she never seen one before?

She threw the paper in the back seat. She made one more trip, passing him again, and loaded one more box before confining herself into the seat. He finished and accelerated away. Back home she let him unload and took the steps in twos, bypassing, smash and grab, right into his office. The cabinets seemed to be filled with educational documents. Printouts. Effects of nuclear weapons. Emergency childbirth. Crop rotation. Finally in the bottom cabinet...

DEBORAH CORBIN

Tax return and...

DEBORAH CORBIN

Bank statement and...

A quick trip to her room, no need to pack, she was her father's daughter. She had a Get Out of Dodge bag leaning against the wall and a duffel at the ready. She flew back down the stairs.

"Why is everything addressed to Deborah Corbin?" Molly asked as he unloaded the last box.

"Well see that way we're safe. That way Uncle Sam doesn't really know who or what is here. We pay what we need to and that's fine. The PO box is it. There's no trace."

Did Jonathan Corbin have any sense of how beautiful his daughter was? Could he tell, even in that moment where he thought everything was A-okay? Was he blind to the doom showing on her face? Maybe it was fatherly delusion. Maybe it was wishful thinking. Maybe it was denial. Maybe it was disguise. Maybe it was the clothes.

Beautiful either way, Molly Corbin was not a tomboy. She may have been wearing an army jacket over an open flannel shirt, but it worked the other way. Maybe it was the fingerless gloves, maybe the freckles under her eyes.

Molly's elbow connected with glass. The drivers' side window of the truck was knocked out. She picked up a cinder block with both hands, used arms as a pendulum and tossed it over the hood and into the windshield. She did not even watch the fracture. The passenger side window was rolled down. She reached in, and grabbed the knob, cursing as her fingers hit a shard of glass but toughing through it to roll the window up halfway. She looked at the wound, pried out a piece of glass, stuck the cut in her mouth, tasting blood, and merely swung her other elbow into the half up window. She withdrew the spraypaint from her pocket and raised it with her left hand, pausing, removing her injured finger, and switching it to her right. "I AM AN ASSHOLE" she unleashed on that side, then the other, knowing the 75 miles to the repair shop would provide enough of a public viewing.

Jonathan Corbin dropped the box he was holding. He did not gawk in shock. He was coming toward her. She recognized his direction before he could even get within twelve feet. Molly Corbin yanked her favorite Sig from her side, not just a gun but a beautiful machine, years of practice and all grown up, no longer the dinky .22, 9mm, trained straight for him, center body mass. Whoa, he almost said with the exhale, the freeze, the neuron crash of the biological operating system.

"What's your plan for this?" Molly said.

He took another weak step and Molly pumped two rounds straight into the ground three feet from him and a third into the formerly intact windshield. Crack. Crack. Crack. Crash.

He cursed with a wail, a shuddering spasm of limbs.

Legs shuddered, bowels failed, sweat trickled, and he cowered.

"What's your plan for this?" Molly Corbin let herself scream. "When the shit hits the fan we'll do this and when everyone else is dying and thugs are killing everyone we'll be safe here, no one will die... But what's your plan for this? Can't you realize part of surviving means *not* making your daughter kill you?"

He sunk to the ground, almost as if he had been fake shot in an old western movie, that cowboy buckling, but Molly didn't need a bullet to strike flesh for the same effect. She did not need to bleed blood. She left him whimpering on the ground, and rockcted away in the vehicle he had once given her.

Molly headed for the very last place he would ever follow.

⊠　　　⸬　　　⊠　　　⸬

MONDAY MORNING, SECOND SEMESTER junior year, Chloe readied herself. Here we go. She texted Efram one last time. "Don't do it. People are going to attack you. You'll probably go to jail. Come on."

She told them all to meet her there early. Spring was showing. Lauryn was attempting a bare shoulder while Michelle was still shivering in a boy's hoodie. Jess was MIA.

"Things could get bad today," Chloe said to them.

"What things?" Michelle asked. Lauryn ignored both of them.

Through the doors. Through the metal detectors. Through the first obstructed part. The first visible television screen was a foreboding blank field. No schedule, no updates, no friendly greetings, no sponsored reminders on nutrition or tolerance. Twenty minutes before the bell. He would probably do it soon, timing the beginning while enough people were milling through the halls. First hallway, another blank screen, they were synchronized.

"Wait here!" Chloe told the two, "and find Jess!" Eye rolls.

Three more screens were blank, dull background radiation, dark energy.

No response from Efram.

She stopped in the middle of a hallway intersection, four screens. The image twitched but stayed blank. Chloe saw Marcus walking past. She almost threw him against the lockers.

"Where is Efram?"

"God. I don't know. Probably on a plane by now."

"It's not a joking thing, Marcus. I need to talk to him."

"It wasn't a joke." Chloe took her hands off of his shoulders.

"What?"

"He's gone. He left."

"Where?"

"Apparently he got into a couple boarding schools in England and Switzerland. Who knows if he was telling the truth. But he's gone. No one can reach him since yesterday. Dude is gone."

The voyeuristic audience still fixated on what could make Chloe put Marcus into the wall. Chloe let go and fled back. She rounded right past Lauryn and Michelle, annoyed, and brushed them off with her hand. ("What's her deal today?" or whatever.) Chloe's homeroom had a display panel outside above the door facing the hallway. She hung under it.

Blank.

Nothing.

It could be coming now. He had fled, god knows if they could prove anything, he had set the bomb and gotten the hell out. Untouchable. Chloe cursed herself. She shouldn't have tried to influence him. Shouldn't have given herself away.

Classmates pushed past, she had to lurch out of the way, teacher shuffling inside. A look through the door. It was time. She still looked up. Plus one minute.

Blank.

Nothing.

"Chloe, we're starting."

The screen stayed blank.

"I left something in my locker," she said.

This was a lie. She kept looking up.

By the end of second period, Chloe worried it would be days. At the short break in between third and fourth periods, Chloe actually did go to her locker. The combo turns, the click, and right above her books was a matte black box. It was six inches wide, four inches high, and seven inches deep. "CHLOE" a label maker sticker said from the top. She held it in her hands, its removable top waiting and wanting. Without looking inside, eyes constant on the screen above, she pulled the top as fast as she could, a squeeze for the trigger.

Nothing happened. Or. Something happened.

Baseball Practice 3:45 p.m. South Field.

This is an 'A' week.

The screens had reverted. Fixed to their supposed purpose.

Inside the box, was another box, even smaller, a withered thick slab of overtaped cardboard. It went into her bag. And then under her bed.

The EDEI was offline. His profile page disappeared. The texts went unanswered. "WHERE IS EFRAM DANIELS?" started in a week. The private school kids chimed in: "He's disappeared before! He SHALL return." They made animations and signs and memetic gifts. The skaters plastered "HAVE YOU SEEN HIM?" stickers with Efram's likeness under a paddy hat on all architecture in a six-block radius.

Chloe monitored. Day after day. TGT posted photos of Efram's lifeless house. "UNSUCCESSFUL," he said.

Anton Hotz said he heard that Efram had been sent to military school. Lauryn spouted some bullshit about how he had been a huge drug addict the whole time, and was now in some rich kid rehab place in Arizona where they took away his ability to talk to anyone. Chloe did the unthinkable. She walked into Mr. Winters' office after the last bell. She could see the miniature drones hiding on top of the row of shelves on the wall, landed and dormant, flightless. He asked what he could do for her.

"Did you know Efram Daniels?"

"Who?"

"The kid who got kicked out of all those private schools. He's gone."

"Oh. Him. I was told about him. But nothing happened while he was here."

"Why did he leave?"

"I don't know. I didn't know he had."

"Can you find out?"

"Not really. I know he wasn't expelled or suspended or anything."

Winters absentmindedly hit the keystrokes, figuring there would be no privacy to violate.

"Yea, it says he withdrew."

"What's the deal with all the new screens in the halls?" she asked.

"Those aren't really my job. I don't know. In our last meeting someone reported on it being a citywide thing."

Once again, Chloe ran away.

At home, it started all over again.

Natalie Joy was tagged in two photos. "I crave sunglasses," Isabelle Phillips said. Ben Alexander liked this. "You are such a loser not showing up Carolyn and I are going to the salv and other fun places," Isabelle commented back. Ben Alexander liked this too. Lauryn had linked horrific daily updates of meals every three hours, and started a thinspiration program of skeletal images. "Lady bug get off my lamp lady bugs don't belong on lamps!" Emily Guerin said. Chloe had to look up whether it was song lyrics or an actual sentiment. Someone named Pleasure Island unanonymously asked The Great Toscano a question—

"I had a dream where Marcus was president and you were his CIA director…"

"I think Marcus being president might be the only time I'd ever find it cool to work for the cops. My first plan of action? Rounding up all the Jews. And reputting them in charge of all the money," TGT answered.

Someone named Sol Hurok ran around telling thirty-four people, both male and female, that they were "really really ridiculously good looking." Private schools handle their business privately.

"The jean shirt, jean pants combo is a classic, his gesticulating made me wanna vomit," Natalia Carpene said about Ethan Wells dancing all thug. Lauryn bought a burner off of Emerson and started relentlessly calling Anna Maddamama Davis an anorexic bitch and a hoe, and then said the boys weren't talking to her because it had spread around how bad her pussy smelled. Kevin

Williamson "fucked bitches and got money". Bridgette Becker told everyone she was proud she had a pornstar name. Anthony responded that Bridgette could fulfill both German and Ebony fetishes. She winked. Uzo Nwagwu got a football scholarship. "Go fuck a goat," Hannah the Starchild posted.

"IF THESE CHILDREN ARE SO INVISIBLE HOW COME I KEEP SEEING STATUSES ABOUT IT #HYPOCRITES" Emerson said.

"I CAN'T BELIEVE YOU'D SAY SOMETHING LIKE THIS," Johnny Halpern commented, "YOU'VE BEEN BORN WITH LITERALLY EVERY PRIVILEDGE."

"IT'S LIKE, GTFO MY FEED, I'M TRYING TO MASTURBATE." Emerson came right back. Chris Kendall, Jack Xirau, and two others like this.

But, along with it all—

"Where is Efram?" Meredith Sadin.

"where did efram go yo?" Sophie Bewley.

"efram daniels is our class's personal jesus Christo," Aziz Fawaz, despite not being Christian.

"where is he?"

"MISSING"

On. And. On.

Once again, back for you, Maret, Sidwell, GDS, St. Albans, et al, wondered if they were next. But common sense had begun its creep. Wasn't public school the last straw? He had missed so much time at this point, was he even a junior? Did he even need to go to college with all that money? It passed squarely from legend to story. Past tense. For LeMay, Efram Daniels became something that had happened. Something experienced and now over.

Chloe fell asleep and the bombs started going off. She was burned alive three times. Smashed to bits twice. Five times she threw up blood and lost hair until she blacked out, only to be stuck on repeat.

Streak.

Contrail.

Flash.

Heat.

Blast.

Boom.

Wind.

Echo.

End.

All repeated in an endless song.

The updates swarmed in with first consciousness. She opened her eyes and then glued them to the screen.

"I woke up this morning feeling spiritually empty, so I put on extra lipstick," Faran Brostoff said.

PART

6

And, lo, there was a great
earthquake; and the sun became
black as sackcloth of hair, and the
moon became as blood;
And the stars of heaven
fell unto the earth...
                    —The Book of Revelation

Tell me what you know about dreams, dreams,
Tell me what you know about
        night terrors, nothin'.
You don't really care about
        the trials of tomorrow,
Rather lay awake in a bed
        full of sorrow.
                    —Kid Cudi, "Pursuit of*
                    Happiness (Nightmare)"*

‡ ‡ ‡ ‡

TWENTY-NINE DAYS BEFORE THE end, Steven stood at Gettysburg. He walked the line of stones representing the high water mark of the Confederacy. He scoped the mixed foliage from Little Round Top. There were stone outcroppings every twenty feet or so, and then random breaks of vegetation turned to dust. Pickett's Charge had heaved across the fields toward Cemetery Ridge, preceded by an unprecedented attempt at massed artillery bombardment.

Steven left the path and wandered into the middle. His hands sunk into the earth. They bathed in the dirt that had absorbed the blood. People focus on the battle, the fighting, the war, the strategy, the generals, the guns, the uniforms... everything but the actual dying. Steven saw the aftermath. The blue and gray taken over by white bandages taken over by red. He saw boys and old men get hit, and then—not like you think, not die and crumple immediately—they staggered, they went to the ground, and they wailed.

Bleeding out takes minutes. Most did not pass out. They soiled themselves. They prayed. They wept. They relived the worst moments of their lives, not their best. The luckier ones drowned in their own fluids, spared the wait. The luckiest had their heads cleared right off by cannonball, or were pierced straight through by bayonet. A boy of fifteen lay disemboweled, lifting up his uniform, watching his internal organs ooze across his trousers, only succumbing once his eyes could see him. The battle was over, the "buffs" don't care about this part, but the gangrene took hold in the gashes and holes. The surgeons' saws sliced through muscle and ground through bone, limbs thrown into wheelbarrows, teeth gripping wooded dowels so patients would still have tongues. Half their souls left on the table. And then another third, sewn up, saw themselves turn red, purple, green, and black. They fevered and coughed and held on, bacteria feasting on flesh, bed ridden in lines, whole tents, whole camps of the dying. Their faces moaned as they waited and plead to be touched or saved. To be taken or forgiven.

Steven's coat flowed in the breeze over the empty grass that would not support crops. He was alone standing in the bloody lanes, where the green ground turned to pale beige brush along the socket fences that zigzagged next to the paved access road. Four field artillery pieces stood on the other side, black sentinels against the trees.

A car pulled up and all the doors opened. A family of four, emerged, taking pictures with their feet still on the pavement. They did not stray from the vehicle. Steven saw the husband, the father grab his left arm. He sat on the back bumper, the wife, the mother, coming to him. He told them that he was okay, felt better, and regained his feet.

Steven started walking toward them.

The man took three steps, and then seized, pulsating like he was being electrocuted, his tongue and lips bouncing up and down making a cartoon slapping noise.

The elementary boy and tween girl laughed, thinking their father was joking. But then he hit the ground.

Steven knows ER nurses call a certain type of heart attack "The Widowmaker." They can happen to anyone. It doesn't matter how low your cholesterol is. It doesn't matter how fit you are. A lesion spontaneously develops in the left main coronary artery, no one knows why, medical mystery, and the body does its job. It takes days, but the cells plug the hole. The lesion clots. But that clot, as it forms, blocks more and more of the artery, until it is completely shut off by plaque.

And then...

Steven knows this has happened to drivers in perfect health on their morning commute, and their hearts have stopped before the car even crashed.

The wife lunged for her husband as he fell, failing to catch any part of him. The kids went silent, stuck solid.

She started to roll him over, gash now on his head, insult to injury, but seeing the foam coming from his mouth stopped halfway. The daughter called 911, the son still a statue. The man's breaths, half snores that sounded like they had been recorded and then sped up, blew bubbles with each exhalation. His eyes went white.

Steven reached the pavement.

It was already over in truth, though it did not look it. Passed out and shivering, what's your emergency, the mother told her daughter to get a blanket.

Steven did not wait for them.

The man started to lurch, to rattle, chest bucking up, everything trying to get oxygen in one last thrash.

Steven dropped his coat over the man's head, and walked away.

⊠   ⊠   ⊠   ⊠

HERE WE GO FIRST semester senior year, the first day, the same-old same-old, the gravimetric flow inward through the doors and metal detectors. There are fewer school shootings in urban areas because they actually have had to deal with violence on a sustained basis. LeMay's first year in existence, before Chloe ever got there, there were several low-scale incidents of black vs. Latino violence, as if this was California or somewhere. But that was a thing of the past. Stomped out with each class year. Murder Capital no more. Only Southeast and PG County still rocking. Throw your hood up high.

Being a senior, a top feeder, had its limitations. Planned obsolescence. The countdown clock started in Chloe's head, and it only got worse. She had no interest in discussions of kings and queens and proms and colleges.

The first assembly of the year was on "vandalism." This deserved to be put in quotation marks. The Efram Daniels Experiment had directly or indirectly caused, or maybe only correlated with, an explosion of creative and artistic energy. Battles of bands and fashion shows and grandiose works of visual machinery had been planned and executed. Some freshman nerds made a pact to build a trebuchet on the first day. A science teacher agreed.

Every surface was being decorated. It was not exclusively scrawling dick jokes and capping tags, though those certainly had their own music and beauty. A cinderblock wall next to the chemistry lab had been painted with a mural of fake oil portraits on dark wooden walls, each fake gold frame housing a school administrator as if they were a nineteenth century head of state. Landed gentry.

The seniors rolled their eyes better than the rest, having been through round after round of "don't do this," and "improve our community," and "let's open this up for dialogue." The air in the gym was saturated with transmission, wave and particle carrier pigeons shooting bits to the nearby cell tower and then straight back to that building. Walls were nothing in the face of the telecom leviathans. The banners proclaiming athletic conference triumphs could not muster a single flutter despite the extreme flow of conditioned air battling the September humidity. Dress code violations were ignored.

"Stickers are as harmful as ink," they were on it now. Old men and dragons and Hello My Name Is and…

"WHERE IS EFRAM DANIELS?" was everywhere, again and again, in plastic vinyl, in positions on ceilings and walls that should have been unreachable. Adhesive colonization.

Lauryn and Michelle talked as if they had been friends with him. Jess kept her mouth shut, once again. Despite the heat Jess was wearing sleeves, a tattered white boy's dress shirt rolled and disused and crumpled for effect. Her stringy hair was up. She did not seem to sweat.

The imitators had sprung up. The faculty lounge had been besieged by rotting onions hidden in the ceiling boards above. Science classes were an exercise in avoidance tactics. Original pranksters weren't so original anymore. The school was explored like it was an ancient castle. Skip parties were thrown in the boiler room. Sprinklers attacked during gym class. The clocks all moved distorted.

Now the talking heads were explaining that defiling school property hurt your education, how it took money that could have been used to hire more teachers or buy new team uniforms. Chloe knew budgets didn't work like that, certainly not in Our Nation's Capital, taxation without representation, but she kept her mouth shut.

An ICBM made its hypocenter over the national mall. There were no windows in the gym, so the light did not exist. Instead, the roar came right before the walls started coming down. The ceiling made for the floor in a giant rip of wind. Bodies flung and baked between seconds on the frozen clock. Michelle's phone died in her hand from the pulse, and then Michelle died from the crush. Chloe's body kicked up into the air, floating, a brief bird's eye view of six warheads striking Our Nation's Capital in gorgeous succession.

Then it returned back to normal.

"The consequences will be serious for those who are caught, but we also want you to take stands with your friends, to help us do this together. Take responsibility to make this school a wonderful, clean place."

Chloe rubbed her head. Two hundred and eighty two days remained in the school year. Fortunately, only twenty-six days were left before the end.

☰　　☰　　☰　　☰

ONE WEEK INTO FIRST semester senior year, they decided to meet. The texts unanswered, the mailbox full, every person they asked had the same answer and then the same supposed rumors. Rehab. Military school. Sitting on a beach with or without his mother.

Almost dusk, they gathered on the sidewalk. Woodley's Raj Chaunduri finally pulled up, meeting Evergreen's Ami Virilio, LeMay's Mario Toscano (aka TGT)—all seniors now—and junior Jennifer Savage of Van Ness Day School. TGT was trying to climb the fence as Raj showed last and calmly walked up to the gate and entered the code.

The metal swung open, and Ami abandoned her sly lean, The Savage left her cross-legged seat, and Raj held up on the walk for her.

"We sure no one's here?" Ami asked.

"There's a one in twenty-thousand chance his mom is here," Raj said.

"He has a mom?" TGT asked, but down the slope a motion detecting light ignited and froze him. "The cops are gonna blame the black kid."

"And give the Indian a job," Ami said.

Ami and TGT started toward the front steps, but felt the other two tracing around the curve of the driveway.

Raj pulled out his keys, fingered the one, and unlocked the back basement door.

"You have a key?"

But the noise sprung forth as soon as the door swung, a beeping warning of the impending alarm. There was no panel down here, but Raj took off up the stairs through the labyrinth to press the code in time. And the wailing ceased.

There is nothing more sacred than a teenager's room. No space more slaved over and defined and revealing of a soul. But Efram Daniels did not have a singular room. Efram had slept on couches and air mattresses and sleeping bags all over the house. Space is the most valuable commodity for a teenager, and Efram Daniels was fucking rich. There was no central hunting area for clues. The Savage and TGT took the hard drives in the basement, scouring directories on the screens. The lower zone still had its ramshackle assortment of furniture. Cracked leather, high-backed chairs ringed the walls, misshapen ottomans strewn across the makeshift chaos zone and dance floor. The upper half still had most of the equipment. Hard cases upon hard cases of audio gear, perfectly locked down and racked, desk banks and lounging arenas. The closet where some of his clothes lived was still full of never-worn kicks and bespoke blazers wreathed in drycleaner plastic. A long desk shelf combo was crammed full of large graphical books on art, graffiti, graphic design, noise, fashion, and naked attractive people. More shelves entered into the breach, with tomes of comics, zines, and music. There were boxes for Japanese remote control tanks that shot airsoft pellets. There was a whole set of shelves devoted to electronic parts, blue boxes of transistors and resistors, motors and microcontrollers. A colony of vinyl toys, bright colored transmuted monsters in hip-hop poses, lived next to a ground level window. Vintage lunchboxes ringed around an ancient television next to an ancient computer, more shoeboxes filled with game cartridges far older than Efram, a line of brand new snapbacks covering an unused turntable. One soaring shelf of vinyl records sat behind the main computers and servers, undisturbed, sample fodder resting at slants within the cubed cells. The miniature kitchen still had a healthy arrangement of frozen pizza products and packaged snack food, like he could return at any moment.

"Is there any paper?" Ami asked. A prayer for a syllabus or school correspondence.

Raj held up a shoebox full of receipts from junior year. He found another one full of crumpled dollar bills.

"We aren't going to find him this way," The Savage said.

Ami sat on the cement floor, amid the scrawled drawings of demons and deformed figures with tagged names and crude poetics, right next to her contribution—

I am Efram's floor,
He's the only man I adore.
I see him scheming and gleaming,
Wanking, fucking, and spanking,

For I am Efram's floor,
He's the only man I adore.

Raj tried to remember Kevin's last name. He hunted for obvious contact info for Efram's mother. He wracked his brain for others. Mailer demons and network alerts told him Asshole Joe's numbers and addresses were obsolete. So Raj went back and typed in the name.

☦   ☦   ☦   ☦

IN WORTHINGTON, OHIO, A teenager's body entered a toxic state. Barricaded in his room, twenty pills deep, smart enough to have taken an antiemetic beforehand to prevent vomiting, committed enough to swallow enough before losing consciousness. His organs failed.

The old woman at the rest stop played backgammon, so Steven obliged. She did not remember her own name at that point, and called Steven her "Sonny." Her wrinkles were a landscape of golden brown, victorious over three rounds of skin cancer, a series of lines for a topographical map. She was ahead by four, and doubled, so Steven doubled again, rolling and catching double fives, clicking his pieces around the corner, reinforcing his wall.

"Ah, Sonny," she said, "You're wonderful. Truly wonderful."

She picked at the wood of the bench before each roll, as if wearing down her fingers to bone would give her an advantage.

Steven rolled doubles again.

"Oh, well," she said, "It was time for me to go anyway. And I'm sure you must be getting along on your way, as well."

"Yes, ma'am," Steven said, adopting an even more American twang.

"Now get it over with and give me a hug. Say hi to your sister. And don't forget to call your mother sometime."

Steven leaned in, and his hands grazed over the scenery of her back.

The dust flew as he pulled away.

Twenty days before the end, Steven accelerated across the plains. He watched the light reflect off the wheat, the machines harvesting, mechanical scythes digging into genetically engineered stalks. Not a cloud above, a quick darkness passed over the car, a floating, thin body fuselage eclipsing enough of the sun to cast a moving shadow.

Flight 3232 from St. Louis to Lawrence, Kansas, a short hop, low cruising altitude, ten minutes without the seatbelt sign, suffered a catastrophic loss of hydraulics on its left side. Autopilot engaged, nothing happened, until the computer automatically corrected for altitude after a thermal patch, and the elevator, instead of slightly adjusting its angle, jammed all the way down. Steven watched the spiraling descent, the structural forces gnawing at the metal, the wings bending both directions but managing to stay connected. Four hundred feet above the ground, engines flamed out, the pilots or God managed to throw the wings level, the elevator sinking back. But there was no thrust, and that brief moment of optimism, the twenty-six in their seats realizing that being able to see the ground was not the same as being alive and well, standing on it.

Steven watched the airplane spin, nose dipping in an attempt to gain speed, but without enough altitude for a stall. Hands on yokes, the pilots wrestled it into their best version of a glide for the seconds they had left. They died on impact, heads thrown right into their instrument panel. It almost struck the ground like a pancake, nose first, and rolled slightly to the left. The fuselage broke immediately, three passengers dying when their heads went straight into what had been the ceiling, the front half severed and crushed, the back half ripping off and spinning, the engines crunched to the ground and igniting the fuel. Four passengers were thrown from the plane when it broke, colliding with the ground, the broken metal leaving them bleeding, severed, or brain dead, and scattered within the crop.

Steven walked down the aisle, the twisted structure now alight in the places close to where the wings had been, smoldering and melting like a forge in hell. Overhead compartments exploded. Bags grew in disfigured piles.

Brains swelled.

Spines compressed.

A teenage girl's earbuds hung from a disconnected armrest, wrapped around the torn fabric, swaying, still playing a song.

Rockies on the horizon, swimsuited bodies ran toward the lake. Two groups of four. They played a game, inhaling and exhaling and trying to hold their breath the longest. They all went under, one did not come up. The breathing reflex did not trigger. Blackout. Panic.

Steven knows that if you can hear someone call for help while swimming, they're probably going to be all right. It's the ones who go quiet, the ones who disappear, they're the ones you ought to worry about.

He drove away as the firefighters were hauling out the body.

New Mexico had emerged from a decade of relative drought, eighteen nights before the end. The sunlight showed that the desert had turned green, kind winters of ski tourism snowfall combined with a generous streak of summertime thunderstorms.

The access roads in White Sands Missile Range were two-lane looping conduits through the nondescript high desert planes, bisecting and multiplying to form uneven polygons where the elevation changed. Nothing for a mile or so, and then there was a fake structure or box, a target from decades past, timber and cement outlines without ceilings. Its circle was in the middle of the route. The road went around it instead of going through it, afraid of trespassing on holy land. The Trinity Test Site was wreathed in a large circular fence. It was slightly bigger than the crater had been. At 05:29:45 MWT all those years ago, pink and gold and white illuminated every peak and valley on the horizon, and the glorious orange and red ball ascended. Even at the safe observation points it felt like being thrown in an incinerator for several seconds. At the center they found a ten-foot-deep crater of glass, a circle with a diameter of 1,100 feet. They called the light green rocks trinitite. Most had been bulldozed and buried when they resurfaced the land. But signs told you not to take the remainders, allegedly because it was still mildly radioactive. Really it was because so much had already been stolen and sold. Twice a year the ground was opened to atomic tourists, cold warriors and southwestern randoms who got to walk the site and take their pictures.

There was a second fence around Ground Zero, the first Ground Zero, the real one, now just an oval with Park Service signs and educational plaques. But then, at the center, marking the hypocenter, right under where the tower that held the gadget had stood, was a thirteen-foot-high obelisk of red rock so dark it could only have been come from the furnace of the earth. This was the origin, it looked like anywhere else, but it was the holy birthplace. Bethlehem was a nondescript city in the West Bank. Steven had been there too, eight years before the end. Lumbini was a tourist and pilgrim trap. Steven had not been to Mecca. At least at Trinity, the earth had actually moved.

Steven knows that park rangers, pilots, and early risers saw the sky light up and the earth shake. The fallout quietly blanketed a free-form, pluming, concentric area that almost reached Santa Fe and Albuquerque.

Steven knows that two months later, it took Tokyo almost a day to realize what had happened. The signal line along the rails simply went dead. The phones went unanswered.

☶ ☶ ☶ ☶

RAJ WAS NOT IN Our Nation's Capital, was not in London, and was not in Mumbai. He was not waltzing into history class at Woodley. Instead, Raj was strolling through Mantua, Italy, the place of Romeo's banishment. Raj was also aware that Virgil was born there, but that was not the purpose of his visit, nor was the House of Gonzaga or the Army of Italy. He had no time for the Piazza Sordello or the Palazzo del Te.

Raj was a twig floating in a river, a way too tall and way too Indian sight for Northern Italy, stuck in the current toward Stadio Danilo Martelli. It was his dress perhaps, his open sweatshirt wreathing a T-shirt that read "Woodley Soccer." Then a man next to him asked on the walk—

"Giuseppe?"

And he shook his head.

"Raj," he pointed at himself.

"No, no." And then one pointed at his shirt, "Giuseppe?"

"Raj?" he patted his own chest again.

"No," and a finger toward the stadium, "L'americano?"

Ah. Ear to ear grin. Si. L'americano. I'm looking for l'americano. And they loved it, they cheered, they passed the word, the young men and working class devotees buzzing with his presence—he was here for the American. They jabbered at him and patted him on the back and led him closer, a badge of honor.

Montova F.C. used to be A.C. Montova, back before its first, second, and third bankruptcies, and various bouncing promotion and relegation stints between Serie A, B, and C. Insolvent and restarted one more time, it now resided in the Lega Pro Seconda Divisione, the fourth tier football league of the Italian football pyramid. Raj took the last crosswalk with the throng, ants in a line. The short walls of the stadium had heavy fences ringing the top, a prison, lest the flares and fights spill out onto the nearby traffic.

Raj made a move away from the flow, but they halted him, so he pointed to where the ticket window was in explanation. But they all said no and led him inward. These were the diehards. Red and white and ready for battle. Furled banners in backpacks. Reaching the entrance the mass ushered forward into a line, and then three peeled off to talk to an usher and policeman. They mouthed and pointed at Raj and the faces of the authority held immediate recognition, and the usher rushed forward and said—

"Americano? Here to watch him?"

"Yes," Raj smiled and made sure to speak slowly. "I am his friend. From school. But he doesn't know I am here. Surprise?"

"Ah! School friend. Surprise!"

Raj pulled out a wallet indicating he needed to buy a ticket, but the short bald man put his palms up frenetically in denial and led him through the gate. Raj gave thankful waves to the flock that had led him there, and they cheered before restarting their songs.

The seats were maybe half-full, thinning in the corners, but the steward led him around to a section on the far side, under the shade directly behind the home bench area. Raj entered the land of the WAGs, the family members, the club employees.

Treviso was the visiting team, in their away black with light blue piping, already warming up. Behind their goal a group of the young had organized themselves among the sparse edge of the crowd into the shape of a massive arrow pointing toward the net, all while holding neon arrow signs vectored on the target.

The steward was pointing him to a seat. The man tried to find the English words.

"No goal for us in four games," he said. Raj made sure to laugh. "But your friend is returned. He have the strappo muscolare. Bad leg a few days, not bad, but is here now."

"Right," he said. "Grazie."

Some of the others in the section pointed at their new teenage 6'4" Anglo-Indian-American comrade, but word spread fast—l'americano. His nearest neighbor, in her designer sunglasses despite the fallen sun, shifted over a seat, took his hand like it was as frail as a napkin, and pointed onto the pitch.

Asshole Joe was twisting on the grass with one leg hanging over his side, held static by the trainer stretching him. Raj's neighbor handed him a program page, the roster, which showed nineteen names with Italian flags, one with the Swiss cross, and then one with stark Stars and Stripes next to the name of Joseph Kaplan.

"Eccolo," she said.

Raj stood to get a better look as Joe took warm-up runs under the lights, number nine on his back. Joe turned back around, and despite the distance, recognition gleamed across his face. Asshole Joe trotted behind the bench to the fence line, and waved Raj down. He waded down the aisle the fifteen rows, right up to the barrier.

"Nice shirt. You fucking got taller," Joe said.

Joe looked more terrifying now, his locks shaved down to a nothing set of hard lines, his shoulders broader and his legs cannons.

"My sister sends her best."

"To what do I owe the pleasure, Raja? How the fuck did your parents let you come here alone? Earliest early acceptance in the history of academia?"

"Where is he?"

"Where is who?"

Raj's face contorted into a stoic death stare.

"What?"

"He disappeared. No contact with anyone."

"I don't know where he is," Joe said, and Raj found it unusually convincing for Joe, normally he would lie for the sheer giggles of it. "You didn't have to come all this way," he continued, but that was too nice, suspicion returned.

"And miss all this? Do not play dumb, Joe. Where is he? You either know or you can find out."

It was almost time, the three overseeing yellow shirted minders testing the ball. The teams were retreating back to the tunnel so they could march out again in unison. Joe nodded a giving ascent, grabbed Raj's hand by the thumb, and brought his arm around him in a hug, and made for the tunnel. Raj moved back up to his seat.

The hardcore supporters' five note Jack White adopted chant, waaa-wa-wa-wa-wa-wa-waaa, morphed into a slowly dying pause, one by one. And then Raj thought he was imagining something: a quick chorus of Yankee Doodle sounded from one side of the stadium, and then was quiet again before the chants resumed, the horns. The teams were coming. Joe touched the grass, the dead music played, and they waited. The dots took their spaces, and the whistle blew…

And the uproar came back the moment he took the ball…Raj did not need the Italian words. He made up his own.

> *Joseph Kaplan went to town,*
> *A-sprinting 'cross the gra-ass,*
> *Faster than your whole defense,*
> *Just give him a nice pa-ass.*

> *Joseph Kaplan, Asshole Joe,*
> *Yankee Doodle Dandy,*

Mind the midfield and the ref,
And with the girls be handy.

The second the curled shot was headed to the upper ninety looping over the poor goalkeeper, the human arrow vibrating with joy, and the singing spread.

The Savage knew that the earliest version of Yankee Doodle Dandy was not about Yankee Doodle at all. It had no Macaroni wig. She knew, so then Raj knew.

The earliest, the first, goes—

Brother Ephraim sold his Cow
And bought him a Commission;
And then he went to Canada
To fight for the Nation;

But when Ephraim he came home
He proved an arrant Coward,
He wouldn't fight the Frenchmen there
For fear of being devour'd.

Two and a half hours, showered and triumphant, Asshole Joe led Raj to his small bedroom above the restaurant where the team met afterward, a boarder with the owning family. He opened a tattered laptop.

‡ ⊗ ‡ ⊗

FOURTEEN DAYS BEFORE THE end, Steven ditched his car in an abandoned lot that once housed a supermarket, hemmed in by a menacing ridge. The fence only existed in spaces. He climbed. A slow sea of lights grew to the left, the late-night remnants of Great Falls, Montana stretched out along the too-dry river. But the other side of the slope hosted the more interesting site. The hike revealing that it was more a mesa than a mountain—a flat curving summit, resembling a massive C plopped down into the ground, a brush from a map editor. A second set of fences at the top had fallen, and the dirt became cement.

Steven knew that from 1953 onward, over 260 Nike missile sites were built to protect the populated areas of the United States. They occupied blocks and badlands, sat upon mountains and islands, and now had become parks, prisons, paintball fields, power stations, air traffic control centers, and storage yards. The missiles that used to preside over them, arrows toward the heavens, had been stripped and retired leaving only the shells that once held them.

Most of the buildings were gone from this particular site, but there was still a cluster of cement boxes hanging in the wind, covered in graffiti and ringed in broken glass. There were ancient teenage messages of curses and love, two or three decades old now, alongside big burners and straight tags. The tallest remaining structure was a single wall, all that was left of a storage bunker, sixteen feet of height extending for forty feet on the far side, only interrupted by a single empty doorway. It had been fully given to the scrawl, layers of paint flecking off of earlier attempts, but along the top, the outer reaches of reach, in fresh red marks against the cement read—

FOURTEEN DAYS
BEFORE THE END

So. Here we go. Here we are. Now.

Fourteen days before the end.

Steven lets his eyes wash over it and walks through the phantom doorway. And here is the real destination. The ridge ends again, and is an overlook. In the zigzagging of farmland is actually a missile field. Someone like Steven can see the pothole pattern over miles and miles. He knows that down the road is a large farmhouse surrounded by chain link fences, a radio tower, and guarding Humvees. And underneath that is a command center with men in little holes, trained to know when to end it all. It is cold down there. They are bundled in robes and blankets. They are watching episode after episode. Clearing level after level. Drilling. Waiting.

Steven comes to rest against a broken concrete slab. Twenty feet to Steven's left, Molly Corbin sits atop a boulder next to her tent, protected from her father's pursuit by the sentinels under the ground. The problem with going straight to Aunt Linda's in Texas is it's the first place he'd look. She needs to wait it out. To give enough time for him to conclude that is not where she is headed, and then in fact head there.

Surveying a missile field is exactly the same as gazing at any other big piece of American land. Except that when you know what is there, it isn't like any other at all. You know the ground could shake and the sky could light.

Offense or defense. It's like being on safari. Watching a massive lion relax from your jeep does not stop the pit of your stomach from understanding that, if you would just make that small leap to the ground, those rehearsed movements... The basking beast becomes a different thing entirely. Who hasn't stood on the edge of the train platform while the horn is blowing, thinking that if I fire my nerves and jump like I have a thousand times before then that's it. Crunch.

Steven and Molly both know that the most likely target for a strike, conventional or nuclear, is not a city but a missile field. The latter half of the cold war was all about figuring out how many warheads it would take to knock out all of their warheads, ground burst PSI versus reinforced silo door concrete. The most threatened cities for those decades were not New York and Washington. They were Omaha, Great Falls, Sturgis. They were the towns, bases, and swaths of ground where the good stuff was. In Omaha, for a good thirty years there, you were literally the walking dead. Three or four hundred commie rockets and bombs were specifically trained on your ass. Strategic Air Command. General Curtis LeMay. Go Huskers!

Molly and Steven get to look down death's door. They get to sit on the rim of a sleeping volcano. They get to climb the trees of a forest begging for a fire. They are surfers during a tsunami warning. Rafters waiting for a flood. Base jumpers on the North Tower and South Tower eyeing each other waiting for the planes to hit so they can jump in style.

Chloe knows that there is beauty, being pretty, being hot, and then there is punch you in the fucking stomach gorgeous: the unfair embodiment of mental and physical traits, developmental mixed with genetic, the kind of attraction and attractiveness that brings fear and anger as often as lust and obsession. Not everyone has to like it, be into it, want to love or fuck it—it is less about that and more about the acknowledgement. The kick in the gut. The eyes popping out of your head. The 'holy fucking shit—seriously?'

Steven is like that. Tall mesomorph, broad shoulders cutting straight down to a perfectly proportioned waist and perfectly proportioned legs; he has muscles without trying, strength without being over the line, and a stupidly symmetrical face and eyes that hold nothing but a terrifying void, over a jaw worthy of an ancient roman commander. Skin dark and taut and perfect. Brooding with expressions evocative of knowledge of the hidden world.

Molly is like that. The preposterously constructed body of a silk-steel athlete. A big cat, a killer, a warrior, cheetah, leopard, lioness, long legs—toned smooth hydraulic levers. All this packaged with the most easy-on-the-eyes face, wavy hair changing color in darkness, skin wrapped around all that tone and curve in a soft shimmer. Shoulder blades poised to spring. Elegant fingers, smooth paws belying powerful claws.

They only look at each other for a moment. An acknowledgement. A "yes I understand I am not the only one who came to the missile field tonight." And they turn back and look into the void, sharing that, even over the twenty feet.

Steven leaves first, hiking back to the car. Fourteen days before the end.

⚏   ⚏   ⚏   ⚏

FRESH OFF THE PLANE, Raj steals one of Efram's cars. Friday afternoon, he gathers The Savage, The Great Toscano, and Ami. An hour-thirty outside Philly, Buckstown Friends resembles a college and has an endowment to back it up. The lawns stretch between buildings, discipline-specific cathedrals from fundraising drives of yore. Weekly Quaker meetings for worship still occur. The teachers are called by their first names. The dorm rooms and lockers have no locks. Students leave their jackets and bags overnight in a corner, able to find them the next day.

For years, Buckstown Friends was cool as fuck, a high degree of freedom along with the IB, athletic, or arts directed academic rigor. Sex in the woods. Drugs in the laundry room. Vice versa.

But now the new headmistress runs a reign of fucking terror, mostly on drugs, but disproportionate time is spent dealing with the "sexual policy," an anachronistic holdover, which states that any act of embrace between students is against the rules. This creates a devastating difference between the day students and the boarders, merely outsourcing all illicit activity to sheltering day students' houses on weekends.

But this week, the students of Buckstown Friends spend their days in constant physical contact. They walk between structures with their arms around each other. Couples and sporadic hookup friends make a show of in solidarity making out. It is now an effective pick up line, tongue in public for the cause.

They drive in circles, arguing over whether they should park. Ami appeals that they need to be cool, to keep the element of surprise, to not look like outsiders. They zag through a post-practice line of parents picking up the day students overseen by a staff member.

The Savage rolls down her window.

"I'm looking for, uh," she looks down at her phone, "'Holmes Sullivan?'"

"And, who are you?"

"I'm his sister?" The Savage says.

"Bail," TGT whispers repeatedly, "bail, bail, bail."

"Oh never mind, he's calling!" The Savage holds up her phone even though no part of it indicates an incoming call..

They yank around a cul de sac, now tramping back outward between Elysian athletic fields under the gray sky.

Raj slams on the brakes. And Efram is sitting there, under a tree against a rock, dark jeans, T-shirt, blazer, white oval women's sunglasses.

The window is open. TGT sings "Waaaaaaatt-ttuuuuuuup Holmessss?"

So there we go Efram, first semester senior year.

"Took long enough," Efram says, and gets in the backseat as Ami scoots into the middle before tackling him. The Savage is in front with Raj, girlfriend rule upending all other shotgun claims, but jumps through the middle onto the pile. TGT pulls off Efram's sunglasses and puts them on. Instead of the interrogation, instead of what, or why, or a grand immediate recounting—

"Where do you want to go?" Raj asks.

"West," Efram says, "let's go west. We have to go west." He points to the electronic compass on the dash.

"Okay," Raj says, "but when do you have to be back here?"

Efram reaches forward through the center, over the bodies, and hammers the GPS out of the dashboard. He plugs, enters the address, lets it calculate, and The Savage pulls back up to her seat and sticks it to the glass.

The estimated arrival time reads 14:03, but Raj does the twenty-four hour conversion and knows that right now, 5:16 p.m. means it's 17:16. And he wonders for a minute how that could be possible and then understands.

"Do you need to get your stuff? Pack or anything?"

"Did you all pack?"

They shake their heads.

"Good. We'll buy clothes on the way."

The Savage tells her mother she is staying at Ami's. Ami tells her parents the truth. TGT had already lied to his parents that he was going on a college visit with Raj for the weekend. Raj doesn't tell anyone anything.

"You sure about this?" he says.

"Yea. Look, worst-case scenario you miss school Monday. I'll fly you all back."

"We have to stop at a toy store," TGT says. He wants an arsenal for the trip.

"I didn't know you were a bend over boyfriend sort of dude," Ami responds, but he is now already hotwiring a new set of beats into the speakers, from the wire passed back by The Savage. She leans over to kiss Raj on the neck, and resettles, scratching the back of his head.

Raj accelerates off of the shoulder and follows the voice and arrows.

    ✉   ✉   ✉   ✉

THE SAME TWO GUNMEN chase her through Metro Center, tossing grenades and hooting behind their masks like owls. Superviruses put her in hospital beds, coughing, skin turning to liquid, massive epidemics shutting down airports and highways, leaving the shotgun toting immune to sort out the rest. It rains until it floods, drowning her, letting her body float through intersections in decomposition. Superstorms, snow hurricanes, full-on ice ages, she freezes to death, cut down in the snow while running south to escape. Then the opposite: thirst, hunger, crop failure, drought, the endless glory of the dramatic climatic catastrophe, dust and desert let loose on her world. She chokes from poisonous clouds. She spends too much time in the sun when the magnetic field disappears, birds dropping from the sky. A caldera kicks up and douses the hemisphere with ash. She burns in a pyrotechnic cloud and starves in a parking garage basement. A tank runs her over on North Capitol Street. She is beaten, raped, and scalped by wasteland bandits. The rapture comes true, and the earth breaks apart, and she burns while watching asshole evangelicals float to the heavens, so psyched at having not watched too much porn. At least in that one she wakes up laughing. She wanders through the ruins of endless cities and wraps her head to counter radioactive dust once she reaches the suburbs. Incendiary bombing runs. Her house turns into a furnace. The air ignites. She becomes a charred body among hundreds of thousands. Meteors and comets do the job too, detonation, quake, tsunami, dust, heat, cold, starvation.

All this, and still there are the self-inflicted blasts. Large scale, high-megatonnage, single airbursts take out the whole city. MIRV spread saturation attacks. Dirty bomb sprees. The blue, the purple, the orange, the white. That illuminating moment before she is put in an oven and the air becomes the enemy. The boy from the school stalks her. Hunts her. Haunts her.

She wakes up to bloody sheets, having scratched her skin thinking it was peeling off (because, it had been peeling off, melting as she vomited).

Chloe reaches down under the bed and retrieves the box Efram had left in her locker. No longer afraid, she opens it, unearthing the plastic gray box, ancient, from another era, not even a color screen. She flips the switch and the Kremlin materializes.

Chloe begins to play the video game. She presses the buttons. The seven tetriminoes fall from the sky into the brick gash. *Music A*, "Korobeiniki," Russian folk music blares in eight-bit form. Chloe makes lines. Her structure reaches for the stars in imperfection before its height is cut down in triumph. She learns to click offenders into position under overhangs with last second rotations. The rain speeds up. She figures out that clearing four lines at once gives more points. She starts stacking everything to the left side, willing to go higher and riskier to allow single width gaps for when the flat girders would come down. The pieces become people. The gaps become obstacles, social and political problems, issues of isolation. She makes errors with a spat of Z- and S-shaped vectors and her first game ends. She closes her eyes. And then she feels it. She sees it. Her brain is still playing Tetris. Her mind is seeing the falling blocks. Booting up another, starting on level eight this time, no need for the slow, they rain down again...

Faster and faster, hands clapping to the tune, the polyominoes now shooting down like lasers. Put all objects into their place. Make the structure a structure so it can vanish. Take every element and give it order, and once there is order, there is glorious nothing. Meditative bliss, a complete line off of your mind. She can see the preview of what block is coming while dropping the next perfectly into place. She curses errors, banging the ceiling when it got too fast after a tricky run of inefficient leaves.

When does she stop playing and when does she go back asleep?

Unconscious, all she sees are objects given to gravity, geometric shapes tracking down the black background, waiting to be rotated into place. Skyscrapers go higher than any screen could accommodate, previous floors vanishing in line-ending haze, floating orbital platforms, superstructures. Organize everything into its place. Put it all where it is supposed to go. No end. Keep going.

Only once does the scene melt into the experience of suffering through a detonation, of watching Jess burn to death while she hides under a minivan.

"What are you doing?" Lauryn says to Chloe in the hallway, and she looks up from her phone, ported, as she guides blocks downward. Lauryn looks at the screen and walks away.

Chloe does a full two hours before sleeping the second night, and sees nothing but sinking foursomes under gravity's pull. Awake, new visions torture her. Nukes falling while watching a teacher whine or pretending to listen to Michelle pretend to complain about some boy's cock. Chloe needs more. To make the screen scroll another direction, make her float above the land as a god.

⊗   ⊗   ⊗   ⊗

MOLLY SPENDS THE NIGHT in a highway rest stop parking place. She creeps southeast, only stopping for food and bathrooms.

Her sleeping bag is stretched across the very back part of the trunk, her legs poking through a folded-up pass to the backseat. She is thankful for the tinted side windows. Thorough paranoia has its uses. From the windshield it looks as if the vehicle is empty.

Eyes open, squinting through the tint, Molly can tell it is still the middle of the night. The watch says 3:45. She rotates her head carefully above the line of the window and completes a full 360-degree search for anyone close by.

This is a truck stop. She is unsure of the legality of sleeping in a car here. Being sixteen could make even the slightest suspicion catastrophic. Molly does another rotation, finds her jacket, and exits the car from the back. The lot lights wash out all traces of red. To her right, big rigs house other slumbering bodies. The building is not small. The gift shop section, overflowing with the worst possible doodads of Americana, screeching eagle sculptures and motorcycle models, is mercifully closed.

She tiptoes down the hall, finds the restroom, surprisingly clean, and then makes for the larger opening. The food options are typical gas station fare, but magnified by greater architectural scale. She sizes up the aisles, taking stock of the fat man about to make his purchase and the skinny redneck, possibly methed out, waiting behind him. She times her entrance with the last exit. Molly takes another opportunity for the glory of pure junk food. She grabs a large bag of pretzels, a large bag of popcorn, a chocolate bar, and a pack of skittles. Even though there is enough water in her car for a desert breakdown, she grabs another bottle from the refrigerated, windowed doors. She picks up magazines by which covers look interesting, moving quickly. A fashion option, a car option, and an interior home design option. She cradles it all in her arms.

The clerk is a girl, young, maybe twenty or twenty-two. The girl's eyes are unblurred by the time, no obvious effects from working the nightshift, no exhaustion on her face. A TV putters away next to her, unmuted, commercial break unleashing an infomercial for a window-washing squeegee.

"Hi there," the girl says as Molly puts her things forward.

"Hi," Molly says. Don't draw suspicion by being weird or quiet.

The red light scans the barcodes and emits its laser beeps.

"You're not from around here are you? Just passing through?"

"Yep. My family's in the car. Brother and sister passed out." That was good. Nice. Detailed.

Molly catches the police car circling without moving her head, maneuvering around for a spot.

"Lemme guess," the girl says, "New York? Or is it LA?"

Molly tries to see if she had accidentally picked up some item that would have led to such a conclusion, but could not muster a reason. No comprehension.

"New York," Molly says, "But how did you know?"

"You have that look about you," she says. "I really love your hair."

Molly runs a hand through the mess upon her scalp. Seconds before it had been enshrouded in the mummy hood of down synthetic subzero ready nylon.

"Thanks," awkward, but good enough.

"Have a good night now," grab the bag.

"You, too."

A cop, or trooper, Molly guesses, has parked on the food mart side of the pavement, the side with the eastern lanes of I-15. Molly reasons she can safely come back the way she came, through the hall to the dead gift shop. But the low volume crackle makes Molly stop. The late night local news is stuck on repeat, and it shows white smoke.

"The fire crossed the border?" Molly asks.

"Oh yea, you hear about that? Yea, it crossed a couple days ago and looked like it was done but then the wind picked up suddenly and it kept going west. It's huge. Maybe the biggest ever around here."

Home footage of the wall of flames approaching a roof.

The news graphics announced the area covered three states. A door opens on the side the police car had parked. The TV says the fire could track southwest all the way to Spokane, but for now the hazard yellow on the map is confined to the northern and western edges of the panhandle. Molly does the trigonometry.

She makes for the car and keeps her head down.

⠒ ⠒ ⠒ ⠒

THERE'S BEEN AN HOUR or so of vintage moogtronica, a deathset of garage and rockabilly, a roving backyard jam of o.g. DC Chuck Brown go-go, endless jumping playlists of thugged out gangster melodies and emotive road-trip ballads, but not yet any Balearic house, Mancunian percussion, teutonic techno, Croydon deathstep, or guerilla radio drum and bass. Much later on, they'll begin blaring ancient rock and roll through the desert, knowing the music of their parents and grandparents better than they ever could have. But they're fifteen miles outside of Kansas City, burning on a mixture of ambient IDM psychedelia being released at the lowest possible volume. For the first time, they've stopped the updates on the educational institutions of yore, on the media of media and the end of days. The Savage is driving clad in little boy clothes from the toy store, a pajama top covered in talking anthropomorphized multicolored racecars, with green glitter on her face. She's the most awake, inscrutable, having entered a state of borderline narcoleptic unconscious during the elongated sunward evening so she would be able to stay awake and drive without energy drink enhancement. TGT is out cold in the middle, eyes wide shut under old person drugstore sunglasses, and Raj is on the verge of sleep behind The Savage, eyes open but losing focus. Ami is leaning back in the far corner and watching the window like it's the greatest show on earth, wearing a hideous drugstore bought XXXL T-shirt with a giant American eagle looming over an eighteen-wheeler.

Efram is riding shotgun.

"So what did you do this summer?" The Savage asks in a quiet indoor voice, but drained and drowsy Raj laughs, and not a nice laugh, and says—

"That's the first real question we are going to ask him?"

The Savage shoots a pair of evil, discolored eyes through the rear view mirror, and waits for Raj to revise. Ami readies with a turn of the head. TGT's head suddenly droops with a soundless snore.

"How about 'Why did you leave Efram?'" Raj says.

"You don't need to answer that," The Savage says.

And Efram Daniels puts his leg up on the dash and leans a head against the window.

"And then how about 'Why did you stop talking to all of us?'"

"What, you didn't get my telegrams?" Efram says.

And The Savage preempts Raj's mouth from opening, with her arm squeezing between the door and the seat and grabbing his knee.

"Don't be a bitch, Raj. He fucking left because of Operation Plop. Wakey rapey bakey," TGT says, apparently more awake than his face is, almost drooling in slack.

"It wasn't called Operation Plop," Efram is laughing.

"Well that's what it ended up being. Plop. That Chloe bitty got to him. She's the queen gnome," TGT says.

"Queen gnome, Mario?" Ami asks.

And TGT sticks out his tongue his mouth open in a faux-exhausted pose, jerking his whole body forward and flailing his arms. Raj shoves him.

"Wait," Ami asks, "Chloe, the LeMay girl who came to that one party?"

TGT does the shuttering affirmative again, still hasn't opened his eyes

"What do you mean, 'got to him?'" The Savage asks.

"She gots her hooks into him, her lady hooks, her vag teeth. Thought it was normal Chloe shit, but not with Efram Daniels, there's nothing she could put out on him. So really it wasn't her. It was him. Efram messed up. You fucked up E. Never like actually love 'em. Shit."

Ami punches him.

"Wait," Raj stops, and forces the remaining lids to open, "you fucking left because you were in love with a girl?"

"No. I wasn't in love with her. I just liked her, that's all." Efram says. "And leaving was the only way to get her to trust me."

But Ami is laughing, hard—like, hysterically—a Hyena on PCP. And they all turn, except The Savage, who has to keep them gliding down the lane.

"Oh, Efram," she says.

"What?"

"Chloe, the girl from the party last year with her friend who they said you should date to fuck with the school?"

"Yea…"

And she's laughing again and waving her hands.

"I'm sorry. It's not funny."

TGT closes his eyes and starts flailing again to make her explain.

"Efram. She's not into dudes."

"You say that about every girl." TGT says. "She's like the main girl in the school, or whatever. You know I don't really pay attention to that shit, but she like has all these boys running around her, and all the girls scared she's going to steal their man, or whatever."

"Says the guy who thinks there are no gay boys on the football team."

TGT gives a fake snore. Ami keeps going—

"No, she's into chicks. She's obsessed with women. I mean a bunch of that type secretly are, even if they don't know it. All those cliquey female groups are more homoerotic than the boys wrestling team. The power plays, the obsession with sharing and being shared to—especially about sex. God, all the magazines and gossip and picture stuff. Look at the ratio of images of beautiful women to beautiful men. They're all obsessed with the ideals of the female form, the flattery and the self-demeaning comments. Think of the breakups. I mean they have fucking breakups!"

TGT exaggerates a yawn. Ami hits him. Raj puts a sweatshirt over his head, retreating from the conversation.

"Listen, Theresa," Ami imitates, "the three of us came here today because like, you're never there for us. You went a whole week without texting me to find out how I was. Like that isn't okay?" She switches back to her normal voice. "What the shit is that? Being a friend is like, about that. It's being there when someone needs them. But all these girls create friendships under romantic terms and pressures. Obligations and expectations. Fuck. They all really want to fuck each other. I shouldn't generalize, I know. Only some of them want to fuck each other. And your one, Chloe, she is at least real about it. She wasn't, like, pretending. She knows what she wants. She was scoping out every girl in the room, Efram. That's who she was looking at. And she was all over her friend. Possessive and shit."

"I wasn't into her like that," Efram says.

"He couldn't dooooooooooo it," TGT says. "And dummy dainty Efram just wanted to be liked, awwwwwwwwwwwwwwww. Operation Plop."

TGT tells Ami, The Savage, and Raj (if he's awake) about the suspected social network surveillance aggregator that had been assembled at LeMay. Consensus is he avoided arrest and a public, cable-news show trial by not following through with it. But Ami doesn't buy it. Some people who tell the tales of Efram Daniels exaggerate.

TGT starts shooting Nerf pellets at where Raj's head should be. They stick to the window when they miss.

◩   ◩   ◩   ◩

CHLOE BREAKS BRICKS ON her phone in history class. The ball flies into the wall of multicolored blocks. Her paddle snakes back and forth under her desk.

"They planned the music for the formal," Michelle says.

"Oh yea? I'm so interested in that, I can't think of something that would change my life more," Lauryn replies.

Chloe builds a skyscraper in math class. She puts shops and movie theaters above the lobby—a mall—with ten floors of offices before the luxury condos start. The elevators shoot up and down, their sounds muted. She starts her hotel on the far side, single rooms in a block, housekeeping in the basement next to a security center. She kicks out low renters in favor of higher paying tenants, upping lease rates every year and renovating degenerating purchases. Another ten floors and she can pick a sculpture garden, an ice-skating rink, or a television studio to take up her courtyard. She already has a media company as tenant. Her scaffolds reach for the top of the screen, the windows turning from light blue to the purple of dusk. She builds twenty-four hours a day. The workers aren't pictured. Express elevators are moored in the new lobby on the sixtieth floor. A gym and a pool. She jacks up rents.

"Sarita fucked Christian," Lauryn says.

"Christian Perez or Christian, uh, the sophomore," Michelle asks.

"Perez."

At lunch, Chloe sets up towers and defensive emplacements, letting the goblins wade into the kill zone. Her castle gains turrets and pinnacles with each level, rising higher and spreading wider. A chapel heals her archers. An engineer puts engines on her walls. A banquet hall doubles her cartoon knights on the walls. The goblins bring orcs with the next wave, and the green freaks are decimated by the storm of steel, coins going into her purse when each gets knocked off the plain.

Paulina Miartusova walks past their table, face blank, and Lauryn swallows a gasp.

"Yea I heard!" Lauryn says to no one.

"I didn't, what?" Michelle asks.

"She got roofied last weekend," Lauryn says. "It was really fucked up. Date-raped and then almost ODed."

"Should we say something or do something nice for her?" Michelle asks.

Chloe climbs into her bed.

"How about this one?" Anton asks, link embedded. This one message Chloe does not ignore.

Chloe infiltrates the facility. She waits in shadows for guards to pass. She rewires cameras and hacks electronic doors. She pickpockets keycards from slumbering workers. She scales walls and climbs through windows. She talks her way in and talks her way out. Alarms cease to function.

Eyes close, and she does it again, she plays on, penetrating office buildings, police stations, hospitals, Chloe steals with stealth, pulling plugs and taking files.

"I hate it when people tell me I'm pretty as if I don't know I'm hot," Lauryn says.

One hundred and eighteen other new updates lie unread in Chloe's feed.

"OH MY GOD GIRLS NEED TO STOP COMPLAINING ABOUT GETTING REPLACED IN MY PROFILE PIC. IT'S A CYCLE, EVERYONE GETS A TURN," Emerson says. His hair is now short.

TWELVE DAYS BEFORE THE end, Molly Corbin walks through the hospital doors in Spokane. She skulks up to the desk.

"I'm here for Jonathan Corbin," she says, no eye contact.

"Are you Deborah Corbin?" They ask her.

"Ummm, no?"

"You aren't Deborah Corbin, Kentworth Gardens, 4530 Lorraine Terrace, St. Louis, Missouri?" They look at the file.

"No," Molly said, "I'm their daughter."

Whispers. Corrections. Rattling of keyboards. They print her out a badge and start talking.

He had been trying to make his own firebreak, they tell her. She imagines him starting up the tractor in the shed, attaching the minidozer, and felling and moving the trunks between the house and the tree line. He did not realize that the fire had jumped the main road eight miles away and dipped down along a ridge line, and would now attack from the south in its quest to gain elevation. This meant that it ignored the clearing he had been laboring on, and swept upon him as he drove or ran, at the same time it circled up the other side of the oval and threatened the house. The smokejumpers found him, they tell her. There was no way to get him out for three hours, but eventually by road he was taken to Boundary Community Hospital, and then airlifted there, to Spokane. She had tried first to get to the house, but met the roadblocks and did the math.

"Your dad's in very bad shape," they say, "second- and third-degree burns. He has head injuries from a fall. We're keeping him sedated. Do you know what that means?"

Molly asks to see him, and they lead her into the room. Molly cannot remember if he had visited her when the situation was reversed. It must have existed, there must have been a time where her form was broken in a hospital bed, hanging from a hospital ceiling, and he was next to her, but the image is unsummonable.

The ventilator lets out a gentle hiss. He has an IV in each arm. His skin is still swollen and red where it still exists, so much is slathered in gel or bandage. They probably expect her to say something. To hold his hand. To ask when he can come home. Molly does neither. This is a dead man not walking. Molly reminds herself she is a minor. They will not be asking her about a living will, or giving her the absolute truth. And they will not be pestering her about insurance or treatments. She is a passenger. Molly Corbin does not always remember that she is a kid. He had at least trusted and treated her to that extent.

Approaching the bed, half of his bloated and torn face is concealed under strings of bandage, the white ending taped to the tube entering his throat. His chest, in need of too much treatment for clothes, is a mangled structure of the weight he gained over the years. Blood starts to pool. His eye is shut. But when she leans in, and can hear what is left of his body, when she is close enough to actually touch some unaffected part of him, she hears movement behind her.

"I'm glad you got a quiet moment with him," a nurse says sliding from the curtain. And there are beeps and two more enter as Molly backs into the corner. They leave again, and Molly is alone with him once more.

She pushes her brain into aggressive overdrive, a search for what she is supposed to say in this situation, a steeplechase through the obstacles of the paralysis. She shuffles back up to his body. No prayer, no saying, no message of love in his ear, no brush of the forehead (if he had a forehead). Molly takes a breath. And turns.

Back in the waiting room they ask her about her mom and family: who would be taking care of her?

"My aunt is on her way to pick me up right now," Molly says. Code for not calling social services. They believe her.

She shifts out of her seat while the receptionist is on the phone, makes for the elevator. The automatic doors give way to a torrential downpour, a wall of water that might allow her passage back to the house.

⊠   ⊠   ⊠   ⊠

CHLOE WAKES UP AND goes to school.

First class and Jess is sitting between these two kids who usually spend the whole time hitting on her, but this time were serenading her with songs from cartoons.

"Stop acting so homo," Lauryn says.

This half-white, half-black, Rastafarian dude is staring at Jess from the side, and she starts toying with the edge of her shirt, revealing enough skin to make him think he is about to get the beginnings of nipple pigment, and then she stops, staring off into space.

Someone draws a swastika in the boy's locker room.

Freshman Jana Hendry decides that Sheena Maroni is irreconcilably uncool. The enormous frosh empire is instructed not to speak to her.

Sheena sits down at lunch and the entire table moves. The young'uns do good.

Chloe escapes through the side door. She plays and she falls asleep.

Chloe's town survives the apocalypse. They build in the ashes. First a fort, a citadel of aluminum siding, a headquarters in an old barbershop. She sends scouts to salvage the ruins. She stockpiles bullets, food, and water. Her villagers get the sawmill up and running. The carpenters raise bunkhouses. The walls are reinforced. The treasure is buried.

Chloe assembles real teams to venture out, to comb the wreckage of once civilization for anything useful. Her squads are picked, a medic here, a soldier there, a technician, a scientist, a criminal, a brute. They are outfitted with clothes, rations, weapons, and gear.

She leads them through the wastelands, through the scorched deserts that used to be jungles, the jungles that used to be cities.

She waits for the bandits to attack, to come across the evil empire's borders. For the dead to rise, or the radiation to breed unimaginable monsters.

But her parties encounter nothing. Empty space. Skeletons.

She loots, and moves on.

⊗   ⊗   ⊗   ⊗

MOLLY CORBIN LEAVES HER tent. It's set forty feet from the house on a flat patch of grass, ringed by the now dead forest. Some green is still visible. About half of the house still stands, the reinforced walls doing their job, but the kitchen, the porch, and the slanted roof are now charred remnants on the ground. After careful testing it is clear the bottom floor had held. Jon's shelter withstood the heat. The hard boxes from his bedroom and office had caromed to the ground once the supports gave way. Molly's gloved hands rescue them, caught under the wood and metal, and remove the medicine, the papers, gold, and guns. She finds her birth certificate and social security card in a file in the ruined clutter, ten feet from where the office used to be. Next to it are her medical and educational records. But then there is also a folder marked "Deborah." Molly's shell mother apparently has a bank account with an ATM card, along with a photocopied living will. Molly crams it all into a neoprene sleeve.

The large shed with the vehicles was obliterated, but three of the smaller sheds by the vegetable patch and field survived. They give her some tools to use before she penetrates underneath. She clears the last pieces away from where the basement stairs should have been, finding their cement elements scarred by drying water. She walks back to the tent and puts on her rubber boots. A precaution. She takes one last look at what was above, making sure no heavy objects are left waiting to cave in on her. There's a small pool of water before the first door. Molly comes back up, steals a pump from the irrigation shed, and covers her ears while the rainwater moves. She leaves it set up in case the first sanctum suffered a similar fate, and balances on the step as she opens the door. The pantry, more or less, has made it. There is an inch or two of water pooled in one corner, having snuck in through part of the ventilation system, but the rows of food and seeds are right where they had been left. The smell of smoke had made it down. She does not dare open the walk-in fridge, since it might have been without power for too long, avoiding the stench of the spoil. She ignores the food and comes to the second door. This part she knew would be intact from the beginning.

The blast door opens and the air rushes. The fuel cell generator is on standby. The independent ventilation is running. The server meant for backing up Jon's hard drives gives its friendly beeps. The shelves with the gear, the guns, the bullets, the clothes, the emergency provisions, and the tools all lie ready for her.

Molly's vehicle benefits from being a Jonathan Corbin reject. It had been modified with two secret panels under the backseats and back for traceless transport. Molly Corbin fits a carbine, a rifle, flashbangs, grenades, and three handguns, plus spare parts, casings, oil, and ammunition in the space, along with a small case of gold and cash. Daddy's girl. She sets aside the rest of the valuables—minus additional stashes of cash in the glove compartment—under the front seat, and in each of her five bags. She has a red civilian looking hiking backpack, small, for her everyday travel needs. The leftover magazines, a wallet, keys, her mother's Bible/bug killing weapon of choice, a water bottle, and a stack of cash hidden in a black zipped bag, all join a toiletry bag. She has the large duffel she first left with and the chosen clothes, the ones that survived in exile, joined by the utilitarian additions from the basement. It has her favorites: the red mesh shorts stolen from Luke, the special forces shemagh David wrapped around her face, the childhood T-shirts that stretched but still fit, the bras she bought herself as soon as she had a license, and the greatest hits: dresses, hoodies, jeans, and skirts Jonathan had allowed her to pick every birthday—the same present every year, perfect for the father who does not know what to get his daughter. Any clothes you want, he said, and then he drove all the way to a real city store. Or, later, they would sit at the computer together as she made her choices.

She has a second, large, duffel that can be converted into a large backpack and holds all the secondary camping and survival gear. Extra outerwear, iodine tablets, MREs, blades. It is accompanied by her original military grade

ACU camouflage G.O.O.D. bag, restocked, repacked, and ready to run. Last she has an almost empty black 3-Day assault pack, MOLLE webbing with custom pouches and holsters attached, and a bladder for water supply. Curled inside its main compartment is a matching MOLLE tactical chest rig also outfitted with holsters for possible aggression. She applies to its blank strip of black Velcro David's INFIDEL patch, the black letters across the olive, ranger tab-shaped background.

Molly takes the remaining arsenal, a dozen hard cases, and box after box of ammunition, and lifts them onc by one into the large rectangular hole she has already dug and insulated with a tarp. She centers the weapons cache under a tall pine that survived on the border of the clearing. She sweats, stripping down to hiking boots, dirty baggy work pants, and a black sports bra. After the last lift, she fills in the grave. She paces back to the house, counting, in case the tree is felled, memorizing that number. Then she locks both doors to the basement, with double padlocks harvested from the sheds. She hides an extra set of keys in the agricultural shed.

One last hole, twenty paces from the house, in the grassiest square, is given to the remaining gold and cash. She jacks up her legged bathtub from the wreckage with a chain winch, loads it onto the trailer, and four-wheels it over to the packed dirt.

She breaks down her miniature campsite, and adds the larger tent bag and her sleeping bag on top of the rest.

Molly spins around one last time.

She smells the trees.

She strips down to nothing, shivering, discarding her sweaty, ashy, and muddy rejects, pumps the ground spigot connected to the hose, and showers over the last grassy part of the lawn.

She listens to the woods and stalks back to the car.

She pulls a three-sizes-too-big shirt over her head and bites her lip.

Molly Corbin places a large envelope with "Dad" written on it in a waterproof black bin, and leaves it on what used to be the doorstep, just in case.

Ignition.

The day you were born changed my life, the parents say. They make your birthday a pin number and an alarm code. That's how much they care about you.

Thank god it's all automated now, no IDs necessary, and Molly walks into the bank, swipes the card, and enters her birthday in place of the pin, and the teller hands her the statements.

"Anything else I can do for you, Mrs. Corbin?"

Molly almost corrects her. And then realizes.

She rifles through the pages and sees the rhythm, every month, each payment in clockwork step. "Kentworth Gardens" they say. The search box finds her apartments in San Francisco and a gated community in Florida, but then, third down, a long-term assisted care facility in St. Louis.

But first.

Twenty-six hours to Texas.

THEY'RE A MISSILE NOW. They take states like falling dominoes, driving and sleeping in shifts, lined up like Rockettes. They live off of packaged snacks and fast food wreckage. Efram's credit card besieges gas stations.

This is the true Fortress America. A system, a network, the clustered replication of franchises coast to coast. Roads connect one giant mall made up of all the smaller ones, nodes with nodes with nodes. Brand name, brand name, they can stop and get anything. They know that Albuquerque will have what Oklahoma City did.

Four days before the end, first semester senior year, 3:48 a.m. there are 58,758 human beings directly en route to California. They grip dirt, pavement, and tarmac on six continents, float over four oceans, loop over the North Pole, all taking advantage of the curvature of the earth, all in orbit. 9,268 of them are listening to music. Eleven have hidden earbuds under hoodies so they can keep jamming during takeoff and landing. The Savage doesn't need to sleep. Efram is driving. She is lined into the car directly, letting her loose on the system with actual control, not ever a passive playlist. In the back, Ami stretches out, using TGT as a pillow, and Raj takes advantage of the legroom The Savage gave him by moving up. She is sitting cross-legged, lit by the touchscreen, manipulating pitch and beatmatching deaf, no cueing needed, knowing each note and beat of each song so well that she doesn't need headphones and can do it by sight and feel alone. So The Savage coherently assembles songs related to California into one streaking set. And she doesn't announce its beginning. 104 people on the way are bumping *California Love*. 135 are bouncing to *Goin' Back To Cali*. Biggie is winning that battle. Of the eponymous entries, fifty-six are swatting to Led Zeppelin's acoustic ballad, four are passing out to Low, eight are knocking out Wiz Khalifa, six are humming to Rogue Wave, and eighty-six are listening to Phantom Planet rock the state (combining the original, secondary, and live recordings). A really cool twenty-two are smart enough to pick Mates of State covering Phantom Planet. Four are listening to either version, beginning their journey walking the streets of New York City, joined by another seventeen Gotham residents who are listening to it without travel aspirations. Three were weird enough to listen to Al Jolson do the originating deed.

California here we come.

There are another thirty-eight listening to songs titled *California* so useless, unfortunate, or awesomely obscure that they do not deserve mention or betrayal. A whopping 175 are listening to a Beach Boys song. Another 2,224 will at some point during their journey. *California Girls* is in the lead, with ninety-two. Thirty-two nod to R.E.M., Forty-four acknowledge superiority with The Dead Kennedys, and of course you've got your scores of Red Hot Chili Peppers, Eagles, and Mamas and Pappas/Jose Feliciano devotees. Eleven are eyeing *Beverly Hills*. Five are watching the sun come up. Twelve are headbanging to *Los Angeles* with Frank Black. Thirty-four are pretending they are *Straight Outta Compton*. Fifteen receive their *Welcome To The Jungle*.

There are many others of course, one offs, one hitters, garage bands, social network experiments, random downloads, and location-specific melodies that attract and shift the numbers this way and that. Route 66, far from Folsom Prison, on the way to the dock of that bay.

But The Savage gives Efram all of them and goes further. This is Efram Daniels. He is onto something else. He listens to bands that don't even exist yet.

Efram thanks The Savage for coming. For making them find him. For being willing to do all this.

And she does this very Savage thing, where she hangs her arms off of the seat with a leaning look in his direction. And she thanks him for finding Raj, for finding her, and for giving all of them everything.

Literally everything, she says.

You've only seen the parts, the instances, but imagine it in real time, she says. Imagine being stuck in that place, the worst place—youth, adolescence, high school, call it what you will. And then imagine the barriers going away. Space. Money. Materials. Motivation. We were all rolling the dice. Getting lucky or unlucky with our student bodies. And then given everything and everyone we could ever want.

It's like being a hated orphan, made to live in a broom cupboard under the stairs, and then being told you're a wizard.

Like, if The Savage had had one cool sibling or friend before the age of fourteen, her life would be completely different. She could and would have known things earlier, started sooner, felt music in a different way. If only she'd had a parent who put headphones over her young ears and given her something real. And then the reverse happened. She got all the music. All of it. But once again: luck, which is really another word for chaos. Discord. Indeterminacy. Efram Daniels is all of these things.

The embodied notion that you, individually and collectively, are not in control.

So thanks for that, she says, shifting the equalizer filter on the beat and bringing a drift effect on the hounding vocal, mixing the next song over the last.

Ami begins to stir in the back. California here we come.

She's up, driving next.

‡   ‡   ‡   ‡

ONLY SEVEN MINUTES INTO recess and eight-year-old Eliza's body is aching from boredom. The collected sports and adventures seem no more preferable than sitting in the corner, kicking the ground. Eliza's stomach burns with the desperate wish that the school day would pass more quickly, that the clocks would bend to the will of speed, a return to the blissful ease of summer. It is acid in her veins and a needle in her head. She is alone because her best friend Maggie has not shown up to school today. Maggie is sick, or faking. Eliza has never faked being sick. Standing against the brick of the building under the dead

Texas flag, Eliza scans back and forth and then notices some boys sneaking through a gap in the locked chain gate of the fence behind one of the soccer goals. They aren't actually escaping, but instead laughing as they try to squeeze through, their clothes or flab or height snagging them every time. But I'm smaller than them, Eliza thinks. The boys leave for other pursuits, right on cue. Maggie lives so close to the school, Eliza remembers. When she goes over after school, the drive is almost nothing. In fact, it never had made sense to Eliza why they drive. It's a shorter distance than her own walk to the bus stop every day, but each play date always consists of Maggie's mother or father showing up at the circle.

Reaching the fence, Eliza waits for the soccer game to migrate to the other end. She locates the minding teachers, waits for them to turn away, and, in an all or nothing swipe, clumsily dives under the fence and starts furiously walking to the front of the school.

In her head, she tries to remember the route to Maggie's house.

Walking along the big road could get her caught, so Eliza takes the smaller road that runs parallel, peeking down each street she crosses to get her bearings. She doesn't need to hide, all the houses seem dead. On her second block, a teenager races by on a silver bike, but does not show any sign of having noticed her. A block later, Eliza feels eyes. An old lady sits on a porch, but instead of rising and scolding her, the woman holds up a hand in a wave. Eliza returns it and keeps going. The old lady doesn't call after her. Another lucky break. It's supposed to be this way, Eliza thinks. I'm supposed to see Maggie today.

Suddenly the road curves ahead. Eliza considers turning around and taking the last cross street back to the main road, but realizes that it's going that direction anyway. The growth gets thicker around the houses past the bend, but then she sees and hears the traffic of the main road as her angle increases. The actual pavement does not connect, it ends in a circle. Eliza sees a path on the side of two long gray houses, which she knows must spit her out on the main road, right by the turn onto Maggie's street, which should be a crosswalk or two away.

The path only has a fence on one side, and the wall of a house on the other. It stretches up the slope, compensating for the elevation she had lost by going down the curving street. Ahead it looks like it dead-ends into some sort of road, but she finds a row of thick wild bushes that zigzag her inward, depositing her in a wide rectangle next to a house. The traffic is louder, so she thinks she's close. Following the path farther, she ends with a turn into a small courtyard in which there is a bench surrounded by tall ugly trees and rusted sheds and two men passing a glass cylinder between themselves. The windows are totally dark, covered in trash bags it looks like, but the door to the square building is open, and inside it looks like a mad scientist's lab, a messy and wrecked assortment of tubes and glass visible from her approaching angle.

The two men are skinny, their teeth are a mangled beige, and they look at her so differently than a teacher or parent. It's like they're scared.

"Are you lost, little girl?"

I'm trying to find the main road, to my friend's house. And she points to where it should have been, to the source of that sporadic *whoosh* of the cars going over forty miles an hour, but her eyes are fixated on the open door and the structure inside it. She stares. One of the men looks over his shoulder through the portal, and she looks down at her feet and takes a step toward the next turn in the path, keeps going forward, but the two men look at each other and move.

"We'll show you how to get there," one maybe says.

But so big and fast, suddenly there is a hand over her mouth and a hand over her eyes. Caught between trying to manufacture tears and trying to inhale oxygen, Eliza's legs move but hit nothing. She feels a surface against her back. The hands go away and she is given a millisecond of perceived light before she feels the slab, and darkness presses down on her. It's a pillow, she realizes, but a big one, like in her mom's bed. The feeling of the fabric goes all the way down to her knees. Her left forearm manages to escape and feel air, but nothing else. It's like a hold your breath game, hold your breath through the tunnel, but she can't. She hadn't known to inhale beforehand.

Eliza, like most children, knows she is about to die in a way that not even the most fatalistic or fearful adult is capable of experiencing. It is a primal feeling divorced from language or *this isn't happening to me* delusional gripping. It is not founded on a specific phobia or selection bias. It is less a fearful feeling than a pounding, twisting scream aimed at the heavens. Please. Help me. I'm dying.

She wishes for her mother, for her father, for her brother Simon to start throwing rocks at the windows. She wishes she had been paying attention when Luke was teaching Simon how to fight. Hopes for something. Anything.

And then, it comes. There is a muffled exchange and light seeps in, a "what" or "don't" is happening, and not from her mouth. Someone is helping her, and she sneaks what feels like a quick breath from the side of her mouth against the uneven shifting pressure. They're arguing. She lets loose a moaning wail with the air she sucked into her lungs.

But the muffled exchange ends. And the pressure comes back down, nose, mouth, stomach. Then there is a race of the mind when Eliza can only feel her tear ducts and cannot remember who she is, or who her parents are, or how she got there. She feels the veil. And then there is blackness.

Nine minutes into class, Ms. Abrams becomes suspicious that Eliza has not returned from recess. The principal, Mrs. Watson, conducts a search of the school by 1:15 p.m. Molly Corbin's once-uncle, Martin, is about to begin teaching his tenth grade class, when he answers the phone and confirms he has not picked up his daughter. Aunt Linda's phone buzzes while she is waiting for her number to be called at the county DMV, and she gives up her place in line to rush to the school. Mrs. Watson calls the sheriff at 1:17 p.m. to inform him they have a missing child on their hands. By 1:50 p.m. they have searched the school, interviewed the teachers, and patrolled the surrounding ten blocks. Despite the fact that no teacher had witnessed any adult or strange vehicle around the recess field, abduction is considered the most likely scenario. Runaways rarely if ever occur that young.

Steven knows an AMBER alert activation requires there to be evidence and a description of the abductor or the abductor's vehicle. Not that it would have helped Eliza Edwards. Steven knows she has been dead for over an hour.

A 'missing, feared abducted' line is broadcast to local authorities and media. The local highway patrol and next-door towns send extra cars by 3:45 p.m. The total lack of witnesses results in concerns that it is a hoax by the parents, or the child is in a hiding place. None of the children has seen anything. She was there, and then was gone. Ms. Abrams explains that her best friend is home sick, the one who should have been glued to her is not there that day. Maggie's house is searched along with Eliza's.

Aunt Linda breaks down for the first time when she has to provide pictures for the bulletins. Eliza's face first takes to the airwaves at 4:00 p.m., interrupting local programming. The first news truck spiral goes up outside the school at 4:17 p.m.

Then for a long time, nothing happens except erroneous reports and fruitless searches.

At 9:17 the next morning, Thomas Walker, who had seen the girl's description, photo, and outfit on the eleven o'clock news, calls the police to tell them he saw a small child's shoe floating down the stream behind his house. He thinks it is probably nothing, trash, but makes the decision to call anyway. Thomas Walker has daughters.

Eliza's body is found half a mile down the flow, where a drainage ditch bypassing a road meets the stream. She had been eight years, two months, and three days old. Aunt Linda drives to the county seat and identifies the body under the sheet, and then restrains from touching her dead child for the sake of preserving forensic evidence. There is no mutilation. No trace of sexual assault. No signs of a struggle, save red eyes suggesting asphyxiation.

The county sends backup. Dallas, Houston, and Austin send men and women with microphones. The nationals are on their way.

The youngest deputy, Brian Chavez, is sent to Maggie's house for the second time to interview the parents of the best friend. He has a revelation pulling down that grid. He weighs the local geography and gets pretty close to the truth. "She disappeared in one of the worst drug areas in town, hell, in the county," he tells his superiors. He breaks out a crime map. "Maybe she wandered off and saw something she shouldn't have."

Sheriff Tanner ignores him. It's ridiculous. She walked into a drug deal or lab in the middle of the day? The county backup and the federalis arrive, and he shops his theory around. He is met with derision. Only an assistant D.A. seems mildly interested and asks him to write a report.

Frustrated, Brian Chavez finds a reporter...

The hypothesis is leaked and the rumor spreads. Break down. Cable news breaks in. Steven watches.

For the ninety-six hours the big three networks are in town, the county and town police put up a furious theatrical performance of evidence collection and random drug raids. They pursue every possible angle. Too bad both parents have confirmed absolute alibis. Her older brother could not have done it.

The locals cannot summon a specific confidential informant. Interrogating squeezes, snitching offers, and corner raids yield nothing. Sex offenders give nothing but theories. No neighbors had heard little girl screams, or—correction—concerned citizens over a fifteen square mile radius said they thought they heard something. They volunteer suspects from among the local drug addicts, criminals, and adolescent troublemakers. In a panic, three teenage boys—spray paint can flamethrower making, pot leaf pendant wearing, minor burglars—are arrested and accused of a goth-and-devil-music-and-violent-video-game-descent-into-Satan inspired killing. And then the cameras leave. And the three are released when it is discovered that, at the time of the crime, they had been caught on tape attempting to break into a closed-in-the-middle-of-the-day strip club.

Steven knows Eliza spent her last moments held down and smothered with a pillow. She was so small that the strength required was minimal, nothing that would bruise. In her third week of having lost a child, Aunt Linda tries Jonathan Corbin's landline only to find it disconnected.

✉️   ✉️   ✉️   ✉️

"WHERE ARE YOU?" LAURYN asks.

Chloe does not respond. Chloe is busy. Chloe is a dot on a map on a screen. Mouse and keyboard.

She has a weapon floating in front of her. A gun. A full clip. A targeting reticule. A compass. A heads-up display that tells her precisely how many bullets she has left before she has to reload. Her peripheral vision goes unused.

The screen blinks as a light burns out. The mousewheel brings options—knife, pistol, assault rifle, sniper rifle—you know how it goes. She stalks.

Chloe strafes around a corner and sees movement. Her tongue curls into her cheek. Trigger depressed, the muzzle flash illuminates the hall, bullets colliding with the chest of the gray target, each strike kicking up dust from the wall or blood from flesh. The physics engine pulls the corpse to the ground. Chloe keeps moving. Always keep moving. She floats through the corridor, the display bobbing with virtual steps, changes of direction coming with a twitch.

"Lauryn wants to know where you are," Michelle says.

Chloe is along the southwest boundary of an abandoned factory shooting a twelve-year-old boy in the head. His curses crackle in her headset.

"So does Jess," Michelle lies.

Chloe crouches behind a half-wall, releasing the key to pop up, only to find the alcove empty. She feels the enemy before she sees or hears him. The edges go red as she is hit, but she hurtles onto a crate, and then onto another, feigning a full upward retreat. Then she is reversing direction, jumping straight back down, tossing grenades and spraying bullets. The sound effect death symphony plays, the kill bringing the exhaling grunt of the defeated and the victory notification into her ears.

She shifts to a sprint through the maze of shipping containers, clearing corners, rapping keys twice to dodge, and then, without warning, the screen bursts red, and the perspective shifts to watching her headless body become a dead puppet splayed on the pixelated floor. Or, not her body, but her warrior's body. The camera shows a man with a mask. He cackles in her ear. She respawns and he is camping at the site of her resurrection, a headshot cleaves her neck, sending her right back into the countdown, staring at the leaderboard.

"Fuck you," Chloe says.

And he and they recognize the pitch of her voice. A girl is in the game.

"Stupid fucking slut," he says. "I'm gonna fuck the hole I put in your head."

Her avatar is revived, and Chloe twists and turns, ignoring the rest of the players, cutting through the furball of flying projectiles on the lookout for the hovering name. Floating in red over the mask, she pumps lead into the torso under his mask.

"You fucking fat cunt," whines in her ear.

Chloe climbs a ladder onto a hanging gantry, scoping down, picking off others with alternating headshots. She finds the mask again, and clicks.

"Hey," the phone glows.

Sound and bullet hit his body at the same time. And again. And again.

The next map is a residential neighborhood. But in her head it repeats. And when she sleeps it starts again. Which one is which gets all mixed up. A crossbow bolt cuts through a neck. A rocket launcher tears off a limb. Accelerated plasma and spinning chainguns. Chloe spits fire and lead, awake and asleep.

Dreaming, she moves her warrior into position, her slender avatar of black and gunmetal.

"Seriously, where the fuck are you?" Lauryn asks the ignored phone.

⊗   ⊗   ⊗   ⊗

MOLLY DRESSES HER BEST version of a teenage mess, and goes straight to the high school Eliza would have attended had she made it to fourteen. Molly Corbin has never been inside one before. She walks into the fray and navigates the halls like she belongs. It's easier than she thinks. She stereotypes, profiles, and with flirty desperate eyes asks the oldest, wrecked, obnoxious, wannabe, all-over hoodie kid she can find.

"Hi," she says, "I hear you're the person to ask…"

And he smiles, because they all smile, but are still, somewhere in their skulls, scared. As they should be. He tells her not only the place to go, but all the places where she can get it. Who is making what. He offers to go for her. In return for…

She selects the correct options from the dialogue tree.

Who used to make that stuff by the elementary school?

And he tells her. He says where they've moved. With an imitated tweak, she gets up and leaves.

Molly's load out is complete. She ditches the car on the opposite side of the block, and blazes a path through a yard's underbrush. She cuts the fences for a direct escape route, and settles on the overlook.

First, she walks up to the house. She's wearing jeans and a plaid button down. She puts on makeup so she can smear it. She knocks on the door. Like it's nothing. The narrow man who opens with his mesh hat and black holes above his cheeks looks down from the two steps and already knows…

She asks for it.

He tells her to come in, but she stands outside shivering. For a second he floats at the center of her targeting reticule, weapon undrawn, Molly considers going for it right there. But she reconsiders. He's mad, but something stops him from yelling or lunging at her or telling her to scram.

How much?

And so he tells her.

I don't have that much, she says.

Well you can pay for it other ways.

He looks at her but Molly makes sure not to look at him. He is a collection of pixels, a syphon of visual information, a bullseye. Before he can think to grab her, she runs away like the spaz that she is. And he shakes his head, and doesn't know that she has not left, and is now dressed in all black, with all manner of destruction hanging from her body.

She watches for three straight hours, hidden under two bushes. She counts four, two visible inside despite the improvised shades, and another two that enter while she waits. Three men and one woman. Targets. She ignores their hair color and cut, their clothes, their eyes, the way they walk and talk and banter and act. They are shapes. Cans and ring boxes. Containers of water to be pierced. She can see one of the men move to the upper floor bedroom with the woman, and rotates to a second spot, closer. She adjusts her scope. The one unsheathed window gives her an occasional view of the two fucking before they've even remotely stripped down—a leg here, a bobbing head there. She can't hear the cheeks spanking or the television volume blowing up downstairs. Two new marks open the front door, let's make that six total, and jump up and down and twitch as they light cigarettes and look at the dilapidated half-woods around them. There are no grand pines down here.

It isn't the plan, wasn't the plan, but Molly Corbin acts.

Two shots ring out and collapse the first—mid cigarette draw, with the firelight lightning bug beacon on his lips—with center body mass hits that obliterate his internal organs into mushy, unsustainable goo. The other one surges up, confused at the sight, and makes it three steps toward the door before he is nearly decapitated when the third bullet hits the back of his neck. Dumbass hick number three gets the bright idea to open the front door with his shiny, shitty handgun. Her first round passes straight through his throat while the second tears off the lower left side of his face, the third slamming into his chest.

The two assholes upstairs are still going at it, the sound of skin slapping and speed enhanced moaning making them too fucking dumb to hear the shots. She knows there is at least one, if not more, in there who might be cowering. Or, worse yet, sprinting to grab the couple and assemble numbers—if they aren't passed out or dead or in the basement cooking.

Molly covers a hundred yards in eleven seconds. She stays elevated, settling on a ridge with the closest sight through the window, with the carbine now, and unloads lead that will ignore the shattering glass. Molly catches sight of the blood and mangled skin—confirmation.

The front door is still held open by the two bodies inside it. She checks the bodies in the yard. Her boots never meet blood. Crouching against the side of the door, she thinks for a second about yanking at her chest, fingering a pin, and tossing a flashbang, but the slightest burst of heat could explode the house. That would come. But not yet. She checks the door from both sides, seeing what she can. Picking the first partition, she clears one side of the room before exposing herself, and dives in, settling against the far wall, zooming to the corners on instinct, automatic pilot. The ghetto chemistry set is exposed on a large dining table. She can hear the cook. Crouching behind the couch, the man who answered the door shudders. She can only see the top of his head and a bit of his shoulder, but she takes no chances. The couch and those visible bits of him come apart, foam fuzz ripped off along with flesh and hair. He is still alive, survivable, and she pulls out her sidearm to finish him off. She has no moment of remorse or acceptance, no emotional acknowledgement of the act of killing. She does not consider the moisture in his blue eyes. The paleness of his skin. The narrowness of his skull. The thickness of his neck. The flag on his T-shirt. The jewelry around his wrist and neck.

She fires straight into his brain.

Someone charges at her, an extra number. She hears him before she sees him and spins to see him emerging from the kitchen.

Double tap.

Fire two shots so close together that it's like being hit with two at once, and then a third carefully aimed blow higher, severing the spinal column and ending all movement.

Steven knows that somewhere in the order of four decades before the end, a Rhodesian mercenary named Mike Rousseau unexpectedly took a corner and ran into a FRELIMO guerrilla with an AK and instinctively double tapped, only to find his target still advancing. He aimed for the head to end it, but slipped, instead smashing straight through his neck and severing his spinal cord.

So Molly goes shotshot-shot. Onetwo-three. Chestchest-head. Not even doing the failure to stop version where she assesses before the last shot. She decapitates his nervous system. She does a quick clearing run around the lower floor. She checks closets. She keeps an eye out for hiding toddlers. The only upstairs room is that single bedroom and a bathroom. She kills the light. Back down the stairs, and Molly drags the outdoor bodies into the house. The bloodstains on the dirt will not matter in a few seconds. The bodies are sacks. They are workout weights. They are not people. They did not have parents. They did not have first steps or first kisses. In the kitchen, she fires up the oven and opens the door, and then blows out the pilot lights on the stove. She sniffs to make sure the gas is leaking. She grabs a bottle of alcohol and smashes it on the wall above the couch, not that she needs more accelerant, but just in case the reputation for flammability in meth labs is oversold. She tosses a match onto a cushion.

Molly throws a grenade under the table and a flashbang on top, and dives through the door at the greatest possible velocity. She is not sure it will work, though the couch is already burning. She needs not worry.

The inferno borders on plasma, and then, in that moment, she sees the people. She sees round faces and decaying bones and washed out blue jeans.

Only dental records will be left.

Molly grabs the casings from her initial perch. She breaks down. She zips her hoodie over her torso and balances the loaded duffle on her back. Running away, dogs now barking, calls being made, she cuts across the lawn behind the house across from which her wheels are waiting. As she skips over the fence, there is a piercing siren in her head. A boy's face presses against a window, violating bedtime, watching her all along.

Molly waves.

Then runs.

Then drives.

◧　　　◧　　　◧　　　◧

KYANA GREENE WALKS BY, squawking into the pink and rhinestone pod held in her gloved hand. Her own minions trail her. Daddy got her a vocal coach and a stylist. If Kyana gets famous, when she gives her first big magazine interview and is asked (they always ask) whether people were mean to her at school, Chloe will be the figure in Kyana's answer. Kyana got a smidge too popular after the freshman talent show, so Chloe superimposed Kyana's face on her mother's colossal body, and told her, to her face, to enjoy her fatass future.

But this time, Chloe keeps her face down in her phone.

"Mia was in New York and saw James, uh, what is his name, from..." Michelle struggles.

Chloe understands why dudes would want to be famous. Girls are being socialized to starfuck. And boy is it effective. Michelle could not remember the name of the movie. This didn't seem to matter. She tells the story anyway, basking in the light of celebrity by association by association.

But Chloe's virtual westside gang is the best virtual westside gang. Controller in her hand, Chloe lords over the southlands. She owns the city. It is hers. Her very image has been grafted into the game, exact height, exact weight, exact wardrobe.

But she wants them to be more than criminals. Chloe tries to play the game differently than intended. She deals drugs and battles for turf at the beginning, but reinvests the cash in legitimate businesses. She hires vigilantes. She donates to the police. They become toothless. It's on her men to keep her turf safe. She gives her gang members a corporate structure. Benefits in virtual cash.

The game does not respond.

They run through the streets stealing cars and beating pedestrians. They casually hold assault rifles as if they were umbrellas. Prostitutes congregate on her street corners. Her employees become pimps.

She goes on a rampage, killing her own men, running them over, a pistol propped out the window. But her empire splinters, the cat's away, and violence envelops the territory. Her former lieutenants split into miniature fiefdoms, their pawns wreaking havoc on the citizenry, bands of outlaws unhindered. Scores are settled. Chloe goes to the highest overlook and watches it burn.

And she dreams, and it repeats.

⠇⠇   ⠇⠇   ⠇⠇   ⠇⠇

EFRAM'S BURNING RUBBER THROUGH the changing, Northern SoCal elevation, and finally they see the blue and peel off, up against a wooden fence laced with barb over the cliff. It's a hill, and the sun is clipping the horizon, so The Savage and Ami and TGT rip, running down the horizontal road toward the turn to the beach. Efram and Raj stand overlooking, skidding on the perch, and Efram puts his arm around Raj's shoulder and gives a real *we made it* squeeze, and Raj nods, jerks his head to his right, and starts his walk to follow his girlfriend. Raj leaves the frame, and suddenly there is a vision twenty feet to Efram's left: a faerie, a nymph, a siren, a NuCalifornIA girl, with sun-kissed skin and Apollo halo hair, absentmindedly kicking the ground. Raj looks over his shoulder and gives the *of course* rolling eyes smile and accelerates his long stride down the mountain.

Who are you?

Whoever.

Efram waves and mouths *Hi* and closes the distance with his head down, collar ruffled, blazer dirty, hell on earth. He decides to say nothing, and five feet away from her turns and crosses his arms and looks out into the blue, and then looks back and she laughs, pointing at the license plate on the ditched vehicle.

"Yea," he says, "a long way."

But then it all happens in noises. There's the sound of multiple footsteps, first against pavement then against dirt. The waddling, sagging wobble of sweaty clothes and soggy skin, stomachs full of alcohol having their own distinct vibrato. The deep bullshit husk, sample of, "Who are you talking to?" and, "What the fuck are you doing talking to my girl?" Then there's the pleading, hoping, praying shout of the western maiden: "Nothing. He stopped." There's the snare of knuckles cracking, the bass of muscles shifting, a grinding rhythm section of teeth. They are closer now, three, you can hear three, and she tries one more time. "He's not... He's gay!" She says. "He had his arm around a guy. Please!" But there's the answering mutter, if a mutter can be a roar: "Oh, so a fucking faggot was talking to my girl!?" And then there is the sound of her trying to stop him. And at this moment Efram turns from the ocean, deep blue sea, and it's not sound. Efram gets the punch he's always wanted. He finds the real bullies and the real bullets. He slackens. He smiles. The calls are now a symphony as the first fist collides with his relaxed stomach. And the next. And the next. A flurry of blows. He can taste the blood and smell the air despite being unable to breathe. The drumming adds elements: a bending knee, a flexing foot, a tackling shoulder, and, after hitting the ground twice, he collides with the fence, piercing his hands on the barbed wire, strung up. A heavy strike connects with his head, this should be a normal blackout, but the kick propels the base of his skull into the wooden pole. The next fist is already on its way.

There's real screeching now, and not only from her. Something is wrong. Raj and TGT are racing back up the hill, and the three are retreating, hauling their princess with them. Raj tries to untangle Efram from the fence, to get his slacking, drooling, oozing skull on the ground, but he finds it is too hard without ripping the skin on Efram's outstretched arms. Raj hastily tears off his shirt and tries plugging the wounds, talking, trembling, trying to get a response from the unconscious sack of swelling flesh. TGT goes after them, single, suicidal, ripping off his shirt and throwing it to Raj on the way, locking on their path like a short muscled missile. The Savage and Ami have better fight or flight responses than Raj, avoiding shock, dealing with disaster. He collapses when they arrive, paralyzed. The Savage searches the car for any kind of useful first-aid while Ami tries to staunch the bleeding. The wounds aren't the enemy; the trauma is in there. The phone call is made, the plea, the hope, but the brain is swelling and the diaphragm is crippled. The pulse, the boom-boom, the second part of that awesome beat— boom! boom-BOOM! cha! *Be My Baby* or *Just Like Honey*, it's the middle part, looped on repeat, pumping blood through his veins: boom-BOOM, boom-BOOM, boom-BOOM, boom-BOOM. But the countdown clock hits zero. The progress slider hits the end, ready for the next. Efram can't hear Ami's questions, or feel her wet hands, or see TGT return unvindicated, or smell the sweat seeping from The Savage as she labors over him.

Efram Daniels dies. Just like that. Three days before the end, 221 days before his eighteenth birthday, first semester senior year.

PART

7

There was silence in heaven about
the space of half an hour.
            —The Book of Revelation

And we'll all float on, okay.
And we'll all float on, alright.
            —Modest Mouse, "Float On"

THURSDAY AND IT MUST be bulimia awareness month here at LeMay Senior High School. The character building assemblies have been an eating disorder festival for three straight weeks. The twigs must be running scared or shuddering from laughter—but Chloe's peasants are well fed at the moment. Her faction, the Satsuma, own the southwestern coast of Kyushu. When Chloe closes her eyes, everything goes black as she sees a campaign map. An isometric bird's-eye perspective of the islands of the Japanese archipelago, complete with terrain, weather, reflective water, towns, cities, roads, and farms. Armies are signified by human figures holding banners, towering sentinels, accompanied by agents of subterfuge and reconnaissance who scour the map independently. The fleets are on the sea in third period. As news of Efram Daniel's fate spreads, ships are bobbing in the digital froth, the age of steam and iron making the wind less of a factor in battle. Her fingers move the pieces around the board.

Chloe the gamer has ruled empires for thousands of years. She has started revolutions, invented writing, raised hundreds of cities out of the ground, razed hundreds of cities to the ground, and saved the planet from satanic, fantastical, extraterrestrial, and villainous threats for all eternities. She has been a Navy SEAL, a Pharaoh, a cast-off, gun wielding scientist, a trapped medical experiment, a general, and a thief. She has killed demons, ghosts, terrorists, dragons, giant spiders, zombies, aliens, and uncountable legions of pixelated men with guns. She has won World War II for the Axis, defeated Washington and Rochambeau at Yorktown, spent the eighteenth century unifying India from within and the nineteenth century colonizing Europe from the outside. Not to mention all the glorious wars, unburdened by historical geography, she won in randomly generated scenarios.

Do you remember when the Mayans nuked the French?

Chloe does.

Lucifer fell on Reims and Marseille first, smashing cities and armies alike. Chloe was fine with the digital mushroom clouds and radioactive lands playing through her head, from God's view in orbit. That she could endure, as she slept and took over the world again and again and again. Maps and movements on the slumber screen. Blocks ejected from the sky.

But a day later, now four days before the end, Chloe is running through hallways, shooting the minions of a breakaway terrorist warlord, spraying bullets and taking fire. She takes the objective, and boards the Blackhawk she rode in on, rotors spinning above her head. EoD and NEST are en route, but then, of course, out of nowhere—

There's that same old thermonuclear glow. Dust and dust and dust. Her ride is spinning, and she's dizzy, but she can feel the heat. She slams into the ground. Fade to black. Curtain up. Crawl, no gun now, and then die. And now she's sitting in her room and there's another glare. Her window becomes broken missiles of sharp glass, and her flesh melts. Her body is tossed through the windtunnel as her bedframe crumbles in the air.

And it's like parallel mirrors. Infinite. She dies on the screen and then dies in real life only to find that to be the screen. She conquers the alternate history French Empire, incinerating fake people in fake cities, irradiating the ground, running up the score. And then the warheads fall on her.

Chloe cannot sleep. When she does, she is caught in the loop. The tetronimoes become collapsing buildings or tumbling bombs.

So Chloe starts it up and keeps playing.

Her soldiers let bullets fly.

Sickness takes most of them. Plague and pestilence, children almost never making it to eighteen, brutal meteorology taking care of the rest. War makes appearances, background radiation and chaos kill more. Throats are slit, kings and beggars alike. Death strolls hospital hallways, he floats next to shipwrecks, he stalks battlefields.

Steven read once that all warfare is based on movement, but he doesn't know what the hell that means. Napoleon moved all over the place—feint left, go right, disappear, exile—but that didn't stop his army freezing to death in the end. Molly, on the other hand, doesn't just understand that all warfare is based on movement, the notion is embedded in the connective tissue of her body, hardwired into her nervous system. She cuts across the country on back roads that have not seen tires for weeks. She is among trees and fields and rusted abandoned hulks. The only faces she sees belong to children. They smile, or wave, or even try to follow.

Steven knows that seven decades before the end, a British bastard of an English lawyer and his Burmese mistress—a boy named Alexander—slammed flat into the ground of El Alamein, and squirmed into a four-inch groove in the earth. Caught outside of a foxhole, Armageddon enveloped him. It was enough, that dirt fold, and Alexander lived. The metal flew every other direction but toward his body. A few months later, in a hospital bed in Gibraltar, a killer fever split Alexander's head and liquefied his skin. But Steven watched him survive. Alexander entered the Foreign Service, and met a deb named Alice from a secretly catholic family. The union yielded no offspring. Alexander left her for a much younger British woman named Nell Penley, and fifty-two years before the end, brought Norman into the world. Alexander died of a heart attack three weeks after the birth of his only "Anglo" son. Steven knows the exact way Alexander's body trembled in his last, futile gasp for oxygen.

Twenty-eight years before the end, Norman witnessed death for the first time. From a rooftop half a klick or so away, Norman watched there as six rebels were cut down, first from a machine gun, and then from a mortar. Smoke and bodies tumbled from that distance, figures withering on the ground. Steven watched his father, back when the wars were cold and the living good, and the nation-state a healthy institution the globe over.

Nineteen years before the end, Norman sat on a beach next to a small set of inland dunes, southwest of Jakarta, watching sand being mined into lines.

"Your wife is enjoying her stay?" One of his minders asked.

"Yes," Norman said. "Bali."

"Yes. Very beautiful. She is American?"

"Yes," Norman said. It was the man's job to know the nationality of his wife.

"It is good you married an American," the watcher said.

"Oh yes?"

"Of course. It is always very good business to marry an American."

The large mansion was a blend of Hollywood and Jakarta, plain white walls allowing the scale of the architecture to speak for itself. House arrest. A palace for a prison and a prison for a palace. An Australian jazz quartet, expertly imported, sounded off the walls. The dignitaries, the local politicians and, the random business contacts buzzed around the family members. The smiling general sat at the head. Norman accepted his hand, and then wandered.

There was a terrace, and Norman walked out onto it, and there was a woman there.

She was shorter than Norman's normal type: darker skin, long brown hair that bent to the ground and eyes of copper. She rested an elbow on a curled hand, leaning against her own ribs, her wine glass hovering by her shoulder.

Steven watched Norman open. Watched Norman close. Steven watched the genocides, the pulses stop, the chests shot, the heads severed by swords, the corpses tossed into rivers. He watched her laugh. He watched Norman blab. He watched her say no until she said yes.

No international incident. Nothing. Deterrent for deterrent. Dust for dust. Genocide for genocide. Destruction for destruction. All to keep the peace. Steven watched himself be conceived the following night in a Bali hotel room. He watched the other baby cross oceans and jetways. He heard the wails as she was born in a private room of the hospital. He rode on the truck to the orphanage. He held her hand during the showcase for the prospective adoptive parents. He took the brochure with her picture on it.

⁝   ◩   ‡   ⊗

THE DAY BEFORE THE end, the body of Efram Daniels sits in a California morgue. But his disciples are in a three-bed hotel suite. It was seven hours at the station before Kevin the lawyer rescued them and became the shield of *in loco parentis*. He told them they could handle their own families but that transportation would be provided when they needed it. In the glove compartment, Ami found an envelope with more cash than should ever be in an envelope, labeled JUST IN CASE FRIEND. She was the only one brave enough to retrieve the car.

They told their parents in a mixed haze of revelation.

Yes, I am in California.

Yes, I am okay.

Yes, my friend Efram is dead.

No, you do not need to come here.

It elicits various responses and various degrees of panic.

Raj tells the rest to go.

They say they are staying put.

Chloe doesn't need to sleep, or need to try to sleep. She doesn't need to play a game. Thirty hours before the end, she's seeing it wherever she walks. Every person is a starved, concaved version of themselves. Their skin is flaking. They are swept away in tsunami tides and swallowed by the fissures of the earth. A mall is taken in a sinkhole. Suicide bombers start taking out coffee shops. Imported child soldiers orchestrate massacres at fast food chains. Indigenous child soldiers fight back. Chloe watches a mother smother her infant daughter so she won't have to live in this world, an act of murder and compassion as the bombs congregate around her. Down come conventional two thousand pounders, knocking down buildings with the same ease with which they cut down trees, even a few thousand yards from the crater.

The schools have become Efram Daniels' wet dream. LeMay is an arena. All day, they sprint through the halls shooting each other. They take damage. They die. They respawn. The currencies could be collapsing. The war could be coming. Steven plods through the industrial muck. There's another five percent dip and a huge bump in volume. Lauryn and Michelle kill each other for the thirty-seventh time in math class. The school receives its fourteenth tactical nuclear strike of the day. Earthquake. Back to normal. Chloe is sitting at break with the rest of them. Lauryn is talking about something.

"He likes them all, one of those guys, but only certain types, curly blondes, the true ones, the fake ones he hates. Even natural blondes who look like the plastic cliché of the fake blondes he doesn't like..."

Chloe waits for the evening when she can paint targets.

Jonathan Corbin dies in his hospital bed, twenty-four hours before the end, finally succumbing to third degree burns and annihilated lungs. Jonathan Corbin was a survivor. For thirteen days he kept on technically living, kept pumping blood, kept moaning through the drug-dimmed pain—a record, the doctors thought. He really did not want to die. No one can figure out where the medical bills should go until, through Mr. Corbin's billing history, they settle on an address for his wife, Deborah. Kentworth Gardens, 4530 Lorraine Terrace, St. Louis, Missouri.

Norman's dilapidated, hairy arm reaches up and claws at a taut escort's ass under a London roof and a London sky after dinner and drinks. All-night girlfriend experience. He doesn't realize her moans and calls and pleas are fake. Maybe it's the accent, that's why he buys it. She's from Poland he thinks, but he hasn't asked because he thinks it would be impolite. London will be the first to go, Steven knows. It always is. He works the back end of the cycle. The NIKKEI goes totally fucking apeshit. Floods hit Bangladesh. Hindus riot and beat the life out of some Muslims. Some Muslims bomb some nightclubs. A cult commits suicide. Another day during another night.

Norman snores, midevening crash, stamina not what it used to be, even with the drugs, while his wife Mary fingers an empty pill bottle in the early Annapolis afternoon. She walks into Steven's "room," knowing the quotation marks exist, and starts opening the drawers. Steven's abandoned clothes hit the floor, as her bathrobe struggles with movement, and she wheezes with the exertion of muscled work. There's nothing there. Nothing else she hid away. She checks the spare closet, and goes to the floor, wilted, a sidesaddle seat morphing into a splattered starfish of limbs. But then she sees it. Under the bed, the tub with a case. Her nails break and her limbs stretch but she manages to pry it out, scraping against the wood. Forget the clothes, she goes for the briefcase. Her husband left nothing. Nothing. Nothing except this. She picks up the gun, tastes the metal, the barrel, not knowing if it's loaded, not knowing how to load it, and waits for the bullet.

Molly Corbin makes the last turn the kind robot voice instructs and leaves the car on the side of the road, lot be damned. 4530 Lorraine Terrace, St. Louis, Missouri. Kentworth Gardens. It looks like an apartment building, fifteen stories stretching up. Reception is the open glass bottom floor, and now at least it has some characteristics of a hospital. A security guard opens the door for her, so she does her best to enter like it's no big deal, bee-lining for the desk where two women recline behind screens.

"Can I help you?"

"I think so," Molly says, but says nothing after.

"Is it your first time?"

Molly nods.

She puts her driver's license on the table.

The eyes drag up. A phone comes off its hook.

Two nurses emerge from an elevator.

"We'll take you," they say.

Molly figures out that the floors correspond to various levels of ailment. The top and bottom are for the more able-bodied, able-minded citizens. The middle, well, it's for the rest.

On the fourth floor, they hold the elevator door like it's a door that needs manual opening, and now it really looks like a hospital, glimmering floors and blank walls. A cart is picking up dishes from defeated lunches, at least for those who can still eat. No one goes on strolls on this side of the building. The doors are all closed. The two women lead down the row of cells, and they are cells: wooden gates with single block windows, blocked by beige shades.

At the end, second to last, a block from the corner, one turns the knob.

"Here she is."

Molly Corbin cannot recognize Deborah Corbin. The figure on the bed with the tube in her mouth and the pipes in her arm, the machine with shut eyes and inflated, unused skin.

"Has she ever woken up?" Molly asks.

The nurses look at each other.

"No. She's in what's called a persistent vegetative state. But you can talk to her. Hold her hand. She moves sometimes."

But Molly does not approach. She is fixed to her spot.

"Why keep her like this?" Molly asks.

"We have a legal obligation."

Molly knows that soon the bills will stop being paid. She does not know what that does to the legal obligation.

"We'll give you some time with her," one says.

Molly's mother is, after all, even without brain activity, technically breathing. Molly can see where they've shifted her to minimize bedsores. Her chest expands and contracts. The daughter takes a step. Then another. The body on the bed only knows the horizontal. It owns no kinesthetic traces, no evidence of movement patterns. It is flattened. The skin spiders with veins and flakes. Eleven years brain dead.

Molly Corbin starts pulling plugs from sockets. She expects alarms and readies running muscles. A body. Just another body. Just another sack of flesh. The artificial breathing seems to stop. The blood no longer pumps. And then she hears the steps. Molly makes for the door, catching one look at the tall, male orderly with gray eyes, mask over his mouth. She plunges into the stairwell and exits through an unmarked door, her internal compass guiding her straight to her car. She is spit out on a loading dock next to a dumpster. She escapes the property through the bushes.

≝   ‡   ⊗   ◳

THE NIGHT BEFORE THE end, the disciples of Efram Daniels sprawl on the balcony overlooking the ocean. No one cries. The Savage holds up Raj, despite the size differential. TGT sits on the railing.

Efram Daniels automatically posts to three walls. His robot likes three statuses. TGT and The Savage manifest a set of portable speakers and wire up a soundtrack. The music starts as the bright orb meets the water.

And five years before the end, first quarter, eighth grade (here we go!), Efram Daniels called Kevin Longhil and asked him to be his lawyer, his own lawyer. Child Efram Daniels, the one who started reading the markets at age ten—chip off the old block, destined for Ivies and margins—had proof. It would be Kevin's job to figure out how Efram Daniels could effectively implicate his father, while simultaneously cutting a deal to protect the family assets.

And six years before the end, C.W. Daniels sat in the back of the sedan with his son Efram, stuck at the intersection between school visits.

"Where are all the buildings?" Efram asked.

Our nation's capital doesn't have real buildings. It has imitations. Diminutive piles of mush, built by people afraid that if they go too high, God will knock them down. Not a real city and not real architecture. That's what his son was saying.

"Hong Kong makes New York look like a pancake," C.W. responded. It was all relative.

"And why is everyone driving so slowly?" Efram asked.

As if to give an answer, a single teal pickup truck made a right into the opposite lane, chased by a blinking police siren. They pulled over exactly opposite Efram's window. The cop punched the keys to look up the record while the driver reached for the glove compartment. The officer of the law climbed out and took his steps forward. He made it to his own headlights when the driver, the perp, flung open his door, extended a handgun—a real one, right there, black in front of Efram's fixated eyes, totally illegal back then in Our Nation's Capital—and let three loud, thunderous cracks of fire into the cop's body.

C.W. Daniels was already ducking after the initial shock. He had, in his memory, grabbed and yelled for his son to get down as well. Noise had come out of his mouth, he was sure of it. Except his son was not held in his arms.

The cop had been hit in his groin, his left thigh, and his right arm, and was on the pavement, down, bleeding. God knows how close the bullet in the leg was to an artery, with the shooter closing, the finishing headshot next. And everyone else remained ducking. Afraid to look. Crummy witnesses. Except the door in front of C.W. Daniels was wide open.

And his son, Efram, was somehow already across the street, standing in front of the cop, facing the shooter.

He was a twelve-year-old boy standing there. Staring down the barrel. While everyone else cowered.

His twelve-year-old son: The one who constantly needed a haircut to compensate for his unfortunate curls that tended to bend toward a mullet or rat tail, who in the seventh grade wore sweatpants and turtlenecks to school, who had never been kissed, who had struck out at every school dance and at every little league at bat, wallflower, who had literally airballed every attempt at a basketball hoop in his entire life (do you know how difficult that is?) He was the only kid in that first kindergarten game who would swing a foot at a soccer ball and connect with nothing but grass and laces, the kid who at age seven cried when a cartoon got too scary, whose idea of fun was covering his mother in stuffed animals as she slept, who built spacefleets out of Legos, making extra sure that every piece was the right color, who could bear to look at a computer screen for hours but a set of human eyes for only seconds...

He, Efram Daniels, was staring down the barrel, staring at the bullet, staring at the trigger, staring at the finger, and glaring up at the mind aiming it all at him, and them. The cop was stirring, struggling. But Efram was in between. He was the shield.

The sirens were coming in the distance. C.W. once again imagined grabbing for his phone, he had that memory, but found it untouched in his pocket. Someone else had done it. The sound, the music, was coming.

Decision time.

Efram stood his ground. Body steady.

And the shooter retreated to his car, and peeled out.

Broad fucking daylight, Efram turned around, twelve-year-old body, and knelt to the ground in front of the bleeding uniform. Someone should be out of a car now, running to help. C.W. was still ducking. Pinned. Curled up. Evolutionary reaction. A vegetable. Someone should help. Put pressure on the wounds.

Cushions are stolen from the sofa and layered on the deck. Raj, Ami, The Savage, and The Great Toscano blast and broadcast over the ocean in the rising wind. The waves increase in magnitude, the noise, the haze, the spray, the static. The vocals report in. The rhythm accelerates and deepens. The Savage lets it go. The heads bob in the water in their wetsuits. Norman sends another email. Steven sleeps in a motel bed. Molly slumbers in her car, rest stop parked, knife close, one in the chamber. Chloe no longer dreams.

The map is wireframe green. The countries are outlined. The silos are bright triangles of color, the color depending on allegiance. The air defenses are brilliant rectangles with chads, representing ammunition. The cities are faded opaque diamonds, size depending on population. The score is ready to measure megadeaths. When the rockets cross their hemispheres, they'll make the screen into a rainbow, the dashes showing the path gravity gives the missiles, mouse clicks targeting millions for an end, creepy ambient soundtrack giving faint cries and coughs. Chloe sets her defense condition. It's a tricky game, the trickiest of games, since launching too early renders you defenseless, having lost your deterrent, your threat. But launch too late and there may be nothing left for you to put in the air. She targets New York and Our Nation's Capital, a limited frontal assault. She moves submarines in three oceans.

Sunset before the end, West Coast time, the ocean becomes infested by the low end. The fusion ball reaches the horizon, bright orange afterglow, nice pink clouds, and they huddle next to the speakers in the wind. They turn it up, final moments, and The Savage pulls a nice high-low cut, backspins, fingers on the record, the real record, hand to actual noise. She moves the needle in the groove, one ear to headphone, extension cord through the sliding door, speakers from the heavens. She holds that opening stab, moves the fader slightly over and rocks it back and forth, under enough. She cuts the lows from the interloper, hits the on-off switch, lets it gasp as it strangles to death, and then lets the new song go with a thrust into its signature. The waveform spikes and scrapes the sky. The first six bass hits hypnotize, and the ripples comply and the surfers stop as the surf tries, because for Efram Daniels, there's life after death when one is ready to die.

⊠   ⋮⋮   ⊗   ‡

EVERY DAY IS EXACTLY the same. Go to school. Go to the office.

Cheer as the bombs are about to fall!

Tremble with excitement at the possibility!

Michelle spends the morning talking about a dream in which she was stuck waiting at an airport during a delay, and ended up at a party with the rich and famous. The dream has crushed her. Changed her. At least for an hour. Senior year cannot compete with the vision. Her future, her known future, its wildest delusions cannot meet what she saw. Chloe targets defensive installations, airbases, logistics centers. She strokes the touchscreen map in her hand, selecting primary and secondary targets with bloodlust gleaming from her shadowed eyes. She does not notice Jess's dress.

"Shut the fuck up about your stupid dream," Lauryn says to Michelle. But Michelle cannot shake it. Efram Daniels might have had a shot at living that life. Efram Daniels and maybe some of the outliers he found. The artists. The hidden geniuses. Efram Daniels had been trading in commodities. Chloe understands this now. He was assembling assets. Because with everything he had, even that wasn't enough to end up where Michelle wanted to be. It's useless to be rich and alone. You need to bring everyone with you. But even for him, it didn't work. Michelle wants the money and glamor. Lauryn wants it even if she's annoyed right now. Jess wants it, even if she is afraid of it, since she is already an object of it. The boys they pass in the hallways are all desperate for it.

That world of seamless modern architecture, beautiful people, beautiful people who say wonderful, interesting things. Giant paintings stretched above obsidian dining room tables. Yachts filled with hard bodies of the desired sex. Food arranged in colors worthy of botanical gardens. The locational freedom, city after city.

If we can't all have that...

If we can't all get to sip wine on the French Riveria with glamorous scoundrels and thieves, if we can't go to private VIP previews of art fairs with Bey and Hov, if we can't bomb Tokyo arcades with Skateboard P, if we can't have bodies actually look the way they do in editorials, if we can't have skin shimmer color-corrected orange or blue like it does on film, if we can't drape ourselves in loopwheel cotton and supple leather and custom silk, if we can't project movies, if we can't design games that design games, if we can't go back to see punk or hip-hop or rock and roll born in the first place, if we can't feel the sweat of moshing like it's 1991, the alive feeling of skin on skin because your clothes are soaked, if we can't have a moog in our house, if we can't all have that perfect record collection, if we can't go on Los Angeles prank sprees with OFWGKTA and go to the ballet with Yeezy and swim in pools with Kendrick, if we can't have the actors and actresses live up to the characters they play, be that sexy, that smart, capable of that dialogue without their writers, if we can't all shoot guns and have it not matter, if we can't all save the world and feel like we did, if we can't all watch it end and revel at the view...

If we can't all be music video rich, surrounded by the toned bodies of scantily clad professional dancers with costume changes and money dripping, if we can't

all be that, private jets and vineyards and design so good
its porn, Tribeca lofts and Miami mansions, if we can't all
have that...

FUCK IT. LET IT BURN.

And so the status updates scream it.

And the Efrapp goes live a minute after midnight.

Steven ditches the car in the suburbs, the last stop
commuter lot, no days before the end. This far out,
they're above ground. It could be anything.

The traders look at a possible currency collapse. A
debt implosion. The news director orgasms. In assembly,
the prism of signals is visible, called this time because
some freshman was in the hospital with holes in his
wrists.

Be kind children.

Oh be kind.

Chloe organizes a massed group of ICBMs into
one command and control protocol, and instructs them
to cluster their payloads on civilian targets. She makes
no effort to knock out our missiles. What's the point?
She selects lower megatonnage multiple independent
warheads instead of single high megatonnage tips. On
the map on her lap, her SSBNs slip through the sonobouy
net. She wishes she had the game's sound, instead of
having the accompaniment be the breathing, digesting,
wanting-to-fuck, waiting-to-shit biorhythms of a
thousand high school students.

The gym supports buckle. Chloe sees the background radiation coming up through the earth. She smells her genetic material coping, proteins making mistakes, copy, copy, G, T, C, A. Lauryn tries to have a real conversation with Michelle about how she should lose some weight. Michelle calls Lauryn a slut to everyone but her. Chloe waits for both of them to die. She prays for it this time. She pauses and looks up and asks for salvation. For judgment. Come down from the sky, please. Rain down upon us. Burn us. Make us stars.

Another four warheads destined for Our Nation's Capital. For spite.

The speaker conducting a requiem for the freshman who slit his wrists wraps up.

"Thank you," Mr. Winters says, "and now…" but Chloe is busy rearranging her interceptor forces into escort groups. She decides to spare the west coast despite its naval assets. She has no gripe with them. Cali kids are probably alright. Better to use the western trajectories against the strategic military assets in the mountain states. Fallout aside, the lower and upper Midwest and the West Coast will largely be spared. At least in her initial plan. Lord knows once the other players join the fray.

A new woman shows advertising on a projector. Unrealistic expectations. Airbrushing. Here we go. She holds on an ad showing a model stretched out on a couch, topless, denim tracing her lower half, beautiful denim, indigo over dark skin. The model is kissing one man, strategic arms covering her breasts, while another man is kissing her stomach, and another is holding him, kissing his neck, and completely ignoring the girl. The lecturer is talking about how skinny the girl looks, but she's missing the point. The ad is amazing. Brilliant. It guns at everything. Bisexuality exists. Beautiful men exist. Beautiful men may want to kiss each other instead of the beautiful girl. Beauty actually exists. Shame is your own fucking problem. Chloe knows the ad actually does more good than any criticism of it could do. But it doesn't matter. She prays again.

Her missiles won't kill the network. She thinks about that. "My missiles won't kill the network," Chloe updates. Efram Daniels likes this.

Back in the assembly, it's Q&A time. The woman answers a teacher asking about how students and parents can effect change through consumer habits. Chloe gives a look to her flock, then a look at the minor apostles at the bottom of the stands, mourning. Maria Price-Marcos, Anton Hotz, and the rest looking like parents of a runaway, his hallowed form in the blank space of honor, leaning back in a bespoke suit, hands stretched out on the step, lounging. They're whispering in his car. In spite of resurrection, Efram Daniels won't fight this or any fight. He never did anyway. He just showed up and let others do it. Okay, sometimes he may have helped others do it. He's gone now, but here we go. Chloe's hand fixes into an erect monument, in fact her legs find themselves standing up, skipping the nonexistent line. An image of a magazine cover with a skinny maiden in a sundress is still large on the projector, hanging over the room.

"Do you believe in relativism?" Chloe does not shield herself from the big word. The heads turn.

The woman struggles. "Can you be more specific?"

"It's not that hard. Do you believe in universal truth? Do you believe that what your senses perceive is what everyone else perceives? That everyone sees the same thing?"

"No."

"Well then how can you argue that there is a distinct physical world, separate from the mental world? That physical beauty is distinct from mental beauty, beauty on the inside, or whatever you want to call it? They are obviously related. They are constructions of certain values, decisions a subject makes in dress, grooming, and lifestyle."

Lauryn is tugging at her leg.

The woman's microphone tussles with ums and breaths for three or four seconds, so Chloe almost starts going again, but the microphone squeaks out a riposte—

"Can you be more specific?"

"Well, the reason people are attracted to people who are in shape surely is not purely aesthetic. There is a value there. An association is made. I would assume even an evolutionary imperative."

Efram Daniels smiles because Raj smiles.

"But wouldn't you agree that there is a point where valuing that goes too far? And it isn't desiring a healthy trait?"

Chloe gives a beat. Still stands. Parry. Flank. Move the carriers into the North Sea.

"Does art have value?" Chloe makes sure to project.

"Yes. I think it does. Of course it does. But I don't..."
The woman trails.

"So basically we are allowed to make judgments about what is beautiful in art, but not what is beautiful in people?"

"Not when those judgments are destructive."

"So you believe in censorship? That destructive art should be banned?"

"No."

"But you believe that beauty is genetic, so there is no cultural bias?"

"Of course there is a cultural bias. That is the point. Our culture is biased toward unhealthy images."

"So you can judge cultures? You can judge behavior? You can say, for example, that homosexuality is an unhealthy image? Or interracial relationships, they are unhealthy images? You get to say there are good cultures and bad cultures? You can say certain cultures are uncivilized for example? You can impose your values on them."

Chloe feels it. She feels the crowd turn. Their shoulders touch her shoulders. Some of the teachers smile. Chloe, that mean girl, that devious operator. Chuckle, shake your head, thank your God(s) and idols.

"I am all about acceptance, tolerance," the woman says, and Chloe makes sure to visibly scoff at that part. "But yes, I can critique our culture. The culture you and I belong to."

Coup de grace time.

Chloe crosses her arms. Her pupils lock into her target, gnawing at flesh and soul. They go to the edge of their seats. She gets the appeal. He gets the appeal. They are chomping at the bit. Get her. Bully her. Take her down. Make her feel like nothing. Maybe, just maybe, she deserves it.

Chloe's eyes make an overdramatisized sweep, looking the woman up and down. She trains them on every thread of her horrible department store pantsuit, every crusty layer of her neglected skin, and lingers over every hint of unworked flab.

"You and I don't belong to the same anything," Chloe says.

She makes her move down the aisle. And she gets that feeling, better then Efram ever got it. Sporadic applause, even if it's confused. Even if it's misunderstood.

A teacher rises to interrupt her exit, but Mr. Winters visibly overrides. The lights flicker, go off, glitch, the dying slow-down sound of all the hard wired mechanicals sputtering, here we go again, and then back to life.

Chloe goes out through the exit doors at the top, down the external escape stairs, to the grass. She feels the warhead hit the gym. She hears the school shooter start his work. She smells the vomit in the bathroom. She tastes the blood from the plague. She sees the first crops fail.

Chloe the truant scrapes the sidewalk toward the next target. She heads northwest. Steven boards his train at New Carrolton.

David is on the range. Achilles reborn, he is prone, stacked with a carbine, calmly firing shots at a distance past the limit of the round's penetrating range. Following orders, including impossible ones. He has been knocking out bullseyes for over an hour on the normal targets, so maybe now they're trying to take him down a notch. Humble him.

The spotter has no curses this time.

They pull back the target, always a human outline— the real thing don't come with archey targets painted on their clothes—and pull it down. It's a discussion, the superiors analyzing like normal, but longer. They show him. No accusations.

Bullseye. Bullseye. Bullseye.

"It's not possible," one says.

"Well clearly it fucking is."

David removes his helmet, risking the chewing out, and rubs his hairless head.

He tries to miss on the next round. Thousands of yards. The bullets keep hitting. His arms won't let him jerk the shot. His finger won't fuck up the trigger pull. Straight back, every time, a subtle squeeze, perfect. "It isn't possible," he whispers to himself, over and over, weapon after weapon, shot after shot, distance, windage, whatever. But he knows it's possible. He knows what has happened. He wants to whisper it, wants to say it, but refuses.

Raphaelle dances in a club in Paris with an older man, who is a successful artist with kind eyes. He grabs her midspin and begins kissing and trying to force her teeth open with his tongue, getting a good eight seconds before she can pull away. She shakes her head, and he grabs again, so she flees, making for the door, going straight into the night air. She takes her first few steps on the cobblestones, but he bounds out after her, taking her arm, pulling her into an alley. First he says he wants to talk, and lights a cigarette, relaxed, and she crosses her arms and readies escape routes. But right before she interrupts to bolt he throws her against the wall to try again. The lit cigarette in his hand, stinking and smoking, smolders into the skin on her left arm. She can feel the layers melt, the horrible itch, she whelps at the pain, bassline still audible through the wall. His mouth reaches her neck and she readies her scream, her knees already gathering strength to slam his crotch. But then, with his fingers bundled in her hair, pulling, and his leg grinding between hers, he withdraws back, hacking, coughing, total incapacitation. He hits the ground on his knees, blood coming from his nose, saliva pooling in his mouth, foam and then nothing. He is seizing, twitching, veins in his neck dilated rivers, a puddle on the ground. He bucks up again and again, hands holding, but cannot breathe. His eyes hold nothing. She takes the chance, the reprieve, and runs. A block and a half away, she remembers the burn and inspects her arm, only to find the skin pristine.

OUR NATION'S EDUCATIONAL INSTITUTIONS are experiencing anomalies this morning. We apologize for any inconvenience. Unauthorized music is roaring through PA systems. Faculty lounges have become weapons factories.

Did you know Efram Daniels can make a catapult from paper clips, rubber bands, and plastic pens? He can turn a stapler into a machine gun. Registry settings have been destroyed. Mice only navigate one direction. Wireless networks crumple under the weight of nude photos. A massive water fight breaks out at a school in Mississippi. A bike race takes over an Illinois hallway. Four grades leave class at the same time to throw a pool party in Nevada. Principals' offices stink with rotting vegetables hidden in ceiling boards. Libraries find volumes signed by dead authors. The Woodley School is invaded by engineering team robots. Van Ness Day School suffers a furnace that will not stop burning. Evergreen faces a complete ADHD revolt of its younger charges. The sod dries up. The renovations fail. The computers go on the fritz. Texting in classrooms. Chaos.

He is risen, and he cranks the knob and lets the reverberation pump through the eighteen-inch subwoofers. He pulls into the node, the wonderful institution, the prestigious academy, the amazing learning opportunity, whichever this one is. He yanks into the faculty lot and throws the parking pass on his mirror. A crack, and then shined shoes hit the pavement, mere compliments to the Saville Row suit, gray, with pink dress shirt and matching pocket square. Jeans and a T-shirt one day. Old school tracksuit the next. No routine. By the time he leaves the lot, five tires are flat and one is off its axle completely. Several trunks are ajar. He wanders through the foaming sea of fist pounds and compliments, a receiving line, as the tar-black asphalt gives way to the plaster floors of the faux-arcade exterior halls. He tosses a stack of stapled papers down the stairwell. He detours down four flights and into one of the middle school hallways, reaches up and taps an emergency EXIT light that has been glitchily buzzing for the past week. It stops, but then all the lights die in the hallway, one bulb too many.

Chloe sits on the stage where she last spoke to Efram Daniels. She basks in the shadow of the school she does not know. A hundred feet away, bolted to its brick wall, is a ladder, a tower to heaven, a way to the roof of the school on the hill.

After the fall of the wall but before the fall of the towers, back when they were younger, the world tilted. It was no different than it had been, though the parents believed the broadcast that the nonexistent war had lapsed into oblivion. But Chloe, all at once, knew better. At any moment, you could be gone, and not some dumb speech about living life to the fullest. Everything could go up. Poof! In one instant, one spark, everything incinerated. Within the blast radius at least. Not the individual, the species. Poof! or… Bang! or… Flash! (most appropriate) and the end, goodbye. The ultimate proof that Mommy

and Daddy cannot keep you safe. That you are not and
never will be safe. That there is no such thing as safe.   .

A decade,

Now,

Can you see Steven sitting on the roof?

He has no such fears.

Back resting on an exhaust vent, acknowledging
modern ventilation and air conditioning are the sole
requirement for the education of young minds. Our
Nation's Capital was a swamp before a city, and the
government ceased to function properly once air
conditioning was invented. Now, representatives are
content to take their time and block each other, as
opposed to getting through business quickly, in order
to rush home and escape the humidity and the malaria.
Two thousand are below him and one with him, above.
Chloe's pose is more of a crouch, but they both have eyes
turned upward, understanding they should watch the
conclusion.

A sight, something Steven has wondered about,
daydreamed about. Chloe has seen it a million times.
Being far enough away so you could see, really was far
worse. People say brighter than a thousand suns, but
they really have no idea. Quoting the Bhagavad Vita
is not sufficient. Tests in the desert do not denote the
proper surreality. One cannot grasp what a detonation
looks like in its natural habitat, but trying is necessary.
You are sitting from a fixed position, actually watching

the sky, enjoying the trappings of your surroundings, when a sudden glare followed by an ever-expanding cloud mushrooms to the heavens. Resting on a bench, watching the most beautiful sunset, taking in the skyline from the upper deck of a baseball game, or walking home from school scanning the horizon, you, a lucky one, are suddenly blessed with the chance to witness. It appears, a complete picture of your world changed forever, a sight more breathtaking than what caused you to look in the first place.

Force yourself. Imagine it, right now. Look around you, noticing the tranquility, the normalness. If you are inside, imagine the light through the windows, the feeling of your building shuddering. If you are outside, gaze around you and envisage from every angle your awe at seeing existence change on the horizon, untold millions instantly sentenced.

But don't worry! Don't Fret! This is absurd. The bombs won't come.

Chloe's eyes turn to the north. No cloud, no blink, nothing over Baltimore.

The generals wished for a weapon so powerful it would defy four thousand years of military theory. They were tricked.

The iliadic beauty of warfare utterly decimated in the shit of Verdun and the Somme. The last vestige of chivalric combat confined to knights of the air, who would eventually evolve into the harbingers of absolute destruction. Instead of getting their reprieve, their renaissance, they were left with a useless weapon. It was a big stick to threaten with, while always extending the carrot. Fallout rendered modern warfare into a game of I'll show you mine if you show me yours. Perhaps suburbia followed, spreading out so at least some, the smart, the fit, the lucky, would have time to escape whichever direction the wind was going.

But the world caught on, and moved back to the cities. The last days of the superpowers brought with them a far better system. Not one big stick, but a rocket that at the last moment would split into eight. Eight targets over one spread. Eight Hiroshimas covering one city, one greater metropolitan area. Multiple independent reentry vehicles. The ultimate phallic interpretation of the ICBM, ending with an ejaculation over the target. Steven and his Chloe finally face each other. Their faces reflect the blaze of light.

And it starts.

The Middle East explodes. Iran and Saudi Arabia pollute the skies with wreckage. Tel Aviv becomes a crater. Tehran becomes a cemetery. Mecca becomes glass. Rockets enliven the desert. It spreads to Europe and Asia first. Suicide bombers in Shanghai. Indo-Pakistani fun. Launch codes turned over to local commanders. Himalayan glaciers into battlefields. Avalanches triggered by explosives. A dirty bomb detonates next to a tube station. Gunmen light up Madrid. The small scale before the large scale. The airborne early warning centers see the launches, they sense the flocks of birds. Plumes become visible. Start the clock. Start the snapcount. Fifteen, maybe twenty minutes for a missile to cross a hemisphere.

Or maybe the storms finally come. The carbon in the atmosphere becomes too much. The math goes wrong. The coasts disappear. The buildings become reefs. The Midwest becomes a bayou. Crops fail. Decamp to the Northern Rim.

Or it goes the other direction. The glaciers advance. The northern wealth freezes to death. The mammoths take the business corridors. The polar bears hunt the survivors.

Or the water stops. No more clouds. No more rain. If you survive the thirst you still won't survive the hunger. Nothing lives. You live off of leftovers until they run out. Another dead planet floating in space.

Or the meteor hits. It is just another sort of missile. Wave of dirt, wall of water, and endless winter. We starve where we do not burn.

Maybe the earth beneath us grows sick of being so relatively stable. It decides, once again, to spit fire, to open and shake. Waves crash and wipe us from our homes, drowning and slamming until we are no more.

Maybe somewhere in Southeast Asia, a sick cow brushes the dying carcass of a pigeon. The farmhands spread the infection first. The new mutation tips in that impossible direction. It takes two weeks for symptoms to appear. Kills in four days. Eighty- to ninety-percent mortality. By the time they think to shut down the airports, it's too late. No one can keep down their meals. The uninfected hide. The markets close. The prices soar. The cities crumble while the bodies decompose.

Or maybe somewhere in Moscow, a deranged ape, bloody eyes, bites a young research assistant. She turns first. And it isn't like the movies at all. The walking dead are not dead, they are alive, bloodlusting, infected, cannibalistic. Grab that shotgun or chainsaw you've always wanted.

Or the laws of the universe change. The sun goes supernova. A radiation burst from the center of the galaxy immediately bakes the lot. The gravitational constant reverses. Time changes its flow. Dark energy combusts. The light switch flips. At a certain point, with understanding, it ends, ceasing, click.

Or the dead rise another way. The stories become true. The day of return comes. Hands become swords. Lying, murder, violence, adultery, and greed rule the world. The path disappears. The trumpets sound, lightning shoots from east to west, the clouds part, the winds blow, and the heavens shout. The armies of both sides gather. The hooves hit the ground.

And He who has seen the truth of humanity, Death, will cut through their ranks and let Hell fill the gap behind him, War will from place to place to incite challenge and ravage, Famine will do her endless work, and the King of Kings stands again and spreads chaos and strife.

The world ends or it doesn't. Our Nation's Capital burns or it lives.

Steven and Chloe sit on the roof over the school on the hill. They hang in the radiation and surf the shockwave. Her eyes target missiles and his target souls. They all go up now: angry, fat, old men shouting into hotlines, young men in holes turning keys, the sky is given to them and all the others.

Three thousand miles away, the highest disciples of Efram Daniels watch the water, see the rumbling, the boil, waiting for him to surge to the surface. The network is built to survive, but he's in the lines. In the cables. In the fibers. He rides the data and crashes the nodes. Inhabiting the servers in their bunkers.

Somewhere between the coasts, Molly Corbin leans against the hood of the car studying the map. The road is dirt, single lane. There have been no curves or turnoffs for five miles. The fence is three long planks of wood, stretching between half posts, extending on either side to the horizon. Trees dot at scenic increments. Her shoulders brush leaves. They know she is coming, but there is no obvious entrance. She ducks through one of the spaces in the fence, and walks on the grass, following the trace outline of a footpath. The topography changes, shallow hills ballooning, making her feel better about not seeing any buildings. An old barn comes into view, around the corner from a cut of trees, three buildings gray and decaying. Not quite abandoned, rusting equipment aside, she slides through the opening and into the lined stables. The first few are empty, despite the stacked hay, but she keeps walking. She can hear the beast breathing. The horse hangs its head over the gate and flares its nostrils, giving a slight bow. She reaches out her hand.

Acknowledgements

My endless gratitude to Tyson Cornell, Julia Callahan, Alice Marsh-Elmer, and Angelina Coppola of Rare Bird, all of whom are brilliant and hardworking. A special thanks to William Goldstone and Marina Dunjerski for making it possible to actually read this text.

I am forever indebted to Bayh Sullivan, a freakishly gifted editor and wonderful partner in crime, who saved this book multiple times from total destruction. Likewise, Andrew Mellen delivered an indispensable assist in initiating the communication that would lead to this novel's publication. He should add literary agent to his resume.

Rodrigo Corral and Rachel Adam are the best designers on the planet. The quality and beauty of their art continually astounds me.

Lauren Cerand is a divine publicist and fabulous human being. Christopher Toregas provided excellent and indispensable financial guidance.

Kirsten Reach fought very hard to make this book a reality, and was there at its earliest genesis, even if neither of us knew it when we were 16.

Sascha Feldman, Eli Dvorkin, and Sophia Martelli all plodded through early and deeply flawed drafts and delivered invaluable advice and support. Benjamin Samuel, Mary Morris, Durga Chew-Bose, and the entire Edwards/Wiseman family all generously offered their wisdom and help over the past five years.

Aubrey Hesselgren and Ashly Burch were particularly heroic in making my video game dreams for this book come true.

Thanks to Clare Hipschman, Alexander Zimmerman, Morgan Asbridge, AnnaRose King, and Ian Sullivan for assisting a poor monoglot with foreign languages.

Thank you to my parents, for always letting me get as many books as I wanted, to the teenagers who answered my inane questions, to my friends for being totally awesome, and to you, for reading at all.